SEA OF EXILES

THE EXILED CHRONICLES
BOOK ONE

PAIGE ANNABENTLEAH

ISBN 979-8-9911559-1-5 (PAPERBACK)

CHARACTER, SCENE, & SPECIAL EDITION DESIGN: MAGDALENA CHERVENYAKOVA
SOCIAL MEDIA: @CHERVENYAKOVA
PAPERBACK COVER, CHAPTER & PART PAGE DESIGN: LUCIE DUCLOS
SOCIAL MEDIA: @LUCIEDUCLOS
DEVELOPMENTAL & LINE EDITING: KATE SEGER
PROOFREADING: SAMANTHA ROBINSON
FORMATTING & MAPS: PAIGE ANNABENTLEAH

To Matthew, my rock, my home, the other half of my soul. Without you by my side, none of this would have been possible.

&

To Samantha, my biggest ~~bully~~ *supporter, number one fan, and one of the best friends a girl could ever have.*

CONTENT WARNING

This story contains mature themes and may not be suitable for all readers. Please be advised that *Sea of Exiles* includes:

- Graphic depictions of violence, including combat and injury.
- Explicit sexual content and intimate scenes.
- Graphic depictions of sexual assault.
- Themes of memory loss and its emotional consequences.
- Themes of survival, trauma, and psychological tension.
- Strong language and intense emotional dialogue.
- Fantasy elements, including magic, mythical creatures, and supernatural phenomena

Reader discretion is advised.

A full list can be found here:
https://paigeannabentleah.com/

CONTENTS

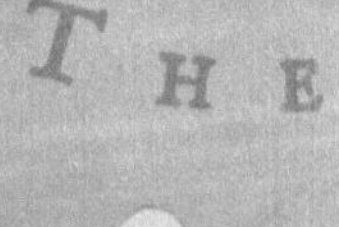

The Realm
of
Faerie
AETHERIC
OCEAN
STORMWING
ISLES
MYRWOOD
SUNFIRE
AERIE
REVERENT
WASTES
THALASET
CARAMIS
EXPANSE
OF
MIRRORS
MOSSGLADE
HYTHE
Valmora
SHADEWILD
THE
WHISPERING REACH
DREADWOOD
Nyxtrae
AETHERIC
OCEAN
SILVERBROOK
ELOWEN

ICEBORNE
SANCTUM
NYTHOR
Lythoria
SILVERMIST
LAKE
VELARUNE
MISTWOOD
BRINWYL
EACH
TIRIANOR
ALDERMOOR
CALANTHA
ILINDOR
WYNDHELM
EVENDELL
EBONREED
SWAMP
SEA
EMBERLIGHT
SHALLOWS
SIREN'S
BAY
THE
SUNDERING
TITANHOLD
ER
Zaranor

Liriel's Tears
The Island of Caramis
The Tempest Sea
Grotto
The Manor
The Garden
Caramis
The Deadwalk
The Tempest Sea
N

You may not control all the events that happen to you,
but you can decide not to be reduced by them.

— MAYA ANGELOU

1
FAERIE

MARGOT

TRUST YOUR INSTINCTS

SHADOWS WHISPERED HER NAME, their cold, breathless voices curling around her like inky tendrils of fear. Their hushed resonance carried wisdom—terrible wisdom that wanted so badly to be heard. And try as she might, she couldn't silence them.

Listen, they echoed.

The ground beneath her feet trembled; the earth pulsed with a rhythm that matched her racing heartbeat. Cold, damp air clung to her skin, carrying with it the scent of decay and something far worse—something she couldn't quite place but knew instinctively to fear.

Listen to the sounds.

But she didn't want to listen to the sounds—she wanted to wake up.

This wasn't the first nightmare she'd had, but it was the first time she could feel the glacial mist on her face and taste the sodden land on her tongue. Her mind insisted it wasn't real, but even so, she was terrified.

Her breath puffed in the cold as she tried to warm her hands, nearly chilled to the bone. If only her subconscious had been considerate enough to put her in weather-appropriate attire rather than the tank and shorts combo she typically wore to bed, then this situation would have been more bearable.

Look.

Wind whipped her hair wildly, the errant strands stinging her eyes as she struggled to make sense of her surroundings, which were unlike anything she had ever seen. Gnarled black trees twisted, their thick vines seeming almost angry. Through the dense canopy, twin moons peeked between the leaves—one larger, casting a silvery lavender glow, and the smaller, a simmering amber. Black flowers with purple centers nestled between curling blades of blood-red grass, their petals frosted with ice so fine it looked like glass. Warbling birds sang to one another quietly while insects chittered, hidden from view.

That's it.

As if she were a black hole, the forest leaned toward her, making the shadows darker. The living woods were corralling her, stealing her space, her air. It was like this place had sentience and was doing what it could to let her know she wasn't welcome here, which only added to her mounting horror.

Gather your wits.

Blood *whooshed* against her eardrums as she turned in a slow circle, searching for a way out, searching for a ripple in reality that showed her bedroom where she knew she was currently sleeping. No matter where she looked, she was only met with the unknown. She huffed. Tiny crystals of condensation floated in front of her face, twinkling like diamonds. If she had a second to spare, she may have marveled at the sight, but she had no idea how long she'd be trapped in this eerie limbo, and standing still felt like inviting the darkness to swallow her whole. With no clear direction, she chose the path to her right, hoping it might lead to something—anything—other than the oppressive shadows closing in around her.

Don't let them in.

Unrestrained gusts pushed against her with deafening howls, as if telling her to turn around, to return from whence she came.

But she couldn't. There was nothing for her there but more woods, more darkness, more unease that sent shivers down her spine. Moving forward was the only path that made sense.

Thinning trees gave way to a cliff with a sheer drop. She inched closer, so carefully, then peered over the edge. The thrum of her pulse tightened her neck. Sea spray spritzed her face as indigo waves thrashed against water-worn stone, licking up the cliff's face with an ire that had her scrambling back. Her foot slipped upon the slick debris, but her fingers found purchase around an exposed root. Breathless, she righted herself and scurried back the way she came.

Trust your instincts.

She scanned the wood, finding the crooked tree that had a particularly large burl sticking out from the trunk, and went left, making sure to count her steps. Trees grew denser, the brush wilder. Nocturnal animals peered at her with gleaming golden eyes. One resembled a squirrel, but its ears were large like an elephant while its paws were sharply clawed. Another glowed like bioluminescent algae, but it flitted through the forest with the wings of a butterfly as its humanoid body radiated a spectrum of colors. She desperately wanted to follow the rainbow creature, but bit back the urge. She didn't know this place. Curiosity would have to wait until she knew she was safe.

Good.

Seven thousand two hundred and forty-five paces later, she heard galloping in the distance. She slowed, quieting her feet, until it sounded as if the creatures were on top of her, and she hid behind a tree. Straining her ears, she listened.

"I got a read," a man said, his voice rasping like sandpaper.

"You sure?" another asked. He sounded young.

Mere feet from her, they stalled, sending adrenaline pumping through her veins. "Positive. It was only for a second, but she's here. Must be almost corporeal, too, judging by the analysis. Here. Look."

Her breath caught in her throat. *She?*

The young man grunted. "We heading north then? Nothing over that way but the sea."

"If she's over that way, it'll make it easier to snatch her." The man with the grating voice guffawed. "What's she going to do? She jumps in, she dies."

"True enough." The young one clapped his hands, and they started to move. "Let's ride!"

With her back pressed against the tree, she slowly rounded its trunk so as not to be caught as the riders passed her. She doubted another woman was hiding in these woods, and given that this was her dream, she knew they were looking for her. Once she was sure they drifted far enough away, she started back toward the knobby tree.

As she retraced her route, the forest shifted around her like a living, breathing entity that sought to disorient her. The trees now appeared more menacing, their branches reaching out like skeletal fingers waiting for the moment she came too close. The whispers grew louder, more frantic, urging her to flee.

Her heart thundered as she realized she could no longer hear the riders in the distance. The silence was more unsettling than the noise of her would-be captors. She was alone—truly alone— and in her panic, she hastened her steps, but the vegetation became more tangled as she pressed forward, her movement more difficult with each passing second.

Suddenly, the ground beneath her feet gave way, and she tumbled down a steep incline. Dirt and leaves cascaded around her as she scrambled to stop her fall. She came to a jarring halt at the bottom, her breath knocked from her lungs. Dazed, she lay there for a moment, staring up at the rustling, leafy roof, trying to gather her thoughts.

Before she could fully recover, a deep, resonant growl shook the ground, making her blood run cold. With trembling hands, she pushed herself up, looking through the dense foliage for the source. It was then she saw it—a pair of glinting silver eyes watching her from the shadows. Frozen with fear, she could barely move, her breath catching in her throat. The creature, whatever it was, remained hidden within the darkness, its gaze unblinking and predatory. Her mind screamed to run, but her body refused to obey. The eyes narrowed, and just as she thought the creature might lunge, the surrounding forest erupted with the sound of rustling leaves and snapping branches, and the creature with the penetrating gaze vanished as quickly as it had appeared.

Now that's *an interesting turn of events*, the voices rang out, taking on a surprised tone that caught her off guard.

Inhaling a shaky breath, she clambered to her feet, taking note of the trampled undergrowth that looked as if something massive had recently passed through. From the trees, invisible watchers tracked her every move, and she had never felt more exposed. A shudder crept up her spine, pimpling her skin. She couldn't stay here—not with whatever monsters lurked nearby, likely eager to make her their next meal.

She ran.

As she sprinted through the forest, the eerie silence was punctuated only by the frantic thudding of her heart. She could feel those silver eyes locked in on her, never blinking, never relenting. The sensation of her being hunted gnawed at her resolve, urging her to run faster, to escape unseen predators that seemed to close in from all sides. But no matter how hard she pushed herself, the forest appeared endless, the path ahead an unchanging maze of darkness.

It would seem I made the right choice.

Her lungs burned with the effort, and her legs threatened to give out, but fear kept her moving. *Cold. So damn cold.* She refused to look back, too afraid of what she might see, but the intensity of that silver gaze bore down on her—a constant reminder that she was not alone.

It's almost time.

Then the world tilted, and she stumbled, her vision blurring as her surroundings morphed into something unrecognizable. She gasped, desperately clawing at the air, but there was nothing to hold on to, nothing to stop her from falling into the shadows that opened beneath her and swallowed her whole.

And then—nothing. Everything went silent. No shadows, the whispers long gone, and for a brief moment, there was only the umbra veil clouding her ability to see. She felt like she was floating in a void, her senses dulled, her mind unable to process what had just happened—until she was thrust awake, her body drenched in sweat.

2

WELCOME HOME

"I was going to ask if you wanted to come to the bar tonight for the costume contest... but you kind of look like death, Margot," Janey whispered, just out of earshot of the last browsing customer. "Still having those nightmares?"

Margot pushed off the counter with a sigh and looked her beautiful friend straight in her brown, almond-shaped eyes. "They're getting worse." She scrubbed her face as if the act could rid herself of the exhaustion riddling her bones. "I don't know what to do."

Janey tilted her head, lost in thought, her pin-straight black bob swishing with the movement. "Maybe you could talk to someone?"

"I—" Margot started but nudged her chin at the customer coming toward them. Janey stepped to the side so the middle-aged woman could put up her stack of books. "Did you find everything you were looking for?"

"And then some. I've lived in this town my whole life, and this is the first time I've stopped here. Your selection of used books is fantastic!"

Margot grinned and nodded toward Janey. "That's all Janey.

She has impeccable taste. Let's see here..." She checked the stickers on the books. "That'll be twenty-five even."

Margot traded the woman for her cash with the brown bag of delightful reads, and much to Margot's surprise, the woman reached out and patted her hand. "Get some rest, dear, ya hear?"

"I'll do my best." She forced a smile as the woman made to leave. "Have a good night."

"You too," she said over her shoulder as she left.

Janey sat on top of the counter and motioned with her hand toward the exit. "Even the customers can see you're a wreck. Like I said, you should see someone."

Margot crossed her arms and frowned. Despite doing her best to avoid mirrors, she knew what she looked like—a ghoul. Her face sunken in and sallow. Dark circles ever-present. Unable to eat, she'd lost an unhealthy amount of weight. Honestly, she didn't know how she was still standing, let alone coming to work every day.

"I wish I could, but I haven't been able to find a therapist that accepts insurance around here. Do you know how much they charge? It's like they don't want people to get better."

"Maybe a few days off then? Sleep. Take care of yourself. Can't have you dying on me."

"My landlord raised my rent last month, and I have, like, thirty bucks to my name." A bitter laugh slipped past Margot's lips. "I'll probably need to get a second job. I'm barely surviving."

Janey quirked her eyebrow. "What the hell? Didn't he just raise your rent six months ago? Is that even legal?"

"Yeah, he did. By a hundred bucks and again by another fifty." Margot shrugged. "Doesn't matter. Virginia doesn't have rent control laws. He can raise rent as often as he wants."

Janey locked the door and clicked off the open sign before turning back to Margot. "That's absolutely insane." She tapped her chin. "Are you on a month-to-month lease?"

"Nope. Yearly. Have about... three months left. Why?"

"I was thinking about fixing up the second floor of the shop...

if I do that, would you move in? Please? I would give you a *really* good deal." Janey twirled and bent at the waist, wagging a finger at Margot. "Think of it as a best friend discount! Mom would love it, too. We wouldn't have to worry about the apartment being destroyed by assholes, and we would make some extra income to subsidize the store." She gripped Margot's hands tightly, her eyes pleading. "What do you say?"

The thought of change—a more stable, comfortable living situation—was tempting, almost too good to be true. She could finally have a place where she didn't have to worry about the leaky ceiling, the neighbors arguing through thin walls, or the draft that turned her tiny apartment into an icebox every winter. Living above the shop, so close to her best friend, with the added bonus of helping to keep the store afloat, felt like a lifeline thrown in her direction just when she needed it most. Turning Janey down would be not only foolish but possibly the biggest mistake she could make at this point in her life. The offer was more than just a better living situation—it was a chance to rebuild, to find a little bit of stability in a life that had felt increasingly precarious. How could she say no?

"God, Janey," Margot wiped a tear from her lashes, "you have no idea what that would mean to me."

"Consider it done, Ms. Hawthorne." She grinned. "Besides, I really need you to get your shit together so you can go back to being my wing woman."

Margot snorted. "You've never needed that in your life."

"No, I guess not. What can I say? Men dig the exotic look." Janey gestured to her petite frame and flawless Korean skin. "I just hate going out alone. Always safer in pairs, you know?"

"You're not wrong." Margot pressed a button on the register, and the till opened with a *ding*. She took the first stack of bills and started counting them down. "Hey, Janey?"

"Hm?"

"Do I really look that bad?"

"Terrible. Like one foot in the grave kind of terrible." Margot flinched. "Sorry, babe, but it's true." Janey huffed and gently pulled the stack of bills from her hands. "Take a few days off *with* pay." She held up her hand when Margot opened her mouth to protest. "I'm your boss. For the next three days, you won't be welcome here. Have you tried any sleep aids?"

Margot's shoulders slumped as she leaned against the counter. "I haven't had the extra money."

Janey softened, her usual teasing demeanor giving way to genuine concern. "I know, but you can't keep running on fumes like this. It's not just about the money—you're going to burn out completely if you don't take a break." She squeezed Margot's hand. "I've been there, remember? Before Mom and I took over the shop, I was working two jobs and barely sleeping. I felt like a zombie. It took me ages to realize that sometimes, taking care of yourself is the only way to keep going."

The gospel Janey was preaching had Margot biting her lip. "I just... I don't want to be a burden. You and your mom have already done so much for me."

"Never think that. You're not a burden. Not at all. You're my best friend. I'll always be there for you no matter how shitty the situation. And honestly, I'd rather give you a few days off with pay than see you collapse from exhaustion. We need you here, but we need you healthy, too." Janey's voice was firm, but there was a warmth that made Margot's heart clench.

After a long moment, Margot nodded slowly. "Okay... maybe you're right. I could use some sleep that doesn't involve waking up in a panic."

"That's the spirit! And who knows? Maybe a few days of rest will do wonders for you. Don't worry about us. We've got this covered." She gave Margot a playful nudge. "Now, go on. I'll finish up here, and you can head home. Stop by the pharmacy on your way." Janey narrowed her eyes. "And promise me you'll actually rest."

"I promise," Margot said, a small smile tugging at the corners of her mouth. "Thanks, Janey. For everything."

"Anytime. Now get out of here before I change my mind and put you back to work." Janey winked, shooing Margot toward the door with a lighthearted laugh.

Margot grabbed her purse and looked back at her best friend. "I'll make it up to you, I swear."

"You already do, just by being you. Go take care of yourself. I know you'd do the same for me."

As Margot stepped out onto the street, a blast of icy wind bit at her cheeks, numbing her skin within seconds. She tugged her cream sweater up to her chin, burrowing into its softness as if it could shield her from the unexpected chill. For Halloween night, the cold was sharper than expected, more like a winter preview than autumn's last hurrah. She felt a pang of guilt for skipping out on holiday fun with Janey, but the truth was, she wasn't sure she'd live to see another day after a night of drinking, considering how dead she felt. But Halloween had always been their night, and this year, she was ruining it. Somehow, she'd make it up to her.

Outside of the pharmacy, Margot grumbled as she checked her account balance on her phone. Twenty-seven dollars. Not even thirty. She stabbed at her screen as if that would magically add a zero or two. If Janey really could make the apartment above the shop livable, even in the barest sense, she would take it in a heartbeat. Living like this wasn't feasible, and her landlord was a dick for squeezing her for all she was worth. But honestly, who could blame him? She was letting it happen. Shaking the thoughts from her head, she went inside, her bones instantly thawing.

Behind the counter at the back, a bald, old man was restocking the shelves that housed prescription medication. Deep wrinkles lined his forehead and creased his eyes and mouth—he looked deep in thought. Margot shifted her weight from one foot to the other, wringing her hands together. She didn't want to interrupt him, but she didn't know what product to buy and didn't have the luxury of picking up a few to test them out.

After a few minutes, she cleared her throat. "Excuse me?" The man adjusted his glasses with arthritic fingers and squinted at her as he leaned forward. "Could you help me find something to help me sleep? I've seen ads... but I don't know what's best."

The old man hobbled around the counter and waved for Margot to follow. For someone who was clearly in pain, he moved quickly. He scanned the shelf, found what he was looking for, and handed her a purple box. He gave her a gentle nod. "This brand is excellent. Something on your mind that's keeping you awake?"

"It's not that I'm not sleeping..." She gave an empty chuckle. "I'm just having nightmares. I hope this can help me sleep so deep I don't remember them even if I *do* have another."

He plucked the box from her hand and swapped it with another, tapping it. "Extra strength. Come on, I'll ring you up."

The ancient-looking register flashed sixteen thirty-six. Margot wanted to die. She didn't get paid until next Friday and would have to stretch every cent. Reluctantly, she handed the old man her card. At this point, she would pay any amount of money to have her sleep back. Hell, she'd even sell her soul.

"Good luck to you," he said, handing her the bag and her card.

"Thanks. Enjoy the rest of your evening."

Margot took her purchase and cursed under her breath as she left the store. She'd barely been inside for ten minutes, but the temperature plummeted. Her breath plumed in front of her face, and she hugged her body, trying to keep warm as she picked up her pace. At least she remembered to put the heat on in her apartment before leaving for work.

The stench of stale air slapped her in the face when she entered her building. She curled her upper lip at the mildew creeping up the walls and the chipped paint. Her landlord couldn't even be bothered to provide a safe and habitable space for the tenants. *What an asshole.* She strode past and headed to the second floor, wiping her shoes on the mat before heading inside her apartment.

Leaning on the counter, resting her chin in her hand, she

drummed her fingers against the cracked laminate. The purple box taunted her, looking so smug as if it were a cure-all. There was no way sleep could be this easy. Down some magic liquid, and then magically, Mister Sandman poofs back into one's life, giving them a blissful night's rest. She pinched the bridge of her nose and rubbed her eyes before pouring the concoction into a little plastic cup.

"This better work," she muttered as she downed it, slamming it back onto the counter harder than intended.

Margot opened her fridge, grimacing at its contents before promptly closing it—she wasn't hungry, anyway. Truly, she didn't know how much more she could take.

Restless, she wandered around the room, unsure what to do with herself. Dusting had been taken care of the day before yesterday, her plants were watered earlier, and she caught up on all her shows last night. *Idle hands are the worst.*

Margot changed into a pair of shorts and a tank top and threw her long, ashen hair into a messy bun and made for the bathroom. Gripping the sink, she debated whether to wash her face or brush her teeth—she didn't have the energy to do both. She sighed and squeezed toothpaste onto her toothbrush. Her skin would survive a day without cleansing. Cavities were far worse than pimples—more expensive, too. Once she was done, she picked up her trashy pirate romance novel and slipped beneath the scratchy sheets of her twin-sized bed.

Eventually, the heaviness in her limbs won out, and Margot drifted into a restless sleep. At first, it was a merciful darkness—no thoughts, no worries—just the soft hum of oblivion. But soon, the shadows twisted and distorted, shaping into something terrifyingly real.

A shimmering figure rippled before her, vaguely human but ethereal, its form shifting with each step closer. It tossed its long hair over its shoulder, moving with unnatural grace, and leaned in, its voice a soft, chilling whisper in her ear: "The time is now, Margot. Welcome home."

3

WE CAN'T STAY HERE

MARGOT'S EYES flew open as she gasped for breath, her gaze darting wildly, trying to make sense of her surroundings. She knew where she was—this was where her nightmares *always* brought her. But this time, something was different. Pain shot through her as she lay on the ground, dirt clinging to her skin, snapped branches and jagged rocks digging into her back. Her last visit had still carried the hazy, surreal quality of a dream, but now it felt fully realized. *Too real. Too* damn *real.*

Her thoughts spun. The voice. *That* voice. It whispered her name, pulling her here, trapping her in this place that felt too solid to be her subconscious playing tricks on her. *Welcome home.* The words echoed in her mind, colder than the dirt pressing into her back. There was something about it—something that made her skin crawl. Like it knew her. Like it had always known her.

Who was it—*what* was it—and what did it want?

The silence around her felt heavy, suffocating, as if the voice was still lurking, waiting. She pushed herself up, ignoring the sharp pain that flared in her spine. Whatever she saw had been nothing more than a blur, but the voice... that had been real. It wasn't a memory, but it felt familiar—like she should recognize it.

Her heart pounded as she scanned the shadows, half-expecting to see something, anything. But there was nothing. Just her, the dirt and trees, a three-eyed chipmunk, and a rabbit with a corkscrew body. The creatures mostly ignored her—a few were more curious, daring to get closer, like the rabbit. It approached her, tilting its little head to the side and wiggling its nose before hopping away like a pogo stick, but she never felt threatened.

A gust of wind whipped through, making her bare legs pimple and her teeth chatter. It was so much colder this time, bone-chilling. If she didn't find shelter soon, she'd die of hypothermia. *Do I even know how to make a damn fire?* She didn't. She quit the scouts the month before the big camping trip where she would have earned her badge. *Figures.*

Rubbing her arms to keep them warm, she thought back to the last time she was here. The men who nearly caught her said they were going north, toward the sea. If this dream was repeating itself, they were to the south. North and south were off the table, but she had no idea where she was or how to tell which direction was north in this strange world. She couldn't remember where the moons had been in relation to her, which meant she was fucked. With a sigh, she tossed her arms in the air, picked a direction, and started walking.

The ground was uneven, littered with roots that pinched her skin and rocks that seemed deliberately placed to trip her up. Every step was a struggle. Frigid air seeped beneath her skin, making her joints stiff, and her breath came out in small, visible puffs. She kept a steady pace, though. It wasn't like she had any other option.

As she walked, the forest grew denser; the trees twisting into unnatural shapes, their branches clasping hands with one another high above her head like a gnarled cage. Every so often, a rustle or a distant crackle in the underbrush would make her stop and listen. Nothing ever followed.

The creatures from before were gone now, replaced by a silence so thick it pressed on her ears. Not even the wind stirred the air anymore.

She glanced at the sky, trying to glimpse the moons, hoping for some sign of direction. But they were hidden beneath the thick canopy. A thought gnawed at the back of her mind—was this even the same dream? The same place? *It had to be, right?*

She shook her head and kept moving. Her muscles ached from the tension coiling inside her. But she couldn't stop. Not yet.

Suddenly, the snap of a branch echoed far behind her, followed by the unmistakable sound of hooves. She froze, her heart hammering in her chest. *Don't look back.*

But the beasts picked up their pace, heading straight for her. *Shit.*

Without a second thought, Margot took off running. Blood oozed from the soles of her feet, but she didn't care—*couldn't* care. She needed to get out of here fast. Fear coursed through her veins, her heart pounding in sync with the deadly party closing in. She doubted she'd survive if they caught her. *What if they trafficked me? How awful would* that *dream be?*

Wake up, damnit.

Heavy brush stung her face and exposed limbs as she sped through the forest. Rasping breaths tore from her throat as she pushed herself harder than she ever thought possible. Desperate to gauge the distance, she risked a glance over her shoulder—but in those few seconds, her foot caught on an exposed root, and she hit the ground hard.

Tears streamed down her face as she clawed into the moist earth, trying to right herself. But her momentum was gone, and she knew it was over. In a matter of minutes, the men would reach her, and her life—or worse—would be taken. Accepting the inevitable, she rolled onto her back and wiped the wetness from her cheeks, smearing dirt across her skin. She inhaled deeply and shut her eyes tight. She was tired.

So. Damn. Tired.

"V'eshka renar," a man's voice said. The strange words

dripped from his mouth like honey, the syllables flowing together in an impossibly smooth way.

Margot heard a soft *shh* sound and felt the sharp metal tip press against her throat. She whimpered. *Please wake up.*

"Perhaps Common?" He huffed after a few seconds. "Well?"

Margot forced her eyes open, staring blankly at the man peering down at her through narrowed silver eyes. Terror seized her, realizing the creature that had stalked her the night before was, in fact, this man—at least six and a half feet tall, towering over her. She scrambled to back away, but the sword in his hand pressed harder against her throat, freezing her in place. She stifled a cry as blood beaded beneath the blade and snapped her eyes shut again, as if she could ignore the pain simply by not being able to see.

His black hair was neatly pulled back into a ponytail, and he scratched the stubble on his chin, the muscles in his massive arms shifting. "We can't stay here. What's your name?"

Please wake up. Please, please *wake up.*

"Did you not hear me?" The anger in his voice made her shudder. "Ears don't work?"

"Margot," she whispered, her bottom lip trembling—and not from the cold this time. "My name's Margot."

"Margot... that's not a fae name."

Peering through her lashes, she cocked an eyebrow at the man. "What's a fa—"

Before she could finish, the man scooped her up, tossing her over his shoulder like she weighed nothing, and sheathed his sword. He pinned her arms tightly against her body so she couldn't move them. With her legs being free, she kicked them wildly, hoping to land a solid hit. But her attempt was weak—she was far too exhausted, which was unsurprising considering she wouldn't be caught dead working out.

He jostled her, jerking his shoulder back and forth until she stilled. She peered at him as best she could, given her position. He placed a finger against his lips and said, "Shh. Listen."

Despite her pulse pounding in her ears, she strained to hear and caught the galloping barreling closer. The two men were coming in fast.

Before she could react, the man sprinted, still carrying her slung over his shoulder. She tried to crane her neck to see which way they were going, but she was being rattled too much to see clearly.

The terrain grew rocky beneath his heavy boots, and she watched jagged boulders flash by, wondering how her captor—or savior, she still wasn't sure—managed to avoid tripping. But she kept silent. He was an unknown, much like this place. He wasn't killing her now, but that could change in an instant, and she wasn't going to give him a reason to by causing a scene.

The man pressed on, hauling her for what felt like miles at an inhuman pace. He didn't even seem winded. His athleticism was astounding—he could probably run multiple Ironman Triathlons without breaking a sweat. No human could do what he was doing so easily. As if he sensed her thoughts, he picked up speed, leaping forward. Her gasp turned into a high-pitched scream as she watched the cliff's edge disappear beneath them. They dropped like an anvil and she could feel her guts in her throat. If there had been anything in her stomach, she would've lost it.

He grunted as they landed on a narrow path ten feet below, his stance never faltering, and set her down and turned to her. "I need you to be quiet. Do not speak. Do not breathe. The fae will pass in two minutes, and they cannot know we are here. Nod if you understand."

Margot tried to stop herself from shaking and nodded. She didn't know how the man knew these... *fae...* would be here shortly, but sure enough—after what she assumed was two minutes—she heard them directly above them. Broken stones dug into her skin as the man's arm pressed her against the cliff's side, barricading her in place. She held her breath as instructed. If he was right about the men being here, he was probably right about a lot of things, and it would be wise to listen to him. For now.

"I thought I saw him go this way," the young man said, followed by a rock being kicked off the cliff. Margot tensed as she watched it tumble down. "This is a dead end."

"Ravara won't be happy," growled the gruff voice. "He's been tracking the girl for some time. Wait a minute—" A loud sniff filled the air. "—Do you smell that? She was definitely here... do you think—"

"Where would they go?" the young man interrupted. "There's nothing out there but water. I didn't see a ship. Did you? What does the locator say?"

"Can't say I've seen a ship... let me check." There was a rustling sound. A few seconds later, slow, measured beeps came at consistent intervals. "Just says she was here, but the signal isn't strong enough."

"Maybe she went west? Let's go that way."

"You better hope she went west. If we don't find her, it'll be our heads."

Margot didn't dare move. Her back stung, and the man's arm was a rigid barrier holding her in place. Her lungs screamed for air, but she couldn't risk even the quickest breath. The men—no, *fae* —were so close, and if they heard even a pin drop, it'd be over.

She could hear the clatter of hooves and the faint, fading murmurs of their voices as they left, but she stayed still, counting the beats of her heart, unsure how long they should wait. Every second felt like an eternity.

Finally, when the sound of the fae was completely gone, the man released her. She gasped, sucking in the air, her chest burning and lungs constricting as she coughed.

"They're gone for now, but they'll come back," he murmured. His silver eyes scanned the area, constantly alert. "We need to keep moving."

Margot's legs wobbled beneath her, adrenaline still coursing through her veins. She swallowed hard and nodded, too shaken to speak. Questions burned in the back of her mind but asking them now felt dangerous. They were still being hunted. *She* was still being hunted.

"Where... where are we going?" she finally managed to ask, her voice strained.

"Somewhere safe," he said, though the hard edge to his voice made her doubt there was any place safe from whatever the fae were.

Margot took a step away from him but thought better of straying too far when she looked down and only saw her death. He didn't seem to notice.

"You were there..." She worked hard to clear the lump lodged in her throat. "You were there before, weren't you? Watching me."

He turned toward her, staring for a moment before he spoke. "Yes."

"Why?"

"Ravara's coterie have big mouths."

Without another word, he threw her back over his shoulder and crouched, launching them into the air, and landed on another cliff below. She didn't scream this time, afraid her voice would travel, and the men would hear her and return. While she didn't feel safe with the man carrying her, the others were actively looking for her—ready to take her back to whomever Ravara was.

He continued down ledges, using one large, nutmeg-colored hand to stabilize himself. Despite the precarious terrain, he was careful not to drop her as he navigated the craggy shelf. The path eventually widened into a small landing, and crisp, salty air filled her lungs. In the distance, indigo waves crashed against the rocky wall.

They'd finally reached the sea.

4

THIS IS NO DREAM

MARGOT CLUNG to the man as he carried her past the landing and into a small cove. His hold on her was firm, but almost gentle in a way that felt forced. Tears pricked the corners of her eyes, wanting nothing more than to wake in her warm bed.

His boots sloshed in the shallow water until he carefully stepped across the most suspect-looking bridge she had ever seen. Nearly rotted planks were strung together with frayed rope, several boards cracked in the middle—enough to give any sane person pause. But the man leaped over with a cat's grace, landing on the one board that wasn't on the verge of snapping in two, balancing on one foot without wiggling. The bridge groaned under their combined weight. He waited a second before clearing the rest, landing on the other side.

As they rounded a corner, a modest-sized ship came into view, bobbing at the end of a dock that was hidden from the cove entrance thanks to jutting rock formations. It was impressive that the man had managed to navigate such a ship into an area that dangerous.

He strode up the gangplank, grunting as he lifted her from his shoulder and set her down on the deck. Curious, she glanced at

39

her surroundings, but a low growl commanded her attention, snapping her focus back to the man standing before her.

"I'm going to ask you a few questions. You *will* answer." He narrowed his eyes. "Who are you?"

Margot raised an eyebrow. "I already told you. I'm Margot."

"And where do you come from, Margot?" He gestured to her clothing. She looked down at the shorts and tank she had put on for bed and blushed. They didn't fully cover all her parts, but it wasn't like she expected to be going out for the evening. "Clearly, you're not from here... with these strange clothes."

"I... I'm from Virginia."

"What's Virginia?"

"Virginia is a state in America."

The man huffed and crossed his arms; his leather chest piece stretched tight across his muscles. "*Where* is America?"

Margot pinched the bridge of her nose. If this line of questioning continued, they would never get anywhere. "Maybe you should answer *my* questions."

He cocked his head to the side, amusement dancing across the planes of his face. "Why should I?" He stepped toward her, then leaned in close enough for her to feel the heat radiating off his body. "If you recall, *I* saved *you*. I owe you nothing. In fact, you owe *me*."

"Saved me from what! Pretty sure you kidnapped me!" His expression hardened at her outburst, making her stumble back. Fists balled at her side, she exclaimed, "God, just tell me where we are!"

"The gods won't help you," he chuckled darkly. "The fae, girl. I saved you from the fae. And this is their land." He gestured with a grand sweep of his hand at the expansive ocean before them. "Welcome to Faerie."

Oh, God. Margot fell into the ship's railing, gripping it hard for support as her legs momentarily buckled. *Faerie?*

When she was a girl, her mother used to read her stories about Faerie, and not all were pleasant. But one thing that persisted in each tale was that the land was breathtakingly beautiful. She took in the twin moons filling the sky—one large, the color of lavender fields, and a smaller one, a simmering amber—their light reflected off the sea's surface, seemingly coming to life in the form of bouncing orbs that moved in time with water's ebb and flow.

"No... this is a dream," she muttered under her breath, shaking her head as she took in the otherworldly scene. Faerie wasn't real. It was a story. Folklore. This was her mind's way of keeping her close to her childhood, close to her mother. "This isn't real."

"I assure you, this is quite real."

Dragging her gaze up the man's body, she took a moment to take in *his* strange attire. Clad in black leather, he had blades strapped to his sides and a quiver and bow slung across his back. Compared to him, she looked positively normal. There was no way she ended up in some far-off land of make-believe, standing in front of a gorgeous man with an entire arsenal attached to his person. How would that be possible? An easy answer—it wasn't. She was sure this was a dream. It had to be. The medicine she took made her imagine smutty pirates in a world she knew from her mother's bedtime stories. That's it. There was no other logical explanation.

"Just going to stare at me, or do you have something to say?" The words rumbled from his chest as he toyed with a bone-adorned dagger.

"I kept having the same dream—*this* dream—I was hoping the medicine I took would help stop the nightmares and finally let me sleep..." A chill ran through her as she fidgeted with the hem of her tank top. "But it seems it only made it worse." She looked down at her bloody feet. "This is the first time I've ever been able to feel pain, and it's so cold... I usually wake up by now." *At least I think I usually wake up by now.* She swallowed thickly and her gaze snapped to his. "I just want to go home."

"This is no dream." The man shrugged. "I've sensed you for a while now, coming and going, but this is the first time I'd ever seen you whole. The last few times you've been wandering through the Dreadwood, you've been nothing more than a ghost. But now that you've actualized... well, clearly, Faerie wants you here." He sheathed his dagger and circled Margot. "Which means you won't be getting back to wherever you call home."

"I don't understand." Tears stung Margot's eyes. She tried blinking them back, but they spilled over, painting her cheeks. Cursing herself for crying in front of him, she swatted them away. "What do you mean I won't go home? This is just a dream. I'll wake up. I'm going to wake up."

Why would this time be different?

"Like I said," He hoisted the anchor from the water with ease, "this is no dream."

"Stop!" Margot lunged at him, grabbing his arm as he held the dripping anchor in the air. "I can't... I can't go with you." She glanced over her shoulder at the foreign landscape. "I need to..."

Beneath her palm, his muscles tensed. She immediately released him, sucking in a sharp breath.

"Look, Faerie is the realm of fae." He secured the anchor and turned back to Margot. "Magic reigns supreme here. Whether or not you want to be here, the gods and goddesses—or *something*—brought you here for a reason." He leaned into Margot, exuding a palpable warmth that made her uneasy, but she was so cold she couldn't muster the courage to shy away this time. "You're more than welcome to go with the fae, but I guarantee you'll be safer with me than Ravara."

"What's so bad about the fae? Are you not fae?"

"Me? Fae?" He tipped his head back and laughed, eyes crinkling at the corners. "No, I'm not fae. I'm the furthest thing from their kind. But I promise you, the fae are not to be trusted. Especially not Ravara's cabal. I've seen them do horrendous things, and with how desperate they were to find you... Well, I can say with certainty they weren't looking to crown you queen."

"And you expect me to, what, trust you? How can I do that?"

Her voice was weak and small, and she knew the answer to her question before asking but wanted verbal confirmation.

The man took a long pole, which he used to guide the ship out of the cove, giving Margot no choice—at least no choice that was decidedly safer—than to go with him.

She trembled against the wind as they drifted out to sea.

While the man navigated the vessel, she took a moment to look around. The ship looked like something straight out of the dog-eared adventure novels she used to reorganize at the shop— the kind with gilt-edged pages and illustrated ships battling sea monsters on their covers. Those books had been her escape during slow days at work. Now here she was, living something stranger than any story she'd shelved. "How can I trust you?" Margot asked again.

He turned to her, the corner of his lip twitching. "You can't. But we have something in common: we were both brought to this strange land against our will. And I find it quite remarkable that two exiles like us found one another. Still alive, that is."

"Exiles? I'm not an exile."

"Sure you are. You're stranded in Faerie, same as me. I'd say that makes you an exile."

Margot huffed a laugh. "I guess."

"What's your name?" she asked as she walked to the ship's side and peered into the darkness.

The man dropped a scratchy blanket over her shoulders and leaned against the rail beside her. "Cillian."

"Kill-ee-an," she said, drawing out each syllable as she snuggled into the blanket. "That's a nice name. Rolls right off the tongue."

Booming laughter burst from Cillian's chest, and she couldn't help but smile. He grinned back, displaying rather sharp canines. "You're the first person ever to tell me that." He gently tugged her arm. "Let's get you inside to warm you up. I'm sure I can find some food for you, too."

Margot's mind raced. Cillian's easy grin and that hearty

laughter temporarily disarmed her, but now, with her feet firmly planted, doubt came rushing back. Her skin prickled in the cold air, reminding her of the biting wind and her lack of options. Was she really going to follow a man with sharp teeth and corded muscles into the unknown just because he *smiled*? Undoubtedly, trusting him was stupid. But what were her alternatives? Jumping ship and freezing alone in the cove, or worse, not even making it out of the water? Starving to death? Letting the fae, whatever they were, catch her?

She glanced at Cillian, who stood there patiently, grin fading into a pleasant smile. Something was unsettling about him—more than just his size or those dangerous eyes. Yet, he hadn't hurt her, not even when he could have easily let her plunge to her death during their escape.

Then, her stomach growled, reminding her she hadn't eaten in what felt like ages. She exhaled slowly, hoping the tension in her shoulders would ease—it didn't. "I'm not going to be your prisoner, or whatever it is you're planning."

Cillian chuckled softly, the sound deep, almost warm. "I'm not in the habit of keeping prisoners, Margot. But you can think what you want." He tugged on her arm once more. "There's no reason to die out here in the cold. Come inside. You're shivering."

"I—"

"You're here," he cut her off. "There's nothing you can do about it. I gain nothing from hurting you. Do what you will with that information, but don't be stubborn with your life. It's the most important thing you own."

She turned from his piercing silver gaze, focusing on the ship's deck. The further out to sea they went, the colder it became. Realistically, she didn't know how long she could survive in flimsy shorts and a tank. The blanket helped, but not enough.

"You coming?" Cillian asked over his shoulder and Margot sighed.

A blast of warmth enveloped her as she followed him into the cabin. The heat against her skin, the rough wood beneath her feet, the scent of herbs and wood smoke—it all felt viscerally real in a way her previous dreams never had. She heard of astral projection before, but she was pretty sure that was just your spirit leaving your body... not your body physically entering some other realm. Whatever this was, it was starting to feel less and less abstract and more like real life and *that* was something she didn't want to think about.

There was a large bed pushed against the wall to the left, a fireplace in the center with a coffee table directly in front of it, surrounded by two cushioned armchairs. To the right was a little kitchenette with a sink, a wood-burning stove, an icebox, and a pantry. Honestly, it was nicer than her one-bedroom apartment. Carved wooden figures decorated the mantel, drawings of fearsome creatures hung on paneled walls, and the most out-of-place object for the giant man to own was sitting in front of Margot on the center of the coffee table: a sage-colored vase hosting a single black flower.

"Sit, make yourself at home," Cillian said, motioning toward the chairs. "I'll get you a drink and something to eat. You look like you could use it."

"Did you decorate this place yourself?" Margot asked, choosing not to be offended by his comment. She knew what she looked like.

"I've been on the sea for a long time." He shrugged and turned back to the counter. "Figured I should make the place my own."

"It looks good." She rounded the worn olive chair and sank into its comforts.

Soft fibers from the plush cream rug felt like heaven against her feet, though the cuts and scratches from her forest flight still stung. The woods had done quite a number on them. Just another reminder that this was more than just a dream.

"Here." Cillian handed her a chipped plate piled high with bread and cheese, along with a cup of something warm. "It's not much, but it's all I have now. Haven't restocked."

Margot set the plate on her lap and held the cup between her hands, gently swirling the liquid. She glanced between Cillian and the tawny brew.

"Oh, come on!" Cillian gave her an incredulous look. "I didn't poison the damn thing."

She sipped tentatively, her eyes widening. "This is fantastic."

He grinned. "My special blend of herbs and spices. What better to warm you up than a cup of tea?"

"It's doing its job, that's for sure." Margot took another sip. "How... how are we talking right now?"

Cillian groaned as he sat in the chair next to her, cracking his neck from side to side, as if releasing the tension from their earlier journey. "What do you mean?"

"Well, when we first met, you spoke to me in a strange language. Then you mentioned Common... what is that?"

"Ah... that. The first language I spoke was Fhalian—the fae language. Though nowadays, only the royals still use it. In hindsight, I should have just led with common tongue, but Ravara's men were after you..." His voice trailed off, and he cleared his throat before starting again. "Common is an ancient language, woven into Faerie's fabric by deities at the time of creation."

Margot grimaced. "I... don't know what that means."

"Common is innate. Any being entering Faerie can speak and understand it, regardless of their primary form of communication. This is basic knowledge... you should know this." Cillian eyed her curiously. "What species are you?"

Margot's chewing slowed, and she set down the hunk of bread, her brow furrowing. "Can't say I've been asked *that* before. I'm human."

"Damnit," he muttered, dragging his hands over his face in frustration. "You're not safe here. I was going to drop you off at the next port town... but that won't work."

"You were just going to *leave me*?" she asked, her voice rising with disbelief.

Cillian nodded slowly. "Being with me is dangerous. Those in

Faerie fear me—and for good reason. I can defend myself, but you? You're weak. Fragile. Faeries consider your kind lesser beings." He glanced at her. "No matter where I took you... it wouldn't be safe."

Margot bristled at his words, her hands curling into fists in her lap. "Weak? Fragile? I didn't ask you to drag me here, and now you're telling me I'm a burden?"

"It's not about being a burden. It's about survival." Cillian leaned back in his chair. "Faerie isn't like your world. They'll see you as prey—or worse—a prize to be hunted. If you stay here, you'll need more than luck to survive."

A cold pit settled in Margot's stomach. She wasn't sure if it was from realizing just how much danger she was in or the fact that Cillian spoke with such certainty as if her fate had already been decided.

"So, what am I supposed to do?" she whispered. "Just sit here and wait for the next fae to come for me?"

He leaned forward, resting his forearms on his knees, his jaw tight. "No. I won't let that happen." He grabbed the rest of her bread and thrust it into her hands. "Eat. I've decided you'll stay with me for the time being."

"And now you're asking me to trust you again." She nibbled at her food. "You were ready to abandon me."

"Yes, but now you're my responsibility. Better me than the fae." He hesitated, his gaze locking with hers. "I don't fail, if that has you worried."

"Is that why you're feared?" she asked, her voice barely audible.

His posture stiffened, his expression hardening into something dangerous. Without a word, he stood and strode to the door. The sudden shift in his demeanor left the cabin feeling ten degrees colder despite the crackling fire.

Margot sat in silence as loneliness crept up her spine—familiar, in a way that reminded her too much of home. *Home...* If this wasn't a dream, what would she do? A life she could never return to. Her dingy apartment, the job she loved, the small town where everyone knew each other's business. Her life hadn't been perfect, but it was *hers*. And now? She wasn't sure what this was.

The only silver lining was that she wasn't completely alone. But could she trust Cillian? Her heart said yes, but her mind threw up red flag after red flag. The only thing she truly knew about him was that he was dangerous—but apparently, so was Faerie.

She tried to ignore the tightness in her chest as she finished her food. For such a simple meal, it was surprisingly good. Despite the uncertainty of her situation, the meal helped settle her nerves, and her eyes grew heavy. Her breathing slowed, and slowly, she let herself drift, the warmth of the flames lulling her into sleep.

THE CABIN DOOR OPENED, SMACKING AGAINST THE wall. The sound jolted Margot from her slumber, sending the blanket to the floor.

"Sorry." Cillian winced. "Not used to having anyone here. You should go back to sleep."

"Where did you go?" she asked, wiping crust from the corner of her eye.

"To make sure we're on course. We have a few days before we reach the next town." He looked up and down her body. "You need clothes."

"Clothes," Margot's face reddened as she covered her chest, "would be nice."

Tears pricked her eyes, and she quickly turned away, not wanting him to see. She had hoped, prayed even, that when she woke, she'd be back in her warm bed, safe in the world she knew. But she wasn't. And that was more terrifying than anything.

Her lips trembled as she returned her gaze to the hulking man. "This really isn't a dream, is it?"

Cillian shook his head, giving her a sympathetic smile. "No, it's not. I'm sorry."

After pouring himself another cup of tea, he returned to the chair next to her, and the two sat in silence. Margot tried making sense of things, but everything felt surreal. Things like this didn't happen. They just didn't. But here she was, whisked away to a magic land, unable to change what happened to her. Perhaps making the best of an unpleasant situation would help until she found a way to return home.

The hairs on the back of her neck stood on their ends, and she shivered, feeling Cillian's eyes on her. She looked at him. "You didn't answer the question I asked earlier. Why are you feared?"

He hesitated, inhaling sharply before speaking. "I'm... a demon—a powerful one." He tapped his cup's handle. "My kind isn't welcome here either."

He watched her intently, as if to gauge her reaction to this learned information. She stared at him, feeling her jaw go slack. *What the fuck?*

"A *demon*?" The tips of her fingers dug into the armrest. "Like angels and demons?" She dropped her voice to a whisper. "Do you know the devil? Oh god." She dropped her face into her hands. "I'm in hell. This is eternal damnation, and you're going to have me burned for eternity."

"What are you talking about?" He set his cup on the coffee table. "I don't know who—or what—the devil is, and I'm not going to burn you for eternity."

"But demons are *terrible*... and *not* real."

"I'd have to agree that most demons are terrible." He scratched his head, giving her a puzzled look. "But they're real, Margot. I'm a demon, and I'm right in front of you. Do demons come from hell in your world?"

"That's what the stories say." She glanced at him. "Please don't kill me or steal my soul."

"I'm not going to do either of those things, promise. I don't come from hell." He clasped his hands together, resting them between his knees. "I come from Olvath. My brethren cast me out for *radical views*."

"They cast you out..." she mumbled. "How did you get here?"

"The same way you did, I assume. Through the veil." He cocked his head to the side. "Are you afraid now that you know the truth?"

Margot shifted in her seat. "Scared? Yes. Of you? No. You've been nothing but kind to me." She ran her fingers over the newly formed scab on her neck. "Aside from holding me at sword point."

"I won't apologize for that. I needed to know who you were, *what* you were. Fae lands are dangerous, even for me. It took me a few moments, but after inspecting you, I could tell you weren't fae; you're beautiful but not perfect."

Margot snorted. "Gee, thanks for letting me know I'm not perfect."

Cillian sighed. "That's not what I meant. When you see the fae, you'll understand." He paused for a moment, staring at her. "You look young."

Her brows shot up in surprise. "I'm thirty-four years old, Cillian. I could only have thirty-four years left to live, much less if I'm unlucky. And luck doesn't seem to be on my side." She shook her head. "I don't know how much you know about humans, but I'm not a child. Far from it."

"Admittedly, I don't know much about your kind." Cillian gestured to the bed. "Do you want to get some more sleep?"

"Actually... I'd like to talk some more if you don't mind." She brought her knees up to her chest. "You know, learn about the man who apparently saved my life."

"I *did* save your life." He rested the side of his face on his fist, a smirk playing on his lips. "I'd rather learn about you. Tell me about your life before Faerie."

"There's not much to tell, honestly. I was born in a rural town in Virginia and lived there my whole life. I work—*worked*—at a used bookstore, making just enough to get by." The realization that she was speaking about her life in the past tense made her chest tighten.

"What about family or friends? Lovers? Comrades? What are you leaving behind?"

The slew of questions Cillian rattled off made her head spin. She couldn't remember the last time anyone had been so interested in her. She let out a heavy sigh, pausing to gather her thoughts.

"My mother died of cancer, a human disease," she added quickly when she saw him furrow his brows. "That happened a few years ago... I miss her. When she was diagnosed, my dad left. Said he couldn't handle the stress and wished me luck." A tear rolled down her cheek. "No siblings, so I cared for her. All the way to the end. God, that was... really hard." She shook her head, trying to clear the painful memories. "Other than that, I've got Janey—my best friend. She and her mom own the bookstore we worked at. No husband. No boyfriend. No... *comrades*." She shrugged when she saw Cillian give her a questioning look. "Small town, small dating pool. Never really clicked with anyone. I guess I'm just leaving behind Janey and my plants."

"Kind of sounds like you didn't have a very good life."

"No, I guess I didn't, huh?" She took a breath before changing the subject. Talking about her life as if there was no going back hurt. "Anyway, I still don't get where Faerie is, though. Is this another planet or something?"

"Another planet... not exactly. Ah, how do I explain this?" He rubbed the back of his neck. "Faerie and Earth co-exist in a sense, as does Olvath, as do others. Imagine sheets of parchment, all stacked on top of one another. Each sheet is a different world, separated by layers of magic. I don't know how many worlds there are... but if I were to guess, I'd say a lot."

"You mentioned the veil... how exactly did I get here?"

"Occasionally, humans possess magic, which is to be expected considering how intertwined Faerie is with Earth. When a human possesses magic, it is taken from Faerie, typically unknowingly. Faerie wants to regain its lost magic, so it pulls humans through the veil."

"Is that what happened to me?"

"You said you were asleep, right? The veil between Faerie and Earth is thinnest during a dream state."

"Okay... but that would imply I have magic. I feel like I would know if I had magic."

"You have magic, Margot. I can smell it on you," he said as he took Margot's cup and walked to the kitchen to brew more tea. "When I found you, you smelled fae. If I'm being honest, you smelling fae is probably what saved you more than me."

Margot gaped. "You can *smell* magic? More importantly, *I have magic*?"

"I'm a demon." Cillian shrugged and turned to lean against the counter. "We train at a young age, nearly from birth, to smell fae magic." He sniffed in her direction. "You definitely have magic. Stronger now, too."

"How do I use it?"

Cillian handed her a fresh cup and sat back down. "You mean your *stolen* magic?" He laughed when Margot glared at him, then shook his head. "I don't know. You'll have to figure that out on your own. I know little of how it works."

Margot hummed to herself and inhaled the steam, hoping it would calm her nerves. The amount of information she was being given was almost too much. Not only was she stranded in Faerie, but now she apparently had magic. Where, exactly, was the apparent magic? It wasn't like she felt it. She certainly couldn't access it, not that she'd know how to go about that anyway. She sighed.

"Well, what of your people?" she asked. "Tell me about Olvath."

"It's a horrible place, full of pain and anguish. A world of jagged stones and molten fire. Black ash rains down across the land, smothering vegetation, poisoning the water. Suffering is a rite of passage."

"Kind of sounds like hell to me," Margot whispered. "That's terrible."

"It is."

Silence lingered for a moment, and Margot fidgeted in her seat before grabbing the blanket off the floor and spreading it across her lap. She cleared her throat. "Why were the fae after me?"

He shrugged. "Probably the same reason they're after me—we're exiles."

"Why would they be looking for you?"

"*Hunting*, you mean." He gave her a pointed look. "Look around you." He gestured to the sea through the porthole, the twin moons, the impossible beauty. "Who wouldn't want this? My people spent generations trying to claim it for themselves. Demons dreamed of escaping their hellscape for..." He caught himself, jaw tightening. "But that's ancient history now."

"Okay... but why are they hunting you?"

"Because I don't belong here." He met her gaze, his voice cold and matter of fact. "Neither do you."

Margot flinched but pressed on. "I can see why they would want to come here if where you come from is as awful as you described, but why would they exile you to a place they want to invade? It seems they did you a favor."

A bitter laugh rumbled from his chest. "Because the fae *hate* us. The demons knew the fae wouldn't stop chasing me until they killed me. But here I am, all these years later, alive and well."

"What did you do that was so awful that they needed to exile you?"

"Something... something that goes against a demon's very nature." He breathed out slowly. "I suggested we make peace with the fae. If we were on better terms, perhaps they would let us enter Faerie if they didn't fear us." Cillian gulped his tea, holding it in his mouth for a second before swallowing. "The Dread Lord didn't like that."

"The Dread Lord?" Her eyes widened in surprise. "You were someone who could hold an audience with a *lord*?"

Cillian gave her a sidelong glance. "I thought we were talking about you?"

"Just answer the question," she said, hiding her smile behind her cup.

"I was his general," he said. "A title earned through combat."

"War?"

"Many. Too many to count. And all of which are stories for another time." His silver eyes held her gaze. "You're handling this rather well for a human... for anyone, really."

Margot laughed, but her heart wasn't in it. "I don't know. Maybe I'm in shock." She looked away from him and picked at a loose thread on the chair. "Or maybe the idea of a new life isn't as scary to me as it would be for others."

Setting her cup on the table, Margot pulled the blanket tighter around herself, her eyes drifting to the crackling fire. The entire night had been such a whirlwind; she hadn't had a moment to process how this might affect her. Being in Faerie should have terrified her. But it didn't. Instead, she was pulled toward it, like she belonged. *Maybe it's my magic.* The thought was both comforting and unsettling.

"Take the bed and get some sleep. It's more comfortable than the chair," he said, pulling Margot from her quiet rumination as he headed toward the door.

"Where are you going?"

He smirked. "Gonna miss me?"

"Just curious."

"I need some air." He nodded toward the bed. "Now sleep. Those dark circles tell me how tired you are. We can talk more tomorrow."

Margot watched him leave, half-expecting the loneliness to creep back in, but it never did. She knew she should feel angry or upset about her situation, but the truth was, Cillian had been right. Her life back home kind of sucked.

Maybe this new one wouldn't be so bad after all.

Maybe this new one wouldn't be so bad after all.

5

DON'T MAKE ME GO

FOR THE FIRST time in weeks, Margot slept like a log, only to be interrupted by soft snores from across the room. She squeezed her eyes shut, determined not to let slumber float away, but failed miserably. Sitting up cross-legged, she looked at Cillian in the dwindling firelight. The warmth from the dying embers cast dancing shadows across his peaceful features. She took in the slight curve of his nose, the shape of his lips, and the cut of his jaw. His ebony locks were slightly wavy and rested below his shoulder. The strands looked soft, silky. Like her fingers could brush through without hitting a single snag. She blushed as she thought about the way heat radiated from him like a furnace, and she wondered what his body would feel like pressed again—

"Like what you see, Margot?" The deep timbre of his voice brought her back to reality, sending a shiver down her spine that had nothing to do with the cool night air seeping through the cabin walls.

She laughed, trying to mask her embarrassment. "Sorry. You look good and I was just appreciating you. You're truly a work of art." The wooden boards beneath her creaked as she shifted, suddenly aware of how intimate the small cabin felt.

"If you think I'm a work of art, you should see the fae." His mercury eyes caught the firelight, gleaming with something that made her breath catch.

"Are they really that good looking?"

"Yep. They're beautiful. All of them. Their skin? Flawless and glows softly in the light. Their eyes are brilliantly colored like priceless gems. Delicate things, really. Stunning, nonetheless," he said as he put his hands behind his head and propped his feet on the table. The casual gesture did nothing to hide the coiled strength in his muscles.

"Maybe I don't like delicate. Maybe I prefer large, muscled brutes with chiseled jaws." The words slipped out before she could stop them, hanging between them like smoke.

Cillian cocked an eyebrow, his expression darkening. "Do you?"

Her heart thundered in her chest. "I dunno. Never thought about it. I like the way you look, though." Margot stretched her arms, desperate to break the tension. "Do you have a bathroom? I'd like to wash up and use the... facilities."

"You mean the water closet? If so, it's just through the door to the left of the hearthstone. Hold on." He jumped up and rummaged through a small wooden dresser. "Let me see if I have something for you to wear... here." He handed her a bundle of fabric. "It's just a tunic, but you're small... I don't know. Maybe you can make it work."

"Thanks."

When Cillian said water closet, she expected something dreadful—perhaps a pot in the corner that stunk like shit. But to her surprise, the space was quite lovely and far more spacious than she'd imagined. A sink, toilet, *and* shower, all crafted from sanded and sealed wood, adorned the room. It was rustic yet elegant.

She turned the knob in the shower, and to her delight, the water was instantly hot. No waiting, no cold bursts. *Must be magic.* She grinned at the thought.

Margot stepped into the shower after emptying her painfully full bladder and groaned as the hot water hit her skin. The warmth worked its way into her tired muscles, a balm for her aching body. Steam curled around her like wisps of smoke, fogging the glass and thickening the air until it clung to her lungs with each breath. She watched, mesmerized, as rivulets of water raced down her arms and legs, carrying away the grime and blood from her time in the forest. The evidence of her ordeal swirled down the drain in muddy spirals.

She grabbed the round bar of soap from its dish, her fingers sliding over its slick surface. When she lifted it to her nose, an earthy, herbal scent filled her senses—notes of lavender mixed with citrus and leather. It smelled like Cillian. As she worked the soap into a lather across her skin, his scent enveloped her, transforming the small space into a sanctuary. She closed her eyes, savoring the quiet moment and vowing never to take simple comforts like this for granted again.

She turned off the water and grabbed a towel from a shelf above the toilet, wrapping it around herself. Her pale blue eyes caught in the mirror, and she poked at the lines threatening to crease her forehead. Her gaze lingered on the smattering of freckles across her nose, and she smiled. It had taken years to appreciate them, but now she wouldn't trade them for the world.

Looking around for toothpaste, she found a copper container filled with black powder. She scooped some onto her finger and sniffed. It didn't smell great, but it was all she had.

"Can this powder clean my teeth?" Margot asked through the door.

"Yeah." Cillian laughed. "Just use your finger."

The powder worked well. Her mouth didn't feel as clean as it did with her electric toothbrush, but it was far better than not cleaning her teeth. She slipped the tunic over her head. The collar kept sliding down her shoulder, far enough to reveal the swell of her breast, leaving little to the imagination. After a few minutes of trying to fix the shirt, she released an exasperated breath and exited the bathroom.

"Hey, Cillian?" she asked as she fought with the tunic. "Do you have a belt or something? Maybe a rope?"

Margot looked up at Cillian, noticing his nostrils flaring as a deep growl rumbled from his chest. His mercury eyes locked onto hers, burning with an intensity that felt like flames devouring her whole. It was as though his gaze alone could set the air on fire, each slow step he took toward her fueling the heat between them. Her heart raced, panic tightening her chest. She stumbled backward, her hand instinctively reaching out to steady herself against the wall.

She chuckled nervously. "Cillian, is everything okay?"

Without a word, he closed the distance between them, slamming his palms against the wall on either side of her head, caging her in. His nose brushed against her cheek, and she caught her breath, fear coursing through her veins. *He's not a man.*

Her hands pressed against his chest, trying to push him away, but it was useless. He was solid muscle, unmoving, a force she couldn't budge. Her pulse quickened as she looked at him, and he moved even closer, so close she could feel his breath ghosting over her lips.

"Cillian, please," she whispered.

He fisted the back of her hair, tilting her head as he trailed his tongue up the column of her neck. She struggled for air as he crushed her into the wood, his knee pressing against her center.

"Please stop!" she pleaded, gasping, trying to fill her lungs.

A yell tore from his throat, and he staggered away from her, running his fingers through his hair. "I'm sorry, Margot." He swallowed thickly and kept his eyes down. "Primal urges... I-I'm still a demon. You look good in my shirt."

Margot took shaky steps toward the bed.

"I need a minute," she muttered.

With trembling hands, she sank onto the bed, her mind reeling from what had just happened. The ghost of his touch lingered on her skin, a reminder of how quickly things could shift between them. She was playing with fire—real, demon fire—and part of her wanted to burn. The rational side of her brain screamed danger, but her body thrummed with an entirely different message. The ship's gentle rocking did nothing to calm her racing thoughts.

Cillian stepped in front of Margot, and she stiffened. He held his hand open and presented her with a golden cord.

"This will look nice against the black. Please forgive me, Margot."

She took the cord and stood to adjust the tunic before wrapping it around her waist. Once she got it into position, she cinched it, causing her breasts to protrude more while emphasizing her figure.

"Oh, come on." Cillian groaned. "This isn't fair."

Margot shot him a dirty look as she walked over to the kitchenette and poured herself some tea. "You gave me this to wear. Excuse me for having a body. How much longer do we have until I can get some *appropriate* clothing?"

"We still have days," he said flatly.

"Then I guess you'll need to control yourself since I can't go back home. I like you and enjoy your company. Mostly, I feel safe with you. Please don't become what I fear in this strange land."

Cillian moved to his chair and slumped down, holding his face in his hands. "This is hard, Margot. I'm going against my nature. Part of me wants to *own* you. Maybe... maybe this *was* a bad idea. Maybe we should set you up in town."

Uneasiness simmered. What would she do if Cillian really left her? Would the fae treat her as poorly as he suggested? There were so many questions that she didn't want answers to. She didn't want to leave Cillian. She enjoyed him. He was charming in a rough-and-tumble kind of way.

"You don't mean that," she said.

He slid his hands down his face and looked at her. "Margot, I don't know if I can control myself forever—and I have *great* self-control. But I'm not perfect. Look at what just happened." He gave her a sad smile. "I know a life with the fae probably isn't what you want, but I feel like I'm out of options here. I don't want to hurt you."

"No," Margot said.

"What do you mean, *no*?"

She crossed her arms, locking eyes with Cillian. "No. I won't go with the fae. You told me yesterday how horribly they would treat humans. I'd rather take my chances with you."

"I don't think that's up to you." He narrowed his eyes. "Maybe you forgot, but this is my ship."

Margot sashayed to Cillian's chair, gripped the arm, bent over, and pushed her bust into his face. "I. Said. No."

His gaze dropped to her chest, causing his own to rise and fall haphazardly. His pupils were blown. Despite his warning, Margot leaned closer.

"Are you going to hurt me, Cillian?" she breathed, her lips grazing his ear.

She stepped back, and his eyes snapped to hers. Anger and lust fought for the upper hand. A scowl etched his face. He snatched his cup from the table and threw it across the room. Margot winced as it shattered against the wall. His eyes never left hers as his fingertips dug into his knee so hard his knuckles turned white.

He snarled. "What the fuck do you think you're doing?"

"I'm trying to prove a point here."

"How about you don't?"

"But I already have."

"And what point would that be?"

Margot gave him a lopsided smile and plopped into the seat next to him. "I'm still alive, whole, and untouched."

He deadpanned. "Barely." His fingers relaxed, and he sighed. "Margot, there's a chance life with the fae won't be awful."

"And what's the chance that it *will* be awful? Is it higher?"

He didn't respond.

"Cillian, you're my best shot at a life that isn't absolute shit." She sucked in a quick breath as she stumbled through her words. "*You* saved me from the fae... not the other way around."

Cillian walked over to where the cup had broken and picked up the pieces. Margot stifled a sob. He glanced over his shoulder. A pained expression crossed his face.

"Please." Her bottom lip quivered. "Don't make me go."

Dumping the last bits of ceramic into the wooden waste bin, he let his shoulders fall. He turned to her. "If you could, would you want to go back home?"

The question took her aback. She assumed she wouldn't be able to go back home because that's what Cillian had told her, but she never considered *if* she wanted to go back. Would anyone miss her? Janey. Janey would definitely miss her and would probably raise absolute hell when she found out she was gone. Was that enough for her to give up an unbelievable adventure and return to her mundane life?

"Margot?"

"I hadn't thought about it." She laughed nervously. "I'll miss Janey. And my plants. Without me to care for them, they'll surely die. But I think I'd like to stay with you if you'll let me."

He crouched in front of Margot and took her face in the palms of his hands. "I've been alone for far too long... I've enjoyed your company. If you are to stay, there are conditions. Should I find it too difficult to control myself, this partnership will cease, and I will find somewhere *safe* for you to live out the rest of your days. Do you understand?"

Margot squealed, threw her arms around Cillian's neck, and tightly hugged him. "Thank you, thank you, thank you! Thank you for not leaving me to the fae. I would have rather died." Before she fully released her hold on him, she gave him a quick kiss on the cheek. "You won't regret this."

Cillian's laugh warmed Margot's soul.

"I may already regret this. Another mouth to feed, someone else to protect. I'm getting the short end of the stick here." He smirked. "This is going to be much more work for me."

"If it makes you feel any better, I'm an excellent cook," she said with a toothy grin. "Well, at least I am when I have ingredients to work with."

"My, my. Tempting a demon with the one thing they love. Who would have thought humans were so underhanded?"

MARGOT FELL INTO THE RHYTHM OF LIFE AT SEA OVER the next three days, though "falling" wasn't quite the right word —it was more like being thrown in headfirst. Each morning before the lavender sun peeked over the horizon, she'd join Cillian to check the nets and lines. Her hands grew red and raw, blisters forming despite her best efforts to be careful. But she bit back any complaints. After all, sore hands were infinitely better than being captured by the fae—or anyone else.

Between tasks, Cillian taught her about navigation and weather patterns. She absorbed every detail like a sponge, desperate to prove she wasn't dead weight. Sometimes she caught him watching her with those mercurial eyes, his expression unreadable—somewhere between amusement and concern, with something deeper she couldn't quite place.

True to her word, she took charge of cooking, or at least, that was her plan. She'd grossly underestimated how different cooking would be on a moving vessel. Worse still were the foreign ingredients—she couldn't tell one grain from another or what herbs might complement the strange vegetables she found in their stores. That first night, the meal was an absolute disaster. Still, Cillian ate every bite, though she noticed how often he reached for his cup to wash it down. By the second day, she'd at least mastered keeping the cookware from sliding off the stove, and her fish stew actually earned her a genuine smile.

They sat together on the deck the following evening, sharing the leftover stew as the twin moons cast their ethereal glow across the waves. The salt spray on the breeze reminded her how far she was from home, from everything familiar.

"You're adapting well," Cillian said, breaking their comfortable silence. "Better than I expected."

"Did you think I'd be completely useless?" She tried to keep her tone light, though part of her wondered if he really had.

"Honestly? Yes." His laugh was warm when she feigned outrage. "Most who've never been at sea take weeks to find their legs. You're... different."

"I've always been a quick learner." She paused, stirring her stew. "And I have an excellent teacher."

The words hung between them, heavy with something unspoken. Cillian cleared his throat and stood, gathering their bowls.

"Storm's coming," he said, nodding toward the horizon where violet clouds were gathering. "We should secure everything below deck."

Cillian triple-checked that the tools and spare parts were secure. As he was tying a knot, his entire body went unnaturally still. He looked out of the porthole. Margot followed his gaze, unease prickling at the back of her neck as the wind picked up, carrying with it a faint, high-pitched hum.

"What is it?" she asked, but Cillian didn't answer right away.

Instead, he shook his head. "Probably nothing." But his grip tightened on the rope.

Margot watched him for a long moment. His jaw was clenched, shoulders tense, and though he tried to appear casual, she could tell something was wrong. The strange humming grew louder, vibrating through the wooden planks beneath her feet. A shiver ran down her spine as the sound seemed to come from everywhere and nowhere at once. The wind howled outside, but this was different—abnormal. She opened her mouth to speak again, but before she could form the words, a screeching whine sounded, and something crashed into the side of the boat, sending it swaying perilously from side to side.

Margot held onto Cillian, steadying herself. "Please tell me that's normal."

Cillian grimaced and shook his head. "Not normal. Stay here. I'm going to check the deck."

Margot snaked her arm around his. "There is no way I'm staying here by myself. I'm not dying alone."

Cillian huffed and let her follow him. She shielded her eyes from the light rain. Lightning streaked across the blackened sky in the near distance. She knew it was only a matter of time before all hell broke loose.

The sea was rough and unforgiving as they clung to the ship's side, trying to keep themselves upright. Cillian's eyes darted back and forth, scanning the inky depths of an endless ocean. Margot's nails dug into the wood, splintering it as fear coursed through her veins.

Something massive sent waves crashing against the hull, making the entire ship shudder. Each impact jolted through the wooden planks, threatening to tear them apart.

Margot's feet slid on the rain-slicked deck as she struggled to maintain her balance. Then, the ship pitched violently to port, sending unsecured barrels rolling across the deck and forcing her to grab the railing with white-knuckled hands. Salt spray stung her eyes as she peered into the churning depths below.

"Are you okay?" he asked, placing a hand on her shoulder. "You should really wait in the cabin."

"I'm fine, and no. If you're here, I'm here."

"Stay," he said before running to the other side of the ship.

The water below bubbled, and the ship tilted to the side as a giant snake-like creature rose from beneath the surface with thousands of razor-sharp teeth on display. Purple algae slid down thick blue scales, catching on the creature's fins. The head moved slowly until its soulless black eyes focused on Margot. She couldn't breathe, she couldn't *move*.

It's going to eat me!

An arm wrapped around her waist, and she shrieked. Cillian tightened his grip.

"Wha-what is that thing?" she stammered.

"A leviathan," he said through gritted teeth. "And before you ask, it means we're in serious trouble."

6

TOO MANY TEETH

"GET INSIDE THE CABIN," Cillian demanded.

"I'm not leaving you!"

Cillian turned Margot around and backed her into a wall away from the ship's railing. "Don't be stupid, Margot. This is dangerous and we're running out of time!"

"I'll be fine!"

"Damnit, Margot! I can't protect you right now. I need to prepare the harpoon. Please, *please* go inside. I'm begging you."

"I'll be okay. Just go."

Cillian mumbled under his breath, gave her one last glance, and ran to the other side of the ship. Once he was out of sight, she kept wide eyes on the creature. Wind whipped wildly, rocking the boat as the angry sea beat its walls from all sides. The creature reared its head back, baring too many teeth. She knew this stalemate wouldn't last much longer.

Margot spotted Cillian's dark figure through the downpour and exhaled in relief. Pressing herself against the wall, she inched toward him, each step precarious on the slick deck. He held the harpoon steady, his focus locked on the monster. Her eyes flickered to the creature, and for a moment, she swore she saw anger

69

burning in its gaze as if it were furious that they dared enter its domain.

Without warning, the fiend dove into the water, its massive body colliding with the boat as it went under. The impact nearly capsized the ship, throwing her violently from one side to the other. She slammed into the cabin wall, gasping for air as the leviathan struck again and again.

The ship lurched, and Margot slid helplessly across the deck, the rain-slick wood offering no grip. Desperately, she reached out, grasping for anything to stop her momentum—but her hands couldn't find purchase. Her feet went over the edge, her body following in an instant. She could hear Cillian yelling her name; his voice carried away by the wind and the storm.

Margot's gaze dropped to the frigid, churning waters below, the icy spray stinging her face. Panic spiked, her body completely horizontal. If she didn't find something to grab onto—fast—she *was* going to die.

Then, like a switch flipping, the familiar calm of crisis settled over her. The same steadiness that had seen her through her mother's worst days wrapped around her like armor. *Assess the situation. Identify solutions. Keep breathing.* Her mind clicked into gear; she had mere seconds to save herself.

That's when she saw it, a large dowel jutting out from the ship wall. She contorted her body, muscles aching. A cry sputtered from her lips. With one last stretch, her fingers wrapped around the peg. She moved her other arm forward and gripped the wood. Like a pendulum, her body swung out and then swung in. Her chest and limbs smacked into the wood. Hot tears fell from her cheeks, mingling with the rain.

But she'd faced worse. She'd clawed her way through unemployment, endured the crushing weight of debt, and survived. This may have been the most dangerous experience she'd ever had in her life, but she'd survive it, too. She'd make sure of it.

"Margot!" Cillian shouted.

He was close, but Margot was losing her grip. She just needed to hold out until he reached her. Everything would be fine. She searched the wall with her legs for any kind of ledge. If she relieved some of the weight she was holding, she would make it. *Hold on*.

The monster surfaced on the other side of the ship, dipping Margot's side further into the sea. Her hold on the dowel faltered. and she slid down the ship's wall.

"Cillian!" Margot wailed as her feet skimmed the icy water.

The boat righted itself abruptly, and Cillian's hand shot out, grabbing hers just in time. Pain surged through her as she slammed into the hull, a strangled cry escaping her lips, but the relief of being alive dulled the agony. Her chest heaved, each breath mingling with the sting of her bruised ribs, but she clung to the fact that she was still there—still breathing.

"I've got you," Cillian reassured her. "Hold on tight."

Tears streamed down Margot's cheeks from the pain she felt every time she inhaled. He quickly but carefully pulled her back onto the deck, and she collapsed on top of him. Wiping her sodden hair from her face, he cupped her chin.

"You need to go to the cabin and let me deal with this. I am no longer asking you—I'm telling you. You're not equipped to handle this—I am."

Margot wept, her tears falling onto Cillian's hand. "You'll die."

"I won't, but *you* will. I've dealt with this before. Please, Margot. Go to the cabin and wait for me where it is safer." Cillian's head jerked toward the leviathan as it screeched. "*Go! Now!*"

Cillian helped Margot up and ran toward the creature. Her chest rattled as she inched toward the cabin. One arm braced her ribs, which were surely broken, and the other held out to balance herself.

Deafening roars overtook rumbling thunder.

The boat struggled to remain afloat.

Cillian shouted in the distance.

Margot sobbed.

She opened the cabin door, quickly closed it behind her, and gaped at the wreckage. The room was a mess. Shattered porcelain littered the floor. Charcoal and ash covered everything. Blankets and pillows were strewn about. The furniture remained in place. Nailed to the floor, she guessed.

Margot sighed and untied the cord around her waist before slipping off her soaked tunic. Jagged shards of glass and splintered wood littered the floor, and she carefully avoided them, spreading the tunic on the coffee table to dry. She groaned as she bent over to pick up the blankets and pillows. Climbing into bed, she buried herself beneath the covers, hoping nothing would crush her as she listened to the chaos outside.

A DOOR OPENED AND CLOSED, WAKING MARGOT FROM A restless sleep. Her gaze drifted to a bare-chested Cillian, hunching over a chair. She tried sitting up and winced before promptly laying back down.

He looked at her, eyes weary. "You're hurt."

"I don't belong here," Margot said, looking away.

"No. You don't."

The sincerity of his tone caused tears to prick the corners of her eyes. Before coming here, she had always felt like an outsider, spending her days living vicariously through fictional characters. Knowing nothing had changed, even though her situation had, hurt.

"Do you want to go home?"

She stayed silent for a few moments before mustering up the courage and whispered, "I don't know."

Footsteps shuffled across the room. The solid pressure of his arm caused the bed to sink as he knelt beside her. She turned to him. Lines of exhaustion etched his face.

"The answer to that question doesn't matter as much as you may think it does, Margot," he said, petting her head. "I've been trying to get home for years. I think... I think we're trapped here."

"Why would you want to go back to Olvath?"

"It's a terrible place, but I wouldn't have to run anymore. I've been running for a long time. It's tiring... I'm tired."

"If you find a way back... are you going to leave me?"

He shook his head. "No. You're growing on me, and I don't trust the fae for a single second." He clasped her hand. "Margot, I need you to trust me. You don't have to do anything else but trusting me is non-negotiable. Most of my life has been spent fighting or commanding others to fight. So, when I tell you something, I need you to do it. Can you do that for me? This injury could have been prevented."

"I can do that."

"Now we need to tend to those broken ribs. They need to be wrapped. I warn you; it's going to hurt."

Cillian moved to lift the blanket. Margot panicked, quickly pulled her arms out from beneath and slammed them down, preventing him from removing her armor. He eyed her curiously and went to remove it again.

"You can't," she whispered.

He huffed and ran his fingers through his hair. "Margot, I can't bandage you without seeing the injury."

She flushed. After her brazen act earlier, she didn't know why him seeing her bare bothered her so much. More than a handful of men had seen her naked. But Cillian wasn't a man. Not really. And if she really thought about it, if she really dug deep, she knew what she would find—fear.

Fear.

The flippant attitude she tossed about so casually was the biggest lie she ever told. Cillian terrified her. But as scared as she was, she was equally excited and intrigued by the person who saved her life. She couldn't think of a single man back home who would have done what he had.

"Margot?" Cillian asked.

She glanced at him. "You can't because I have no clothes on."

A low growl rumbled from his chest. His nostrils flared as he eyed the creamy skin of her exposed arms. "I will behave myself." He swallowed. "I swear. This needs to happen. It isn't something you can do effectively on your own."

"I read once that doctors don't even wrap rib injuries anymore. That wrapping a broken rib can cause more harm than good."

Cillian rolled his eyes and placed an amber-colored glass container on his lap. "I'm assuming a doctor is some kind of healer in your world, but it really doesn't matter. This is Faerie—not Earth. What I have here," He tapped the container on his lap, "is something you can't get anywhere else."

"What is it?" Margot asked.

A faint hiss seeped from the jar as Cillian pried open the airtight lid. An earthy, sulfurous scent filled the cabin, causing her stomach to turn and nose to wrinkle. The pungent aroma only got worse as he unraveled the murky brown bandages.

"My own special blend," he said proudly. "Doesn't smell great, but it'll fix up those ribs."

"That's the understatement of the century. You can't expect me to let you wrap me in those. They smell downright foul."

"It's only bad now. Once they've aired out a bit, they'll be less revolting."

"No." Margot turned her head away from him. "I'd rather take my chances."

He gripped her chin, forcing her to look back at him, and narrowed his eyes. Then his body went preternaturally still. He didn't speak—only stared. Her heart raced. She wanted nothing more than for him to say something. The tension was so thick it could be cut with a knife.

Fear.

Cillian groaned. "This is ridiculous. You're a liability if you don't let me fix you. An even bigger one than you already are, given that you're human."

A shaky breath rattled from Margot's chest as she tried propping herself up on her elbows while still holding the blanket against her. Cillian rushed forward, placing the bandages on the floor before helping her sit up. She scooted to the edge of the bed the best she could and let the blanket slide down her taut stomach. Cool air instantly pebbled her nipples. She glanced at Cillian, his gaze unblinking as he stared at her body. He grunted and adjusted himself below his belt. She tried to avoid looking, but curiosity got the better of her, and her mouth ran dry when she saw the sizeable member lurking behind his leathers.

Cillian gave her a knowing smirk. "You ready?"

Margot nodded. With the bandages in hand, he sat beside her, his knees touching hers. As he unfurled the dressing, she memorized each dip and swell of his muscled chest. His form was much like a Greek statue. A god. A *demon*.

He leaned in, the heat radiating from his skin nearly suffocating. Her breath hitched, turning ragged as she locked eyes with his hardened silver gaze. With the flick of his tongue, he wet his bottom lip before he squeezed his eyes shut and drew in a deep, controlling breath.

"I'm going to touch you now, Margot." His voice was low, rough. "Remove the blanket."

She nodded and did as he said.

Cillian shifted position, kneeling on the floor before Margot, gently nudging her legs apart to settle between them. His large hands rested on the tops of her thighs as he leaned in, inhaling her scent. A shiver rippled down his spine, visibly shaking his broad shoulders. He paused for a moment, holding himself still, before finally beginning to bandage her carefully.

His hands worked meticulously around her tender belly; his touch was surprisingly delicate. She whimpered as he brushed against her nipples as he worked through the fabric. Her core heated. She wondered what it would feel like for more than just a brief, accidental touch.

Cillian quickly secured the bandage, fled to the cabin's

other side, and rifled through a drawer. His heaving chest shook his body. Margot watched. Perplexed. Why had he run away from her? What was he doing? As if in answer, a tunic fell in her lap.

"Put that on," he said as he looked at the ceiling. "I can smell your arousal, and when you look like that... just—just put it on. Please."

Her mind was a veritable gutter, and she should have felt embarrassed, but she couldn't bring herself to care. Cillian was a beautiful man. She wanted to know what it would be like if he begged for her. Begged to touch her, to taste her.

"Margot, *now*." He shot her a warning glance, and she gave him her best *fuck me* eyes.

She slipped the shirt over her head, but nothing could stop the puddle forming between her legs. It had been far too long since she had been with a man and never with one like Cillian. She squeezed her thighs together, trying to curb the painful throbbing between them, when a moan slipped past her lips. She snapped her mouth shut.

"This is torture," Cillian said as he threw himself into a chair, adjusting himself once more.

She cleared her throat. "Did you kill the leviathan?"

He stared at her. Desire, rage, and concern flashed in his eyes. "I didn't. They're hard to kill. I simply annoyed it enough that it left. We were lucky."

"How long until we get to town?"

"A day or two. Depends on the currents."

"If the fae are looking for us, isn't going into town risky?" Margot asked.

He tilted his head and considered the question. "A small town like Elowen should be fine. The fae there likely won't report us as they need to make a living. Gold is gold. But really, no place is truly safe, so we'll need to stay alert."

"I see."

Margot shifted on the bed and moaned again as some pressure

relieved from her broken ribs. At that, Cillian shot to his feet, letting his eyes rest on her chest before heading for the door.

"Where are you going?" she asked.

He opened the door and shot a look at her over his shoulder. "Away from..." He waved his hand in her general direction. "This. Get some rest."

When Cillian didn't come back, she lay back in the bed. Her body was so tightly wound, and she couldn't stop thinking about how badly she wanted to run her tongue along his muscles or taste his skin as she worked his shaft. If Cillian, a demon, had better self-control than she had, what did that make her?

She didn't care.

Fully aware of how wet she was, she palmed her breasts before dipping her hand below. She bent her knees, careful not to aggravate her ribs, and circled her clit. There was no denying that she wanted Cillian when she moaned his name. And through the wall, she heard him grunting, groaning. She knew he was thinking about her as he pumped himself.

Margot curled two fingers inside her, imagining what it would be like to have all of Cillian. What it would be like for him to push into her center, to feel his weight on top of her. How it would feel to have his hot mouth pressed against hers. She didn't know she could want someone—let alone someone she just met—so much, but the fire had been stoked, and she couldn't stop it.

She didn't want to.

Hearing Cillian's muffled grunts drove her, and it didn't take long before her orgasm crested. Wave after wave crashed over her, and she lay there, panting and covered in sweat. The best orgasm she ever had, and he hadn't even touched her. Despite her injury, she couldn't help but smile as she fell asleep, completely satisfied.

MARGOT STARED AT THE CABIN'S INTERIOR, dumbfounded. Last night, it had been in shambles, but now it looked as if nothing had happened. Pictures were placed back on the walls. Soot was cleaned from the floor. Another flower had even been placed on the coffee table. The clanking of dishes drew her attention, and she found Cillian hunched over, rummaging through the kitchenette cabinets.

"Making food?" Margot asked as she slowly sat up in bed. She was surprised by how much better her ribs felt after a night's rest with the ointment on her skin. "I could use some, if you don't mind."

He glanced at her over his shoulder, gaze lingering on her breasts. Margot promptly adjusted the tunic. Thoughts of yesterday whirled through her mind, causing her to blush. Objectively, Cillian was attractive. She didn't think anyone alive would think he was bad looking. Tall, dark, and muscular with bronzed skin the color of nutmeg. Then there were those eyes. Piercing silver, unlike anything she'd ever seen, made her knees weak. It had been a while since she had been intimate with anyone, a fact she'd become hyperaware of since being around Cillian.

"I figured you would be hungry," he said, returning to his task. "Just a few more minutes.

Margot crawled out of bed and sat in the cozy chair in front of the fireplace. As he worked, the muscles in his back moved beautifully. Admiring his form was something she could spend hours doing—he was perfect. If she were any good at painting, she would ask to paint him nude like Jack painted Rose.

Cillian walked over with a plate piled high with cooked meats, cheese, and bread.

"This is the last of the meat," he said, handing her the food. "Last night was rough. We deserve it." He sniffed and wearily glanced at her. "Why are you doing this to me?"

She shifted uncomfortably in her seat. "I—"

"Margot, it's forbidden for demons to consort with humans," he interrupted her as he sat and ate from his own plate.

She took a bite of cheese and tried deciphering her feelings. It wasn't like she wanted to marry the guy; she just wanted to have some fun with him. A feeling that was obviously mutual. Having regular sex would at least make this adventure a little less lonely.

"Who's going to stop you?" she asked. "I mean, as you say, we're exiles. Is the big, bad Dread Lord going to pop in and slaughter you because you had sex with someone you weren't supposed to have sex with?"

"There's more to it than that." He sighed, his eyes softening when he looked at her. "I could kill you. Humans are fragile... and more often than not, sex triggers the transformation."

"What do you mean?" Her eyes widened. "What do you turn into?"

He laughed. "A bigger demon? I mostly look the same, save for the horns and wings—which I keep hidden most of the time—but my body gets larger. *Much* larger. And that means *everything* gets larger. Understand?"

Margot choked on her food. "I... think so."

"As much as I would love to... experience you, a human's body isn't made to take something that size."

This was *not* the conversation she thought she would have first thing in the morning.

"How much do you know about humans? Be honest."

He cocked an eyebrow. "I know a bit. Why?"

"You know," she said, biting back a chuckle, "humans have babies, right?"

"I assume that would be the case, yes."

"Well, I doubt your penis is as large as a seven-pound baby."

Frustration twisted his face, and he huffed. "Regardless, it is forbidden, and I'm done with this conversation."

Margot didn't hide her smirk. Clearly, Cillian knew nothing about human biology. Accepting the small win, she silently agreed to shelve the topic.

He took a big bite of sausage and pointed his fork at Margot. "We need to discuss how you should act once we're in town. I had to adjust course because of the storm, so we have some time before we arrive, but we need to be on the same page."

"I'll act like I normally would, obviously."

"You will *absolutely not* act as you normally would. The fae will try taking you if they think you're acting of your own free will."

"Hold the phone. What do you mean?"

"What's a phone?" He gave her a puzzled look before shaking his head. "Never mind. I think you know what I mean. You need to act as if I own you."

"So let me get this straight. You were going to hand me over willingly to the people who would abduct me if I weren't your *slave*?"

He shrugged and gave her a wry smile. "I didn't know you then."

"You barely know me now!" She snorted and set her plate on the table. "No way. There is no freaking way I'm going to pretend that you *own* me. It'll be fine."

Cillian rested his head on the back of the chair and slowly exhaled. "You won't be fine, Margot. The fae are stronger than you—even the weak ones—and if they see you walking around on your own, you'll *really* be someone's slave."

"Why don't they capture you?"

"I'm a demon." He gave her an incredulous look, as if this were something she should have known. "The fae are almost as fragile as humans. Almost. I've been in Faerie for a long time. There is a mutual understanding between many of the fae and me." He narrowed his eyes. "I don't raze their villages. They provide goods and services to me. A fair exchange and not one I'm looking to upset because you can't play pretend."

Cold sweat beaded along Margot's forehead. The thought of Cillian destroying an entire community was terrifying. She knew nothing about demons, fae, or this world. Though she was uncomfortable with his plan, it would probably be unwise to go against his advice, considering how well standing against him during the leviathan attack went.

She swallowed thickly, and her mouth suddenly felt like sand-paper. "Would you actually do that? Raze a village?"

"If I had to. Margot, our lives are all about survival. The sooner you understand that, the better. This plan here is the only option that guarantees you stay alive and with me."

Quiet minutes passed as his words weighed on Margot. Reluctantly, she met his eyes and nodded. Living was definitely something she wanted to continue doing.

7

MANACLED

MARGOT'S STOMACH twisted as Cillian entered the cabin, leather manacles and collar dangling from his hands, a thick leash connecting the two. He knelt before her, his silver eyes pleading as if begging forgiveness for what he was about to do.

"You need to wear these. Fae law recognizes the bearer of the rein as the rightful owner of... the individual wearing the constraints."

Margot looked between the shackles and Cillian. "You're kidding, right?"

"No."

"Why do you even have these?"

"Just in case."

She deadpanned. "Just in case you need to own a slave?"

He shrugged, giving her a sheepish smile. "You never know."

Margot sighed and held out her wrists.

Cillian carefully put them on, but the act came easily to him. A little *too* easy for her comfort, as if he had performed the same motions hundreds of times. She chose not to dwell on the thought. His life before she collapsed into his world was none of her business. It wasn't her place to judge.

He closed the collar around her neck, and tugged at the leash,

83

making sure it was secure. "We're still on Nyxtrae. Elowen is south of where I found you in the Dreadwood. I'd have liked to go somewhere farther away... but you can't keep walking around dressed like that, and Elowen is the closest place to get what we need."

The leather collar was suffocating, its rough edges digging into her skin with every shallow breath. Margot slipped a trembling finger between it and her neck, the small gap offering little relief from the mounting pressure. Her pulse quickened, each thud echoing in her ears as she fought to quell her rising panic.

She glanced at Cillian. "Why did you want to go farther away?"

"Ah... well." He frowned as he watched Margot struggle with the collar. With nimble fingers, he loosened it a notch. "When I was in Silverbrook, I heard Ravara's men talking about you. They'd been looking for you for weeks—that's how I knew where you were."

"Why would you care?"

"Purely selfish reasons, truth be told." A groan rumbled from his chest as he pushed himself off the floor. "I simply wanted whatever they were after. Ravara is a damn bastard and has done nothing but complicate my life." He shrugged. "I wanted to return the favor."

He moved across the cabin, grabbed a black canvas sack, and slung it over his shoulder. "The issue with Elowen is that the town is close to Silverbrook. So, you need to keep your head down and say nothing."

Margot scoffed, and he glared at her as he secured a jingling pouch to his belt. "This isn't a joke, Margot. You need to act timid, scared. Don't give them a reason to suspect you."

"This is ridiculous."

"*This* is Faerie." He glanced out the porthole and tugged on her leash. "Come on. Time to go."

"Wow," Margot breathed as they exited the cabin.

Through a thin veil of fog, she saw the jagged coastline dotted with thorny brush and gnarled trees whose bark was the color of dried blood. Their branches reached toward the lavender sky like knobby fingers, leaves rustling with whispers carried on bitter winds.

"Not all of Faerie is beautiful," Cillian said beside her, the leash coiled loosely in his hand. "Nyxtrae is rather grim, but there are some brilliant spots to sightsee. If we have time, I'd love to show them to you."

"I'd like that." Margot lifted her shackled wrists, showing off her bracelets. "Preferably without these, though."

Cillian chuckled, his gaze flicking to her restraints. "I don't know," he said, his tone teasing. "I kind of like the way you look bound."

Margot's eyes widened, heat rushing to her cheeks. He caught her reaction, and the corners of his mouth tugged into a wicked grin.

"Relax," he said, tipping his head back as laughter spilled from him.

She picked a particularly interesting spot on the deck to stare at and waited for the chilled air to cool her down.

Dense fog clung to Margot's skin as they made their way toward Elowen, each step deliberate on the treacherous ground. Loose stones shifted beneath her bare feet, threatening to send her tumbling. Every slight movement had the collar chafing against her neck, a reminder of her supposed place in this world. She couldn't shake the feeling that this wasn't just an act—that somehow, this was a glimpse of what could have been had Cillian not found her first.

Through the mist, Elowen's silhouette emerged like a fortress risen from nightmare. Unlike the organic shapes of the Dreadwood, the town was all sharp angles and high walls, as if carved from the bones of the earth itself. Thick stone towers punctuated the skyline, their peaks disappearing into the low-hanging clouds. Between them, buildings of dark granite pressed together like teeth, their windows gleaming like dying embers in the dim light.

"Stay close," Cillian murmured, his fingers flexing around the leash. "Something's wrong."

Margot tried to slow her breathing, to appear as docile as possible, but her heart thundered in her chest. "What do you mean?"

"Too quiet." His silver eyes scanned the empty streets ahead. "Market day in Elowen usually draws crowds from all over southern Nyxtrae. But look—" He nodded toward the abandoned stalls lining the street, their wares covered in a fine layer of dust. "It's like they're waiting for something."

Acrid smoke curled through the air, carrying with it the metallic tang of blood. Music drifted from somewhere deeper in the town—a haunting melody that made Margot's skin crawl. Every instinct screamed at her to run, to get as far from this place as possible.

"Maybe we should try somewhere else," she whispered.

Cillian's jaw tightened. "We don't have a choice. You need proper clothes, and we need supplies." He glanced at her, his expression softening slightly. "Just stay quiet and let me handle everything. The sooner we get what we need, the sooner we can leave."

They approached the town's entrance—a massive metal gate hanging open like a maw. Carved into the stone above, words in a language Margot didn't recognize seemed to writhe and shift in the shadows. The sight made her dizzy.

"What does it say?" she asked.

"Nothing good." Cillian's voice was bleak. "It's an old curse. 'May those who enter unwelcome find only death within these walls.'"

Arctic wind swept through the streets, reminding Margot of home—of autumn leaves scraping against sidewalks and the familiar creak of her apartment's heating system. But here, in Elowen, even the wind felt wrong.

Margot sneaked glances when she could but never got a good look at her surroundings. Instead, she kept her eyes on the ground. The few fae they passed kept their distance, but their stares lingered too long on Margot. She could feel their gazes burning into her skin, studying her like she was something foreign —which, she supposed, she was. Back home, being stared at in a store meant you had toilet paper stuck to your shoe or spinach in your teeth. Here, it could mean death.

God, what she wouldn't give for something as mundane as embarrassment. For the comfort of Janey's laugh, or even the annoying drip of her bathroom faucet that never quite stopped no matter how many times she tried to fix it.

Cillian tugged gently on the leash, drawing her attention back to their trek. The streets had narrowed, buildings pressing in on either side until the sky was barely visible above. Somewhere ahead, that haunting melody continued to play, its notes distorting as they bounced off the stone walls.

They turned a corner and Margot nearly stumbled as Cillian suddenly yanked her into a shadowy alcove, his hand clamping over her mouth. His body went preternaturally still against hers, and she followed his gaze to where two fae in dark leathers crossed the street ahead. Their armor bore an insignia—a twisted tree wrapped in thorns.

"The girl can't have gone far," one said, his voice carrying clearly in the still air. "Ravara wants every town in Nyxtrae searched."

"I say we kill her and be done with it." The second fae spat on the ground. "She's not worth it."

"Careful." The first fae's voice dropped lower, but Margot could still make out his words. "She's worth it to him and he wants her breathing. Something about her magic."

Cillian's grip tightened on the leash as the fae passed. Once they were out of earshot, he released her mouth but kept her pressed against the wall. "Do you believe me now?"

Margot said nothing, not knowing what to believe. Hell, she could barely believe she hadn't woken up yet, and with each passing day, it seemed more and more unlikely she ever would.

The bitter laugh threatening to escape her throat died as another pair of fae walked past their hiding spot.

Cillian's eyes narrowed as he watched them pass. "They're crawling all over this place." His finger traced the collar around her neck, adjusting it slightly. His fingertips lingered on the sensitive skin for a second too long, making her pulse quicken—and not from fear. "We need to move fast. There's a merchant near the center square who owes me a favor. With any luck, we can get what we need and be gone before anyone looks too closely at you."

The center square was a mockery of the small-town plazas Margot remembered from home. Where there should have been benches and flowerbeds, stone altars lined the edges, their surfaces stained dark with what she hoped wasn't blood. Instead of a cheerful fountain, a massive statue dominated the center—a fae warrior standing atop a pile of twisted bodies; his sword raised triumphantly. The sight made her nauseous.

Vendors' stalls formed a maze around the statue, most of them empty or abandoned. The few that were occupied housed merchants who looked more like prisoners, their movements jerky and nervous as they arranged their meager wares. The music haunting them grew louder here, its source still hidden but its melody more discordant than ever.

"This isn't right," Margot whispered, her voice barely audible above the twisted song. "The way they're acting..."

Cillian's response was cut short by a sudden commotion near one of the larger stalls. A fae merchant was on his knees, blood trickling from his nose as one of Ravara's men stood over him.

"You'll tell us if you see her," the guard snarled, yanking the merchant's head back by his hair. "A human girl. Anyone caught helping her will answer to Ravara himself."

The merchant's eyes darted around the square—and locked onto Margot. She saw the recognition flash across his face and saw his mouth begin to open.

Cillian cursed under his breath and jerked the leash, pulling her back toward the narrow alley. "Change of plans."

They hadn't made it three steps when a shout came behind them, "The girl! By the western arch!"

Everything happened at once.

The discordant music reached a fever pitch as guards seemed to materialize from every shadow. Cillian shoved Margot behind him, and he drew his sword, the metal singing as it cleared its sheath. The first guard who reached them went down with a gurgling cry as Cillian's blade opened his throat in one fluid motion, painting the cobbles crimson.

"Run!" Cillian growled, pushing her toward the narrow street that led to the docks. She stumbled, the manacles making it difficult to catch her balance. Behind her, steel clashed against steel.

The dock was in sight when her foot caught on a broken cobblestone. White-hot pain shot through her heel as something sharp sliced deep. She stumbled but kept moving, each step leaving a small smear of blood in her wake.

"They're cutting us off from the ship!" Cillian shouted. The sounds of combat followed—metal against metal, grunts of pain, bodies hitting stone.

Through tears of pain, Margot saw he was right. A line of Ravara's men had formed between them and their vessel, weapons drawn. An arrow grazed her arm, drawing blood.

Cillian's body began to change, bones cracking as he grew larger and horns sprouted from his head, curling down his skull. "Hold on to me!"

She didn't hesitate. Despite her fear of his demon form, she wrapped her arms around his waist. At that moment, Margot realized how much had changed since they first met. The demon who had once held a sword to her throat was now her only protection against forces she barely understood. She should have been terrified of his transformation, of the way his bones broke and reformed, but instead, she found comfort in his inhuman strength. When had that happened? When had she started trusting him so completely?

He charged the line of fae, his massive form bowling through them like they were nothing more than pins. The impact sent fresh waves of pain through her injured foot, but they didn't stop until they reached the gangplank.

"Kill the demon!" someone shouted. "But take the girl alive!"

Another arrow struck Cillian's shoulder as he practically threw her aboard. He roared—a sound that shook the very air—and leaped onto the deck. "Cut the lines!"

Something strange happened then—time seemed to slow, and Margot felt an unfamiliar energy pulse through her veins. The surrounding molecules shimmered for a split second, and the next volley of arrows curved away from them as if deflected by an invisible force. She blinked, and everything snapped back to normal speed. Had she imagined it? But Cillian's sharp look told her he'd noticed something too, though there wasn't time to discuss it now as she fumbled with the knots on the mooring rope. The ship lurched as Cillian raised the anchor, and she heard him curse as she ran to the helm.

The vessel pulled away from the dock just as another wave of Ravara's men reached it. They launched arrows and hurled magic, but Cillian had already guided them beyond their range. The dark towers of Elowen grew smaller behind them, along with any hope of supplies or proper clothing.

Her body ached, every muscle screaming in protest. She slumped against the rail, watching the cursed town disappear into the mist.

"What do we do now?" Margot asked, her voice barely above a whisper.

Cillian leaned against the ship's rail beside her, his silver eyes distant as he considered their options. "We need somewhere the fae care more about profit than politics. Hythe, maybe." His jaw tightened. "It's a longer journey than I'd like, but the merchants there... they're different. More practical."

"How do you know?"

"I've dealt with them before. They're not loyal to anyone but their coin purses." He glanced at her. "It'll mean a few more days in those clothes, but we'll plan better this time. No rushing in. We'll watch the town first, make sure it's safe. I... underestimated how badly Ravara wanted you. I'm sorry."

The care in his voice, the way he was already strategizing to protect her, made something warm unfurl in her chest. It was strange how quickly he'd become someone she could rely on.

"It's not your fault," she said weakly. "Can you help me into the cabin? I'm tired."

"I've got you." Cillian held her as if she were something fragile. "You're safe." He placed her down on the armchair. "I'll wake you as soon as I get us to safety. Rest."

Margot nodded weakly, exhaustion finally overtaking her.

"Let me see your foot," he said, his voice rousing her from sleep. She shifted against pillows and blankets, groaning as she sat up, swinging her legs over the side of the bed. He must have moved her.

Margot winced as he inspected her foot, rotating it from side to side. The cut was deep—an ugly gash across her heel that still oozed freely.

"This needs to be cleaned and wrapped," he muttered, more to himself than to her. He reached into his pack and pulled out a small bottle and some bandages.

She hissed through her teeth as he poured the liquid over the wound, unconcerned that it was getting on the wooden floor. "I thought we were going to be safe there."

"Nowhere in Faerie is truly safe." He began wrapping her foot with practiced efficiency. "But Hythe... it's different. The fae there keep to themselves and run their businesses. They don't care about Ravara and the chaos he sows as long as they're making money."

"And if they recognize me?"

"They might." He secured the bandage and sat back on his

heels. "But gold speaks louder than allegiance that far north. We'll need to be careful, but it's our best chance at getting what we need."

Margot moved to the chair and leaned back, exhaustion seeping into her bones. "How far is Hythe?"

"A few days' journey, if we're careful. We'll need to avoid the major sea routes." He settled beside her. "You should rest some more. It won't take long for that foot to heal, but there's no sense in pushing it."

She nodded, too tired to argue. The events in Elowen played through her mind—the haunting music, the guards' voices, the merchant's terrified recognition. "Cillian?"

"Hm?"

"Why would Ravara want me for magic I don't even know I have?"

He was quiet for a long moment, his silver eyes reflecting the crackling fire in the hearth. "I don't know," he finally said. "But whatever it is, it's important enough that he wants you alive. That's something we can use to our advantage."

Margot hummed, her eyes growing heavy as the last traces of daylight faded from the cabin. She worried Hythe would be more of the same. More fighting, more death, more unanswered questions. But for now, instead of letting those worries hold her down, she drifted into an uneasy sleep with Cillian keeping watch beside her.

She dreamed of Elowen's twisted streets and haunted melodies, of blood on cobblestones and eyes in the shadows. But mostly, she dreamed of home—of a world where the biggest danger was missing rent, where the only chains were the ones that were chosen for one's self. Yet even in her dreams, she felt Cillian's presence nearby, keeping watch, and somehow, that made both worlds feel a little less frightening.

8

COULD BE AND SHOULDN'T BE

MARGOT WOKE to the gentle rocking of the ship and the sharp throb of her injured foot. The events in Elowen felt like a nightmare, but the dried blood on the bandage and the lingering ache in her muscles proved otherwise. She hadn't yet attempted to walk since their escape, but the angry red gash across her heel wasn't promising.

Pain shot through her leg as she shifted in the chair where she'd fallen asleep. Early morning light filtered through the cabin window, casting long shadows across the wooden floor. Her throat felt raw, and she desperately needed water, but the simple act of standing seemed impossible.

"Here." Cillian's voice startled her. She hadn't heard him enter. He held out a cup of water and something wrapped in cloth. "You need to eat."

She took a careful sip, then unwrapped what turned out to be bread and cheese. "How long was I asleep?"

"Most of the night." He crouched beside her chair to check her bandages. "We made good progress. The winds have been in our favor."

His fingers were gentle as he unwound the dressing, but she

93

still winced when he revealed the wound. The gash looked worse in the daylight—angry and swollen around the edges.

"That's going to leave a scar," she muttered.

"Better a scar than your capture." His voice was grim as he reached for a jar of salve. "What they would have done to you in Elowen…" He shook his head. "We were lucky to escape."

The ointment stung as he applied it, but Margot was more focused on his words. "What would they have done?"

Cillian's hands stilled. "Nothing good. Ravara's reputation for cruelty is well-earned. And after what his men said about your magic…" He resumed bandaging her foot. "Let's just focus on getting to Hythe."

"Try putting some weight on it." Cillian offered his arm for support.

Margot gripped his forearm, surprised by how the warmth of his skin still caught her off guard, and carefully stood. Even with him taking most of her weight, pain shot up her leg. She stumbled, falling against him. His free hand caught her waist, steadying her.

"Sorry," she mumbled, but didn't pull away. The solid presence of him, the gentle rise and fall of his chest, made her feel safer than she had since arriving in Faerie.

"Don't apologize." His voice was soft, barely more than a whisper. When she looked up, he was studying her face with an intensity that made her breath catch. "You're stronger than you think, Margot."

They stood like that for a moment, too close, neither willing to break away first. His thumb traced small circles on her hip—a gesture so subtle she wasn't sure he realized what he was doing. Her heart battered her ribcage, and she knew he could hear it.

Finally, Cillian cleared his throat and helped her to the deck. "You should get some fresh air. It'll help."

The morning air was crisp with the scent of the sea. Margot leaned against the rail, taking weight off her injured foot as she watched the coastline drift by. The twisted trees and thorny brush of southern Nyxtrae had given way to gentler landscapes—rolling hills covered in silver-leafed trees that seemed to shimmer in the early light.

"Beautiful, isn't it?" Cillian said, coming to stand beside her. His arm brushed against hers, and she felt the same spark of electricity she always did when he was near. "The north is different. Softer, somehow. Even the air feels cleaner."

"How long until we reach Hythe?"

"Two days, maybe three." He glanced at her injury. "We'll need to stop before nightfall. That wound needs proper tending, and there's a sheltered inlet ahead where we can anchor safely."

"We're not worried about Ravara's men finding us?"

"They'll be watching the main ports. The place I know..." A hint of a smile played on his lips. "Well, let's just say it's not on any maps."

THEY SAILED NORTH THROUGH CALMER WATERS, Nyxtrae's coastline a constant companion to their starboard side. Margot noticed how Cillian kept glancing at her from the helm, his silver eyes swimming with emotion that made her skin prickle. But each time she caught him looking, he'd quickly turn away, his jaw tightening as if fighting some internal battle.

The sun climbed higher, and the air grew warmer. Margot relished the added warmth as the simple tunic did little to protect her from the elements. She could feel Cillian's gaze burning into her again but refused to look this time. Whatever was building between them—this crackling energy that seemed to charge the very air—was clearly something he wasn't ready to acknowledge.

"There," he said suddenly, pointing to a barely visible break in the coastline. "The entrance is tricky. Most ships wouldn't risk it."

Margot squinted at the narrow gap between towering cliffs. "And we're going to?"

A ghost of a smile played on his lips. "Trust me?"

She did, more than she probably should. She nodded.

Cillian guided the ship with expert precision, threading through the treacherous passage. The cliffs rose on either side, so close she could make out individual veins of crystal winding through the dark stone. The passage twisted, and sunlight diminished until it seemed they were sailing through twilight. Just when Margot thought they couldn't possibly go any further, the channel opened into a hidden lagoon.

She gasped. The water was crystal clear, showing pale sand and colorful coral beneath. A crescent of beach curved around one side, while the other rose in terraced cliffs draped with flowering vines. A small waterfall tumbled down the rocks, creating a constant melody that echoed off the stone walls.

"It's beautiful," she breathed. "How did you find this place?"

"By accident, years ago." He offered her his arm as she limped across the deck. "I was... running from something. Needed somewhere to hide." A shadow crossed his face. "Seems I'm always running from something."

"What were you running from?"

"What else? The fae." He looked toward the shimmering waters. "It doesn't matter, though. Being on the run led me to this, and I've been keeping it to myself ever since."

"And now you're sharing it with me?" The words came out softer than she intended.

He was quiet. When she looked up, he wore a troubled expression. Finally, he said, "Relax a bit while I set anchor. That foot needs time to heal before we attempt Hythe."

The sudden distance in his tone stung, but Margot had grown used to these abrupt shifts. Every time they drew close, he'd pull away, erected walls she couldn't breach. She watched him move about the deck, all fluid grace and controlled power, and wondered what it would take to make him stop running.

Once anchored, Cillian helped her into the small rowboat. The close quarters meant their legs pressed together as he rowed them to shore, each stroke of the oars making his muscles flex.

Margot focused on the waterfall, pretending she couldn't feel the electricity crackling between them.

The sand was soft and cool beneath her feet when they landed. Cillian insisted on carrying her to a smooth boulder near the water's edge, his hands lingering a moment too long as he set her down. He busied himself building a small fire, though the day was warm.

"The nights get cold here," he explained, not meeting her eyes. "And we should clean that wound properly."

Margot watched him work, noting the careful way he kept space between them now. Always so careful, so controlled. She wondered what would happen if he just once let that control slip.

As if reading her thoughts, he stiffened. "Gotta get some water," he said gruffly, and strode toward the falls before she could respond.

Margot sighed, watching him go. The way he moved, the power contained in every step, drew her eyes like a magnet. This push and pull between them felt like a dance full of foreign steps that she struggled to comprehend. But as she watched him disappear behind the falls, she couldn't help but wonder if maybe he was just as lost in it as she was.

The waterfall's song filled the silence as Margot watched shadows stretch across the lagoon. Everything about this hidden place felt magical, the way crystal formations caught the light, the subtle phosphorescent glow beneath the water's surface.

Cillian returned with a waterskin and fresh bandages. He knelt before her, and she caught the scent of leather and herbs that clung to him. "This might hurt," he warned, carefully unwrapping her foot. "The water's cold."

She hissed as he poured it over her wound, but the sting quickly faded to a dull throb. His hands were steady as he cleaned around the gash, his touch detached despite their closeness.

"Why did you really bring me here?" she asked, watching his face for any reaction.

He paused his ministrations for just a moment. "It's safe. We needed somewhere to rest."

"And that's all?"

He looked up then, his silver eyes reflecting the dying sunlight. "What else would it be?"

"You said you've kept this place to yourself. Never shared it with anyone." She hesitated, then pushed on. "Why me?"

Cillian returned his attention to her wound, but she could see tension in his jaw. "Because you needed it," he said finally. "And because—" He cut himself off, shaking his head. "It doesn't matter."

"It matters to me."

His grip tightened around her ankle. "Margot." Her name was both warning and plea. "Some doors are better left closed."

"Even if what's behind them makes them worth opening?"

He tied off the bandage with more force than necessary and stood, putting distance between them. "Especially then." He stared out at the water, his back rigid. "I'll check the perimeter before dark. Sleep."

Margot watched him disappear again, taking the crackling tension with him. She didn't know which was worse, the moments when he let his guard down, or the walls he built immediately after. But here, in this hidden paradise he'd chosen to share with her, she couldn't help but hope that maybe some of those walls were beginning to crumble.

The sun dipped lower, painting the lagoon in shades of gold and violet. In the growing darkness, the phosphorescence beneath the water grew brighter, creating patterns that swirled and twinkled like stars. Despite her racing thoughts, exhaustion crept in, and the past day's events finally caught up with her.

She was half-asleep when Cillian returned, his footsteps nearly silent on the sand. Through heavy lids, she watched him add wood to the fire. When he thought she was sleeping, his guard seemed to drop just slightly, and she caught the way his gaze lingered on her face, filled with something that looked almost like longing. But by morning, she knew the walls would be back in place. And they would go back to their respective positions of almost and not quite, of could be and shouldn't be. For now, she let herself drift off to the sound of the waterfall, and the quiet presence of a demon who refused to give in to his desires.

Margot woke to the sound of waves lapping against the shore. The fire had burned down to embers, but someone—Cillian— had draped a blanket over her while she slept. She found him at the edge of the water, staring out at the horizon where storm clouds gathered.

"Bad weather coming?" she asked, limping to join him. Her foot felt better after a night's rest, though it still throbbed with each step.

"More than that." His voice was grim. "Look." He pointed to a distant smudge of smoke rising from the coast. "Signal fires. Ravara's men are still searching."

Her stomach clenched. Their sanctuary couldn't last forever, but she'd hoped for more time. "How long until we reach Hythe?"

"If we leave now, we can make it by nightfall tomorrow." He turned to her, his expression carefully neutral. "Are you ready?"

She knew he wasn't just asking about her injury. They were about to sail into a port town filled with fae who might recognize her and turn them in. The relative safety of this hidden cove would soon be just a memory, like her old life on Earth.

"Yes," she said, surprising herself with how steady her voice sounded.

Cillian nodded once, then began gathering their supplies. As they loaded the rowboat, Margot took one last look at the lagoon —at this secret place he'd chosen to share with her. Whatever lay ahead in Hythe, she would remember this. Those brief moments when Cillian's walls had started to crack would forever be etched in her memory.

She didn't look back as they rowed to the ship. She couldn't afford to.

9

HYTHE

HYTHE MATERIALIZED through the darkness like a town pulled straight from the pages of a fairy tale—or rather, what remained of one after centuries of wear. Wooden docks creaked beneath gentle waves, their planks weathered and splitting in places. Torch flames sputtered in rusted brackets, casting uneven light across the small harbor where fishing vessels and merchant ships bobbed lazily in their moorings.

Margot stood at the bow, watching the port town grow larger as they approached. After their harrowing escape from Elowen, even this humble sight felt like salvation. The night air carried the mingled scents of salt and smoke, along with something earthier —like fresh hay and livestock.

"Different from Elowen, isn't it?" Cillian's voice was low as he came to stand beside her. "Hythe cares more for coin and their own. The merchants here have learned to look the other way when it suits them."

"It looks so…" Margot hesitated, searching for a diplomatic word. "Primitive?" She winced at how that sounded. "I mean, it's beautiful in its own way, but where I'm from, ports have electricity—lights that never go out—and machines to help load

101

cargo. They could do so much more with just a few modern innovations."

Cillian guided the ship toward a quiet section of the harbor, away from the handful of vessels currently moored. "What's electricity?"

Margot laughed softly, though there was no mockery in it. "It's hard to explain. It's like... captured lightning that we used to power things. No more torches or candles. No more doing everything by hand." She gestured to the town sprawling up the hillside, where thatched roofs rose in uneven tiers. "Think about how much easier life would be for these people with just a few basic machines."

"The fae prefer their ways," Cillian said as he worked the ropes. "Though I admit, captured lightning sounds useful." He glanced at her with curiosity. "Your world must be very different."

As they drew closer, Margot could make out more details of the town. Buildings of varying heights and states of repair lined the broken cobblestone streets that wound up gentle hills. Most were built from rough-hewn timber and stone, their walls leaning slightly with age. Wooden walkways connected some structures, their boards groaning with each step of the few fae still out at this hour.

"You have no idea," she said, watching a merchant struggle to push a heavy cart up the uneven street. "Where I'm from, we have vehicles—machines that move on their own, carrying people and goods. No horses—livestock—or carts needed." She shook her head. "It's strange seeing a place that feels so... medieval."

The ship glided to a stop alongside the dock, and Cillian secured the lines. He rummaged in his pack, taking out the manacles. "Sorry for this. Though Hythe is different, they still recognize Ravara's laws."

Margot sighed and held out her wrists. He helped Margot onto the pier, his hand remaining on her waist a moment longer than necessary before he switched to guiding her with the leash.

The touch sent a familiar warmth through her, one she tried desperately to ignore.

"First thing tomorrow, we'll get you proper clothes," he said, eyeing her makeshift attire with concern. "But tonight, we rest. There's an inn nearby that doesn't ask questions." He jerked his head toward her shackles. "You won't need to keep those on once we're in the room either."

They made their way up from the docks, following a winding path into the heart of Hythe. The cobblestones beneath their feet were worn and uneven, with weeds sprouting between them. Here and there, torchlight revealed glimpses of the town's daily life—baskets of produce left outside shop doors, farming tools leaning against walls, the occasional chicken-like creature pecking at scattered grain.

A wooden sign creaked gently in the breeze ahead. Its letters were carved deep and weathered by time. The building itself was two stories of timber and stone, with a thatched roof that needed mending in places. A covered porch wrapped around the ground floor; its boards worn smooth by countless boots.

"This is it?" Margot whispered, taking in the sight. Despite its rustic appearance, there was something oddly charming about the place.

Cillian nodded. "The Siren's Rest. The owner's an old salt who's seen enough of the world to know when to keep his mouth shut. We'll be safe here." He tugged on the leash, moving toward the door. "Just let me do the talking and keep your head down."

The door opened with a groan, releasing a wave of warmth and the scent of roasting meat mixed with ale. Margot's stomach growled, reminding her it had been far too long since their last proper meal. As they stepped inside, she couldn't help but wonder what other surprises this quaint town held in store for them—and how many more reminders of just how far from home she truly was.

A large stone hearth and scattered candles in metal holders dimly lit the common room of the inn. Patrons hunched over wooden tables, speaking in low voices that barely carried over the crackling fire. The air was thick with pipe smoke and the smell of whatever was roasting on the spit—some kind of game bird, Margot guessed as she looked at the succulent meat.

A gruff looking fae worked behind a scarred wooden bar, his skin the color of storm clouds and his eyes glinted like copper coins. Though lines etched his face and his skin leathery, he was still handsome. He looked up as they entered, giving Cillian a slight nod of recognition; his gaze lingered on Margot for a few seconds before he returned to his work, polishing a tankard with a cloth that had seen better days.

"Stay back as far as the leash lets you," Cillian murmured as he approached the bar.

Margot listened as they spoke in hushed tones, sneaking glances at the other patrons. The fae there were less ethereal than the ones she'd briefly seen in Elowen, but stunning, nonetheless. These were working fae—farmers, merchants, sailors—with callused hands and weather-worn faces. One woman's skin had a greenish tint that reminded Margot of moss, while a man at the corner table seemed to shimmer faintly like morning dew.

"We have a room," Cillian said quietly, returning to her side. He released her manacles and put the contraption back in his pack. "You don't have to worry here, but once we head into town, they'll need to go back on."

"Are you sure?" Margot whispered, glancing nervously at the fae, expecting them to attack her, but they didn't even give her a second look.

"I'm sure." He placed his hand on the small of her back as he led her to a table near the hearth. "Food's coming, if you're hungry."

"Starving," she admitted, sliding onto the wooden bench that creaked as she sat. She couldn't help but smile. "Back home we'd call this place rustic chic. People pay good money to eat in restaurants that look deliberately old-fashioned."

Cillian raised an eyebrow as he settled across from her. "Your people pay to pretend things are old?"

"Some do. They think it's charming." She ran her fingers along the table's rough surface. "Though I guess it hits different when you don't have a choice."

A serving girl appeared with two tankards of ale and what looked like fresh bread. Her movements were quick and efficient, but Margot caught the way her eyes widened slightly at Cillian before hurrying away.

"They're afraid of you here too," Margot observed quietly, tearing off a piece of bread. It was still warm, and her stomach growled appreciatively.

"They should be." His voice was matter-of-fact, but there was a hint of something else—regret, maybe. "Fear keeps people from asking too many questions."

"Is that why you keep everyone at arm's length?" The words slipped out before she could stop them. Maybe it was the warmth of the fire, or the relative safety of their surroundings, but something made her bold. "To keep them afraid?"

Cillian's silver eyes fixed on her, intense enough to make her breath catch. "Not everyone."

Before she could respond, the serving girl returned with their food—some kind of roasted fowl with root vegetables and herbs. The awkward moment passed, and they ate in comfortable silence, though Margot couldn't shake the weight of his words. *Not everyone.*

"Tell me more about your world," Cillian said eventually, pushing his empty plate aside. "These machines you mentioned— they really move on their own?"

Margot dove into explanations about cars and trains, then electricity and indoor plumbing.

Cillian listened with genuine interest, asking questions that made her realize just how much she took for granted. When she described airplanes, his eyes lit up with wonder.

"Metal birds that carry people through the clouds," he mused, shaking his head. "Your world sounds like magic."

"That's just it though—it's not magic at all. It's science. Knowledge. Things anyone can learn to use." She gestured around the room. "These fae could have so much more."

"Would it make them happier?" Cillian's question was gentle but pointed. "Look around, Margot. They have food, shelter, community. Sometimes simple isn't the same as lacking."

She opened her mouth to argue, then closed it again. The common room had filled as they talked, and the atmosphere had grown livelier. Someone had started playing a stringed instrument in the corner, its melody weaving through the conversations and laughter. The serving girl smiled now as she moved between tables, and even the gruff barkeep seemed more relaxed.

"Maybe you're right," she conceded.

Cillian's laugh was unexpected and rich, drawing a few curious glances from nearby tables. "Come on," he said, standing and offering his hand. "Let's head upstairs. Tomorrow will be a busy day."

Margot took his hand, trying to ignore how natural it felt to do so. As they climbed the narrow stairs, she found herself wondering if maybe she was the one who needed to adjust her perspective. Perhaps there was something to be said for simplicity after all.

The room itself was barely more than a closet but clean, with a single bed that suddenly seemed too small. A window overlooked the harbor, where moonlight painted lilac paths across the dark water. Margot's heart skipped as she realized the sleeping arrangements they faced.

"I'll take the floor," Cillian said, already pulling a blanket from the bed.

"Don't be ridiculous," she protested. "The bed's plenty big enough for both of us." When he started to object, she added. "We're both adults, Cillian. And it's not like we haven't slept near each other before."

He hesitated, and for a moment, she thought he would argue. But finally, he nodded. "Get some sleep, Margot. Tomorrow, we'll find you proper clothes."

As she lay in bed later, listening to Cillian's steady breathing beside her, Margot thought about home, the one she'd left behind, and this strange new world she was beginning to understand. The bed was lumpy, the room was lit only by moonlight, and somewhere below, the last patrons of the night were singing a song she didn't know. Yet somehow, she felt more at peace than she had in weeks.

Maybe that was worth more than all the modern conveniences she missed.

MARGOT WOKE TO FIND HERSELF CURLED AGAINST Cillian's chest, his arm draped protectively around her waist. During the night, they had gravitated toward each other, seeking warmth in the chilly room. His breath stirred her hair, and she could feel the steady thrum of his heartbeat against her cheek. For a moment, she allowed herself to savor the closeness, knowing it wouldn't—couldn't—last.

Cillian stirred. His arm tightened briefly around her before he seemed to realize their position. He withdrew carefully, but not before Margot caught the way his breath hitched and the slight tremor in his hands as he pulled away.

"Sorry," he muttered. "Force of habit."

"What, cuddling with humans?" The words came out more bitterly than she'd intended.

His mercury eyes met hers, dark with something that made her stomach flutter. "No. Just you."

The moment stretched between them, unspoken possibilities lingering in the back of her mind. Then Cillian cleared his throat and stood, breaking the spell. "We should get moving. The markets will be busy soon."

The morning air was crisp as Cillian tugged Margot along through Hythe's waking streets. Vendors were already setting up their stalls, arranging produce and goods. The scent of fresh bread wafted from a nearby bakery, mixing with the ever-present smell of salt air.

"Here," Cillian said, steering her toward a shop tucked between two larger buildings. A sign depicting a needle and thread hung above the door, though the letters beneath were in a script Margot couldn't read.

Inside, rolls of leather and fabric lined the walls in various colors and textures. A tall fae woman looked up from her work at a large table, her fingers stained with dyes and her silver hair tied back in intricate braids. Her eyes widened slightly at the sight of Cillian but quickly smoothed into a professional mask.

"The lady needs proper attire," Cillian said, his voice carrying that edge of authority that seemed to make everyone in Faerie snap to attention. He removed her manacles. "Something suitable for travel. And combat."

The seamstress nodded and approached Margot, circling her with an appraising eye. "Arms up," she instructed, pulling a measuring cord from her pocket.

As the woman worked, Margot caught Cillian watching her in the shop's clouded mirror. His gaze traced the lines of her body as the seamstress took measurements, and the heat in his eyes made her skin prickle. When their eyes met in the reflection, neither looked away.

The seamstress disappeared into a back room and returned with several pieces of leather armor. "Try these," she said, handing them to Margot. "Behind that screen."

The leathers were softer than Margot expected but still sturdy. She struggled with some fastenings, unused to the complicated arrangement of straps and buckles.

"Need help?" Cillian's voice was low, closer than she expected.

"I... yes," she admitted after another failed attempt with a stubborn buckle.

He stepped behind the screen, and Margot sucked in a sharp breath at his proximity. His fingers worked deftly at the straps along her sides, each touch sending sparks across her skin even through the leather. When he reached the fastenings near her chest, his hands slowed, becoming almost reverent.

"Too tight?" he asked, his breath warm against her ear.

"No," she whispered, though her heart felt like it might burst from her chest. "It's perfect."

The outfit was form-fitting but allowed effortless movement. The leather hugged her curves in a way that might have made her self-conscious if not for Cillian's appreciative look. A diamond-shaped cutout at the chest revealed more than she was used to, but she had to admit it suited the overall design.

"You look..." Cillian started, then seemed to think better of whatever he was going to say. Instead, he turned to the seamstress. "We'll need three sets. And appropriate undergarments. And socks and boots."

While the seamstress gathered the additional items, Margot studied herself in the mirror. The woman in the reflection looked like someone else—someone stronger, more confident. Someone who belonged in this world.

"What do you think?" she asked, turning to face Cillian.

His eyes darkened as they roamed over her, lingering on the exposed skin at her chest. "I think," he said carefully, "that we should find the rest of our supplies quickly."

They left the shop with several packages, Margot now properly clothed in her new armor, yet still donning the manacles. As they walked through the market, she noticed the way other fae looked at her—not with suspicion, but with interest. She walked taller, more assured. Even Cillian was lax on the leash and wasn't constantly telling her to keep her head down.

"You're different here," she observed as they examined goods at a merchant's stall. "More relaxed."

"Am I?" He selected a few dried herbs, adding them to their growing collection of supplies. "Maybe it's the company."

"Or maybe you just needed a break from saving my life every five minutes."

His laugh was warm, genuine. "I wouldn't count on that lasting." But his eyes were soft when they met hers, and his hand found the small of her back as they moved to the next stall. "Though I admit, this is... nice."

The way he said it made her heart skip. Nice. Such a simple word, yet coming from him, it felt like a confession. And maybe it was—a small admission that whatever was growing between them wasn't entirely unwelcome, even if it could never be more.

For now, Margot decided, that would have to be enough.

They spent the afternoon gathering the rest of their supplies, though Margot found it increasingly difficult to focus on the task at hand. Every time Cillian moved near her, she felt that pull—like gravity, but stronger. More insistent. The new leather armor didn't help; though it covered more of her than his old tunic had, something about the way it fit made her feel more exposed, especially when his eyes lingered on her.

At a weapon smith's stall, Cillian's hands brushed against hers as they examined a bow. "You'll need to learn," he whispered quietly enough that only she could hear. "I can teach you."

"Is that wise?" she asked, hyper-aware of how close he stood behind her. "Being alone together while you show me how to shoot?"

His breath hitched slightly. "Probably not." But he bought the bow anyway, along with a quiver.

As the sun climbed higher, the day grew uncomfortably warm. They found refuge in a small tavern, tucked away from the bustle of the market. The space was cool and dark, with only a few patrons scattered at various tables. Cillian chose a secluded corner, though the table was small enough that their knees touched when they sat.

"Here," he said, pushing a cup toward her. "It's better than the ale from last night."

Margot took a sip, surprised by the sweetness. "What is it?"

"Honeywine." He watched her over the rim of his own cup, his eyes dark in the dim tavern light. "Made with flowers that only bloom under Faerie's moons when they're at their fullest."

She took another drink, letting the sweetness linger on her tongue. A drop escaped, trailing down her chin, and before she could wipe it away, Cillian's thumb caught it. The simple touch sent a jolt through her, and she couldn't help the small sound that escaped her throat.

Cillian withdrew his hand as if burned. "Margot..."

"I know," she whispered. "You don't have to keep reminding me what can't happen."

His jaw tightened. "Don't I?" He leaned forward, close enough that she could see the flecks of darker silver in his irises. "Because every time I let my guard down, every time I forget for even a moment what I am—" He broke off, his hands clenching into fists on the table.

"What you are," she whispered, "is the only person in either world who makes me feel safe."

Something flashed across his face—hunger, need, desperation —before he schooled his features back to careful neutrality. But his voice was rough when he spoke. "We should head back. It'll be dark soon."

They walked back to the Siren's Rest in tense silence, the air between them charged with everything left unsaid. Their purchases had been arranged to be delivered to the ship, leaving them unencumbered but also without distraction from the growing tension.

In their room, Margot struggled with the buckles of her new armor, unused to the complicated fastenings. She heard Cillian's sharp breath behind her.

"Let me," he said, his voice hoarse.

His fingers worked at the straps, and Margot held perfectly still, afraid that if she moved, if she breathed too deeply, something would shatter. The leather loosened, but Cillian's hands remained on her shoulders, warm through the thin shirt she wore beneath.

"We can't," he whispered, but he didn't move away.

Margot turned slowly to face him, her pulse pounding in her ears. "Why not?"

"Because," his thumbs traced small circles on her shoulders, "if I start, I won't be able to stop."

"Maybe I don't want you to stop."

His eyes fell to her lips, and for a moment—one breathless, perfect moment—she thought he might kiss her. Instead, he stepped back, putting distance between them like a physical barrier.

"Get some rest," he said roughly. "We leave at first light."

That night, they lay in the narrow bed, carefully maintaining space between them despite the magnetic pull that seemed determined to draw them together. Margot stared at the ceiling, listening to Cillian's uneven breathing, knowing he was just as awake as her.

Tomorrow, they would return to the ship, to the reality of their situation. But tonight, in the quiet darkness of their room in Hythe, Margot allowed herself to imagine a different world—one where Cillian wasn't a demon, where she wasn't lost in Faerie, where the growing ache in her chest could find relief in his arms.

Sleep came eventually, but her dreams were filled with silver eyes and gentle hands, with all the possibilities that lay just out of reach.

The streets were quiet, save for the occasional merchant preparing for the day ahead as they made their way back to the ship. Their extra supplies had been delivered as promised—crates of provisions, medical supplies, and the weapons Cillian had chosen, including the bow he'd insisted she would need.

During their time in Hythe, something had shifted—a deepening of whatever connection had been growing since they met. The relative safety of the port town had allowed them to see each other differently, to dare to hope for things that seemed impossible in the dangerous world beyond its borders.

"I'll show you how to use this once we're at sea," Cillian said, securing the bow with their other supplies. His voice was harsh, as if he, too, felt the loss of their brief respite. "You'll need to defend yourself."

"Because you won't always be there to protect me?" Margot meant it as a joke, but her voice wavered.

Cillian turned to her, tipping his chin down and narrowing his eyes. "Because I can't bear the thought of anything happening to you."

His admission seemed to float between them, heavy with implications neither was ready to face. Margot stepped closer, drawn by that familiar pull, but Cillian busied himself with the mooring lines.

"The tide's turning," he said, though his knuckles were white on the rope. "We should go."

As they sailed away from Hythe, Margot watched the town grow smaller from her place at the bow. The sun had fully risen now, burning away the morning mist and revealing the open sea ahead. She touched the leather of her new armor—practical, protective, but also a reminder of everything that had changed in the past two days.

"It was nice," she mumbled, feeling Cillian approach behind her. "Pretending we could just be normal for a while."

His hand found her waist, and this time, he didn't immediately pull away. "Nothing about this—about us—could ever be normal, Margot."

She searched his face, finding his silver eyes swimming with emotion. "Would that be so terrible?"

Instead of answering, he cupped her face in his hands. For one breathless moment, she thought he might finally give in to whatever was building between them. But then his hands fell away, and he stepped back.

"We have work to do," he said, his voice rough. "Starting with teaching you to shoot."

"Why do I feel like I won't enjoy this?"

He smirked. "Because you're smarter than you look. But if you're going to survive here, you need to learn. Rest up." He turned toward the helm and looked over his shoulder. "You'll need it."

Margot watched him walk away, knowing their brief respite in Hythe was well and truly over. Whatever came next would test them both—not just her skills with a bow, but this fragile thing growing between them.

She was ready for both.

TEA RUINER

HELL WAS ON THE HORIZON—OR at least that's what Margot's muscles screamed as she collapsed into the chair by the hearth, her body trembling from exertion. The morning's impromptu archery lesson had left her feeling like a herd of wild elephants had crushed her bones. Her arms ached, her shoulders burned, and Cillian only taught her the parts of a bow and how to pull the string back.

"You did well today," Cillian praised, stoking the fire before settling into his chair. Goosebumps dotted her skin from the force of his gaze. "I bet most humans would have given up after the first two hours."

Margot snorted, flexing her fingers to ease the stiffness. "Maybe I'm not like most humans.

"No," he agreed, his voice dropping lower. "You're not."

Margot shifted uncomfortably in her seat, trying to ignore how his eyes smoldered as he looked at her. "You should let me make tea," she blurted, desperate to break the tension. "It's the least I can do since you're handling dinner."

"I'd really prefer if you didn't."

She arched a brow. "And why not?"

For a moment, he just looked at her, his expression unreadable, before his eyes shifted to the ceiling as if searching for an answer—or avoiding the truth. "It's not necessary."

"Well, I insist." She pushed herself up, grimacing.

"Ah, come on, Margot." He sighed, leaning back in his chair. "You should just get some rest."

She glared at him. "God, Cillian, I may not be able to lift my arms above my head right now, but I'm sure I can manage tea."

Cillian's lips twitched. "If you're sure."

"I am."

She hobbled to the kitchenette, bracing herself against the counter as she caught her breath. The thought of preparing a full meal was laughable tonight, her muscles screaming with every small movement. But tea? Tea she could do. Even if her hands shook a little as she reached for the kettle, she'd manage.

As she worked, measuring leaves into the pot like she'd watched him do countless times, Cillian's voice broke through the comfortable silence. "Tell me about your life before. On Earth."

Margot paused, surprised by his request. "Not much to tell, really. I worked at a bookstore, could barely afford my apartment..." She shrugged, then immediately regretted the movement as pain shot through her shoulder.

"That's not what I meant." He leaned forward, elbows resting on his knees. "Tell me about you. The *real* you. Who were you? What did you do for fun?"

Who am I? The kettle whistled, and Margot busied herself with pouring water over the leaves, buying time to gather her thoughts. "I had Janey, and we would go out from time to time to let off steam... but I was... lonely, I suppose. Had a few relationships that went nowhere. More one-night stands than I care to admit. But most of my time was spent alone reading or something like that."

"One-night stands?"

She couldn't help but laugh at his confused expression. "When you spend one night with someone—intimately—and then never see them again." Her cheeks flushed. "It's not exactly something I'm proud of."

"Why not?" His tone held no judgment. "Demons aren't so different in that regard."

"Really?" She brought their cups over, settling back into the chair with a groan.

"Really." He took a sip of the tea and immediately frowned. "You are abysmal at brewing. Worse than that first meal you concocted." He inhaled the steam and wrinkled his nose. "This is truly awful. Easily the worst cup I've ever had."

She sniffed her own cup—it smelled fine. "Oh, come on. It can't be that bad."

"Taste the tea."

"You just told me it was terrible!" She huffed. "That doesn't make me want to taste the damn thing."

"Taste the tea, Margot," Cillian repeated, his voice firm.

She bit back another retort and took a tentative sip. The acrid taste of rancid flowers mixed with marijuana resin hit her tongue, and she gagged, her throat tightening in protest.

"I burned tea." The blood drained from her face as she looked at him. "Cillian, I burned the damn tea! I didn't even know it was possible to burn tea!"

Cillian laughed as he stood, reaching for her cup. "Hand it over, tea-ruiner." Without waiting for a response, he strode to the kitchenette and dumped the bitter brew. "There's an art to it. The water needs to be just right, and the timing..." He trailed off, carefully measuring the tea leaves as if performing a sacred ritual. "Watch."

There was something almost meditative about the way he prepared the tea—the precise movements of his hands, the quiet focus in his expression. A small smile tugged at his lips as he worked, as though this simple task brought him some measure of peace. It was clear he enjoyed this, took pride in it. Margot couldn't look away, drawn to his unguarded, softer side.

"I want to show you something," he said as he handed her a fresh cup. "A place that's special to me."

"Oh?"

"Sunfire Aerie." His expression grew distant, almost wistful. "It's... different from anywhere else in Faerie. Peaceful. Beautiful in a way that's hard to describe. I never thought I'd want to share it with anyone."

Margot cradled her cup, savoring the light spice of Cillian's custom brew. "Why bring me, then?"

He was quiet for a long moment, and when he spoke, his voice was subdued. "Because you're different. The way you handle yourself here, the magic within you—there's more to you than meets the eye."

"The magic again." She set her cup down harder than intended. "Cillian, I'm human. Just human."

"Are you?" He leaned toward her across the arm of his chair, his eyes intense. "I've seen how Faerie responds to you. Magic seems to bend around you like it recognizes something familiar. Something old."

"But my parents—"

He shrugged. "Maybe there's more to your story than you know." He reached out, his fingers brushing against her hand. "The fae are hunting you for a reason, Margot. And I think Sunfire Aerie might help us understand why."

She stared at their hands, the simple touch sending warmth through her tired limbs. "What makes you think that?"

"It's a sanctuary dedicated to old magic—magic that predates even the fae. If there are answers about your connection to this world, we might find them there."

Though she hated to admit it, something had changed. Every day spent in Faerie made it harder to dismiss the gnawing feeling that she wasn't quite the same as she was back on Earth. They hadn't spoken about what happened in Elowen—the arrows, the impossible way they moved—but if Cillian was bringing magic up now, particularly old magic, it was obvious the memory hadn't faded for him. The idea that she was something other than human seemed impossible, yet here she was in Faerie, drinking tea with a demon.

"When do we get there?"

A ghost of a smile played on his lips. "Sometime tomorrow if the winds are favorable." He hesitated, then added, "There are creatures there—gargoyles, mainly. They guard the Aerie. But if I'm right about you, about your magic, we should be safe."

Her brows shot up. "Should be?"

"Trust me?"

Margot thought about everything that had happened since arriving in Faerie—the dangers they'd faced, the moments they'd shared. Cillian had become her constant, her anchor in this strange world. Even now, exhausted and sore, she felt safer with him than she ever had on Earth.

"Yes," she whispered into her tea. "I trust you."

She glanced at him, catching a glimpse of something in his eyes, something that made her heart skip. But then it was gone, replaced by his usual careful control.

"How are you doing?" He asked, eyeing her foot before he moved to the kitchenette. "You seem to be walking just fine. I'm assuming the ointment worked well?"

She nodded. "Surprisingly well, actually. My foot aches a little, but my ribs don't hurt at all anymore."

"Good. Tomorrow will be another long day of training," he said over his shoulder as he checked on their dinner. "I'd like for you to get the motions down."

Margot groaned. "More archery?"

"You need to learn to defend yourself and this is the first step." His tone grew serious. "Faerie isn't safe, especially not for someone like you—someone with power they don't understand."

"I still think you're wrong about that," she grumbled. "But I'll keep at it. Someone needs to watch your back out there."

Unexpected laughter filled the cabin. He turned to her, a grin stretched wide across his face. "Is that so?"

"Someone has to." She returned the grin. "Though right now, I can barely watch my own back."

Cillian's expression grew thoughtful as he stirred whatever was cooking in the pot. "You don't give yourself enough credit. Most humans would have broken by now—the magic, the running, everything. But you..." He looked at her over his shoulder. "You adapt. You survive. Maybe that's part of why I want to show you the Aerie. It's one of the few places in Faerie I've felt... real. Like I could be more than what others expect of me."

Margot froze mid-sip. This was a side of Cillian she rarely saw —the part of him that wasn't just a demon warrior, but someone seeking his own place in a world that had rejected him.

He nodded, turning back to their meal. "Get some sleep after we eat. You'll need your strength for tomorrow."

As Margot settled her aching body into bed later that night, her mind raced. She couldn't help but wonder what awaited them at Sunfire Aerie. Whatever truth lay hidden there about her nature, about her connection to this world, at least she wouldn't face it alone.

The coming days would bring more training, more pain, and more questions. But it would also bring them closer to understanding who—and what—she truly was. And maybe, just maybe, closer to understanding whatever was growing between them, unspoken but undeniable.

Her last thought before drifting off was of Cillian's hands guiding her through the bow forms, his touch both strength and temptation, and of the way he looked at her when he thought she wouldn't notice—like she was a puzzle he both feared and longed to solve.

In her dreams, she flew through purple-tinged skies toward a distant aerie, silver eyes watching her every move, while something ancient and powerful stirred within her, waiting to be discovered.

11

THE GUARDIANS

WIND WHISTLED THROUGH THE SAILS, and the soft hum of the ship moving through the water filled the air as the first hints of dawn kissed the skyline. Margot set the quiver and bow next to her as she stood at the point of the ship, the cool breeze sweeping through her hair, carrying with it the faint scent of salt.

Ahead, the sky shifted from the bruised purple of night to soft lavender, igniting the surrounding waters with morning's early glow. The vessel cut through calm waters. If she leaned far enough over the side, she could see the slipstream trailing behind them.

"The Aerie's close," Cillian murmured, his voice low and steady. He leaned forward, resting his elbows on the rail beside her, his gaze fixed on the hazy outline of the desert beyond the water's edge. "We're passing Thalaset now."

Margot turned her eyes westward, where colorful domed roofs crowned with delicate finials jutted above the dunes, their vibrant hues muted by distance. Her fingers worked nervously at her cuticles, unease rippling beneath her skin. Another fae town. What if her would-be captors were waiting along the coast, watching for their ship?

121

"What if Ravara's men are there?" Her voice wavered. "What if they see us?"

Cillian leaned further against the rail, the wood creaking under his weight as he clasped his hands tightly together. "They'll likely chase us down," he said matter-of-factly.

Her breath hitched. "Shouldn't we, uh, be worried?"

He glanced at her, calm as ever. "Not really. Hardly anyone ventures into the Wastes. Thalaset keeps to itself—they trade for necessities, but only necessities, with Hythe. The fae there see themselves as divine." His mouth twitched in a faint smirk. "I know little about them, but I'm guessing that's why they settled so close to the Aerie."

Margot's fingers found the bowstring at her side and tugged at it absently. "Have you ever been there?"

"No," he admitted. "And I probably never will. They don't allow outsiders—not even fae outsiders."

"And the Wastes... that's where the Aerie is?"

"Yes."

She turned to him fully, catching the flicker of tension in his posture. "Is everything okay? You're acting weird. We don't have to do this, you know."

"It's not that," he muttered, his lips curving into a faint, conflicted smile. "I'm just being selfish."

Her brow furrowed. "Selfish how?"

He exhaled, the suffocating pull of his thoughts pressing into the space between them. "I want to take you away from all of this, hide you somewhere no one can ever find us. But I know you deserve more than that. You deserve answers—about who you are. And I really think the Aerie is the place to find them."

Margot's fingers stilled against the bowstring. Part of her bristled at the idea of being taken anywhere, as though she had no say, no choice. But another, quieter part, wondered what it would be like to run away from herself. To leave behind fear and uncertainty. To simply be with Cillian.

But then what? Could she really live like that, hiding away, never knowing the truth? She swallowed hard, pushing the thought aside. It was foolish to even entertain the idea. Answers mattered.

They had to.

Margot focused on the shifting sands against the skyline instead of her downward spiral. "What can we expect when we get there?"

"Heat. Silence. And eyes watching from the shadows," Cillian replied, his words tight. "Stay close to me. Always."

The ship sailed smoothly as the day wore on, the rhythmic creaking of the wood and the rush of wind filling the quiet between them. Margot found herself drawn to the distant vista, the desert ever nearing, its sands casting a golden haze against the sky.

She sat cross-legged on the deck, absentmindedly tracing the grain of the wood with her fingertips. Cillian had retreated to the helm, focused on navigating, though his presence was still palpable even from a distance. The silence between them was comfortable enough, but questions burned through her mind like wildfire. She wanted to know more about Faerie and the creatures that roamed its lands, but more importantly, she wanted to know about Cillian. The outcast demon who risked his own life to save hers, a fragile human who was nothing more than a burden.

"Tell me more about Sunfire Aerie," she called over her shoulder to break the silence, unable to hide the curious lilt her tone had taken. "You said you never thought you'd want to share it with anyone. How come?"

"It's... a place of solitude. A sanctuary dedicated to some old gods or goddesses or something—I can't make much sense of the carvings, but that's as much as I gather." Cillian glanced back at her. "It's one of the reasons why I think it'll help you." He returned his gaze forward. "Most fae steer clear of it because of the gargoyles, and it's one of the places in Faerie that feels... untouched." He paused, as if considering his next words carefully. "I wanted to share it with you because you remind me of myself.

A little lost. A little alone. I thought you might need that peace, among other things."

Margot blinked, surprised by his honesty. She hadn't expected him to offer something so personal. "Do you go there often?"

A small smile tugged at his lips. "Only when I need to remind myself of who I am."

The statement lingered. To Cillian, this was a place of quiet reflection, somewhere he felt safe enough to breathe. *Maybe it's the* only *place he feels safe.* She didn't push him further. Instead, she smiled and let the conversation hang, their shared silence somehow more profound than words.

"What about you?" Cillian's voice broke the tranquility. "What do you miss most about home?"

"I'm not sure," she admitted. If he could be honest, so could she. "I miss Janey a lot. I miss the simplicity, too. Knowing what to expect every day. It wasn't perfect, but it was... familiar. Safe."

Cillian nodded, his gaze still fixed ahead. "Familiarity can be comforting. But sometimes, it's the unknown that helps us find what we're really looking for."

As the sun climbed higher, Margot felt the heat settling in, but it wasn't unbearable. Not yet. She pulled the waterskin from her satchel, took a small sip, and leaned against the mast, watching the desert draw closer with each passing moment. It shimmered in the distance like a mirage, golden and endless... and speckled with glimmering purple dots. She gasped and pointed at them. "What are those?"

"Weaveshards." He looked back at her, silver eyes glowing in the sun. "I can't wait for you to see them. They're even more magnificent up close."

"But *what* are they?"

"The Reverent Wastes has an unusually high concentration of magic, which is why there's almost no vegetation. Most of the land is just endless dunes, dust, and emptiness. But all that magic has to go somewhere. Deep beneath Faerie, when veins of magic burst, they form massive glowing crystals. It's the only place I've found where something like that happens—and it's incredible. I'd probably stay forever if it wasn't so damn hot."

Margot shot up and ran across the deck, and craned her neck as she squinted, trying to get a better look. Behind her, she heard Cillian laughing. Faintly, she could make out waves of energy refracting around the Weaveshards. The idea that magic could manifest so tangibly, so beautifully, was mind-blowing.

"They're gorgeous," she murmured, her gaze still fixed on the distant glimmers. "I've never seen anything like it. They look like they're alive."

Cillian came to her side and rested his hand on her hip. "In a way, they are. Weaveshards pulse with residual magic for centuries, maybe longer. They never fade."

Faerie was far different from Earth. She marveled at the stark contrast between her two worlds. Here, the fae hadn't conquered the land like humans had done with her home. Instead, it seemed that the land ruled over them—a living, breathing entity in its own right. She glanced at Cillian, wondering how much Faerie had shaped him. Did he feel the magic around them the way she did now? She hadn't known him long, but moments like this made her want to understand more about the man beside her.

A pang of sadness tinged with guilt settled low in her stomach. *Janey would have loved this place.* Her friend had always been obsessed with fantasy novels, and if she ever found out Margot had come here without her, she'd probably kill her. But not before squeezing every little juicy detail out of her. *Not that there are any.* She smiled wryly.

Running her fingernail along a groove in the wooden railing, she sighed. *No use dwelling on things I can't change.*

She cleared her throat. "Can we get close to them?"

"We'll pass right through a field of them before we reach Sunfire Aerie. I'll take you as close as you like. Just remember—don't touch them. Weaveshards are beautiful, but they can be unpredictable."

"Unpredictable, how?" she asked, a bit more cautious now.

"They store a lot of magic," Cillian explained, his tone shifting to something more serious. "Some are harmless, others… not so much. Once, I touched one that shot out a bolt of lightning strong enough to create a crater ten feet deep. Best not to take any chances."

Margot nodded, her eyes drifting back to the purple crystals, still shimmering like jewels scattered across the golden sands. Part of her wanted to reach out, to feel the magic hum beneath her fingertips, but she also knew how little she understood about this world—how easily it could shift from wondrous to dangerous.

"I'll stick to looking," she promised with a grin, though she wondered what the stones were truly capable of.

Cillian pushed off the rail and started back toward the helm. He looked over his shoulder with a smirk. "Good plan."

The ship glided smoothly toward the horizon, the distance between them and the Reverent Wastes shrinking with every passing minute. The purple crystals grew larger, their glow more pronounced, casting an incandescent light over the dunes that was mesmerizing in the twilit night.

Margot couldn't take her eyes off them, a mix of awe and trepidation bubbling in her chest.

As they neared the edge of the crystal field, a subtle vibration *burred* through the deck beneath her feet, barely perceptible but enough to send threads of energy up her spine, causing her skin to pimple. She looked toward Cillian, who carefully turned the ship's wheel, navigating them safely in the shallow waters.

"Drop the anchor!"

Margot's arms shook as she slowly lowered the chain until she felt it hit the bottom. The boat bobbed lightly against the current as Cillian took his place next to her.

"They really are alive, aren't they?" she whispered, more to herself than to him. The surrounding air was charged with magic, as if the stones were drawing the very essence of Faerie into their crystalline forms.

"The same way that magic is alive. I think they filter ambient magic, storing it until the pressure becomes too great, then they release it and repeat the cycle. It's... unpredictable, as I said. You'll see once we get closer." He turned to her with a sheepish grin on his face. She cocked an eyebrow. "No dock. We're gonna get wet."

Margot shuddered, not wanting to think about the kinds of creatures lurking below the surface. At least the water was clear enough to see straight to the bottom, but the sheer number of strange-looking fish darting around gave her the willies.

Cillian adjusted a large rucksack and slung it over his shoulder. "I know the temperature is comfortable now, but as night presses on, it will plummet." He patted the bag. "I've got a coat for you once we get to shore. Don't worry, I'll keep it dry."

Margot squealed when Cillian scooped her into his arms and jumped off the ship's side, splashing into the water below. She was grateful he had the forethought to carry her. The water that barely came up to his shins would have easily come up to the middle of her thighs, and she was already chilled.

"Figured I'd help you out." He chuckled as he set her down on the shore. "Not like you weigh much."

Sand crunched beneath her feet, and as they entered the heart of the crystal field, the atmosphere grew heavy, rife with magic. Pressure built within her in a way that made her feel both energized and wary. Weaveshards rose from the sands like jagged amethysts, some as tall as she was, others towered high above the dunes on either side of them, and few were short and stout. Their violet light curved across the sandy ridges like a velvet sea.

"Whoa. They're amazing." Her eyes fixed on the glowing crystal to her right. As she stared deeper, a strange feeling tugged at her, something beneath the surface of their beauty. It wasn't fear exactly, but a sense of something... waiting.

A soft breeze stirred her hair, carrying the faintest whisper of sound, barely audible. She froze, glancing at Cillian, who was focused on navigating them safely between the crystals. She shook her head, trying to dismiss it as her imagination, but she swore she had heard it before.

"Stay alert," Cillian warned. "This field is where the magic is strongest. Things tend to get... strange out here."

As if the obelisks heard his words, one exploded in the distance. Margot flinched as the eruption echoed through the air. Her heart pounded in her chest, and she instinctively grabbed Cillian's arm, eyes wide as she watched a fiery vortex swirl high into the sky, only to be swallowed back into the crystal like a nightmare retracted. The Weaveshard's glow returned, as calm and serene as before. Too bad her pulse didn't follow suit.

"What the hell was that?" she said with a gasp, struggling to steady her breath.

Cillian shrugged, but his eyes were sharp. "Unpredictable. Maybe the stones store more than just magic, and sometimes they react to..." His voice drifted off as he gave Margot a sidelong glance.

"To what?" Margot's voice wavered, her eyes darting around, taking in the other crystals. She wondered if they were all ticking time bombs waiting to detonate, hellbent on incinerating her.

His eyes narrowed. "Emotions. Intent. Anything that disturbs the balance of magic here. I don't really know, honestly. But with Faerie, anything's possible. We need to stay calm and keep moving. The closer we get to the Aerie, the stronger it gets."

Margot swallowed hard, trying to quell her racing thoughts. *Stay calm.* She kept repeating the words to herself like a mantra, but the danger became *very* real, and she wasn't strong enough to pretend it didn't scare her. Magic pressed against her skin, testing her limits. She focused on breathing, trying to ground herself, but the violet gleam from the Weaveshards felt like ghosts watching her every move.

As they continued through the maze of crystals, the terrain grew rugged. The sands shifted beneath her feet, and the jutting rocks threatened to topple her; she struggled to keep up. Eventually, Cillian took her hand to help keep her steady. A whisper—so faint it might've been the wind—stirred again. This time, she couldn't ignore it.

"Cillian," she breathed, her voice breaking. "Do-do you hear that?"

He paused, eyes narrowing as he listened. After a moment, he shook his head. "Just the wind playing tricks on you. I swear this place messes with your senses."

Margot wanted to believe him, but the tug in her chest said otherwise. Something was calling to her, distant and haunting. *God, coming here was a terrible idea.*

She bit her lip, forcing herself to focus on Cillian's steady pace.

Her eyes shot to the left, where the faintest flicker of movement caught her attention—just beyond the crystal ridge.

"Did you see that?" Margot asked, her voice hushed as she pointed toward where the shadow had moved.

Cillian's gaze followed her gesture. "See what?"

"There was... something. Over there." The words sounded flimsy even to her ears, but she was sure she hadn't imagined it. "We're not alone, are we?"

Cillian sighed, his expression guarded. "I'm pretty sure we're alone. I'm not picking up on anything. But the stones draw all kinds of creatures. Magic-infused ones, spirits, Djinn. The power attracts them... but they usually keep their distance." He paused, glancing at her. "That doesn't mean we're completely safe, though."

Djinn? Margot's skin prickled. The sense of something watching them—or *her*—remained. Unintelligible whispers returned, louder this time, wrapping around her like a spectral presence. She squeezed her eyes shut, trying to keep it at bay, but it was getting harder to ignore the draw at the edges of her mind.

Then, without warning, the ground beneath her feet trembled.

Cillian spun around, his eyes manic. "Move!" he shouted, grabbing her wrist and pulling her forward.

The Weaveshards around them pulsed faster, radiating in an erratic rhythm. Another explosion rocked the air, this time closer, sending a plume of sand into the sky. Margot stumbled, her blood surging as the fiery tempest whirled, its heat searing even at a distance.

"We need to get out of here," Cillian growled. "*Now.*"

Margot didn't need to be told twice. Together, they sprinted through the crystals, volatile energy pulsing around them. The dreamscape had transformed into a minefield.

Just as they neared the maze of Weaveshard's edge, a massive shadow passed overhead, blocking out the light emitted by the crystals. Margot froze, her gaze snapping upward. High above them, a gargoyle perched on a jagged cliff, its stone wings unfurled, eyes glowing with cold, predatory light.

"Cillian," she whispered, barely getting his name out.

His face tightened. "Sunfire Aerie," he murmured. "We've arrived. And so have the guardians."

12

SUNFIRE AERIE

MARGOT'S HEART slammed against her chest as the gargoyle's eyes locked onto her. It was larger than she had imagined—its stone skin cracked and weathered, but its presence was one of ancient power. The wings, sharp as blades, stretched wide as it watched in silence from its perch.

Cillian's grip tightened on her wrist, his voice low but urgent. "Don't move. Don't make a sound."

Her breath caught in her throat. Instinct told her to run, but Cillian's steady presence kept her rooted in place. She could feel the silent pressure of the gargoyle's gaze bearing down on her, as if it was assessing them, deciding whether they were a threat—or prey.

Seconds stretched into what felt like hours. Magic buzzed around them, gradually picking up pace. The pressure was building again, like the world itself was holding its breath.

Cillian's eyes flicked toward her. "They protect the Aerie. As long as we don't provoke them, we should be fine. But we need to keep moving—*slowly*."

She forced herself to nod, keeping her gaze on the gargoyle. The muscles in her neck coiled with tension as they inched forward, one slow step at a time. The sand crunched beneath their feet, every sound amplified in the silence of the dunes.

Just as Margot crept within mere feet of the weathered stone column, another shadow plummeted from the sky like a thunderbolt. The second gargoyle landed with a deafening crack on the neighboring pillar, its claws gouging into the stone as if marking its claim.

Margot froze, her breath hitching in her throat. The creatures moved in eerie unison, their heads swiveling toward her almost mechanically. Empty, hollow eyes bore into her, and for a fleeting moment, she felt as though they could see straight through her, peeling back every fragile layer.

The whispers surged, rising in a frantic chorus that needled her mind, compelling her forward. Her heart hammered against her ribs as her mouth ran dry, her instincts screaming at her to flee. But the whispers wouldn't relent, weaving through her thoughts like a relentless tide.

She clenched her fists, her knees trembling beneath her. Every fiber of her being screamed to stay away, to retreat from those grotesque, stone-born beasts whose gaze seemed to hold the promise of ruin. Yet the whispers pulled at her with a force she couldn't resist, dragging her closer to the precipice of whatever awaited.

Shoving down her fear, she wriggled from Cillian's grasp, ignoring the curses he muttered under his breath, and took the last few steps to stand before the guardians. She filled her lungs and held it, mouth closed tight, as the gargoyles' eyes flared before dimming. Their stone forms creaked and groaned, lowering their heads, bowing to her, allowing her to ascend the crumbling steps that led to the top of Sunfire Aerie.

Margot glanced over her shoulder at Cillian, his mouth hanging open in amazement. "Have they ever done this before?"

"Have they ever bowed before me? Never." He let out a low laugh. "I knew you were special when I first saw you."

She turned back to the massive creatures, now humbled by

her presence. If she hadn't already seen what Faerie was capable of, she would have thought she was still moving through a dream that she hadn't quite woken up from. But this was her reality now. Unspoken power slid against her skin like a gossamer veil, as if Faerie itself was acknowledging her, accepting her. *What just happened?*

Cillian's words echoed in her mind—*I knew you were special when I first saw you.* Instead of being comforted by the sentiment, doubt and confusion set her nerves on fire. *Special?* She had never felt special. She was a normal woman with a normal job and a normal life. It wasn't until she came to Faerie that she felt anything other than normal.

"What do you mean?" Margot whispered. "What makes me special?"

Cillian stepped forward cautiously, his eyes never leaving the gargoyles, though they remained motionless as if accepting him, too. "I don't know the full answer to that," he admitted, his voice softer now but with a note of reverence. "But Faerie—the magic—reacts to you. And Ravara... Ravara knew. Somehow. The fae, this world—they know something about you that we don't. This," He made a sweeping motion with his arm, gesturing to the gargoyles, "doesn't just happen to anyone." He jerked his head toward the top of the Aerie. "We should go."

Margot swallowed hard, turning back toward the steps leading up to Sunfire Aerie. The ancient stone crumbled beneath her feet as she took a tentative step forward, the gargoyles' massive heads still lowered in respect. She wanted to ask more questions, but the whispers returned, urging her onward.

Her body moved on instinct now, each step feeling both foreign and inevitable as if the path had been waiting for her all along. With each stride, the connection between her and Faerie grew stronger, thrumming through her veins like a current. She couldn't shake the feeling that Sunfire Aerie was somehow *calling* her. She hesitated just before the final step, gigantic stone doors looming over her.

"Come on," Cillian said softly, offering his hand. "No matter what this means, you don't have to face it alone."

"What if this has nothing to do with me?"

His silver eyes met hers, unwavering. "I've seen enough of Faerie to know nothing is ever random here. If the guardians bowed to you, it's because they recognize something in you that's meant to be here. This has *everything* to do with you."

She stared at his outstretched hand for a long moment, then slowly reached out, taking it. His grip was warm, grounding her in the moment as they ascended the final step.

The ancient doors groaned as they swung open, revealing a chamber lined with intricate carvings. Though worn with age, the images etched into the stone walls remained detailed enough to be recognized, each telling a long-forgotten story. Towering columns framed a breathtaking view of the desert beyond along the back wall. From this height, the golden sands stretched like an endless sea of wine, rippling with deep shades of purple as magic pulsed from the countless Weaveshards scattered across the landscape. The expanse shimmered, the interplay of gold and violet turning the desert into something otherworldly, even for Faerie.

Margot ran her fingers over the worn carving of a woman with delicate features and pointed ears, her form regal as she held a gnarled staff before a massive mountain. "Fae?" she asked, her voice tinged with curiosity.

"I don't think they're—" Cillian began, but Margot cut him off as the familiar whisper crept into her mind, soft yet insistent.

"They're elves," she said, her voice barely above a breath, as if the knowledge had been placed there, unbidden. She blinked, her hand hovering over the carving, the whisper still resonating in her thoughts.

Margot stumbled back, her heart racing as the whisper sharpened, growing clearer. The voice wasn't hostile, nor was it kind— it simply *existed*, ancient and unyielding. A chill ran down her spine as she tried to make sense of the presence that seemed to linger. And then it clicked—a sudden, bone-deep recognition.

This wasn't the first time she heard it. *It's the same voice that had brought me to Faerie.* Her breath hitched, the realization settling over her like a shroud. How had she forgotten about the voice? *That* voice?

"Margot, what just happened?" His gaze shifted between her and the carvings, his brow furrowing in concern. "How do you know that?"

"I—" Margot swallowed, shaking her head. "I don't know. I just... *heard* it. The whisper... the same person—*thing*—that brought me here told me they were elves. Didn't you hear it?"

So, you do *keep a demon for company,* the voice said. *Interesting.*

"There it is again!" She looked around wildly, her heart thudding in her chest. "Please tell me you hear it."

Cillian's eyes narrowed as his hand rested on the hilt of his dagger, scanning the room as if something might emerge from the shadows. "Margot, I don't hear anything." His voice was calm, but there was an edge of unease to it. He gently gripped her arm as if to anchor her in place. "What's it saying?"

"It—" Margot hesitated, glancing at Cillian. How could she explain something so intangible? "It said I keep interesting company... that a demon is an interesting companion."

I am sorry to have brought you here. You were the only one worthy.

"Worthy of *what*?" Margot yelled into the air, throwing her hands up.

Cillian gripped her chin, forcing her to look at him. His expression was hard, searching her face. "What's going on?"

"I don't know!" Margot cried, blood *whooshing* in her ears.

I have little time. Stay with the demon. He will keep you safe.

"Wait! Don't go, please!" Margot's voice broke, her plea filled with desperation. "Tell me why I'm here!"

Until the time is right. Stay vigilant.

"What did it say?"

The voice faded, leaving the crackling silence of the ancient chamber around them. Margot's breath came in ragged bursts, her chest tightening as she thought about the final whisper—it felt more like a warning than a reassurance. She stared at Cillian, her fingers trembling as they interlaced with his, seeking comfort in the only anchor she had in this strange world.

"What did it say?" Cillian asked again, his voice low. He searched her eyes as if they held answers she didn't have.

"It said... to stay with you," Margot whispered, her voice barely holding steady. "That you'll keep me safe." A tear slid down her cheek, and she blinked rapidly, trying to process the fear creeping into her chest. "But keep me safe from *what*?"

Cillian's throat bobbed, his eyes softening as he cupped her face in his hands. His touch was gentle, but there was something behind his gaze—a shadow of something darker, something that seemed to weigh heavily on him. He wiped away her tears with his thumbs, and for a moment, the world around them faded. It was just the two of them in the ancient chamber, their fears laid bare.

"From everything." His hands lingered on her cheeks, his fingers brushing against her skin as he pressed his forehead to hers. "I'll keep you safe from everything, Margot. As long as it's within my power... I'll keep you safe."

For a moment, neither of them moved. Her fingers lightly rested on his chest, feeling the steady beat of his heart. Everything around them melted away, leaving only the quiet space they shared.

Cillian tilted her chin upward, his thumb brushing along her jawline as his eyes met hers. The look he gave her was tender, but full of yearning. Slowly, deliberately, he leaned in and kissed her—softly at first. The touch of his lips was delicate, a featherlight connection that made her heart skip.

Margot closed her eyes, letting herself enjoy the moment. His kiss was gentle, almost hesitant, as though he were giving her space to pull away if she wanted to. But she didn't. Instead, she found herself leaning into him, her fingers curling into his leathers.

The sweetness of the kiss remained, soft and slow, each movement careful, as though they were testing the waters of all that went unspoken between them, something forbidden. But the more their lips moved together, the more Margot could feel the heat building between them—a subtle shift, a series of sparks igniting with every passing second.

Cillian's hand slid to the back of her neck, his rough callouses causing her skin to pimple as he pulled her close. His lips pressed against hers again, more insistent this time. What had started out languidly grew more urgent, more heated. The tenderness gave way to something raw, something desperate, like he couldn't hold back any longer.

Her hands found their way to his shoulders, clutching at the leather straps as their lips and teeth and tongues smacked together. Heat radiated from his skin, the way his body responded to hers, sending a rush of warmth through her, making her dizzy.

Cillian moved against her with growing fervor, his hands roaming from her neck to her waist, pulling her closer still. There was no hesitation now, no careful restraint—just a wild need surging between them. His kiss was consuming; it was everything she needed, everything she wanted. She never wanted to stop. The way her body molded against him, the way his fingers tangled in her hair—it was *everything*.

When they finally broke apart, both were breathless. She placed her fingers to her tingling lips, wishing they were still being devoured by the demon who had just rocked her world.

Cillian brushed a strand of hair behind her ear. "I didn't mean for that to happen."

Margot smiled, her chest rising and falling as she tried to catch her breath. "Neither did I."

"I swear it, Margot. Whatever I can do... I'll keep you safe." He cleared his throat and looked toward the overlook. "I wanted you to watch the sunrise with me. Still interested?"

Cillian had just kissed her like she was the only thing in the world that mattered, and now he was offering to experience one of life's simple pleasures with her. Out of all the dates she had ever been on, this wasn't even real, and it was at the top.

She glanced up at him, her smile widening. "I'd love that."

Without another word, Cillian took her hand, guiding her toward the overlook. Frigid air hit her as they stepped outside the Aerie, vastly different from the heat within its ancient walls. He placed his rucksack down beside a weathered column and began pulling out supplies. She watched as he handed her a thick fur coat, its warmth a welcome relief from the frozen temperature. She slipped it on quickly, pulling it tighter around her as a chilling breeze swept through the open space.

Cillian settled himself with his back against the column, spreading a blanket across his lap. He patted the space next to him, opening the blanket with a gesture for her to join him. Margot didn't hesitate and moved to sit beside him, resting her head on his shoulder as he pulled the cover over them both. His arm snaked around her waist, drawing her closer until his body heat seeped into her. The closeness, the quiet, the feel of him beside her... it felt natural.

For a moment, everything was still. The wind whispered softly, and Margot felt her eyelids grow heavy, lulled by the calm of the moment and the steady rise and fall of Cillian's breath.

"TIME TO WAKE UP." HIS VOICE WAS SOFT AS HE nudged her gently before taking the blanket off them, considering the rising heat.

Margot blinked, startled by how easily sleep had crept in. She hadn't even realized she dozed off. "When did I fall asleep?"

Cillian chuckled quietly; his eyes already fixed on the scene before them. "Take a look."

She turned her gaze toward the horizon, and her breath caught in her throat. The sky had begun to shift, the deep purples of night giving way to the soft blush of dawn. Hues of pink and lilac stretched across the sky, bleeding into the remnants of darkness as the first rays of sunlight inched over the landscape. The Weaveshards in the stance caught the light, glowing as though set ablaze, their rich violet hues shimmering like fire against the golden sands.

"Oh... it's beautiful," Margot whispered. She couldn't tear her eyes away from the sight, the sheer beauty of Faerie overwhelming her senses.

Cillian hummed in agreement, his chin resting lightly on top of her head. "It's one of the few things here that always stays the same. No matter what happens in Faerie, the sunrise never disappoints."

Margot snuggled closer, leaning into Cillian to keep the cold at bay. The peacefulness of the moment was unlike anything she had experienced since arriving in Faerie, and for a fleeting moment, the dangers and mysteries of the world faded away. All that mattered was the rising sun, the glowing Weaveshards, and the steady heartbeat of the man beside her.

As the sun climbed higher, painting the sky even more vibrant colors, Margot found herself smiling—a small, quiet smile that felt like a secret shared between them. It was the kind of moment she didn't want to end.

Cillian shifted slightly, his hand tightening around her waist. "I wasn't sure you'd like it out here. But I thought you'd want to see something beautiful despite all the horrid things you've experienced lately."

Margot tilted her head to look up at him. "I do. I'm glad you brought me... for a lot of reasons."

They stayed there in comfortable silence, watching as the desert below came alive with light and magic. And for a little while, they were just two people, sitting together, watching the dawn of a new day.

13

WHAT ARE YOU HOLDING ONTO?

Sunfire Aerie felt like a lifetime ago to Margot. The memory of it lingered in the back of her mind, but everything that happened since was nothing more than a blur. When they returned to the ship, Cillian hadn't spoken to her about it—the kiss, the whispers, how she knew the elves were carved into the Aerie's walls. And she hadn't dared to bring it up, though her thoughts spun with unanswered questions and growing concern.

Cillian had been adamant that nothing could happen between them, that their relationship—or lack thereof—was simply one of friendship. Then he kissed her with such intensity and so much passion that it felt like her lips were his lifeline. And now... nothing. He had pulled away completely, retreating into himself like a man lost in his own world.

For days, he brooded in silence, barely able to hold her gaze. He didn't talk to her unless it was absolutely necessary. The once easy rhythm they'd shared had been replaced with uncomfortable tension, each passing moment making the silence between them heavier. Margot tried to ask him about their plans, where they were headed, but he would just shrug, his voice distant, muttering something about figuring it out.

Her frustration gnawed at her. Deliberately shutting her out was childish, and to make the situation worse, she couldn't understand why. The kiss, the connection—she hadn't imagined it. It had been real, and yet, Cillian acted as though it had never happened. The few glances he gave her were fleeting, burdened with something he refused to voice.

The ship had been sailing aimlessly since they left the Aerie, at least that's how it seemed. They'd gone north of the Wastes, past Stormwing Isles, drifting in the Aetheric Ocean with no apparent destination. Margot caught Cillian staring at the map more than once. She knew from how he looked at the parchment with furrowed brows that something was beneath the surface—something he wasn't telling her.

Margot leaned against the ship's rail, watching the sun dip lower past the horizon, casting long shadows over the water. She didn't want to press him—didn't want to push too hard—but whatever was going on right now between them was suffocating.

She exhaled slowly, feeling the cold bite of wind against her skin. *How long is he going to avoid me?* The question circled her mind, but she had no answer. She hoped he would figure things out quickly before the distance between them became too wide to bridge.

As the ship rocked gently on the waves, she heard the faint sound of footsteps behind her. She didn't need to turn around to know it was Cillian, even though they were the only people on this ship. His presence consumed her, something she noticed before his physical body even reached her. He lingered for a moment, standing just out of reach, the space between them a chasm of unspoken words.

"Margot," he said quietly, his voice low and rough, as though the words had been pulled from him against his will.

Her grip tightened around the wood, watching as stars peppered the sky. Maybe ignoring him was petty, but he deserved it.

"Margot, please." She heard him take a step closer. "Look, I'm sorry."

Oh, fuck this. She spun around on her heel, her long ashen braid slicing through the air like a silver whip. "You're *sorry*?" She tried to keep the anger from her face but knew she did a poor job. "That's all you have to say." A dry laugh slipped past her lips. "You've ignored me for days!"

"What do you want from me, Margot!" He threw his hands in the air, letting them fall back to his sides with an audible *thump*. "What happened at the Aerie... it shouldn't have happened. I can't gi—"

"Give me what I want. Yeah, you've told me." She jabbed at his chest. "But let me remind you, Cillian, *you* kissed *me*. So why don't you give me an actual reason why you can't?"

"It's forbidden," he ground out.

"Forbidden?" With arms stretched wide, she gestured to the open waters. "Forbidden by whom? Reality check, Cillian. There's no one here but us."

"Damnit, Margot." He scrubbed his face. "My entire life... it had been drilled into my head that any species that wasn't a demon was lesser, weaker. That consorting with anyone other than a demon was treason." When he looked at her, all she saw was pain etched on his face and pleading in his eyes as if begging her to understand. "Do you know how hard it is to ignore *hundreds* of years of indoctrination? *I can't.*"

Margot was silent for a moment before she said quietly, "They exiled you, Cillian. They threw you out of your home, left you for dead... what are you holding onto?"

He just looked at her.

She stepped back until she hit the railing and stepped onto the first rung. "Do you believe that I'm lesser?"

Cillian glanced down at her feet before returning to her face. He shook his head. "No."

She stepped onto the second rung, wobbling as she found her balance. "Why do you care about them? They don't care about you."

"Margot," he fretted. "What are you doing?"

Her heart lodged in her throat. "I care," she said, stepping onto the final rung.

The wind gusted, and her footing slipped. Cillian lunged forward as she started to fall backward toward the icy depths. With Margot tightly in his arms, he stumbled back, saving her once more.

He held her close, unable—or unwilling—to put her down. "Are you insane? You could have died!"

She slid her arms up his chest, wrapping them around his neck. "You won't let me die, Cillian." She pressed a kiss to his stubbled jaw. "I trust you."

"What are you doing?"

"Trust me?" She kissed his neck, his pulse fast against her lips.

He groaned, silver eyes dark and swimming with conflicted emotions. She kissed his neck again, feeling his throat bob.

"I trust you," he whispered.

In an instant, Margot closed the distance, her lips claiming his in a fiery kiss. Her tongue brushed against his, coaxing, pleading for him to let her in. For a heartbeat, he hesitated, the strain of lifetimes of brainwashing flickering behind his eyes. But then, as though breaking free from unseen chains, he answered her with raw fervor, matching her intensity with his own.

Strong hands slid up her thigh, curving up her backside before tugging at the leather strip that held her braid together.

"Your hair drives me wild," he growled, his fingers tangling roughly in her unruly ashen locks, pulling her closer. He licked up the column of her neck, biting her earlobe. "*You* drive me wild."

She wrapped her legs around his waist, feeling the hard length of him press against where she desperately wanted him. He walked them across the deck, pressing her back against the cabin wall, pushing into her hard.

The wind whipped around them, sending shivers down her spine, but it was nothing compared to the heat pooling below. His lips moved down her neck, leaving a trail of wet kisses as he drove down her collarbone and toward her chest. Swift fingers unlaced her chest piece to expose her breasts. He groaned quietly, looking at her with desire-filled eyes before he latched onto one of her nipples, sucking hungrily.

Margot moaned softly, clawing at his back, desperate for more. He rocked into her at a torturously slow pace that let her know he knew *exactly* what he was doing—she had never wanted anything more.

Cillian gripped her hip possessively as he returned to her lips, tasting every inch of her mouth. He moved them around the corner, pushed into the cabin, and dropped her on the bed. His chest heaved as he watched her with clear eyes for what seemed like the first time. With practiced ease, he removed his boots and armor, letting them clatter to the floor.

Standing there, he bared everything. Every scar, every bruise, each swell and dip of muscle.

"I won't hurt you," he pushed out.

He took a step toward the bed, and her eyes caught on his erect, uncut cock. Large, but not unmanageable. Her pulse had grown erratic.

"I won't hurt you," he echoed, taking another step.

Margot inhaled sharply, her eyes darting back to Cillian's. He stood directly in front of her. She reached out, running her fingertips across the underside of his penis. With his head tipped back, he sighed before kneeling in front of her. Carefully, he removed her boots.

"I won't hurt you," he breathed as he took off the rest of her garments, tossing them aside.

He gripped her calves and pulled her toward him. The callouses on his hands felt like heaven against her skin as he moved up to her knees. Spreading her like a buffet, he leaned in, inhaling her scent. A low rumble rattled his chest that sent her nerves haywire.

He glanced at her. "I won't hurt you."

Before she could respond, he dove in, flattening his tongue as he tasted her with broad strokes. His fingers dug into her bottom, supporting her as he traced intricate patterns along her folds. Each flick, each lick, made her heart race faster.

She arched her back, her fingers holding onto the sheets beneath her as he explored her most secret parts. His hands glided up and down her thighs, his fingers lightly grazing over sensitive skin, making her tremble.

Her breath hitched as he continued his assault on her senses, each stroke of his tongue eliciting a different reaction. A whine here, a mewl there. Each involuntary sound that sneaked from her throat had him grinning against her cunt.

He delved deeper, curling his fingers inside her as he paid special attention to her most delicate spot. She whimpered and moaned, feeling herself slip away, losing herself in pleasure so good she couldn't think straight.

Cillian looked up at her again, pulling away. His skin glistened with her wetness. "I won't hurt you," he whispered before adding another finger and sucking hard on her clit.

Margot's vision blurred, her body shuddering as she clung to the flimsy fabric, and she cried out as her world came crashing down. Each breath she took felt like an eternity, each movement a wash of lines and colors.

And then another shudder. A gasp. A plea for more.

His eyes locked with hers, drinking her in as if she was an intoxicating sight. She panted with parted lips, and he just watched as she convulsed with pleasure.

The orgasm he had given her was life changing.

He was life changing.

Breathless, she slid to the floor next to Cillian, tentatively taking his cock in the palm of her hand, the head glistening. She gripped him tightly, working his sheath.

"I won't hurt you," he muttered as his eyes fluttered closed.

"I know." She pumped him harder. "I know you won't."

He watched her, biting his lip, her eyes never leaving his. She leaned in closer, her lips brushing against his shaft as she continued to move her hand. His breath caught as she took him fully into her mouth. Her tongue flicked against the underside, and he groaned.

"I won't hurt you," he whispered over and over again, his hips bucking wildly as if he had no control.

But still, she took him deeper, moving faster, sucking harder even though her eyes watered. She knew the rhythm of her own body, the tension, the throbbing, the need. And now, she wanted to share it with Cillian. She wanted to give him everything he had given to her and more.

He was panting now, fucking her mouth hard, his eyes closed as he let himself fall deeper. His lips parted slightly, revealing the tiniest bit of teeth as he fought for control.

But then, Margot felt it. He trembled and gripped her hair as he tried to hold back the release building within him. She hummed an upbeat tune she and Janey used to listen to, her tongue lapping every inch of his cock, driving him higher and higher until, finally, with a loud groan, he came. She felt every pulsing surge, savoring each one as he emptied himself into her eager mouth.

Slowly, she pulled away from him, a satisfied smile playing on her lips. She kissed the tip of his softening cock before sitting back on her heels, waiting for him to catch his breath.

After he composed himself, he pulled her into his arms, holding her tightly. "I didn't hurt you," he said, his voice breaking.

And then, he did the last thing she ever expected.

He cried.

MARGOT WATCHED CILLIAN MOVE ABOUT THE CABIN, his naked form a study in contradictions—powerful yet gentle, dangerous yet vulnerable. The tears had dried on his cheeks, but something had fundamentally changed between them. How he looked at her now carried none of his earlier hesitation, only a quiet certainty that seemed to have settled in his bones.

He handed her a cup of tea and a small plate of tea cookies with what looked to be bits of purple and red flowers in them, settling beside her on the bed. The heat of his body radiated against her bare skin, comfortable and familiar in a way it hadn't been before. Neither had bothered with clothes—there seemed little point in maintaining such barriers now.

"There's something I need to tell you," he whispered, his silver eyes guarded in a way that made her stomach tighten. "About why we've been sailing in circles these past few days."

Margot's fingers stilled around her cup. There was something in his voice—a hesitation she rarely heard from him. She shifted closer, drawn to his warmth, to the solid presence of him beside her. "I had a feeling you weren't just lost," she whispered.

His hand found the small of her back, thumb tracing idle patterns against her skin. "What happened at the Aerie—the whispers, the way you knew about the elves..." He paused, taking a slow breath. "I've been thinking about it constantly. About what it means."

She leaned into him, feeling the steady thrum of his heartbeat. After their shared vulnerability, after watching him break down in her arms, she knew whatever came next would change everything. "Tell me."

"The elves aren't like the fae," he said, pulling her closer as if the mere mention of their enemies might snatch her away. "They're older, more powerful. And I think..." His other hand cupped her chin, turning her face to his. "I think you might be connected to them somehow. The magic I sense in you—it's different from anything I've encountered before."

Margot watched the firelight dance in his gaze, remembering how fierce they'd looked moments ago. "Different how?"

His hand slid up her spine, coming to rest between her shoulder blades. "Fae magic feels... fabricated. Controlled. But yours?" He pressed his lips to her temple, inhaling deeply. "Yours is ancient. Wild. It reminds me of stories I heard in Olvath about the old powers—the kind that shaped worlds."

The words he spoke made her shiver. "Is that why you've been studying the maps? Looking for the elves?"

"Yes." His voice grew hoarse. "There are rumors of an island where they dwell, hidden from the fae. If anyone knows why you have this power, why you were brought to Faerie..." He trailed off, his arms tightening around her.

"But you're worried," she said, feeling the tension in his muscles, the way his heart raced beneath her palm.

"The elves aren't known for their hospitality." His fingers tangled in her hair, still loose from earlier. "They're secretive, dangerous. And they hate demons even more than the fae do." The last words came out barely above a whisper, heavy with meaning.

She pulled back enough to look at him properly, seeing the vulnerability still raw in his eyes. After what they'd just shared, after watching him cry... "You're afraid they'll kill you."

"Not just kill me." He cupped her face in both hands. "They might take you from me. And after this..." His thumbs traced her cheekbones. "I don't think I could bear that."

She set the plate of cookies down and traced his jawline with trembling fingers. "Why didn't you tell me sooner? About thinking I had elven magic?"

"I wasn't sure at first." His breath caught as she touched a sensitive spot beneath his ear. "When I found you in the Dread-wood, you smelled of fae magic. But the longer we're together..." He caught her hand, pressing a kiss on her palm. "It's changed. Or maybe I'm just seeing what was always there."

"And what do you see?" she whispered.

Cillian's eyes darkened as they roamed her face. "Power. Real power, not simple tricks the fae use. When you understood those carvings at the Aerie, when you heard those whispers..." He shook his head. "That kind of magic hasn't been seen in centuries."

"You make it sound like I'm special." She tried to look away, but he caught her chin.

"I already told you; you *are* special." The intensity in his voice made her nipples pebble. "But that's exactly what worries me. The fae want you dead—or worse. And the elves..." His jaw tightened. "If they discover what you are, they might decide to keep you."

Fear coiled in her stomach, not for herself, but for him. After what they'd just shared, the thought of being separated was unbearable. "I won't let them take me from you."

A sad smile played on his lips. "You might not have a choice. Their magic is..." He tensed, something dark flickering behind his eyes. "They could control you, bend your will to theirs."

"Then we don't go." She gripped his shoulder, pressing closer. "We'll find another way."

"That's the thing. There is no other way." His voice was gentle but firm. "Whatever brought you to Faerie, whatever power you possess—the answers lie with them. And if we don't find those answers..." He drew in a ragged breath. "The fae won't stop hunting you. Whatever they want from you, it's important enough that they're willing to tear apart Faerie to find you."

Margot rested her head against his chest, tea forgotten on the end table as she listened to his steady heartbeat. The gravity of everything settled over her like a shroud—the magic she supposedly possessed, the fae hunting her, and now the elves who might help or harm them. "I don't want to put you in danger," she murmured against his skin.

His laugh was low and bitter. "I've been in danger since the moment I was exiled here." His fingers traced lazy patterns down her spine. "But this is different. For the first time, I have something worth protecting. Something that matters more than my own survival."

She lifted her head, meeting his silver gaze. The raw honesty there stopped her breath. "Earlier, when you..." She swallowed hard. "When you cried. Was it because...?"

"Because I've spent centuries believing humans were beneath me?" His tone deepened, rasping with emotion. "Because everything I was taught said this was wrong?" He cupped her face, his touch achingly gentle. "Or because for the first time in my life, someone looked at me and wasn't afraid?"

Tears pricked her eyes. "Cillian…"

"The elves might kill me." His thumbs brushed away her tears. "But not seeking them out will definitely get *you* killed. And that's not a risk I'm willing to take."

"We should start plotting our course," Cillian said, though he made no move to release her. "The sooner we find the elves—"

"Tomorrow," Margot said, cutting him off. She pressed her palm against his chest, where his heart still raced. "Tonight, I just want to remember this. Remember you."

His gaze met hers, and something unspoken passed between them—not quite a promise, not quite a confession, but an understanding.

And for now, that was enough.

14

NOCK, STANCE, AIM, BREATHE

CALLOUSED fingers combed her mussed hair while searing hot kisses peppered her shoulder before climbing up her neck. Cillian nipped her earlobe, the tip of his tongue grazing the shell of her ear, sending electric currents straight to her core.

Margot rolled over, smiling at the beautiful man who had been waking her up the same way every morning for the past twelve days. The perpetual stubble of his jaw scratched at her fingertips as she dragged them lightly along the sharpened edges. His grin stretched wide, reaching his eyes and crinkling the corners with a warmth that made her chest ache.

"Can we just stay like this?" she asked, moving her fingers along faint lines etched on his forehead. Not nearly enough to show the lifetimes he'd lived. "This is perfect." She rested her head in the crook of his shoulder and sighed. "I know we can't. But I'd like to."

They'd pressed steadily north, the jagged coastline giving way to the ominous expanse of the Gloomwater, its dark waves churning just off the shores of Zarandor. Their journey had nearly circled the globe, a winding course dictated by caution rather than convenience. Cillian had insisted they avoid Lythoria at all costs—Ravara's territory, brimming with soldiers and crawling with danger.

Cillian had no real strategy except to sail around until they found the elves. A bold move, considering Faerie had already been charted, but Margot couldn't fault him for the shoddy plan. The land was rife with magic, and if the elves were as powerful as he said they were, then there was every possibility they'd hidden themselves away from the rest of the world.

Cillian spread his fingers across her stomach, slowly inching lower.

"Would you be fine with not knowing?" he whispered in her ear. His breath made the hair on the back of her neck stand on ends.

"I thought about it for a while," she breathed as he spread her with his ring and index finger, using his middle to rub circles around her most sensitive spot. Still no sex, but he seemed to love keeping her satisfied as if it were a consolation prize—not that she was complaining. "I-I need to know."

"You will." A thick finger curled inside her. He languidly pumped in and out as he rubbed her clit with the heel of his hand. With her arm, she covered her eyes, panting hard as he worked her.

"Those sounds you make," he growled against her neck. "Your dripping wet cunt." He bit her shoulder hard, making her cry out. "The way you rock your hips against me." A second finger slipped in, stretching her wide, making her moan low and steady. He worked faster, pinching her nipples with his free hand, twisting them. "You're mine, Margot."

Hearing him say her name was all she needed to send her spiraling. She bucked against his rough palm, and he pushed against her with equal force, rotating his wrist in just the right way to give her the friction she needed to explode.

"Cillian!" she cried out, the last syllable of his name devolving into something unintelligible as her body convulsed.

Her pleasure ebbed, but Cillian didn't stop. Instead, he added a third finger and shifted his body to work himself simultaneously. This wasn't the beautiful experience she had grown accustomed to; this was all demon, his way of claiming her because he wouldn't—or couldn't—do it with his cock.

Drool dripped down her chin as he fucked her, stretching her more than she thought she could to the point where her pleasure was edged in pain. But the furious way he fisted himself, the groans and growls rumbling from his chest, the way he sucked and bit and licked at her neck, her ears, her shoulder, made the discomfort worth it.

A high-pitched whine worked its way up her throat, a noise she didn't even know she could make. Cillian growled in response and worked her faster. Everything went tight, so tight she thought she was going to burst.

"I-I c-can't," she moaned.

He responded with a grunt and another wrist rotation that let him rub her clit with his thumb. He pushed her hood up with one swift motion, touching her directly. She screamed, but no sound came out. *Oh, God. I can't take this.*

Suddenly, he pulled out and slapped her clit like a whip, immediately causing the orgasm that had been building to spill over. He sat up, pushing her into bed with one arm. With a roar, he pumped out rope after rope, coating her chest and stomach.

Sweat dripped down the slope of his nose as he inspected his canvas. He smeared his seed, covering her breasts and thighs before giving her a chaste kiss.

"Where are you going?" she asked, breathless as he pushed off the bed.

"Tea and cookies, of course." He looked over his shoulder, appraising her like one would a priceless piece of art. "Don't clean up."

Margot's cheeks flushed, a wave of warmth spreading as he smirked and turned away, his attention shifting to the cabinets as he rifled through them. The scarred skin of his shoulders stretched as he bent, each movement highlighting the smooth play of muscle across his broad back. There was a raw, magnetic power in how he carried himself, and his effect on her was nearly paralyzing.

She could blame it on her humanity—that ancient, primal instinct entombed in her DNA. The one that made her want to press herself against him, to seek comfort in his powerful arms. It was ridiculous, really, how some long-forgotten part of her, likely born at the dawn of man, reduced her to a needy fool. But that same foolish part made her willing to obey him, even if it meant remaining unclean.

Carefully, she eased off the bed, wincing as she made her way to the chair. In all the years she had been sexually active, she had never been this sore. Not even after that first time with Steve Dawson behind the bleachers during the homecoming game. They had no idea what they were doing, and he basically pushed in with no warning, no prep, and flailed on top of her like a fish out of water.

Earth. Home.

She sighed. If only Janey could see her now. Shacked up with tall, dark, and handsome. Magic working its way to her fingertips, then vanishing like a ghost. Fae trying to kill her. Unbidden laughter bubbled up from her chest.

"What's so funny?" Cillian asked, walking toward her with two handmade mugs in one hand and a plate in the other.

"Just thinking about how jealous Janey would be if she could see me now."

He put the cookies on the center table and handed her the tea. "You think she'd be jealous?"

"Jealous is an understatement. She's *obsessed* with books that are exactly... well, exactly like what my life has become."

Cillian cocked an eyebrow. "Really?"

"Mhm," she hummed, taking a sip. She raised her brows, surprised by the fruity floral notes. "New tea?"

"Do you like it?" He handed her a lavender tea cookie instead of the rose one. "Try it with this."

She dunked the cookie in her tea for a few seconds, then took a bite. Her eyes widened. "This is delicious."

"I'm glad. I... wanted to do something nice for you." He rubbed the back of his neck, glancing away to hide his blush.

Margot froze mid-chew, the cookie's sweetness mingling with the tea's floral taste on her tongue. Her chest tightened, and she swallowed hard to clear the unexpected lump rising in her throat.

"You inspired that blend."

The words hung in the air, simple yet devastating. No one had ever done something like this for her—not in a way that felt so personal, so thoughtful. She glanced at the cup in her hands, the faint steam curling upward like something fragile.

Her grip tightened around the mug. "It's perfect," she said, her voice breaking slightly on the last word. She bit her lip and looked away, blinking quickly.

"Margot?"

She shook her head, forcing a smile as she met his gaze. "Sorry," she whispered, a tremor in her voice. "It's just... no one's ever done something like this for me before."

Cillian's expression softened, and he reached out, hesitating momentarily before placing a hand over hers. "You deserve it," he said quietly.

Her fingers twitched under his, her breath hitching as a faint, bittersweet smile curved her lips. "Thank you."

"Finish up." He sat beside her and took a hearty sip of his own tea. "We've tarried too long. Time to get back to the bow."

"Ugh, do we have to?"

"Yes. It's one of the few things I can do to help you prepare for what's coming."

Margot sighed. Cillian was right, of course.

The close call in Elowen had shaken them both more than they cared to admit. In the days since their narrow escape from Ravara's men, she'd noticed subtle changes in him—the way his hands would clench and unclench when he thought she wasn't looking, how he'd startle at unexpected sounds, how his eyes would linger on her healing injuries with barely concealed guilt.

While she had no doubt about his ability to defend himself, she wondered how long it had been since he'd had someone else to protect, someone whose safety weighed on his conscience. The responsibility seemed to rest heavy on his shoulders, evident in the new tension he carried and the distant look that would sometimes cloud his eyes.

They couldn't afford another close call like Elowen. If—*when* —they found the elves, they needed to be better prepared. Whatever awaited them there, she couldn't remain helpless or keep depending solely on Cillian's protection. She needed to learn to defend herself, even if just enough to avoid being a liability.

She glanced at him and nodded.

This wouldn't be easy, but nothing about survival in Faerie had been easy so far. At least this was something she could control, something she could improve. It was time to stop being just the woman Cillian had to protect and become someone who could stand beside him instead.

WITHOUT WARNING, CILLIAN TOSSED THE BOW AT HER. She fumbled, barely catching it.

"Nice catch," he said, a hint of amusement dancing in his eyes. "Pull the string back."

The bowstring groaned, and Margot's arms shook as she held her stance.

"Not quite." Cillian stepped behind her, placing his hands at her waist. After everything they'd done together, her heart still felt like it was beating in her throat. Strong fingers gripped her elbow, adjusting her position. Then he moved to adjust her hands. He leaned in, resting his palm against her stomach, his breath hot against the shell of her ear. "You need to tighten your core."

He tapped her spine. "Straighten your back; this will help

with stability. Be mindful of your chest and find an angle that works well for you. Don't draw back too far. Otherwise, the string will smack right into the side of your breast or hit your forearm."

"I'm going to release this time?"

He nodded. "I'll guide you. Then, you'll try it on your own. No arrows yet; I want you to get a feel for the bow. Think of it as an extension of your body."

Cillian pressed his chest against her back, his warmth seeping into her as his hands gently enveloped hers. His breath was steady, calm, and he guided her to match it, their bodies moving in sync. The space between them was wound so tight it was palpable, but neither spoke. His fingers curled around hers, and together, they drew the bowstring taut.

"Breathe," he murmured, his voice low and steady in her ear. "Hold your core."

Margot tensed, her muscles straining, and a soft whimper slipped past her lips.

"That's it." He leaned closer, lips barely brushing her skin. "Good girl."

Another whimper escaped her, but it wasn't from the strain this time. Maybe he did it intentionally, distracting her and giving her something else to focus on. Whatever the reason, it worked. The sharp edge of discomfort dulled, and she stood straighter, prouder. She refused to be weak. Refused to let her humanity define her in a world that would sooner see her dead.

Cillian stepped back, crossing his arms as he watched her. His absence made the bow feel heavier in her hands, but she ground her teeth and let out a guttural yell, pulling the string taut on her own. No added strength from him this time—just her. She glimpsed his smile from the corner of her eye, approval flickering in his stormy gaze.

"You're doing great, Margot," he said, his voice steady and encouraging. "Now, as you release the string, focus on your grip. Keep it firm but not too tight. Don't pull back too far—just enough to maintain control. And remember your stance. The goal is to avoid the string hitting any part of your body."

Margot got into position again, her hands trembling slightly as she gripped the bow. She pulled back, feeling the tension build, the bow quivering. Her heart raced, and her muscles burned from the effort. She closed her eyes, forcing a slow, controlled exhale.

When her eyes flew open, her body reacted too quickly—instinct over precision. The string snapped from her fingers, and a sharp, agonizing wail tore from her throat as the bowstring lashed against her arm, sending a jolt of pain radiating through her body.

"Again," Cillian commanded.

The sun had dipped below the horizon when he finally called it quits. Training had been brutal. Despite the constant sting of the bowstring snapping against her skin—about a hundred times during the first few hours—Margot didn't utter a single complaint. Her muscles ached, and her body screamed for rest, but she pushed through.

Determination was a powerful thing, and by the end of the session, her technique had noticeably improved. Each pull of the bow felt more controlled, each release more precise. There was still a long way to go, but at least there was progress. Silver linings amid bruises and fatigue.

She turned to Cillian and grimaced. Even the simplest move-ment was a monumental effort. How much worse would it have been if she hadn't worn armor? The thought had her shuddering. Her kit had at least absorbed some of the shock, but beneath it, she was absolutely battered.

Cillian grinned. "You did well. I think we can try shooting soon."

Margot dropped her stance, the bow heavy in her grip, before handing it to Cillian and promptly collapsing onto the ship's deck. Her limbs felt like lead. Every ounce of strength had drained from her body.

He tossed the bow aside and knelt beside her.

"Margot?"

"I don't think I can move," she murmured.

This was more than tired. This was broken, a hollow version of herself, an empty husk. After everything that had happened and the grueling hours spent training, she had nothing more to give.

"I've got you, alright?"

She managed a faint nod, which was all the encouragement he needed. Gently, Cillian scooped her into his arms, pressing her head against the hollow of his neck and shoulder. His touch was tender as he smoothed her hair. Silent tears slipped down her cheeks, her exhaustion pouring out in the form of quiet surrender.

Cillian carried her to the cabin and placed her in her chair, his fingers brushing away the wetness from her face. With deliberate care, he unlaced her boots and removed her leathers, peeling them away from her body. His jaw ticked. Restraint didn't come easy for him, considering how comfortable he'd gotten touching her bare skin.

He paused for a moment, his eyes lingering on her with an intensity that might have made her self-conscious any other time. But exhaustion had stripped away her defenses, and at that moment, being vulnerable before him felt natural, almost inevitable. The trust between them had grown slowly, like a stubborn flower pushing through stone, but now it bloomed full and undeniable. Each gentle touch, each careful movement as he tended to her, reinforced what she already knew—she was safe with him, perhaps safer than she'd ever been with anyone.

Not for the first time, Margot sat nude by the fire, letting the warmth wash over her bruised and mottled skin as Cillian rummaged through cabinets in search of something to ease her pain. She hadn't expected the bruises to form so quickly or to be so dark. Every small shift in the chair sent sharp jolts of pain through her body, making her grit her teeth.

The pain was all-consuming, worse than her ribs, worse than her foot. Honestly, she'd never been in so much pain before—not even when that jerk Solomon shot her with frozen paintballs when she was walking home from school in sixth grade—and right now, she couldn't tell if training had been worth it.

Cillian returned with food and a jar, setting both on the table beside her. He carefully pried her legs apart so he could sit between them. Plucking a large, glistening berry from the plate, he pressed it against her lips, wiggling it playfully when she didn't respond right away.

"Come on, Margot," he coaxed. "Or do you need me to feed you?"

She tried lifting her arms, but they shook violently and fell back to her sides.

"I can't feel my arms," she admitted, her voice soft with frustration.

Cillian grimaced, then pressed the berry to her lips again. This time, she opened her mouth, letting him feed her. The whole situation was absurd—a beautiful man, practically glowing in the firelight, feeding her berries while she sat naked and utterly spent. A scene of pure hedonism.

And despite everything, the pain and exhaustion, Margot still wasn't immune to Cillian's presence. His closeness was intoxicating. The way his fingers brushed her lips, the intensity of his gaze... God, she wanted him.

A sharp, herbal scent filled the air, and Margot wrinkled her nose.

"I know it's unpleasant." He dipped two fingers into the cream and scooped some out. "But you know it'll help with the pain."

Margot tilted her head back and closed her eyes as his hands roamed across her exposed skin, leaving a trail of cinders in its wake. He never faltered once, not even as his hand caressed just beneath her breast, causing her breath to hitch. She couldn't fight the feeling any more than she could embrace it. His touch was like heroin, and she wanted nothing more than to chase the dragon.

His movements slowed and she looked at him, studying the

lines and creases of his face, memorizing every minute detail. No matter what the future held, she never wanted to forget him like this—the kind, enigmatic demon who saw her for what she was, flaws and all.

He pressed a swift kiss to her lips before grabbing a tunic from his dresser. "You'll feel better in a few hours, but I'd be lying if I said you won't be sore."

Margot laughed as he helped her into the tunic.

"What's so funny?" he asked.

"I was just thinking about how our relationship isn't so different from a married couple back home."

He scrunched his face—it was adorable. "What is *married*?"

"Ah, well, that's... hm. A marriage is a union between two people who love one another. They pledge their lives to each other, committing themselves to the health and happiness of their partner."

He was quiet as he searched her face.

"No... we aren't much different from that, are we?" He sat, stretching his long legs in front of him and cracking his neck. "I've been wondering something... how prevalent is magic on Earth?"

"It isn't."

"What do you mean?"

"People on Earth don't use magic." She shrugged. "There are some people who think they're witches and others who think they're vampires... but none of that's real. At least not on Earth."

Cillian blinked a few times. "What's a witch?"

Margot couldn't help but laugh. What had become of her life? Never in a million years did she think she would have to explain witches and vampires to a demon in a magical land called Faerie.

"A witch practices magic using runes, herbs, crystals... I don't know much about it, really. They use energy from the Earth or the moon for things like prosperity and good health. I don't know. I'm sure some witches attempt sinister rituals, but no one really talks about that."

"Sounds like magic to me," he said. "What about vampires?"

"I don't even think vampires have magic. They're considered more paranormal... anyway, they're people who think they need human blood to survive."

"There are plenty of creatures in Faerie that need blood to survive. Is Earth truly so different?"

"Besides electricity and automotive vehicles?"

"I... yes. I had forgotten about those wonders."

Margot hummed. "Earth also has cellphones, portable devices that allow you to communicate over great distances. They have computers too. Computers streamline learning and provide entertainment... I feel like these, among the other things I've told you, are major advantages Earth has over Faerie."

"Odd. If they're so great, I wonder why the fae don't bring these things over. If humans and the fae fought, who would win?"

Margot gave Cillian a puzzled look. "Why do you ask?"

"Curiosity, mostly. I'm trying to understand why the fae continue to leave humans alone. Varitan Ravara is terribly ambitious."

"From what I've seen, magic is wondrous and horrifying... but humans are terrible, Cillian."

"In what way?"

She sighed. "Humans are smart, ingenious, really. The wars they've waged... well, I'm sure they could rival what you've experienced in Olvath."

"Somehow, I doubt that," he muttered.

"Cillian, humans have created bombs powerful enough to level entire countries, and some nations have enough of them to destroy the entire world." She pointed to the map spread across the table. "And judging by how long it has taken us to travel across Faerie, I'm assuming Earth is ten times larger." She shook her head. "The bombs aren't even the worst of it. They have unmanned drones—metal birds that fly in the sky—that can pinpoint precise locations and kill unsuspecting people below in a matter of seconds. The number of people who have automatic rifles that shoot hundreds of bullets per minute is staggering." She averted her gaze. "Humans may be worse than fae and demons combined."

"Could humans kill me?"

"Can the fae kill you?"

He leaned forward, resting his forearms on his thighs. "Not easily. But yes, they could kill me if I were swarmed. Their magic doesn't affect me, but their weapons... well, their weapons could do the job."

"Then I guess humans could kill you, too."

"How many humans are there?"

"Billions." Margot eyed him wearily. "Why are you asking this?"

"No particular reason." He lifted her from the chair, holding her close to his chest. "Let's get some sleep."

HELL WAS ONLY THE BEGINNING, MARGOT REALIZED.

The past three weeks made those first archery lessons feel like child's play. Cillian commanded her like a drill sergeant. His voice, sharp and unyielding, would cut through the air the moment her focus wavered. Whenever he barked an order, she jumped to action, nocking arrows with practiced speed. The gentle guidance from their first training sessions had given way to relentless demands for perfection. His presence loomed over her, the intensity of his gaze allowing no room for mistakes.

Nock, stance, aim, breathe—she repeated these steps until they were burned into her mind, until her body reacted without hesitation.

The routine became brutal. Every morning at dawn, she'd wake to the sound of Cillian's footsteps pacing the deck, waiting for her to join him. The first week alone felt like it had lasted a month. He wouldn't let her shoot a single arrow until he was certain she had mastered the mechanics. Hundreds of times, she nocked her arrow, felt the click of the string sliding into place, checked her stance, and did it all over again. Her muscles ached from the tension in her arms and shoulders, and her fingers were raw from gripping the bow.

Cillian didn't care.

"You need to be faster," he'd say, his tone emotionless. "An enemy won't wait while you carefully line up your shot."

Every failure stung. Every moment of doubt felt like a pile of bricks on her chest. She wanted to scream in frustration, to throw the bow overboard and call it quits. But she couldn't. Not with how he looked at her or how much he believed in her. Cillian wasn't just training her; it was as if he was preparing her for war.

On the seventh day, he finally relented.

"Now," he said, pulling back from his position behind her. "You're ready."

He had lined up a series of targets across the ship. Their positions and sizes varied, scattered across different levels of the deck. Some were large and within easy reach, placed at the same level she was. Others were smaller, barely visible from her position in the ship's center. A few had been secured on the railing one level above her, forcing her to aim higher than she was used to. Each target felt like a personal challenge, taunting her with its stillness.

"Take your time. Don't rush your shot," Cillian had told her, his voice calm and low for the first time in days.

Her heart raced as she pulled back the bowstring. The familiar tension against her fingers was both reassuring and unnerving. She loosed the arrow with a shaky breath—and winced as it slapped painfully against her forearm, falling short of the closest target. The sting of the fiber echoed through her bones, leaving a welt that throbbed with heat.

Cillian stepped closer, eyes steady on her. "Again."

Margot bit her lip and nocked another arrow, trying to ignore the dull ache spreading through her arm. The second attempt was no better. Another slap of the string, another bruise blooming beneath her skin. Her frustration was a wildfire, growing further untamed with each miss, her confidence crumbling with every failed shot. How was she supposed to hit a moving target if she couldn't even hit a stationary one?

Not for the first time, she considered giving up. She could walk away, tell him it wasn't worth it, that she didn't need this. If she died, she died—so be it. But the thought of quitting left a bitter taste in her mouth. She wouldn't—couldn't—let herself fail. Not when Cillian was counting on her.

As if sensing her doubts, Cillian moved beside her. He didn't yell or chastise her for missing. Instead, he calmly explained what she was doing wrong—how she wasn't accounting for the weight of the bow, how her stance was too rigid, how the wind played tricks on her aim. His voice, though firm, was patient.

Eventually, she learned to read the wind, to account for distance, and to handle multiple targets in rapid succession. Her fingers, once soft and prone to blisters, had grown calloused. The bowstring that so often left angry welts now felt like an extension of herself.

The more confident she became, the harder he pushed.

"Again!" he would command whenever she missed, his voice brooking no argument even though she had been on the verge of tears.

The routine was harsh but effective. She'd wake to find him already on deck, targets arranged in increasingly difficult configurations. Some days he'd have her shoot from the crow's nest, forcing her to account for height *and* wind. Others, he'd set targets on floating debris, teaching her to compensate for the ship's movement.

"How many of these drills did you have to do?" she asked one afternoon, retrieving arrows from the day's practice.

"Thousands." He helped her gather the arrows. "But I had years to learn. You don't have that luxury."

The urgency in his voice wasn't lost on her. Whatever awaited them—whatever she truly was—time wasn't on their side.

Some nights, exhausted from training, she'd catch him

studying the maps, his brows furrowed as he charted their course between the Emberlight Shallows and the Expanse of Mirrors. Those moments reminded her that larger forces were at work. The fae were still hunting them, and the mystery of her connection to Faerie remained unsolved. But she could feel it sometimes, in quiet moments between training sessions. A humming beneath her skin, a tether to something vast and ancient. The magic Cillian insisted she possessed felt closer, more tangible, though still out of reach.

"Your form has improved," he said one evening as she cleaned her bow. "But tomorrow, we add movement. A stationary archer is a dead archer."

She looked up from her work, catching his eyes on her hands as they moved up and down the weapon. Heat coiled low in her belly, a silent promise between the two about what would happen later that night. But now there was something else too, a deeper understanding born from weeks of training together.

"Will I ever be good enough?" she asked, the question carrying more weight than just her archery skills.

Cillian's expression softened. "You're already better than you know."

15

BLOODSWORN

Booming thunder startled Margot from her slumber. High winds howled outside the cabin, rocking the ship precariously as rain battered the wooden walls. Being mindful of her sore body, she eased into an upright position and scanned the room, searching for Cillian. He was nowhere to be found. She kept her stance wide, bending her knees slightly as she used the walls to guide her to the bathroom to wash up and change before heading out into the storm to find him.

Once finished, she used all her strength to push open the door to the deck—and froze in awe. Lightning crackled within swirling purple clouds, branching out like crooked fingers. The bolts bled into an inky fog that crept across the deck, thick and ominous and obscuring her vision. Waves thrashed against the ship, as if intent on dragging the intruders down to the vast kingdom below, condemning them to a watery grave.

The storm's fury rattled her teeth, each gust threatening to tear her from the ship. Her leathers, heavy with rain, clung to her body like a second, freezing skin. She pressed herself against the cabin wall, fingers searching for purchase on the slick wood as waves crashed over the deck. The world had become a maelstrom of tempest winds and stinging rain, with Cillian lost somewhere in the chaos.

Her heart pounding, she forced herself forward. Each step was a battle against the hurricane as she inched along the deck, her boots sliding on the rain-slicked boards. The wind screamed in her ears, a living thing determined to hurl her into the churning sea. Salt stung her eyes as she searched desperately for any sign of him through the curtain of rain.

After a few minutes, she spotted Cillian struggling with the helm. She scrambled to the ship's side and gripped the guiding rope, not wanting to experience another leviathan incident, and made her way toward the demon.

"Cillian!" she yelled, hoping it was loud enough for him to hear her.

His eyes flashed in her direction. "What are you doing out here, Margot? Get back in the cabin where it's safe!"

She pulled herself next to him as the storm exploded, whipping her hair wildly like an untamed flame.

"You need my help," she said. "Tell me what to do."

Cillian gripped her arm and growled through clenched teeth. "Unless you can stop elven magic, you cannot help." He thrust her arm away. "Get. Back. To. The. Cabin."

"Elven magic? We found them?"

"More like they found us!" He roared louder than the storm as he wrestled with the helm to prevent them from capsizing. "Damnit, Margot. Get the fuck out of here!"

His words were knives, making Margot wince as she guided herself down—it wasn't worth picking a fight, especially not now. She figured reaching the elves would have been difficult, but she never expected they would summon whatever this was to keep out unwanted visitors. The magnitude of power the elves held terrified her.

Dread settled in the pit of her stomach as she peered over the railing. The water churned slowly, then picked up speed, forming a vortex. Cillian shouted and slammed the wheel as he tried to prevent the ship from getting caught, but it was too late. The vessel jerked, joining the twisting current.

She gripped the wood so tight it hurt, praying to whatever gods or goddesses were in this world not to let her drown when one finger was pried from the wood. Then another. She tried to bend them back to secure her hold, but they wouldn't move. Another finger was easily removed as if she were a marionette and someone was pulling her strings. Her stomach clenched, and she took rapid breaths but couldn't seem to get enough air in her lungs. This was worse than when she went overboard when the leviathan attacked. So much worse. Something—or someone—was doing this to her, and she was powerless to stop it.

Looking over her shoulder, Cillian's eyes met hers. Tears spilled over, rolling down her cheeks. She was grateful to see him one last time. He shouted something she couldn't understand and took a step forward but seemed to have realized that if he let go of the helm, all would be lost. In that instant, Margot's thumb was released, and she was thrown overboard by some unknown force.

Hitting the icy water felt like landing on shards of jagged glass. Instead of providing her with comfort, the depths were devouring her, pulling her further into their cold embrace. Salt stung her eyes as she opened them, trying to see her surroundings, but it was too murky. She tried moving her arms and legs to help her swim to the surface, but her limbs remained frozen in place. Sharp pains stabbed her burning lungs. That's when she realized she was running out of air. Whatever was controlling her didn't care that she couldn't breathe and continued to drag her deeper and deeper through the water.

Memories flashed before her eyes of the people she cared about most. A woman—her mother, Iris, she realized—before she got sick, happily baking pies in her farmhouse kitchen. Her father, staring lovingly at Iris from behind his newspaper with a grin of adoration crinkling his grey eyes. Iris again, this time after her father left, leaving her a broken shell of who she once was, left to fight off a disease that claimed so many lives—hers included.

Janey, smiling as she dragged Margot to a bar to sing bad karaoke, but not before making sure they were wearing their sluttiest outfits for nobody but themselves. And Cillian. The beautiful, frightening demon who had been kind to her when she needed it the most.

Margot knew she was crying; warm drops mixed with the frigid water against her cheekbones. She knew this was the last minute of her life, and with any luck, Faerie would return her soul to Earth so she could be with her mother. She closed her eyes, expelling any remaining air from her lungs, and let her body drift to the bottom of the sea.

Her chest burned from inhaling a copious amount of saltwater, which led to a spike in fear that morphed into desperation. She clawed at her throat, gasping for oxygen that wasn't there while marine debris blurred in her periphery. As the darkness beckoned, a violet orb pulsed twice before rapidly expanding, encapsulating her—a shroud of safety.

But Margot was still dying.

She stumbled within the shell, looking for anything to help remove the menacing water that wanted to claim her. With no air left to push it out and mere seconds before the element won, she made her decision and clasped her hands together, knowing this was a last-ditch effort and mustered all the strength she had to thrust into her abdomen—it didn't work. All hope seemed lost until shimmering dust swirled before coming together in a sinuous line and making a beeline straight for her gut, forcefully expelling the water through means she couldn't comprehend. Between fits of coughing, she greedily gulped down air. She was grateful to be alive.

"Not whom I would have chosen to inherit Ilphas' magic, but I suppose you will suffice," a mysterious voice echoed, sending a chill down Margot's spine. The tone was familiar, reminiscent of the whispers that had haunted her, yet there was something different about it—an edge she couldn't quite place. It carried a weight, an authority, that made her skin prickle with unease.

Once Margot regained her composure, she pushed against the orb's walls—they didn't budge. She threw her body into it, only to be thrown back. Instead of trying to break out, she flattened her face against it to see if it was moving, but the orb appeared to be in some sort of stasis.

"Are you the one who brought me to Faerie?" she asked, engaging the voice.

The voice scoffed. "I would never do such a thing. *Ilphas*, however, that wild card," disdain laced the voice's words, "*he* thought it was wise to pass his magic to a child of Earth when his body turned to dust."

"So, Ilphas gave me his magic and brought me to Faerie?" *That answers one question, at least.*

"You travel with a demon?" the voice asked, ignoring Margot's question. "How strange. Shall I kill him?"

"No! Please, no." Her bottom lip trembled. "Please... please don't kill Cillian."

The voice sighed. "As you wish. You will sail directly to Caramis without taking detours. There is much to discuss and little time. Do you understand?"

"But the storm—"

"—Will not be an issue for you," the voice declared. "Now go."

Before she could respond, she found herself on her knees as the orb surged toward the sea's glassy surface. The vessel zipped like a jet fighter through the ocean, causing her stomach to churn. It was moving so fast she could feel the skin pulling back from her bones. After a couple of minutes, she burst through the surface and hung in the air, suspended. She looked around wildly, trying to find the ship through the storm.

There it was, just below her. Time had come to a complete standstill. Cillian was mid-shout at the ship's helm, eyes still fixed where Margot had gone overboard. Nothing moved. Not the water. Not the clouds. No rain fell, and the wind did not blow. The entire world just... stopped.

"What did you do?" she whispered.

"You said you did not want the demon to die," the voice said, sounding chafed. "Existence will resume once you return to the ship. Stop wasting my time."

The voice's presence dissipated as the orb descended upon the ship. Whirling water returned to normal, righting the vessel. Though the storm remained, her sphere expanded, encompassing the entire ship, allowing for safe passage to Caramis through the elven storm.

Thunder, heavy rain, and fierce wind raged on, but the sounds were now muffled thanks to the protective barrier. Cillian reanimated. His shout started out strong before quickly dying off. He stood before the wheel, disoriented. A few seconds passed, and he shook off his confusion. His gaze met Margot's, and he stomped across the deck, standing mere inches from her.

"What the fuck happened? One second, you were drowning, and the next, here you are, standing in front of me while the entire ship is surrounded by a magic fucking force field."

She smiled at him sheepishly. "I, uh, guess you were right, and I do have elven magic."

"Of course I was right." He ran his fingers through his hair. The muscles in his neck contracted. "Why don't you explain what happened? Don't leave anything out."

Margot recounted what happened in as much detail as possible. However, she left out the fact that he was the last person she thought of when she thought she was dying. If her tale surprised Cillian, he didn't show it.

"Caramis..." he muttered.

"Do you know about it?"

"Only what I've heard in whispers," he said. "The elven city." He glanced at her. "And they're offering us safe passage?"

"Apparently. It seemed urgent that I get there as quickly as possible."

Cillian laughed mirthlessly.

"What's so funny?"

"They really are going to kill me."

Margot cocked an eyebrow. "They just spared your life. Why would they kill you once we get there? Why not just do it now?"

"The only reason I'm alive now is because you asked for me to live. What's the easiest way to get someone to do what you want? Give them what they're asking for. Once you're there and they can control you. There won't be a reason for them to keep me alive."

The voice *was* rather indifferent when asking if they should kill Cillian. It was clear they didn't value his life. But if they agreed to let him live once, perhaps they would again.

"If it's apparent they have no intentions of letting you live, I'll ask them again once we get there."

His eyes softened as they roamed her face. "Ah, Margot. I've had a good run. If this is how I die, so be it."

Margot could hardly believe what she was hearing. Cillian, the great scary demon, was content with *dying*? Unacceptable.

Unable to stop herself, Margot smacked his chest as hard as she could. "You will not die! I won't let you."

"How are you going to stop them from killing me? You've done well with a bow, but right now, you're a human with elven magic she doesn't know how to wield. They *stopped time*, Margot."

"They need me for something. I could tell how adamant the voice was about getting me to Caramis. I can just refuse to help them unless you live."

Cillian shook his head. "They can *make* you help them. As in, *force* you to do whatever they want against your will."

"I have to try," she whispered.

He tossed a hand in the air. "You do what you have to do, but right now, I'm hungry. Let's get something to eat before we make landfall."

"You go on ahead. I need to think for a bit."

Cillian lingered a moment before heading to the cabin, leaving Margot with her thoughts.

She watched the tempestuous storm through the amethyst sphere. The barrier undulated, warping the clouds, making them look even more otherworldly. Waves erupted up the sides of the shield, climbing at least ten feet high on all sides. The water was a baleful violet rather than the sparkling lavender she was growing accustomed to, leaving her feeling uneasy. The ocean was so rough that she couldn't even make out aquatic life. *Maybe the elves magicked them all away when they created the storm.*

Margot knew her chances of surviving any of this were slim to none, but she wasn't willing to go down without a fight, even if Cillian was. He seemed convinced the elves would discard him, and he could be right, but what if he could be helpful to the elves? What if she proposed Cillian fight on the elves' side against the fae? Surely, if they sided with the elves, they would let him live, right?

She sighed. She missed the calm sea and light-hearted conversations with Cillian. Once they arrived at Caramis, everything would change. Worry skittered down her spine that this was the end, and she would truly never get to fully know the demon. What if they *didn't* let him live and instead killed him in front of her? She shuddered at the thought.

After a few deep breaths, she resigned herself. There was little she could do right now; everything was speculative. Talking to the elves and finding out what they needed from her needed to happen first. If she were lucky, they might teach her how to use her magic. But killing her would be just as easy, and they could wait for the magic to go to someone else, to someone less... *human.* Or maybe all of this was wrong, and the elves weren't as horrible as Cillian thought. Maybe they would even help them both.

She glanced at the sea one last time before returning to the cabin where Cillian waited for her. Errant musings wouldn't save them now.

"Are you okay?" Cillian asked as she entered.

Margot said nothing as she walked to where he stood in the

kitchenette and gingerly raised her hand. He eyed her curiously when she placed it on his chest. Demonic heat radiated through her palm, the steady thump of his heartbeat quickening.

"You can't die," she whispered and slid her hand up to his neck. "You can't die, Cillian." Tears pricked the corners of her eyes as she traced his jawline. "I won't let you."

Heavy droplets fell as she caressed his rough skin. His silver eyes smoldered with every stroke of her hand, deepening the rise and fall of his chest. He never winced or shied away from her touch, letting her explore his body with every ounce of emotion that had been welling inside her since the moment they met.

Cillian cupped the side of her face and wiped the wetness away with his thumb. "Margot, you may not be able to save me."

She leaned into his palm, bringing her hand to his before the sobs she was fighting back erupted. She fell to the ground, beating the wooden floor as if it would change things. Anguished cries reverberated off the walls. Her chest heaved, and her vision blurred. She didn't know someone could feel such sorrow. Even when her mother died, it hadn't hurt like this. They'd known her cancer wasn't treatable, but they still had enough time together to come to terms with the inevitable. This, though... this was a ticking time bomb.

"I h-have to save y-you." The words were wrenched from her as she tried to catch her breath. "Y-you're my p-person."

Cillian sat on the floor and pulled Margot into his arms, pressing a kiss on top of her head. "There... might be a way," he muttered, his voice thick with uncertainty. "But you may not like it."

Margot clutched at his leathers, her heart pounding. She looked up at him, wide-eyed, her breath catching in her throat. "I'll do anything," she whispered, though the words felt heavier as they left her lips, like a promise she wasn't sure she could keep.

He hesitated, his breath hitching. "We—" he swallowed hard, "—we can form a blood bond."

Her brow furrowed. "What's a blood bond?"

Cillian's arms tightened around her, pulling her closer as if afraid of losing her. "We would be bound to one another. Indefinitely." His voice grew hoarse. "There would be very little that could keep us apart. My kind uses the bond to strengthen the connection between..." He swallowed hard. "...mates."

"Mates?" The word felt foreign to her tongue, ancient and primal.

"A demon's blood bond is absolute," he continued, his silver eyes darkening. "Unlike fae who can form multiple bonds in their lifetime, for us, it's singular. Eternal." His fingers traced her jaw. "If we complete the ritual fully, we'll share everything. Pain. Pleasure. Power. Our souls would be forever intertwined."

"And if something happened to you?"

"The elves need you whole, capable. A broken bond..." His voice dropped to barely a whisper. "It would shatter you. The grief alone has driven demons mad. Some waste away, unable to bear existence without their mate." He cupped her face. "But an unconsummated bond, while still painful if broken, wouldn't destroy you."

"And if we did... consummate it?"

"We'd be stronger together. Share power, emotions, even thoughts should we choose." His thumb brushed her lower lip, making her feel heady. "But the risk..." He drew a shaky breath. "If the elves killed me, that connection would tear you apart within. Your magic could become unstable, unpredictable. You might never recover."

Margot pressed closer, her heart racing. "Or it could protect us both. They need my magic—they wouldn't risk damaging it by breaking a blood bond."

"Unless they know something we don't." His expression hardened. "This isn't just about pleasure, Margot. This is about binding our souls together, irreversibly. Are you ready for that kind of commitment?"

Her stomach churned as she processed his words. *A bond? Bound to Cillian? Forever?*

Margot's grip on his leathers faltered, doubt creeping in. "Is this... really our best shot?"

He pressed another kiss to her head, a gentleness in the gesture that made her heart ache. "This is our *only* shot."

Margot stared at the floor, her thoughts tangling like an old ball of yarn. A blood bond. The words themselves seemed to pulse with demonic power, promising something both terrifying and irresistible. Every rational part of her screamed that this was madness—binding herself eternally to someone she'd known for such a short time, diving headfirst into magic she didn't understand. The burden of 'forever' pressed against her chest, making it hard to breathe.

But when she thought of losing him—of watching the elves take his life while she stood helpless—her heart constricted with pain so sharp it felt physical. She'd lost her mother, her father had abandoned her, and now fate had dropped her into this strange world where Cillian was her only anchor. The idea of being bound to him forever terrified her, yes, but a life without him? That terrified her more.

She lifted her gaze to meet his, her voice soft but steady. "I'll do it."

Cillian nodded and helped her to her feet before rummaging through the storage chest. He turned to face her, the dagger with bones strung from the hilt in his hand. The one he had when they first met.

"Are you sure you want to do this?" he asked. "This can't be undone. This is forever, Margot."

"If this can help save your life... I'll do anything, Cillian. I want this."

He wrapped his fingers around the blade and sliced his palm. Faint wisps of smoke rose from the wound.

"Open your mouth," he said as he walked toward her.

Margot hesitated but did as he commanded. Holding his hand above her, a small stream of blood slid down her throat. The coppery tang hit the back of her tongue.

He wiped a drop of blood from her lips. "Give me your hand."

She rested her hand on his and he curled her fingers back, tickling the center of her palm with his fingertips before cutting it open. Cillian knelt before her, opening his mouth. Blood pooled as she tightened her fist, and she held her hand over him, watching her life spill down his throat.

Cillian stood, clasping his bloodied hand to hers, and as soon as their blood blended together, searing pain shot up her arm, causing her to grit her teeth, stifling a cry that threatened to crawl up her throat. The demon in front of her stood stoically, looking at her as if she was the only thing that mattered. Desire raged in his gaze, sending heat straight to her core.

"Flesh of my flesh," he said without breaking eye contact. "Bone of my bones." As he spoke, she could feel her soul, her very essence, intertwined with his.

"Blood of my blood."

Thick smoke filled the cabin. Their hands were so hot she thought they would combust.

"Heart of my heart."

Cillian sealed the bond with a kiss that scorched through her very being. His mouth claimed hers with primal intensity, his body pressing against her as if trying to meld them into one. She met his fervor, fingers tangling in his hair as raw power surged between them like lightning. His groan vibrated through her as his grip tightened, muscles tensing beneath her hands.

The transformation began with a shudder. Bones cracked and shifted, his frame expanding as the change took him. His leathers split and fell away, revealing bronzed skin that rippled with newfound power. His chest broadened, muscles swelling and redefining themselves beneath her exploring fingers. She traced each new contour, memorizing him with her touch as horns emerged, curling from his skull like an obsidian crown.

The bond hummed between them, turning every touch electric. His hands found her breasts, rough and demanding, drawing moans that he devoured with his kiss. She was drowning in sensation, in need, in the overwhelming urge to get closer, to consume and be consumed. Her fingers found his horns, tracing their length before gripping them to pull him deeper into their kiss.

Heat pooled low in her belly as he lifted her, strong hands digging into her thighs. They stumbled across the cabin until her back hit the bathroom door. The wood creaked beneath their combined weight as he pressed against her, his transformed body caging her in a way that made her feel both trapped and utterly safe.

His eyes blazed silver, cosmic storms raging in their depths as he tore at her clothes. The bond thrummed stronger with each layer removed until there was nothing between them but heated skin and desperate need. Teeth grazed her pulse point before biting down. The sharp sting of pain melted into pleasure that had her arching against him, crying out his name.

His hands branded paths down her body, memorizing every curve until he gripped her hips. She could feel him, hard and insistent against her center as she wrapped her legs around his waist, drawing him closer. The silver in his eyes flared brighter, his control visibly fracturing as the bond pulled them toward completion.

Suddenly, he stilled. The demon trembled with barely contained need. He tried to hide his face. Margot reached out, turning him back around to face her.

"Never hide who you are from me. I will never judge you, Cillian." She rocked her hips against him. "I want this. I want you."

His restraint snapped. With one powerful thrust, he claimed her. The bond flared white-hot between them as they joined, their shared pleasure spiraling through their connection. Every sensation doubled, echoed, amplified until she couldn't tell where she ended and he began.

He filled her completely, stretching her in ways that balanced the knife's edge between pleasure and pain, but through their bond, she felt his own pleasure mirroring hers, building between them like a gathering storm. His movements were measured at first, letting her adjust to his size, but soon grew more urgent, more primal.

The bathroom door rattled with each thrust. Her nails raked down his back as he drove deeper, harder. Their shared pleasure built higher and higher through the bond until the boundaries between them blurred entirely. She felt his need, his desperation, his fierce joy at finally claiming her. And he felt her surrender, her acceptance, her complete trust in him, even in his demon form.

When release finally claimed them, it crashed through their bond like a tidal wave. The force of their combined pleasure sent magic crackling through the cabin, extinguishing candles and rattling the windows. She cried out his name as stars burst behind her eyes, feeling him shudder against her as he followed her over the edge.

For long moments after, they clung to each other, trembling in the aftermath. Then, his horns retracted, and his body grew smaller as the smoke dissipated.

Through their newly forged bond, his thoughts caressed her mind. *Thank you.* The intimate touch of his consciousness against hers startled her for only a moment before it settled into place, as natural as breathing. *Flesh of my flesh. Bone of my bones. Blood of my blood. Heart of my heart. Thank you.*

Margot pressed her face against his chest, feeling his heartbeat echo through their connection. Whatever magic this was—demon, elven, or something older still—it had forged something unbreakable.

Let the elves try to separate us now.

16

STUPID GIRL

Warmth lingered in her bones as morning light filtered through the cabin windows. Every breath, every heartbeat shared between one another, a constant reminder of what they'd become. Margot lay curled against Cillian's chest, tracing idle patterns on his skin as she explored the edges of their connection. His thoughts brushed against hers, soft and content, though she could feel tension building beneath the surface.

They were getting closer to Caramis. She could sense it in how the air had changed, heavy with magic that called to something deep within her. The elven power that had saved her from drowning stirred in response, making her skin prickle with awareness.

"You're worried," she murmured, both feeling and hearing his sigh.

"The bond changes things." His fingers tangled in her hair. "Makes us stronger, yes. But also, more vulnerable." Through their connection, she caught flashes of his fears—separation, loss, the terrifying possibility of one needing to survive without the other. "It would be arrogant to ignore the fear."

She pushed up on one elbow to look at him. "Then we don't let them separate us."

His silver eyes met hers, storm-dark with emotion. "The elves are old, Margot. Older than demons, older than fae. They have magic we can't begin to understand."

"But they need me." She pressed her palm to his chest, feeling his heart race. "And now they get both of us, or neither."

Before he could respond, the temperature plummeted. Frost crept across the windows in delicate patterns, and their breath fogged in the suddenly frigid air. Cillian stiffened, instinctively pulling Margot closer as his demon form emerged, horns curling from his skull.

"We've crossed their boundary," he growled. She felt his fear and anger mingling with her own, amplified by their connection.

Through the windows, they watched the amethyst barrier around their ship flare brighter, its protective magic clashing with whatever was out there. The sea itself seemed to part before them, revealing a hidden channel that hadn't been there moments before.

Margot's inherited magic stirred in response, making her gasp. It was different now, stronger, as if the blood bond had awakened something that had been dormant. Or perhaps it was simply Caramis calling to her, recognizing what flowed through her veins.

"Get dressed," Cillian said, already moving to gather their scattered clothes. "Whatever happens next..." He caught her gaze. "Remember what we are to each other now. They might try to make you forget."

A chill that had nothing to do with the cold air ran down her spine. Through their bond, she felt his memories of demon mates that had been torn apart due to loss. She reached for him, both physically and through their connection, needing to anchor herself in what they'd become.

"I won't forget," she promised. "I won't let them make me forget."

THE FRIGID AIR MELTED INTO THICK, TROPICAL humidity as Margot leaned against the ship's bow, watching Caramis emerge through the lavender dawn. Even through the heavy mist, the island's majesty took her breath away. Towering mountains draped in vibrant flora reached toward the sky, their peaks wreathed in clouds that seemed to glow from within. Everywhere she looked, nature thrived in impossible colors—flowers in shades she had no names for, vines that sparkled like scattered gems.

Her mother would have loved this, she thought. The ache of missing Iris was sharp despite their bond still humming warmly in her chest. She could almost hear her voice: *"Sometimes the scariest choices lead us exactly where we're meant to be."* A tear slipped down her cheek as she imagined introducing Cillian to her mother. *She would have seen past the demon to the man beneath.*

The thought of home sent another pang through her. Was Janey searching for her? Had the police already given up, filing her away as just another missing person? Or had time moved differently between worlds, leaving Earth unchanged in her absence? The questions tangled in her mind, but before they could overwhelm her, a familiar presence wrapped around her thoughts.

"Demons yearn for the beauty Faerie offers."

Margot peered over her shoulder at the beast of a man who approached from behind. Dark circles marred his otherwise perfect face; he looked like he slept as well as she did. He stood beside her, his arm touching hers, sending electric currents straight to her center.

Their eyes met, his mercurial storm churning.

Lust.

Desire.

Need.

Her mouth parted, and her tongue swept her bottom lip. Cillian's eyes fell to her chest. His body tensed, his nostrils flaring as he inhaled her scent. His pupils dilated to the size of saucers, and he leaned in, his lips centimeters from hers. The world faded into nothingness, leaving only the two of them caught in a magnetic pull. And then, with a sudden surge of longing, their mouths met in a mess of lips and teeth and panting. She drank him in, her eyes fluttering closed from the taste. A rough hand gripped her waist and pulled her closer. Their bodies molded together as if they were made for each other, igniting a passion that neither had been able to deny. In that stolen moment, time stood still, and Faerie seemed to whisper its approval.

Cillian tangled his fingers in her hair as he deepened their kiss. She lifted her leg and wrapped it around his body as he held it in place while she ground against his thick cock, straining against his leathers, causing him to groan. He slid his other hand down her back, leaving a trail of cinders in its wake as it traveled across her hips and eventually reached the sensitive skin just above the curve of her bottom. She shivered at his touch, feeling as though she was on fire, and the only way she could be extinguished was if she had him inside her. But as quickly as it had begun, Cillian abruptly pulled away, his breath ragged as he stared at her, fighting against what the bond demanded of them.

"Now isn't the time," Cillian said, his voice hoarse.

Looking at the sky, Margot blinked back tears. After a moment, she whispered, "I thought, maybe, just for a few more minutes, we could pretend."

"No use pretending, heart of my heart," he said. "I won't have you smelling even more like me. The elves' senses are keener than even demons'—they'll know exactly what we've done, how deeply we're bound. The more my scent marks you, the more ammunition we give them. A mated pair is far more vulnerable than two individuals."

Margot hummed. She understood, she did. But she wanted him desperately. "If you can control yourself, I guess I can, too." She glanced at him. "I was wondering about what you said earlier when you mentioned demons yearning for beauty. What's Olvath really like?"

"A wasteland that feeds on suffering." Cillian clenched his fists. "Like Faerie, Olvath is alive—but where this realm nurtures beauty, mine craves chaos. War. Death. Every attempt to change it has failed."

Margot rested her head against his arm, feeling his pain echo through their bond. "Then we'll make sure they never send you back."

His finger tilted her chin up, and the sorrow in his eyes made her heart ache. "Things could have been different had we met in another life."

"Stop talking like this is the end." The words came out more desperately than she intended. She wanted to believe the elves would listen, would understand. But doubt gnawed at her confidence, making her next words feel hollow. "I'll figure out how to handle the elves."

Through their bond, his skepticism mingled with her own fear. They both knew she was grasping at straws, but what choice did they have?

A BITTER TASTE OF BILE CREPT UP MARGOT'S THROAT as they neared the shoreline. Pewter gulls soared overhead, their feathers tinged green as sunlight bounced off them, while vibrant hummingbirds flitted between hot pink hibiscuses. But even this paradise felt wrong—too perfect, too carefully crafted. Cillian's mounting unease mirrored her own.

A lonely dock materialized through the mist like a mirage, its weathered planks and rusted nails starkly contrasting the pristine beauty surrounding it. A tattered flag fluttered weakly at its end, the faded symbol barely discernible.

"Time to berth the ship," He gave her shoulder a squeeze. "You sure you want to do this?"

"I don't think I have any other choice."

"We always have a choice, Margot. You just need to be able to live with your decisions. Can you live a gratifying life not knowing if the elves can help?"

She thought for a moment and turned away from him, focusing on the calm waters. "I can't."

Margot tightened her grip on the ship's railing, her knuckles white as thoughts of what awaited them onshore played through her mind. Was this truly a safe haven, or was the calm exterior hiding dangers they couldn't see?

"Got her docked," Cillian said, cutting through her thoughts. "I'm gonna get the brow set up and secure her." The plank thudded against the pier. Cillian walked halfway down and looked over his shoulder. "Everything alright?"

"I-yeah. Sorry. I'm coming."

This is it.

She cast one last glance at the ship, their sanctuary these past weeks. Would she ever step aboard her again, or was this farewell? Cillian's hand found hers, his fingers intertwining with hers like the threads of fate that bound them. She swallowed against the rising tide in her throat, his touch grounding her in the moment.

With each step they took, intricate stones materialized beneath their feet, forming a path that guided them forward. On either side, marble statues rose from the earth—ancient elven warriors and rulers immortalized in stone. Their faces held an unsettling serenity, eyes seeming to track their movement as delicate floral ivy breathed and shifted across the carved surfaces.

Margot shivered as they passed between the silent sentinels. Each statue radiated power, as if the spirits of those they commemorated lingered within the stone. These weren't mere decorations—they were warnings, reminders of the elves' ancient might.

As they neared an ornate gate, thick fog concealing whatever lay beyond, Margot's heart seized. The mist coiled like spectral fingers, reaching toward them. Every instinct screamed that something was very, *very* wrong.

"We should leave," Margot whispered to Cillian.

"A little late for that," he said, jerking his head toward the gate. "Look."

The fog rolled out and her eyes widened as she took in the colorful array of stucco buildings and arched cobbled streets. Many of the structures had tiered garden beds full of creeping bushes that cascaded down the sides between spurting water fountains. Caramis was stunning.

The gate creaked open.

Cillian pulled Margot into his arms, resting his forehead against hers. "Heart of my heart, I am so glad I met you."

Margot sobbed against his chest as if a dam had sprung a leak. The elves scared her. This new world scared her. Cillian was the only one who could keep her safe, grounded. He bent down, pressing a kiss to her lips, but the clearing of a throat startled him, and he pulled away.

She swatted at her tear-stained cheeks and turned to the elf. Like the fae, this man was perfection. His sleek, midnight blue hair complemented his jewel-like amber eyes and his skin, the color of lamb's wool, was flawless, lacking any kind of blemish. His white robe swayed against the lithe body underneath as he approached them. A generous smile spread across his face when he locked eyes with Margot. Though it was shortly replaced with a scowl after he sniffed her. He glared daggers at Cillian, clapped his hands twice, and the demon disappeared.

Margot still held herself as if she could still feel Cillian's arms around her and hyperventilated, not believing what was happening.

"You stupid girl." The elf snarled at her, baring his fangs. "What have you done?"

2
Caramis

MARGOT | CILLIAN

17

WHAT NEEDED TO BE DONE

MARGOT CLUTCHED HER SEIZING CHEST. What had she done? *What had* she *done?* The elf's audacity nearly left her dumbfounded, but an all-consuming rage boiled over. With a banshee screech, she lunged for the elf. Just before she made contact, he held his hand up and spread his long fingers. A wall of force slammed into her, knocking her to the ground. She brushed off her leathers and scrambled to her feet. Then, she tried to run past the man, desperate to get to wherever Cillian had gone, only to be stopped once more. Refusing to give up, she kept changing course again and again, but each time encountered resistance until she was cornered. It was like a mime pretending to be locked inside an invisible box, only this had been real.

A scream tore from her throat as she banged her fists against the barrier. "Bring him back! Bring him back now!"

The elf picked invisible lint from his robe, periodically checking his nails as Margot exhausted herself.

Rivulets of sweat slid down her face. Blood coated her hand from her torn knuckles. But she kept pounding on the wall, breathless. She couldn't keep it up, though. She was losing steam, and eventually, her arms fell limp at her sides.

With one last sweep of her surroundings, she rested her head against her slumped shoulder as she tried to catch her breath. Cillian was gone. The sharp pangs in her chest were proof of that. Focusing on the pain, she closed her eyes, letting it consume her. The ache was incessant, but if she sifted through each jolt, she could feel the slow heartbeat of a certain demon. Although gone, he was at least alive.

"What did you do with Cillian?" she asked.

Margot hadn't expected the elf to answer. Why would he? He owed her nothing. Instead, she kept her eyes closed, directing comforting thoughts to Cillian, hoping they would reach him. After a few moments, pieces of her heart flaked away when there was no response.

"Tell me what you did with him!" she yelled.

"Are you done being petulant?" the elf said. His voice was cold, heartless.

Her eyes snapped to the elf, her upper lip curling. The muscles in her thighs twitched. She dug her heel against the ground, pulled back her fist, then struck the wall as hard as she could. A strangled cry caught in her throat as she clutched her hand, still tingling from the blow.

A *whooshing* sound filled her invisible cage as she drew in an agonizing breath that didn't quite fill her lungs. *I can't breathe.* She flailed her arms, then clawed at her throat, nails tearing skin as she tried to suck in air that wasn't there. Tears blurred her vision, but she could just make out the scowl on the elf's face.

"Are you quite finished?" he asked. "Your only warning: I will not ask again."

As darkness tried pulling her under, she managed a nod. Air rushed in, assaulting her lungs, painfully expanding. They struggled to accommodate the sudden influx of oxygen. She stumbled, falling to her knees as streaming tears stained the cobbled path beneath her.

"Please... tell me what you did with Cillian."

"He is safe. For now."

"Why—"

"Do you have *any* idea what you have done?" the elf snapped at her. "You bound yourself to a *demon*. Even the elves cannot help you undo this... this atrocity."

He snarled what Margot could only assume were vile insults in his native language. Contempt and hatred dripped from his tongue, sending shivers down her spine.

Margot struggled to stand. Despite her trembling limbs and cold sweat dotting her forehead, she didn't want to show any weakness.

"I don't want to be helped. Not with this."

The elf scoffed, narrowing his amber eyes. "Elves and demons do not work together in any capacity. What you have done... is condemnable."

Margot crossed her arms and widened her stance. "Good thing I'm not an elf then, huh?"

"You truly are an imbecile. That brain of yours did not take one second to think about how elements, unbeknownst to you, would affect your being?" He chuckled. "It is laughable, really. A human gained ancient elven magic and was not torn to shreds... and you thought you would stay human?"

The blood drained from her face, and her mouth dried as his words marinated. What he was saying was impossible, improbable, and it *definitely* couldn't be happening. There was no way she could become a different species. Amusement danced in the elf's eyes as the realization struck her.

Magic.

How could she have been so dumb? To her, everything she experienced in Faerie was unimaginable by Earth's standards. For the love of God, Cillian was a *demon*. Why did she choose this time in her life to go with the flow? She should have questioned *everything*. Now the elf was saying she wasn't even human. How could she ever go back home? It was out of the question.

"Do you understand now why this," he hissed as he waved his hand in the air, "*bargain* you made with a devil is problematic?"

"Stop! This isn't a problem! Cillian is different. He's kind. He—"

"—He is a *demon*! You know nothing of this world, of his kind, or what *they* are capable of. He will take everything from you, bleed you dry, and leave you dead where you stand."

"No. No. No! He isn't like that!"

The elf's nostrils flared, clearly annoyed by her denial, but she didn't care. Half her soul had been stolen. The elf *broke* her. She bit her bottom lip to keep the sob that was begging to come out at bay.

Cillian was alive. She felt him. Regardless of what she was now, the demon was part of her, and she would do *anything* to get him back. *That* was what she needed to focus on.

"They are *all* like that. Vile creatures, demons. You will do well to remember that." He moved closer to her and clasped his hands together. "We have a busy day planned, Margot. I rather hope we are through with the theatrics."

When Margot didn't respond, he snapped his fingers and offered his hand. She was reluctant, eyeing him wearily. Demanding anything of the elves obviously wouldn't work, especially when this one wouldn't even listen to her. *Maybe the best way to keep Cillian alive is to follow along.*

"Come now," the elf said. "No harm shall come to you."

Margot sighed and placed her hand against his. Warmth spread throughout her body, bathing her in a soothing calm, dispersing all the tension.

"Is that not better?" he asked.

She hummed in agreement.

"Educating you is my number one priority. But we must also condition your body so you can handle elven magic. Effectively wielding the elements is a physically and mentally demanding process." He squeezed her hand and smiled. "My name is Vesryn. You will be under my tutelage for the foreseeable future. We start today."

Margot fell into step with Vesryn as he gripped her hand

tightly, guiding her through the winding streets of Caramis. She desperately wanted to stall and ask more questions but found herself unable to speak. Whatever he had done to her left her body compliant while her mind was free to wander.

As they walked, she turned her head, taking in her surroundings. Though Caramis was beautiful, the streets had an unsettling emptiness about them. The town was too silent. Even the birds ceased their chirping, and the wind had stilled. Movement caught her eye, and she glanced sideways, but all she saw were shadows slipping behind closed doors and curtains being hastily drawn. Occasionally, she glimpsed faces peering out from darkened windows, their jewel-toned eyes following her progress before vanishing like ghosts. *Where are all the other elves?* Cillian had mentioned they had trouble reproducing, but she figured there would be quite a few openly walking the streets, going about their daily lives. That they seemed to hide, scurrying away like frightened animals at her approach, was... odd. The few elves she did manage to spot more clearly moved like wraiths through the town, heads down, hurrying from one building to another as if afraid to be caught in the open.

Vesryn wore a placid smile as they passed through the main part of town. The serpentine cobblestone paths were lined with unmanned market stalls, their teal and crimson canopies hanging limp and lifeless. Abandoned displays were stocked with gleaming trinkets, exotic fruits, and delicate bottles filled with swirling potions that caught the light which spoke of a market that should have been bustling with life but now stood eerily vacant. The paths twisted like a maze before opening to a large clearing.

A crowd of at least thirty murmuring elves had gathered, all wearing solemn expressions. One by one, they stopped their quiet chatter and turned toward Margot. Their gemstone eyes bore into hers, the colors ranging from deep amethyst to brilliant emerald to molten amber. All she wanted to do was find Cillian and get the hell out of there. She felt the beat of his heart; he felt closer than before. *I don't know if you can hear me, Cillian, but I think I'm in trouble.*

Vesryn cleared his throat, and a light, salty breeze started up as if he commanded it, rustling palm fronds and swaying massive stalks of hot orange canna that peppered the field. Between the cannas were vibrant ginger lilies, which rose from the ground like delicate peach spears, stretching as if they could touch the sun. Beyond the clearing, a dense jungle of tree ferns, cordyline, and banana palms created a barrier between Caramis' high wall and whatever lay beyond.

The island was undeniably beautiful, but the dichotomy between the scenic vista and the elves, whose faces contorted, dripping with disdain, was jarring. As much as Margot wanted to flee, Vesryn's magic had taken root and forced her to physically remain calm despite her mind warring with itself.

One dark-skinned elf came forward as the group split down the center. His steps were calculated, confident. Much like Vesryn, he was tall—not as tall as Cillian—but still a respectable height. Rows of obsidian-colored braids, intricately twisted against his scalp, were pulled into a tight knot on top of his head. A neatly trimmed beard framed his jawline, drawing attention to the thin scar that traced the bridge of his nose and the notched flesh missing from his left ear. While Vesryn wore flowing robes, he wore leathers and had weapons strapped to his frame. *A warrior?*

"This her?" the leather-clad elf asked, his violet eyes jerking to Margot's, sending a bout of terror straight to the pit of her stomach. "I can smell the demon from here."

"An unfortunate turn of events, to be sure," Vesryn said. "Corym, you can dismiss the rest. I will just be needing you for now."

Corym shot Margot a seething look before nodding to Vesryn. He walked back into the crowd, sending them on their way. The group disbanded quickly and rushed back to the city taking roundabout routes as if to avoid Margot at all costs. For that, she was grateful.

Once the clearing was empty, save for Corym, Vesryn walked down the white marble stairs to meet him. Margot trailed behind, despite her attempts to stop herself from following.

"This is Margot," Vesryn said, gesturing to Margot. "Ilphas thought it wise to entrust his magic to a child of Earth."

Corym's mouth formed a thin line, and his eyes fell on her. He shook his head, and Margot could taste the disappointment.

"Why did you do it?" Corym asked. "Why did you form a bond with a demon? It's bad enough that we need to deal with someone from your world having our magic, but now we have to attend to the bond as well... this was a mistake. A big one."

Margot blinked absently. Her mouth wouldn't move. Not that she had an answer for him. She didn't have a good reason for bonding with Cillian, only that she wanted to. Cillian had been so sure the elves would kill him, and the bond might save his life. That reason was good enough for Margot, but it probably wasn't for the two elves standing before her.

"What's wrong with her, Vesryn?"

"Ah, that. This one is highly emotional, and she threw a monumental tantrum. She is under the calming." Vesryn shrugged. "There was nothing that could be done about it."

Corym grimaced. Despite the lines that appeared on his face, he was still strikingly beautiful. Light reflected off his ebony skin, leaving a trail of shimmering sparkles in its wake. The elves exuded a quiet femininity, regardless of sex. Cillian differed from the elves and the fae in that regard. His features were hardened, with bulging muscles and broad shoulders—masculine through and through.

"It's worse than we thought," Corym said as if she wasn't there.

"Afraid so."

"And the plan?"

Vesryn glanced at Margot. "Remains the same. However, as

the issue is severe, we begin today. I would have liked to educate her on our history... but this matter is far more pressing."

Margot's mind raced as she tried to make sense of what the two elves were talking about. Was it about her bond with Cillian? It had to be, but Vesryn said the elves couldn't remove the bond, which only left her more confused.

"I agree. This is something that must be handled with haste. Shall we be off, Vesryn?"

"Lead the way."

They followed the high wall separating Caramis and the field, heading toward the back of the town. Margot's jaw dropped when they stopped in front of what looked to be a mausoleum. Like the rest of Caramis, fine plaster covered the building, but it lacked the colorful array the rest of the town displayed. They walked up the stairs, past white Romanesque columns that lined the front, creating arched entryways fit for gods. Glyphs and runic symbols adorned the large marble door, and when Corym placed his hand in the center, they glowed blue before the door groaned apart, revealing an empty stretch of room.

Once the three of them crossed the threshold, the door shut with more force than it opened, the sound making Margot cringe as it reverberated through her sternum. Their footsteps echoed against the polished concrete floor throughout the hallway. The walls were plain, uninteresting, which she thought was weird considering the amount of detail the elves had put into the rest of Caramis.

"Emotional control is vital when calling upon elven magic, Margot," Vesryn said. His voice cut through the silence like a blade. "When one's emotions are volatile, so is their magic. It is imperative that you learn how to control your outbursts. We would not want your magic to kill you, now, would we?"

Margot would have thrown herself to the ground and vomited if she could, but her body remained forward. A circular chamber opened before them, as plain as the hallway that led to it. Symbols—like the ones adorning the door—were etched into the floor, creating a border around the room. In the center, geometric shapes intertwined forming an intricate pattern within a perfect circle.

Vesryn and Corym walked to the middle, positioning themselves to either side before turning to face her. Her feet moved on their own, trying to catch up to the elf who had spelled her, but another barrier halted her progress. With a swish of Vesryn's hand, the floodgates opened, and every feeling his magic had suppressed came crashing back at once.

The effect was staggering.

Blood rushed against her eardrums, and the only thing she could think about was how she needed to leave this place. Somehow, some way, she needed to get out of there. She never should have sought the elves. Caramis was dangerous, the *elves* were dangerous, and that she thought she could deal with them was laughable. She was so far out of her depth she was drowning. What possessed her to be so brash? Why hadn't she listened to Cillian when he stressed how horrible the elves were? Why couldn't she make better choices? He gave her the facts and she threw them in his face, resigning him to certain death.

And she needed to save him.

With outstretched hands she searched for a hole in the barrier, for any way out of her prison but she kept hitting blockade after blockade. What would she even do if she got out? Freshly bonded, she had no idea how to find Cillian or make the damn thing work. There had been no time for her to learn and she'd been so caught up in the crash of emotions that came along with the bond she hadn't thought to ask.

Margot's throat tightened and she rested her hand on the invisible wall.

She was trapped.

"What did you do?" she croaked.

"What needed to be done," Vesryn said.

The elf gave a solemn nod to Corym, who placed his hand upon one of the glyphs. Indigo rays exploded forth, bathing the room in ethereal light. Chains, born of magic and iron, ascended from the chamber's heart, lifting Cillian in their grasp. The shackles at his wrists soared upward, binding him to the ceiling while a broad metal clasp wrapped around his torso, anchoring him to the earth. His legs, too, were ensnared, held fast by cold, unyielding bands that glimmered in the unnatural glow.

Her demon raised his slumped head, silver eyes meeting hers, and Margot turned to the side, emptying the entire contents of her stomach on the concrete floor.

NOTHING

TABLES APPEARED out of thin air as Corym walked around, snapping his fingers. One by one, horrific-looking tools and contraptions popped into existence. He sorted them, arranging the devices with neat precision. Margot's gaze drifted across the tabletops, dread washing over her as she caught sight of an absurd number of blades.

They're going to torture him.

"Please," she whispered. "Please don't do this. I'll do whatever you need me to do. I'll be whatever you need me to be but leave Cillian out of it. He did nothing."

Vesryn arched a manicured eyebrow and positioned himself in front of Cillian. "Do you know why this must happen, demon?"

Cillian's gaze was vacant, refusing to react to anything the elf said.

"Since you are so disinclined to tell me your thoughts, I will speak in your stead. Our dear Margot has made a *very* poor choice in selecting you as a companion. An even *poorer* choice was deciding to bond with you." Vesryn glared at Margot before he returned his attention to Cillian. "The bond emotionally tied her to you. Normally, I would not care whom the girl bonded with. This is an unfortunate situation you find yourself in, demon, because Margot will be one of us—and soon. Prior to us summoning you to this chamber, I touched upon the importance of emotional control and elven magic. As a demon of... certain intelligence, I would like for you to explain to your dear blood-sworn why this is important. Perhaps if she hears it from multiple individuals, she will start to understand."

"This is insane!" Margot yelled. "Let him go!"

Vesryn stalked over to her, slamming his hand against the barrier. She clutched her side in agony and cried out. Searing pain shot through her abdomen, causing her to fall to her knees. Cillian growled and fought against the chains. The elf tore his hand from the barrier and stormed around Cillian, grabbing a fistful of hair. He snapped the demon's head back.

"Answer the question," Vesryn said with a hiss. "Do not make me ask again."

Cillian grunted, shaking his hair free, and locked eyes with Margot. "Extreme fluctuations in emotions cause magic to be unpredictable and dangerous to both the user and their surroundings."

"Brah-*vo*," Vesryn said as he clapped his hands and circled the room. "See, Margot? Even the demon understands. Because of this emotional tie the two of you just *had to have*, you will need to be well and truly broken. Desensitized to the bond itself. What is the best way to do that? Why, I thought you would never ask! Now you see, the best way to be completely unaffected by the bond is through exposure."

"You're crazy! You don't have to do this. Let him stay with me. Everything will be fine. I swear it."

"Tell her why that will not work, demon," Vesryn said.

Cillian swallowed thickly and softened his expression. "It won't work because the bond strengthens as time goes on. Should something happen to me... grief would consume you, and once you've finished grieving, you would be full of anger and despair."

A sob worked its way out of her throat. "Nothing will happen to him, so that fact is irrelevant." She had to believe that was true.

Even the thought of something terrible happening to Cillian made her want to die.

"Idiot girl," Vesryn seethed. "Nothing is guaranteed in life. Not in your world, and certainly not in Faerie. Living is dangerous for you, for the demon, for me, for Corym." He gestured to the room. "Hells, it is bloody dangerous for us all. You do not get to live in a world where delusion reigns free. I will not allow it." His mouth formed a thin line and moved in front of Margot. "You *will* break. You will not become a liability to our people."

Corym grunted in agreement from the back of the room.

Silent tears dripped from the tip of Margot's nose as a sob caught in her throat. She squeezed her eyes shut, trying to block out the truth that threatened to shatter her. What Vesryn said made sense—her mind could follow the cold logic of his words. But her heart? Her heart felt like it was being torn to shreds, each piece scattered to the wind like ash. The blood bond had transformed her connection to Cillian into something profound and overwhelming, awakening feelings so intense they bordered on spiritual. How could anyone—even Vesryn with all his power—hope to break something that felt eternal, something that seemed woven into the very fabric of her soul?

"I-I thought you said you couldn't sever the bond?" she asked.

Vesryn muttered something to himself about how Ilphas chose the daftest human to assume his power, then shot her an incredulous look.

"Understand that repeating myself is a pet peeve of mine, so I will only reiterate this once more. We are going to break *you*. No one will leave this room until we cast the demon from your mind. The bond, however, will remain intact. It will be useless, but otherwise still there."

Margot sucked in a sharp breath, gripping the hem of her leathers as her mind raced. This was so much worse than she thought. Not only were they going to torture Cillian—they were going to make her watch. And the bond *would* let her forget him.

She was sure. Better to be forgotten than for one's bloodsworn to die.

"There has to be another way," she whispered. "Anything. Please."

"Would you rather I kill you?" Vesryn asked. His voice was flat, as if entirely removed from the situation.

Corym stopped fiddling with the equipment and watched her. Silence filled the room. Would she rather die than watch the elves torture him? She could feel Cillian's heart thumping wildly through the bond. She slowly brought her gaze to meet his. The shake of his head was nearly imperceptible. As if in apology, she shrugged for what she was about to do. Silver eyes pleaded with her; she ignored them.

Margot looked at Vesryn. His jaw dropped as he realized why it was taking so long for her to respond. She straightened her posture and stood tall.

"Yes. I would rather die. Kill me."

Cillian raged against his chains. "You will not fucking die, Margot! Do you hear me? Take it back!"

"You don't get to choose for me, Cillian!"

"Damnit! You don't even realize how imp—" A guttural roar tore from Cillian's throat as Corym stabbed him in the thigh with a scalpel.

The obsidian-haired elf violently pulled the blade from his leg and threw it at the barrier. "Not an option, human. You'll live to see this through."

Margot's eyes darted between Corym and Vesryn, and she banged against the barrier. "You asked me... you asked! Let me die, Vesryn! Let Cillian go!"

The two elves exchanged looks of uncertainty, and Vesryn exhaled, scrubbing his face. "Dying was never an option for you."

"Why even ask if choice is an illusion!" she cried. "Just let me die!"

"I will not *let* you! I will not lose Ilphas' magic to the ether because of some rash decision a *child* made on a whim! There is no bargaining. Any conversation between us has been a courtesy and one I shall no longer entertain. This happens whether or not you want it to. There is too much at stake." Vesryn turned to Corym. "Proceed."

"W-wait!" Margot stammered. Her mind raced a thousand miles per second. There had to be a way she could stop this or at least make the situation better. "How do I know you won't kill him?"

Vesryn rolled his eyes. "We are many things, but murderers, we are not."

"What happens to Cillian once this is over?"

"Once he has recovered, he is free to leave the island."

"Could he stay with me instead?" Margot asked. She looked to Cillian for reassurance. This wasn't a decision she wanted to make without him. Much to her relief, he smirked and nodded slightly, letting her know she was on the right track.

Vesryn pinched the bridge of his nose as if the conversation physically pained him. *That asshole deserves it.*

"If the demon wishes to remain by your side, despite the state your mind will be in, then I will allow it. The other elves will not bother him. This, I promise. Do we have a deal?"

"You have yourself a deal."

"Very well," the elf said as he walked to one of the tables. "Let us begin."

Margot's victory was short-lived as she watched Vesryn peruse the selection of torture devices. The elf's hand tentatively hovered over a tool that looked much like a cattle prod before picking it up. Lightning crackled from the tip as he ran a slender finger along the grip, which was even more unnerving.

Vesryn walked toward Cillian. His face was blank, his form rigid. This obviously wasn't something the elf enjoyed doing, whatever that was worth. Regardless of his feelings, Vesryn pressed it into the wound Corym delivered to his thigh. The demon clenched his teeth and shook so violently in his chains that bits of rock fell from the ceiling.

Unable to stop herself, Margot screamed. She knew what she and Cillian had agreed to, but it didn't stop her from wanting to push through the barrier and rush to his side. To take away his pain, to run her fingers through his hair and tell him everything would be okay.

Vesryn made a face that looked like he was smelling the world's largest pile of shit. He handed Corym the rod and wiped his palms against his robe.

"I truly do not have a taste for this sort of thing," Vesryn said. "I would appreciate it if you performed this task, Corym."

The violet-eyed elf grunted.

Vesryn made his way to Margot, the barrier rippling as he walked through. "Now, you watch. The demon will suffer, and in turn, you will suffer, Margot. No matter what you cry out, no matter how much you beg, Corym will not stop until the bond has been neutralized."

As if on cue, Corym thrust the apparatus back into position. Lightning arced across Cillian's skin, the scent of burning flesh filling the room along with his howls. The elf pulled the tool away, only giving Cillian enough time to take a breath before digging it into the wound again.

And again.

And again.

Corym didn't stop, each blow punctuated by Cillian's garbled screams that tore through Margot's soul like jagged glass. Her hand slid down the barrier as her legs gave out, sending her crashing to her knees. She couldn't breathe, couldn't think past the excruciating pain radiating through their bond. The elves had only just begun their torture, and already she felt like she was dying. Her heart slammed against her ribs so violently she feared it would burst from her chest. Eyes squeezed shut, she tried to focus on the thundering rhythm, only to realize it matched Cillian's desperate pulse beat for beat. Their shared agony created a horrific symphony that threatened to drive her mad. As unbearable as her suffering was, she knew with sickening certainty that what Cillian endured was infinitely worse.

Time lost all meaning as she knelt there, forced to witness his torment. It could have been hours—endless, nightmarish hours of watching lightning tear through his body, hearing his screams echo off stone walls, smelling his burning flesh. Every jolt that wracked his frame sent aftershocks through their bond until she wasn't sure where his pain ended and hers began.

"Please stop," she said, forcing the words past her raw throat.

Corym clicked the tool off and smirked at Margot before walking to a table and carefully placing the rod in its spot. Her eyes darted back to Cillian. He hung limp. Saliva rolled down his chin, his breathing haggard and shallow. There was nothing left of the spirited demon that held her heart.

Corym blocked Margot's view of Cillian and tossed a thin blade before floating three feet in the air. He took Cillian's hand and lifted the blade. The glinting edge illuminated bright orange, warping the surrounding air. He angled the tip, so it was in line with Cillian's index finger, and pushed it beneath his nail. A guttural roar expelled from his chest, shaking the building as the blade cauterized the wound, allowing Corym to continue his onslaught. A stab here, a slice there, using the demon's skin as his canvas. Each strike, a blemish on Margot's soul as crimson ichor stained the concrete. The elf didn't even have the decency to cauterize all the wounds.

Tears streamed down Margot's face, her screams louder than she thought her strained vocal cords could muster. She scratched at the barrier as if her chipped nails could get through if she just tried harder. *There's no way he survives this. This is more than any one person can take.*

"This is only the beginning," Vesryn said. His voice seemed far away, despite his proximity to Margot.

Corym returned to Cillian's fingers, working meticulously through each nail. The elf never flinched or allowed Cillian's jerking body to affect his precision. He worked with the careful finesse of someone who had done this *many* times before. Errant thoughts led her to wonder whom he had tortured previously and what events could have called for such drastic measures.

Vesryn stood with his hands clasped behind his back for an eternity like he was standing vigil over a holy ceremony. But there was nothing holy about what was happening, and if Margot had been religious, she would have believed this to be the work of the Devil himself.

Voiceless screams filled her head, making it impossible to keep track of time as Corym flayed Cillian alive. Her demon's body was caked with blood from the countless gouges in his skin. The elf would wait a few minutes before sealing each wound before continuing again. And whenever Cillian would pass out from the pain, smelling salts were used to wake him to ensure he was aware of the horrors being inflicted upon him.

At some point, Margot exhausted herself. She peeled her cheek from the cold slab of concrete and rubbed salty crust from her eyes. She pushed herself up, shifted her body, and focused on Cillian but quickly turned away. This brutalization was something she couldn't continue to watch. Cillian threw himself on the chopping block to protect her, willingly let his guard down, and was now being destroyed. The blood bond had to be the reason he would put his life on the line for a simple human woman. That was the only thing that made sense.

What was happening to Cillian wasn't right, and she wouldn't let this go on. Regardless of what her demon thought, he still had a life to live and deserved to be happy. Her bloodsworn was barely alive, but at least he wasn't dead. *Yet.* She wouldn't allow that to happen and would save him as he saved her.

Her brain was moving parts, shifting, compacting memories and emotions, arranging themselves in such a way that would better serve her, allowing the bond to dim. Cillian's eyes snapped to hers as the link between them grew numb, colder. The once proud man looked like a child, defeated.

Can you hear me, Cillian?

Margot...

The bond is weakening. This will all be over soon.

Heart of my heart... I will be with you, always.

I know.

I will remember what we had for both of us.

I know.

Margot nodded as she locked away parts of her that would always yearn to be free. They crammed themselves into the deepest recesses of her mind like puzzle pieces that didn't quite fit. The blanketing sadness slowly lifted as she watched a solitary tear roll down Cillian's cheek.

She felt nothing.

Margot stood, brushed herself off, picking bits of dirt and stone from her chipped nails as Vesryn placed his palm against her forehead. Then, the barrier fell, and Corym stopped hurting the strange man hanging in the center of the room. Something in the back of her mind nagged her, telling her she knew this him, but she couldn't place it. Just as she couldn't understand how or why she was in this place.

"Who is this?" she asked.

Vesryn turned toward her with a placid smile. "Ah, this is Cillian. He was undergoing training to ensure he was fit to protect you, our greatest asset."

Margot hummed to herself. Sound logic.

"Corym, do you think we could let the poor man down? It seems he has been through quite a lot."

Corym looked surprised that she addressed him directly and glanced at Vesryn, who nodded. The elf unclasped Cillian's bindings, and Vesryn waved his hand, making the bloodied man vanish.

Margot didn't know where he went, but she couldn't worry about that now, not while confusion lingered. Her thoughts were so addled that she found it amazing she could even form coherent sentences. Stringing complex thoughts together was a bit more difficult. She tried recounting her steps, trying to figure out how she came to be standing before these elves, but her memories were fuzzy. The only thing she knew for sure was that she differed from what she once was.

Vesryn offered her his hand, which she graciously accepted. The robed elf had a pleasant air about him. Sticking by his side seemed like the appropriate road to take.

"Cillian needs to rest, as do you," Vesryn said. "Shall I show you to your quarters?"

"That would be lovely. Thank you."

19

BE WARY OF OUTSIDERS

"YOU DID VERY WELL BACK THERE, Margot. I am quite proud of you, you know," Vesryn said as they meandered through the winding streets of Caramis.

Elves went about their day, sweeping streets, arranging flowers, and setting up wares on display tables. Margot wanted to take a closer look, but there it was clear there was some unspoken animosity between her and the working elves. Whenever she and the elves locked eyes, they'd skirt her gaze, avoiding her at all costs, as if just by looking at her they'd catch some disease.

She shrugged and tilted her face back, letting the morning sun warm her skin. "I'm glad I could help, but I'm unsure of what I did. My thoughts are... unclear."

"No need to fret. I am sure the haze will lift in due time." He chuckled. "Just know that your efforts were not in vain; you are already changing."

"I *do* feel different... I think... compared to how I felt back..." Margot's voice trailed off and her thoughts wandered.

Where had she lived before? When did she meet Vesryn for the first time? She tried sifting through memories. Images blurred, fading into vague still frames in her mind, allowing her to only make out hazy shapes and shadowy blobs. Any conversation associated with each memory was garbled, like someone trying to talk underneath water. *What happened to me?*

"You shall see," he said with a glint in his eye. "It is far better if we keep it a surprise."

They walked up a hill on switchbacks toward a manor. The façade was like the buildings at the city's base level. Creeping vines worked their way up the front, hugging marble columns while bright orange flowers painted the manse in splashes of color.

"Do you live here?" Margot asked, marveling at the beautiful building above.

"I do, but so do others, and so shall you. I believe our accommodations will please you."

The muscles in her calves burned as they continued their uphill trek. Labored breaths pushed through her nostrils, and she nearly kissed the ground once they reached the top. She had never been more grateful to see flat land. *At least I'll be in incredible shape.*

Vesryn motioned her forward. "No one is here now, so introductions will happen later. Showing you around and getting you something to eat is far more pressing. I am sure you are famished."

A rush of scarlet flooded her cheeks. The mere mention of food had her stomach rumbling. When was the last time she ate?

"I suspected as much." The grin he gave her was genuine, warm, and it made her stomach flutter. "We were in the sanctum for two days, after all. Come now, let us be on our way."

Margot blindly followed Vesryn, trying to quell the brewing panic. She had been holed up for two days—*two*—and had no recollection of what had transpired. As if he could sense her inner turmoil, Vesryn gently touched her shoulder, and the feeling quickly dissipated. Gone as if it never existed—a fact she should've found alarming but couldn't find a reason to care.

As they made their way through the foyer, a controlled calm overtook Margot. She didn't feel out of place here. In fact, she felt as if she belonged. Her mind scratched at her, trying to get her attention. She brushed away the irritation, reveling in the contentment that followed.

Vesryn led her around the home, pointing out various rooms, explaining their purpose. He talked of how the whitewashed walls and simple furnishings helped humble the elves. That it was wise not to let material objects blind one of their true purpose in life—a purpose she was told she would eventually learn.

"There is one room, though, where adornment is everything," he said as he stopped in front of an ornately carved door and pushed it open.

When Margot walked across the threshold, her jaw dropped. Limestone floor-to-ceiling bookshelves lined the walls to her right and left. The base of the shelves rippled out a few inches before seamlessly blending into the floor, which was also made of rock. Ancient-looking tomes filled them to the brim. Directly across from her were massive arched windows where gossamer curtains billowed in the salty breeze, giving her a glimpse of Caramis below. She spun around to find light filtering through the room. Sparkling highlights illuminated the furniture, bathing them in an ethereal glow. While all of that was impressive, the most stunning feature of this room was the installation in the center. A golden orb surrounded by three golden rings floated in the center, spinning wildly.

"What is this place?" she asked as she ran a finger along a bookshelf.

"The Grand Archive. This is where I will teach you to harness your magic."

"It's stunning."

Margot meant it. The room was beautiful and the more she looked at it, the more she found. The edge of each shelf had intricate scenes carved into them. Some depicted a struggle between people, while others showed prosperity. She wondered what they truly stood for. Choosing to give up her inspection, she turned to Vesryn. His eyes were distant as he scanned the room.

"I agree. This is my favorite place in Faerie," he said, almost wistful, before he regained his composure. He cleared his throat. "Your room is two doors down on the left, but before I leave you, let us make for the kitchen first. I shall prepare you a fine dish."

Much like the rest of the home, the kitchen was modest, containing only the bare necessities. The elf dug through a chill box, coming up with a bundle of vegetables and protein. He pointed to the wood-burning stove, and a spark shot from his finger, igniting the logs. Would she be able to do that eventually?

Margot took a seat at the café table in the corner and watched him cook. "Where did the man—Cillian—go?"

"My dear, that is not something you should bother yourself with, but if you must know, he is fine and resting here. That poor soul." He shook his head. "He went through much."

"That I could see... why was he hurt?"

Vesryn's eyes didn't leave the food he was sauteing with unexpected finesse. "Our kind is under constant threat. Corym and I needed to ensure he was up to the task of protecting you. I told you this."

Margot furrowed her brow. "You did?"

That nagging feeling returned, and she couldn't help but think she was forgetting something. Something important. She tried and tried to remember but was left with nothing but a dull ache that was slowly spreading from the back of her skull.

The elf slid a plate in front of Margot; the smell made her mouth water. One bite tantalized her taste buds, leading her to forget all about the worry she had moments ago. The beautifully seasoned vegetables still had a crunch to them while the meat melted in her mouth. *This* she could get used to.

Vesryn sat across from her and rested his laced fingers beneath his chin, smiling like a nymph.

"How does the food taste?" he asked.

"It's fantastic. Thank you."

"Rarely do I get to cook for someone, and I am enjoying it far more than I thought I would." He tapped his cheek with his long, manicured finger. "Perhaps we can push back training for a while... I so would love to get to know you more and show you the sights."

"Training?"

"Mmm, yes. Training. Soon, your being will *evolve*. To prosper, you must learn."

They chatted idly about how their days would go once training started as they ate together. Mornings were to be reserved for reading tomes, and after lunch they would apply what was learned. For one hour each evening, she would be with Corym, training her body. Training was to be rigorous—to make up for lost time, he said.

Once finished eating, she pushed her plate forward, and Vesryn made it disappear with a snap. He placed a hand on her shoulder and nudged his head toward the door.

"You look tired, Margot. I suggest you get some rest. Tomorrow morning, I would like to show you around Caramis."

She nodded, bidding him goodbye, and headed toward her room, which was fancier than the others, but not by much. An enormous bed set atop a limestone platform took up most of the space. A canopy of sheer white curtains cascaded down columns that bled into the bed, much like the bookshelves in the Grand Archive.

Margot sat in front of the vanity, which was made of the same white stone as everything else, but a chiseled border rounding the mirror gave it the appearance of a coral reef. She picked up a hairbrush that was made of mother of pearl and ran the fine bristles through her ashen hair. As she worked through knots, she curled loose strands behind her ear and focused on her skin. She turned her head from side to side, inspecting her face. Though she couldn't remember exactly what she looked like, she was positive her skin hadn't been quite this radiant. It was dewy, almost gleaming. And her eyes, they were luminous. A blue so bright it was almost difficult to look at.

What else will change in the coming days?

Her knee bounced relentlessly as she thought. The question

made her uneasy, and she didn't quite know what was happening to her. She had magic, but what was that magic? Every time she tried following a loose thread, she was met with resistance. A solid, impenetrable wall that yielded none of the information she desperately needed.

Restless, Margot stood and paced the room. If she tried sleeping now, her mind would just race. Instead, she made for the wardrobe that was filled to the brim with elegant clothing. Reaching for a pale blue dress, she rubbed the silk between her fingers. Though sleeveless, it didn't detract from how absolutely stunning the piece was. Silver thread embroidered the high collar and bust. The fiber shimmered so brilliantly in the firelight that she thought someone had worked metal into thin strands rather than using filament. She pulled the dress out, letting the flowing white tulle sheath dust the floor and twirled as she held it to her chest, imagining what she would look like wearing such a garment.

After only a moment, she discarded her clothing and put the dress on. If this room was prepared specifically for her, then so were the clothes. That was a good enough reason for her.

She adjusted the bodice and looked at herself in the mirror, twisting and turning her body from every angle to see better.

"How did they add tulle without making it bulky?" she asked herself. "The tulle is so light and flowy, almost like a spider's web."

Margot twirled around the room, the dress swirling around her gracefully. A smile crept across her face. She could've died happy in that dress.

Rummaging through the drawers in the vanity she searched for an accessory and found a blue jeweled clip. As she put it in place, her ears pricked, picking up a muffled noise. Curious, she moved toward the direction of the sound and placed her ear against the wall. Though the wall was made of thick stone, she could make out labored gasps with her. Her thoughts drifted back to what Vesryn said about Cillian recovering here. She didn't think he *actually* meant in the manor.

Margot tiptoed across the room and quietly opened the door before slipping into the hallway. Her ears strained to make out any sound. Once she was sure all was quiet, she pushed toward Cillian's room. How could she leave the man meant to protect her to suffer alone?

Outside his door, she released a shaky breath and pushed the handle down. Much to her surprise, it was unlocked. As she entered, she zeroed in on the man on the bed. Cuts, gashes, and bruises riddled his body. Ragged breaths rattled his chest, tugging at her heartstrings. Whoever had helped him here must have cleaned the blood and cauterized the wounds, but he still looked worse for wear.

She let herself sit next to him on the bed and smoothed his hair. "I'm so sorry, Cillian. I don't know why you had to do what you did, but I'm grateful to you, regardless."

The battered man stirred, and his bleary eyes cracked open. He brought a calloused hand to her face, caressing her cheek.

"Margot," he said, voice rasping. "You look beautiful."

His statement took Margot aback. Was it normal for someone in his position to be so forward? She didn't want to dishearten him by telling him it was inappropriate, especially not when she didn't even know where she stood within Vesryn's home. His condition didn't help, either. So she leaned into his palm, letting his warmth penetrate her skin.

"Thank you for going through this for me," she mumbled. "Is there anything I can do to help?"

Cillian ignored her question and thumbed her cheek. A shiver ran down her spine as his fingertips caressed her arm.

"Your skin, Margot. You're changing."

Her eyes fell, and she nodded.

"I am. I-I'm scared. Will I still be me once the change is complete? Honestly, I don't even remember who I am or was.

Everything is blank. I keep trying and trying, but nothing gets through."

She clasped her hands over her mouth to stop herself from the verbal barrage that poured from her soul. How could she have said these things to a man she hardly knew? But that nagging returned, urging her to say more. To divulge her deepest, darkest fears and confide in him. That feeling was the part of her she didn't understand, *couldn't* understand. Maybe she *should* get to know him, confide in him. Surely, she was about to see a great deal of him going forward. Wouldn't it be better to be friendly with the man?

He jerked his hand away and coughed into it. Blood flecked his palm. He groaned and inhaled sharply, wincing in pain.

"Don't be scared," he whispered. "You're stronger than you know."

"You know nothing about me, sir. Perhaps, in time, you may make a statement like that."

Margot went to stand and take her leave, but he grabbed her wrist. She looked at him over her shoulder, his silver eyes penetrating.

"You're right," he said. "I didn't mean to alarm you with my words. It's just a feeling I get about you, and I *always* trust my gut. Please, stay. I could use the company."

She eyed the man cautiously but returned to her spot next to him. This was the least she could do after the beating he took on her behalf. He smiled, lacing his fingers between hers, and gave her hand a gentle squeeze. Heat crept up her neck, and she felt her face flush. This was beyond inappropriate. She should rip her hand from his, slap him, do *something*. But she stayed. Something about the way her hand felt intertwined with his felt... right.

She cleared her throat as he traced circles on the back of her hand. "Is there something I could get you? Water? Someone to tend to your injuries? Your wounds look... well, they look serious."

"Don't worry about me. I'll be fine. My body heals quickly

and despite what you have seen, the elves treated me well. Having you here is more than enough. It's late, though," he said as he made more space on the bed. "Would you lie with me?"

Margot fidgeted, trying to come up with an excuse to decline his invitation, but the persistent urge returned, advising her to stay close. She couldn't tell him she didn't want to. The words wouldn't come out. Giving into that part of her once more, she swung her legs up the side of the bed and rested her head against his shoulder, facing away from him.

Cillian's free arm snaked around her waist, pulling her into his chest. His nose brushed her hair, and he inhaled deeply. She was rigid in his arms, but as his breathing evened out, she relaxed, finding unspoken comfort in the arms of this mysterious man.

A loud bang echoed throughout the room, and Margot's eyes popped open. Blood pounded in her ears, her heart froze—Vesryn was leaning against the doorframe, looking at the bed with rage-filled eyes and a tense jaw. He balled his fists at his sides, breathing so hard his nostrils flared. His chest heaved as he stared in disgust.

"Have you lost your mind?" he asked, causing Cillian to stir. "I would like to believe that you understand just how improper you are being. Setting the obvious aside, I told you this man needed rest."

Margot stuttered and tried to catch her breath and think of a way to clear this mess. She knew she shouldn't have stayed with Cillian last night. She knew it. How did she explain why she stayed? She doubted telling Vesryn that a little voice inside her head told her it was the right thing to do would go over very well.

"I-I'm sorry, Vesryn," she stammered. "He was in a great deal of pain. I could hear him through the wall! I thought I would just check on him, make sure he was good, but he asked me to stay."

The elf's face contorted, his eyes narrowing to slits and his mouth a tight line. He inhaled, then released a menacing growl.

"This is unacceptable, Margot. Waltzing into a man's room is downright disgraceful, wanton."

Fury dripped from every word he spoke, making Margot

tremble. The only thing she could do was nod in agreement, unable to hide from the shame. Emotions got the better of her, and she'd acted impulsively. Of course, she would suffer the consequences. She deserved it.

"I thought it would be fine since he is to guard me..."

She cut her sentence short and glanced over at Cillian, who stirred. He rolled onto his back, opened his eyes and blinked them against the soft morning light. He squinted in her direction, a dopey look of confusion on his face that belied his masculine form. Then, the realization set in, and a smile stretched across his lips.

Vesryn's amber eyes turned molten as he mechanically rotated his head toward Cillian. The muscles in the elf's forearms twitched as he continued clenching his fists. Margot couldn't move from her spot on the bed, mesmerized by the sheer force of his energy. The room pulsed with tension, the air heavy and oppressive. Her skin pricked, and she fought the urge to intervene —or flee. Fear of the elf's temper held her back.

Cillian seemed completely unfazed by the anger radiating off Vesryn. He simply looked up at the elf with a smirk, as if daring him to say something else.

"It's alright," Cillian said with a yawn. "Margot was keeping me company. She's been a great help, truly."

Vesryn's jaw worked as he ground his teeth together. The elf was so angry Margot could practically see steam coming out of his ears. She couldn't remember if she had ever seen someone this heated, but the sight was downright terrifying.

"His duty is to protect you—not bed you, Margot," Vesryn said, his voice low and menacing and his eyes never leaving Cillian's. "He is to recover, nothing more, and I will be the one to oversee his care. The steps he had taken to serve as your guardian were nearly insurmountable. Interference will not be tolerated."

Margot lowered her gaze. She should have expected this. What was she thinking, giving into impulses on her first day? She opened her mouth to apologize again, but Cillian spoke before she could.

"You should take a step back and consider how your words are coming across, Vesryn. I was the one who talked her into staying. So, if you're looking for someone to direct your rage at, it should be me."

Hearing Cillian defend her so vehemently was odd, as the two had only just met, but she couldn't ignore the quiver low within her belly.

The elf cocked his head, and amusement flashed in his eyes before the all-consuming ire returned.

"Perhaps you should remember to whom you are speaking," Vesryn said. "Do you not recall our agreement?"

Cillian's features darkened. "I understand full well what our agreement was, but you should give us the respect we deserve." He stretched his fingers before curling them into his palm. "Looks like I'm all healed up now. Maybe Margot was exactly what I needed to get my strength back."

Vesryn hissed. The unease in the room was palpable, threatening to combust at any moment. Margot felt like she was suffocating in the charged atmosphere, caught between the conflicting emotions of the two powerhouses.

"You have yet to return to full strength," the elf said, his voice thick. "The extent of your injuries left you quite weak, and you require more time to recover. We cannot afford for you to overexert yourself."

Cillian pushed himself to a sitting position, his muscles visibly straining. "I know my limits, Vesryn. I have to do everything in my power to protect Margot."

Margot watched in disbelief as Cillian rose to his feet, swaying slightly. For someone who had been caked in blood mere hours ago to be standing was incredible. Cillian took a step toward Vesryn, and the hostility between the two men grew, making her feel like she was in the middle of a battlefield. Margot understood

Vesryn was only looking out for Cillian's health, but the way he was handling the situation was causing more harm than good.

"Vesryn, please," she said, her voice barely above a whisper. "I didn't mean to cause any trouble. I just wanted to help. Can we forget about this? I won't do it again."

The elf looked at Margot and sighed, flicking his hand dismissively. "Fine. Water under the bridge. Continue resting, Cillian." He nodded toward the door. "You are coming with me, Margot. We have much to do today."

Sweat dotted her forehead as she finally rose from the bed. She knew Vesryn planned to take her into Caramis, but she was sure their adventure would be anything but easy. She stole a glance of Cillian over her shoulder, who nodded almost imperceptibly. As if Cillian's solidarity was all she needed, she steeled her spine and followed the elf out of the room.

They walked through the manor's halls, and Margot's mind raced with questions. What was Vesryn truly planning, and why was he so angry with her? Why had Cillian been so determined to protect her even though they had only known each other briefly? She couldn't break through the black smog of her mind, but she couldn't help but feel like there was something she was missing. Something that would make everything fall into place.

Vesryn pushed open a door, revealing an imposing chamber filled with maps, charts, scattered tomes, and other oddities. This room was less impressive than the opulence of the Grand Archive, but it was magnificent nonetheless. Rather than an entire wall of floor-to-ceiling windows, there was only one that had a thick burgundy curtain, which was drawn closed. A faded jute rug was spread across the floor, its frayed edges alluding to a lifetime of love for the piece. To the right, there was a hearthstone and to the left, a wall of bookshelves. While the floor and walls were the typical limestone, the walls were adorned with colorful tapestries, making the entire room feel rather cozy. Clearly, this was where Vesryn did most of his work, and a wave of awe washed over her as she appreciated the immense knowledge and power contained within this room.

"Sit," Vesryn said, gesturing toward a chair in the center of his study.

Margot yelped as her body jerked forward, moving on its own volition. No matter how hard she tried, she couldn't stop herself from perching on the edge of the seat with her back ramrod straight. Still as a statue, she stared forward as Vesryn circled her like a predator.

"Vulnerability is an appropriate feeling to be experiencing right now," he said. "Much has happened these last few days, but I would like to think your common sense is still intact."

"I'm not foll—"

"Do not interrupt!" Margot flinched. "Rationality seems to elude you, Margot. Have you been compromised?"

"I don't under—"

"Of course you have been." Vesryn stopped in front of her and gripped her chin hard enough to make her eyes water. He tipped her face, so the elf was the only person she could see. "For I cannot fathom what would compel you to lie with a man you do not know."

Droplets formed at the outer corner of her eyes before spilling over. What she had done was wrong, she knew that, but much like the invisible force making her sit still, she was drawn to Cillian. That man's touch, the way he looked at her... it had all been too much to resist.

"Forgive me," she whispered.

"Forgive you?" Vesryn released a harsh laugh and dropped her chin to run slender fingers through his hair. "How would forgiving you rectify the situation at hand? Hmm? You brought chaos into my home, Margot, and put us all at risk."

"I didn't mean to. I didn't think—"

"You did not think." His eyes flashed with volatile emotion. "That is the problem. You were careless. Irresponsible. That *man* is to guard you—nothing more. What if he gets the wrong idea and considers you something more than a duty? Or is it you find him attractive?"

Margot didn't know what she should have said. What could she have said? Vesryn didn't want an apology. He wanted compliance, but the damage had already been done. All she could do now was try doing the right thing in the future, but if the elf didn't want her to roam the halls, he should have told her so before sending her off alone.

"N-no, I'm not attracted to him," she lied. "I only wanted to help him. I didn't mean to cause any harm."

He put some space between them and straightened his robe. "I know you did not mean to," he said, his voice softer now. "The position we are in is... precarious. We cannot afford to let our guard down, especially where outsiders are concerned."

Margot swallowed thickly. "I understand."

Fragmented memories swirled in her mind's eye, flickering just out of reach the moment she tried grabbing them. She couldn't remember who she was or what happened to her before meeting the elves. There was something *very* wrong, something, perhaps, only Vesryn could fix. Maybe if she complied with his wishes, she could find some way to put the pieces back together.

"If you understand, then you know actions have consequences. Punishing you is not something I look forward to, but exceptions cannot be made."

Her heart sank. "Anything else, please. I'll do anything else to make it right."

Vesryn tilted his head as if considering her. Margot knew he couldn't let her off the hook—that would send the wrong message to the other elves. But he acted as if she had something he wanted, so it was likely harm wouldn't befall her.

"There is one thing you can do," he said. "Though it will not make up for what you have done, it *will* go a long way in proving your loyalty to Elven kind."

Her brows shot up. "Anything." She wasn't inclined to experience any sort of physical violence. Especially not after seeing what they had done to Cillian.

Vesryn's smile was cold and calculated. She shuddered.

"You will become my assistant." He grinned. "Your duty will be to attend to my every need, anticipate my every desire during times of research. When working, you will never leave my side, and you will do as I say without question."

Margot's eyes widened. That wasn't what she expected. She figured he would send her to do laundry or clean the manor, but this... this was a commitment for an unspecified amount of time. But she had no room to bargain when he had complete control of the situation—including her body.

"How long would this task last?" she asked.

"Until I know I can trust you." He extended his hand. "Do we have a deal?"

Margot nodded as a sense of dread settled over her. What was being asked of her was no simple task, but it was the only thing she could do to ensure her safety—and Cillian's. And without the elf, she had nothing.

No home.

No family.

No life.

"Wonderful. Now, shake my hand."

Her arm suddenly felt weightless, lifting on its own. She shook the strange feeling from her limb and wrapped her fingers around Vesryn's icy hand, sealing the deal. A disturbing Cheshire grin spread across his face, and there was a little zap at her temple, which made her wince.

Vesryn, pleased with himself, leaned his back against his desk and crossed his arms. "Now, your studies shall continue—that is a given, but your time with Corym will need to be adjusted. Twice a week should be sufficient. You are in much better shape than I thought you would be," he said as he inspected her body. "This will continue improving as adaptation is achieved."

"As for Cillian, he must be reprimanded for his role in this unfortunate incident. There is one thing that needs to be made clear to you, Margot. That man is not to be trusted. He is an outsider, and we must *always* be wary of outsiders."

Margot cleared her throat. "Can I ask a question?"

"Without questions, we could never expand our knowledge. Proceed."

"You say Cillian can't be trusted... so why ensure my protection to an outsider?"

The elf ran his index finger across his bottom lip.

"Cillian was the best candidate for the job," he said after a moment. "He is a skilled combatant and possesses knowledge that could be useful to us. Additionally... you could say *it is in his blood* to protect you."

What does that mean?

Reluctantly, Margot nodded, her heart sinking. Something about Vesryn's answer didn't sit right with her. She was sure there was more to his reasoning than he was letting on. In fact, it was almost as if he were mocking her.

"Any other questions?"

Margot shook her head, not wanting to push her luck.

"Good. I will discuss the changes with Corym later. For now, I would like for you to change into something more comfortable for our day out. That dress, though lovely, may be cumbersome." He held the door open. "I will come get you in fifteen minutes."

20

BITTERSWEET

MARGOT HAD JUST FINISHED CHANGING into a light green sundress and white leather mules when she heard a knock. Vesryn slowly walked in, closing the door behind him. Instead of his typical flowing robe, he had opted for light leathers that accentuated his lean muscles and tied his hair in a loose knot. A sword hung sheathed on his hip. His eyes glinted with the quiet intellect of the man she assumed he was, but the way he stood with his back resting against the doorframe, one hand on the hilt of his weapon, and his head cocked, exuded the rugged readiness of a seasoned fighter. The dichotomy between scholar and warrior was striking and caught her off guard.

"You look wonderful, Margot. That is a perfect outfit for our excursion."

She forced a smile and bowed. The few memories she had of Vesryn were relatively pleasant, but his reversal this morning left her with more questions and no answers. Agreeing to his demands would keep her safe, but what would happen if she couldn't live up to his expectations? Her gaze lingered on the weapon at his side. What was the elf capable of?

"Thank you."

Vesryn extended his hand, wiggling his fingers for her to take it. "Shall we leave?"

She nodded, letting him escort her.

Dawn's early light warmed her as they stepped out of the manor onto the limestone walkway. Vesryn was quiet. Watching her as she stretched her arms above her head and took a deep breath, letting salty air kiss her skin. The balmy weather alluded to the blazing heat they would feel come high noon.

She walked to the edge of the cliff and rested her forearms on the stone parapet, committing the scenery to memory. Palm and citrus trees swayed in the breeze. Gulls squawked before diving between glittering rays into the violet sea to catch their breakfast. One shot up from the surface with its prey and tossed it into the air before gulping it down in one swift motion.

Vesryn's boots scuffed the stone behind her as he approached. She turned to him, unable to keep the grin off her face.

"I'll never tire of this view. The island is gorgeous."

The corner of his lips twitched before he turned toward the vista. His amber eyes were distant as he scanned the isle. He sighed, letting his head slump forward.

"Seeing Caramis through your eyes... the wonder and excitement that illuminates your face... it breaks my heart."

Her grin faltered. "Why?"

A hollow laugh slipped past his lips, and he shook his head. "Because I will never feel that way again. My memories here... are bittersweet. It has been that way since the passing of my brother, Ilphas."

"I'm so sorry..." Margot wrung her hands together, unsure of what to do in this situation. "Do—do you want to talk about it?" Judging by Vesryn's expression, she was sure she said the right thing.

"That is nice of you, Margot. Perhaps one day I will speak of my past, but for now, let us focus on you."

"You know where to find me when you're ready." She nudged

his arm with her shoulder, trying to lighten the mood. "So, where are you taking me first?"

Vesryn pointed down at a group of stalls. "You see that stand with the teal canopy?"

She stood on her tiptoes and squinted. "I think so. Next to the red one?"

"That is the one. The owner, Almira, makes the best seafood mix. Her ingredients are fresh, so the earlier you get there, the better. Then, after that light snack, I want to take you to the gardens." He pointed to the sprawling tree-covered area just north of the main living quarters. "Elves are proud, and our gardeners take special care to ensure the grounds are well maintained. Once we finish with that, we can take the long way round back to the center of Caramis to enjoy a late lunch at the Coral Reef. A rowdy place, to be sure, but once you get past the brouhaha, it is rather enjoyable."

Margot bit back her surprise. The entire day Vesryn had planned was so... normal. She could imagine him hovering over dusty books and reciting spells, not going to the market to shop, or stopping at his favorite restaurant for a quick bite to eat.

"Wow, a full day, huh?"

Vesryn's laugh was melodious as he took Margot's hand, linking their fingers. "I am excited, dear! It has been a long time since I had anyone new to enjoy my time with. Come now, we must seize the day."

Strolling down the hillside and rounding the switchbacks was much easier than the trek they made leading up to the manor. She didn't even break a sweat by the time they reached the bottom.

They wended their way toward the market on neat, cobbled roads. Elves stopped sweeping their porches and tending to flower beds as they passed by to bow at Vesryn, who would hold up a hand, acknowledging them. Confusion flitted across their faces as they took note of Margot, but one glare from Vesryn had them offering a quick nod or morning greeting.

"Do not mind them," he whispered in her ear. "Everyone was made aware of the situation, but it is still shocking to see a human. Give them time."

"What situation?"

"Do you remember when I explained how absorbing elven magic would affect you?"

Margot's temple throbbed, causing her to wince. Disjointed bits and pieces of conversation with the elf darted through her mind. Something about elven magic changing her, but what she recalled wasn't enough to paint a clear picture. It felt like someone had put her memory of the exchange together with glue, then scribbled over it because they weren't happy with the results.

She frowned. "I don't know... everything is all messed up."

Vesryn placed his hands on the side of her head, concern etched his face as he scanned hers.

"I was afraid of this."

Margot stiffened. "Afraid of what?"

"Well..." His throat bobbed. "Never before has a human acquired our magic. I was worried there would be some kind of side effect. Let me just..." He curled his fingers over her head, spreading warmth that radiated through each of her limbs. Blinding light overcame her vision, forcing her to squeeze her eyes shut, only for it to not make any difference. The entire process couldn't have taken more than a few seconds, but it felt like a lifetime when she felt the elf pull his hand away, and she slowly lifted her eyelids. "Do you remember now?"

Margot attempted to recall the conversation. Clear as glass, she saw the two of them walking along the coastline, the wind whipping her hair, sea spray misting the duo. Vesryn laughed at something she said, and he turned to her, a solitary tear rolling down his cheek as he relayed his worries. How he feared she might not be able to handle the transition from human to elf. How the magic might very well tear her apart. Margot thumbed the wetness from his cheek and smiled, telling him that the alarm was unfounded. Deep in her bones, she knew she would be fine.

"I'm to be an elf?" she asked, sucking in a sharp breath.

"That you are." He wiped sweat from his brow. "As I have said, none of us have seen elven magic entrusted to a human, but I believe that you being here with your newfound kin is accelerating the process."

"Will—will I be okay?"

"I shall make sure of it, dear."

"What about the rest of my memories? Can you bring those back?"

"If only it were that easy." He took her hand again, and they walked toward the market. "Memory restoration is fickle and requires a great deal of energy. The only reason I was able to restore that particular memory so quickly was because I, too, experienced that with you. To restore everything you have forgotten... that would take years, possibly more lifetimes than even the elves are granted. I would have to sift through thirty-some-odd years of experiences and attempt to reconstruct them despite not knowing what order they belong in."

"Will I ever remember everything?"

"This, I cannot know. Only time will tell."

The lump in her throat was so large that she couldn't force it down. If she attempted to speak, she was sure she would burst into tears. Vesryn didn't force conversation. Instead, they silently pressed on, interrupted only by the bustle of elves as they approached their destination. She would have welcomed the distraction of idle chatter. Being left with her thoughts was terribly uncomfortable and depressing. How many years would it take for her to accept she'd never remember who she once was? Would it forever be in the back of her mind, urging her to search for an answer?

Margot's worry was swiftly forgotten as she took in the vibrant market square that was teeming with life. Tents and stalls were lined up haphazardly, creating pathways barely wide enough for Vesryn and her to walk side by side. Flags floated above the colorful array of canopies, denoting what each vendor peddled.

Some were shaped like fish, others like jewels, and everything in between.

Vesryn pulled Margot along, stopping in front of the teal stall he showed her earlier. A pretty young elf with charcoal hair and golden eyes smiled at him as she bowed.

"No need for formalities, Almira," Vesryn said. "I have been frequenting your shop for far too long for that."

Almira blushed as she tossed seafood on a portable grill at her side. "You say that, but it's been ages since I've seen you. So long, in fact, that I've forgotten what your favorite dish is!"

"Almira!" Vesryn feigned hurt by placing his hand over his heart. "You would not dare."

She snorted. "Of course I wouldn't! Why, if I did, you may have me strung up by my ankles for all to gawk at."

"You know I would never do such a thing." Vesryn grinned and nudged Margot forward. "Almira, this is Margot. Today I am showing her Caramis, and it would not be a day worth remembering if we did not have a taste of your seafood mix."

Almira's eyes narrowed, and Margot promptly looked at the ground.

"Ah, this is the human," Almira said. "Never thought I'd see the day."

Vesryn placed a finger under Margot's chin and lifted her head. "Is it not incredible?"

"That's one way to look at it."

Vesryn's body tensed, and Almira had the decency to focus on the food she was grilling.

"I apologize," the pretty elf mumbled.

"Do well to mind your manners in the future. I would not want to find you strung up by your ankles for all to gawk at."

Almira's shoulders shook as she plated their food and handed it to them. Vesryn thanked her before leading Margot to a shaded spot with marble benches.

"I am sorry about that, Margot."

She pushed her food around and hummed. "Why doesn't she like me?"

"That is not the issue." Vesryn sighed and scooted closer to her, letting his hand rest upon hers. "I mentioned how elves are wary of outsiders, remember?"

"I do."

"Well, humans rank among outsiders. Although you are not human, you still come from their kind. It is difficult to trust that your intentions are well-placed. I cannot fault the other elves for their wariness. Though the rudeness... Margot, you deserve to be treated with kindness and respect, regardless of where you come from."

The elf sitting beside her was a far cry from the elf who forced her to shake on a deal she wasn't sure she wanted to commit to in the first place. She didn't know which facet of his personality she should believe—which was the *true* Vesryn? Was he kind and understanding, or was he despotic and cruel?

Vesryn lifted the tiny wooden spear from her hand and stabbed a piece of fish before holding it to her lips.

"Come now, Margot. Almira may be brusque, but her food is divine. Ignore her faults for now, because I am sure once you taste this, you shall let bygones be bygones."

Margot acquiesced and let Vesryn feed her. True to his word, the whitefish was tender, moist, and lightly seasoned. The more she ate, the more she respected Almira, despite her shortcomings. Cooking at this level showed lifetimes of dedication that warranted recognition.

"Try this," Vesryn said as he took one of the lumpy fruits and sliced it with the wave of his hand before handing her a section. "Squeeze this over your next bite but be quick about eating. The acidity cooks the flesh through a process called denaturation. If you wait too long, the fish becomes tough. I promise the flavor is worth it, though."

As instructed, Margot squeezed the citrus over her fish and ate it with gusto. Her knees bounced, her head bobbed from side to side, and she squealed. Vesryn's euphonious laugh wrapped around her like a warm blanket on a cold winter's night as he watched her enjoy his favorite culinary dish. She smiled at him before doing a sweep of the market when she noticed Almira poking her head out from behind a tree. The pretty elf's eyes twinkled, and she nodded once at Margot. *Perhaps Caramis won't be so bad after all.*

Vesryn gestured for Margot's plate when they were done, and he placed them in one of the floating receptacles that were interspersed between the benches. They walked back into the market but veered left at a fork in the road, which ran parallel to the one leading to the manor before curving around a bend.

The path opened to the gardens, and Margot paused, taking in the serene beauty. Ancient trees twisted together with anthurium sprouting from their bark while their branches formed a natural canopy. Sunlight filtered through rustling leaves, casting dappled shadows on the ground, creating a welcome place of reprieve when the heat became too much to bear. Canna stalks and clivia dotted the landscape between sprawling bougainvillea and waxy bushes. A slow-moving river wound through the center of the gardens, adding a quiet susurration to the natural ambiance.

"This is amazing," she whispered.

"I agree." He pointed ahead. "Over there is my favorite spot. Shall we?"

They took a seat on a boulder with a flat top and watched two elflings play. Their parents sat atop a blanket close by, snacking on fruits and cheeses. A few other couples passed by, smiling at the children as one plucked a flower and blew at the petals, turning them into glowing orbs that floated through the air.

"How did they do that?" Margot said with a gasp.

"A bit of magic. Would you like to learn tomorrow?"

"Can I really do that?"

"Of course. And much more."

The sun had shifted noticeably across the sky, letting Margot know it was well past noon. The picnicking family gathered their belongings and headed off for their next adventure. It was a scenario that seemed typical enough, yet it left her with a nagging question she couldn't quite shake.

"Can I ask you something?"

"But of course, dear."

She swallowed and drummed incessantly against her thigh. "Where are all the children? We passed by many elves, but we only saw those two with their parents."

"Those two elflings are the only two males on the entire island. There are three females, likely somewhere with their Ama and Apa. Conceiving, by our very nature, is highly improbable. Even more so when an elf has great power. Magic interferes with the process." Vesryn's gaze dimmed as he focused on the spot where the children had played. "But once in a while, there are miracles."

"So... if I use magic, I won't be able to have children?"

Vesryn furrowed his brow and placed his hand on her lower belly. "I had not considered... what magic may do to one in your situation." The elf said nothing for a long moment, keeping his hand pressed against her body. Her stomach rumbled, and he chuckled, finally pulling away. "Do not worry that pretty little head of yours with such serious thoughts. Let us get some lunch instead."

A worn wall of at least twelve feet tall bordered the path they traveled back to the center of Caramis. Far too high to see over, but from the vines creeping over the edge, Margot could tell it was overgrown.

An hour into their walk, Margot's toe hit a rock chunk, and she stumbled, catching herself on the corner of the wall. She did a double take, thinking her eyes deceived her. This portion of the barrier had crumbled, and just beyond a dirt path led into a veritable jungle.

Vesryn turned on his heel and helped her to her feet. "Are you quite alright?"

"Yes, but... what is this place?"

"So, you can... fascinating," Vesryn mumbled as he steered her away from the ruins. "The old wall seems in need of repair. I shall send someone to see to it as soon as we get back to the manor. For now, food awaits us."

Feeling like something was calling her, Margot glanced back toward the crumbled section, only to find a solid wall in its place.

21

ORGANIZED CHAOS

VESRYN CALLED upon Margot before the sun had even come up that day and dragged her to his study. Tomes and scrawled notes littered his desk while piles of scholarly texts teetered in various locations about the room. The last time she saw him here, it had been much cleaner, nearly pristine.

Margot yawned, taking a seat. "Do you sleep?"

"Rarely. How can one sleep when there is work to be done?"

"What exactly are you working on?"

"Something you said the other day sparked my interest." He pointed to a tome across the room without looking up from what he was reading. Margot jumped up to grab it for him. "I would be remiss to divulge anything yet, but what I am finding is truly astounding."

"Something I said caused a storm to come through here? Look at this place! How do you get anything done?"

The elf's twinkling amber eyes flicked to her before returning to his book. His lip twitched as if trying to suppress a smile. "Organized chaos, my dear. By day's end, we will not even see the floor, I assure you."

"How can I help?"

"Nourish yourself first." He pointed to his desk. "Beneath the silver cloche is some fruit. Then you will help me find information."

Margot hid her surprise. She could read—at least she thought she could—but looking at the covers of the tomes scattered about, she was at a loss, the lettering alien.

Vesryn laughed and beckoned her closer. "Come here, silly girl."

He pressed his index finger to the center of her forehead. Tingling tendrils wrapped around her skull, puckering her skin and forcing her to close her eyes. After a moment, the feeling was gone. She furrowed her brow. "What did you do to me?"

The elf passed her the text he was reading. As she scanned the page, the sinuous lines of the foreign script twisted and shifted along the parchment until it formed words she could comprehend. She looked to Vesryn, who smiled and shrugged a shoulder, and said, "Just a bit of magic."

Margot giggled as she handed the book back and took a seat at his desk. She lifted the tray's lid and plucked a piece of fruit from its vine before biting into its flesh. The sooner she ate, the quicker she could get on with her task, which she was excited about. These books contained a wealth of knowledge about a new world —not that she remembered anything about where she came from —but she was thrilled.

"Sorry to interrupt, but I was wondering about something, too." She peeled the rind from a citrus fruit. "The other day, when we were walking about Caramis, all the elves were bowing. You must be important, right?"

Vesryn hummed. "I suppose I am important."

"Are you a king or something?"

The elf let out a sharp laugh. "King? By the goddesses, no. The only *king* Faerie has would be the self-proclaimed fae king, Varitan Ravara. That brute crushed his own kin to claim an imaginary throne of his own making. Though Vesryn, king of the elves, has a nice ring to it, I must say." Vesryn floated a cloth kerchief and a book over to her. "Wipe those hands and let us begin. I would like for you to search that text for any information regarding humans passing through the veil and living—the living part is important."

Margot froze. "Do—do they not usually live?"

"You must not remember that conversation either. Humans traversing planes is rare in and of itself. Their survival is rarer still. In fact, *you* are the only human I know who has ever survived the crossing. Though, I attribute that to your elven magic. But to be fair, my knowledge is rather limited due to being confined to Caramis and I have my suspicions—hence the research—that there are more humans living."

"And something I said drove you to research *this*?"

Vesryn smirked, pressing the tip of his tongue to the point of his fang, and nodded. "All in due time, Margot. Now be a dear and search for answers. We are burning daylight, and Corym simply will not allow me to reschedule your training again."

Margot pressed the heels of her palms against her eyes. She had been scouring the document for hours, and her retinas burned with fatigue. Twelve chapters on dragons, detailing their emergence, their extinction, and their eventual resurrection, but not a damn thing on a human passing through the veil. Why in the world would Vesryn have her reading about dragons? The closest she had gotten was a quote from some other text that mentioned dragons *leaving* Faerie for other realms. Though it didn't specify *which* realms they fled to, she made a note of the other book, regardless.

There was a soft knock at the door, and Vesryn let the newcomer in. The elf's honeyed complexion complemented her rose quartz eyes. She was wearing a simple frock with an apron and was holding a platter, like the one Margot had eaten from earlier.

"Give me a moment, Tahlsia. I shall clear a spot," Vesryn said as he whisked away tomes from a café table and gently set them down beside it. "Here is fine. Would you mind bringing us some tea?"

"Not at all, sir. I'll be back in a moment."

Vesryn took a seat, looked at Margot, and gestured to the chair across from him. "Come eat and tell me all of what you found."

"Admittedly, I didn't find much," she said as she sat. "Every chapter was dragons this, dragons that. It was exhausting."

"I feared that would be the case. These works are written by some of the brightest minds Faerie has ever seen, yet they continue to focus on those blasted beasts." He sighed. "Help yourself. Research builds up an appetite."

Margot lifted the lid and added the meat pie to her plate, along with crisp vegetables and whipped starch. Two bites in, the elf called Tahlsia returned with a kettle and two cups. She bowed and left. Vesryn looked despondent. *He must not have had much luck either.*

She dabbed away gravy from the corner of her lips and rested her napkin on her lap. "You know, it may not have all been a loss."

Vesryn's head jerked up from his plate. "Really?"

Margot took the notes from the desk and sat back down. "There was a quote from another book in one passage I read. Though the quote still had to do with dragons, it actually mentioned them leaving the veil, which was the first I had read about the veil at all."

"What was the name of the book?"

"*Faerie Through the Ages.* Do you have it?"

Vesryn burst from his chair and walked over to one of the piles of books. He tapped it and shook his head before moving on to another. And another. And another. Until finally, at the bottom of the sixth stack he checked, he bounded over with a thick leather tome. He dropped it on the table with a *thud*.

"First edition." He grinned. "This is huge, Margot. Hurry and finish your meal. I am eager to see what you learn."

As directed, she hunkered down in her spot and opened the new book. Two chapters in and she was sure this would yield better results. The introductory chapters explained the Arcane Weave and how Faerie uses it in order to bolster the veil's defenses.

Unlike other planes, Faerie tapped into the Arcane Weave to create its own source of magic, which is often referred to as the Mana Weave. Apparently, even the gods and goddesses had been dumbfounded when Faerie proved to be more capable than intended, but decided against interfering and left the realm to its own devices.

The next three chapters continued in great length about how difficult it was for beings not of Faerie to pass through the veil because their intrinsic makeup was simply much too different, and their bodies couldn't sustain life once they crossed over. Margot inhaled softly and read the next part aloud, "However, there have been multiple documented cases where humans have passed through the veil and lived to tell the tale. Scholars suspect that humans and the fae are more closely related than previously believed. The fae have even been known to mate with humans, producing offspring at an accelerated rate with the gestational period spanning nine months rather than the fourteen months it typically takes for a faeling to mature within the womb."

Vesryn snatched the book from her hand. His eyes darted from left to right faster than Margot could keep up. She waited silently as he flipped through the pages, gripping his chin between his index finger and thumb.

"Is this what you need?" she asked in a whisper.

His throat bobbed. "I believe so... but more research will need to be done before my assumptions can be verified." He looked at Margot for a long moment. "If I am right, I think you can reproduce just fine."

Margot slowly looked at the disarray surrounding them. Open books, scattered notes, quills, and ink pots covered much of the floor. Stacks had fallen over and were pushed to the side to create a path for Vesryn to pace. By the time her gaze landed on the elf, tears burgeoned, threatening to spill over. "You—you did all this for me?"

"When you asked me if your fertility would be affected... the look on your face broke me. You were both shocked and grief-stricken. Almost as if you had not considered having children, and to have the choice ripped from your womb because of the wondrous gift you received, yet did not ask for, was the worst thing that could happen. I never want you to feel like elven magic is a curse, Margot. It is very much a blessing. So, if there is anything I can do to ease your mind... know that I will do so."

Margot burst from her seat, knocking over a pile of books in her rush to get to Vesryn. She threw her arms around his middle, gripping his robe tightly. Tears flowed freely, wetting the elf's chest.

"Thank you for being so kind. Thank you for caring about me. All this effort... thank you."

Vesryn smoothed her hair before tipping her chin up to face him. His thumbs brushed away droplets from her cheeks. He leaned in, close enough that she could smell minty herbs and honey on his breath. Tracing her bottom lip, he asked her, "May I kiss you?"

Margot's heart thundered as she moved her head ever so slightly to let him know that it was fine, and Vesryn pressed his soft lips against hers. His tongue, cool and sensuous, probed until she finally let him in. He moved languorously, letting his fingers tangle in her hair. She slid her arms up his chest and wrapped them around his neck. The sensation of his body pressed against hers was surreal, as if she was engulfed in both fire and ice, the cold sharpness blending seamlessly with a deep, penetrating warmth that she couldn't get enough of.

Eventually, Vesryn broke their connection and rested his forehead against hers, rubbing their noses together. "I believe I owe you something," he said. "A bit of magic was promised if I remember correctly." Out of thin air, he produced a beautiful violet dahlia and handed it to her before stepping back. "You must look inward, find where your magic flows. Follow the threads to the center."

Margot held the flower in front of her with a frown and a furrowed brow.

Vesryn laughed and massaged her temples. "Close your eyes. Focus on yourself, not the flower." She did as she was told, and he placed his hand on her chest. "Inhale deeply. Picture the way your lungs expand. Good... exhale. Again." She continued, following Vesryn's instructions, when his nail dragged across her skin, making its way down her arm. "Search for the threads, Margot. Find them. They are within you, waiting."

Margot felt a tingling sensation where his touch lingered, a warmth spreading from his fingertips through her veins. As she concentrated on her inner self, a soft glow pulsed at the tip of a wispy tendril. She followed it over the curves of her body, ending at her illuminated center, which resonated gently with each beat of her heart. One by one, the threads revealed themselves, shimmering with an otherworldly light that only she could see. She dove deeper into the intricate web of energy, reaching tentatively as magic surged through every fiber of her being.

A smile tugged at the corners of her lips as her eyes opened. "I did it," she whispered. "It's here. I have magic."

"I felt the weave in you all along. You just needed some help finding it. Now that you have access to some of your magic, know that all comes from Faerie. Imagine the flower sprouting from the soil and its petals unfurling. Imagine the way it sways in the rain, how morning dew clings to each leaf." Margot could picture the scene vividly, with no need to close her eyes. Vesryn pressed on. "As you blow upon the petals, envision their transformation into the very essence of power that created them, radiant beacons whose translucent surfaces flicker with flame."

Margot blew on the dahlia. The petals collapsed in on themselves, forming orbs of energy that seemed almost alive, dynamic forces swirling within, constantly shifting and changing form. They floated lazily about the room before dissipating into the ether. She looked at Vesryn and grinned.

"That, my dear, was your first lesson. All living things within Faerie's domain come from the weave. When they die, be it an elf, a flower, a fish... they must return whence they came to be born anew."

Before Margot could respond, there was a solitary knock at the door. Corym walked in dressed in leathers, with weaponry strapped to his sides.

"Is it already that time?" Vesryn asked.

"That it is."

"Is her gear prepared?"

"Ready and waiting for her in the training hall."

Vesryn sighed and flicked his hand toward the hallway. "She will be out in a moment."

Corym bowed and exited the room.

With two long strides Vesryn reached Margot, wrapping one arm around her back and using his other hand to entwine their fingers. He spun her around, dipping her with a speed that caused her to squeal, and smashed his lips to hers once more. This kiss was unbridled passion, a heat that couldn't be tamed. There were no leisurely strokes, only wanton abandon and teeth and tongue and panting gasps that left her breathless.

"I am sorry," he said as he kissed her softly with a smile. "I just needed to taste you once more." He righted her, brushing her hair into place. "Now go. Corym does not like to be kept waiting."

"Did you hear me, Margot?" Corym asked.

Margot blushed and shook her head. They'd been walking to the training hall, and she didn't even realize they now stood in front of large double doors.

"I said once we get inside, you can head to the room on the right and change into your gear. We'll be going over the basics of sword handling, and then we'll see how well you fare with hand-to-hand combat." He held the door open for her. "After you."

Though the room was empty, Margot could still smell sweat and leather and blood that graced this hall as her footsteps thudded against the stone floor. Banners proudly displayed a repeating motif of an oak tree intertwined with vines. Mounted lanterns illuminated the vaulted ceiling, and racks lined the wall to the right, which displayed a range of weapons, including swords, spears, axes, and many more she didn't know the names of. Armor stands were fitted with cloth, leather, and heavy chain armor, with a wall of shields behind them. To the left, there was an archery range with targets set up at varying distances, and a sparring area was marked off in the center of the room. Heavy-looking bags hung in the back next to thin balance beams and practice dummies.

She found the room Corym mentioned easily enough, her required attire neatly folded on a bench in a pile. Donning the padded underclothing first, she pulled the chest piece over her head and secured the straps on the sides until it was snug. There weren't any pants. Instead, leg protection came in pieces, which she secured to her thighs and shins before moving on to the arm guards. She locked in the shoulder piece, laced her boots, and finally pulled on the gloves, bending her joints to see how well she could move with all this gear on. She was pleased to find she could move relatively easily.

"Corym, this fits well," she said as she walked back to the training hall. "I don't know what all the pieces are called. I guess I can just learn that later." She stopped in her tracks when she noticed Cillian standing in the corner next to the rack of swords. She looked between Corym and her guard. "I didn't know Cillian would be here."

"He'll be helping with hand-to-hand combat after you and I go through sword maneuvers. I can't appropriately teach you if I don't see how you perform."

Margot's gaze lingered on the hulking man. She hadn't seen him since making the deal with Vesryn and had almost forgotten about that nagging feeling, which was back in full force, making her remember what transpired in his room days past. The way his touch sent sparks coursing through her bloodstream and how *good* her hand felt in his. His smoldering silver eyes met hers, a hint of a smile playing on his lips as if he, too, replayed that event over in his mind. She quickly averted her eyes as Corym stepped forward, feeling a rush of heat creeping up her neck.

"To the rack, Margot. You're going to pick a sword that suits you. The swords on the left side are lighter. I recommend you start there."

Margot's fingers trailed lightly along the handles. She hesitated before picking the first one, her eyes flickering between the selections. She couldn't remember if she had held a weapon before, certainly not a sword. The weight of the decision seemed almost as heavy as the weapons themselves. Taking a deep breath, she tentatively reached out for a slender blade near two swords from the left. It felt surprisingly natural in her hand, the grip cool against her palm.

As she turned back to face Corym and Cillian, she saw they were both watching her intently. Corym nodded. Cillian's expression was unreadable, but there was a glint in his eyes that sent a shiver down her spine.

"Good choice," Corym said. "Show me how you hold a sword."

Margot tightened her grip on the sword, feeling hefty in her hand. She raised it up, trying to mimic what she had seen in the carvings around the manor. Corym stepped closer, adjusting her fingers slightly. "You want your hand to be closer," he said, tapping the guard and moving her into the appropriate position. "And your thumb should be placed... like so. This will help with control and precision." His hand hovered over her hip. A pained expression flashed across Cillian's face. "Is it fine if I adjust your stance?"

"Go ahead," Margot said.

"To maintain balance, keep your feet shoulder-width apart." Corym tapped the back of her knees. "And keep your knees slightly bent. We want weight to be evenly distributed. The second you forget this in battle... that's the second you die."

"Are we expecting to go to battle?"

Corym shrugged, shooting a quick glance to Cillian. "You never know. It's always better to be prepared." He unsheathed the sword at his side and walked into the center, dropping into a stance. "Now, we learn to move. Show me what you've got, Margot!"

The elf lunged at her as soon as she stepped into the ring. She stumbled out of the way and lost her grip on the sword, which scraped along the stone, sending sparks flying. She cursed under her breath, getting back into position. Corym bounced from one foot to the other, humor danced deep within his eyes. He had come alive and was ready to make sure Margot never saw the light of day again.

"*Retreat*," he yelled, jumping at Margot again. She barely avoided getting hit but held on to the sword this time. "*Lateral movement!*"

His next attack came for her side, forcing her to dive out of the way. The sword slid across the floor, stopping at Cillian's feet. Margot panted, clutching above her hip as she tried to catch her breath. Her guard handed her the sword, and Corym shouted for her to go again.

After half an hour of dodging the elf's relentless attacks, all Margot wanted was to collapse into bed and sleep for a week. By the end, though, she had started to get the hang of it—sort of.

Corym grinned, sheathing his sword. "You did good for your first time. Next time we'll learn to advance—I'll have Tahlsia bring some books to your room. Time for hand-to-hand combat."

Margot lugged the sword across the training hall and placed it in the rack before heading to the center of the ring. Cillian stood across from her, beckoning her forward with a crooked finger and a sly smile.

"I won't hurt you," he whispered.

"I know." The words felt like sandpaper on her tongue.

"Before you begin," Corym said, "remember that stance applies to physical combat as well. Find your balance."

Cillian raised his fists and circled around Margot. She tried to remember what Corym's instructions were and raised her fists as well, readying herself for whatever Cillian would throw at her. Without warning, he lunged forward, his speed and agility surprising her, considering how bulky he was. She managed to sidestep his attack, but he quickly pivoted and aimed a swift kick at her midsection. She flinched from the impact, but the only thing his attack did was force the air from her lungs.

Margot gritted her teeth and countered with a series of punches, aiming for Cillian's chest and abdomen. Effortlessly, he blocked her strikes with fluid and precise movements. His body was a blur, countering her paltry attacks with calculated strikes that kept her on the defensive. Each blow he delivered was controlled, holding back power so that he didn't do any actual damage—a testament to his skill and experience in combat.

Frustration built within her as she struggled to anticipate his next move. Her muscles ached from exertion. She glanced at Corym, watching from the sidelines, his features an impenetrable façade.

Cillian pressed his advantage, pushing her further back across the sparring area. This man was a force of nature, and Margot was stuck dancing to a tune only he could hear, continually putting her at a disadvantage. He jumped forward with a series of quick jabs; she managed to dodge and countered, landing a kick to his side. He grunted in response, the impact causing him to take a step back. She grinned. It was a small victory, but it bolstered her spirits until he flipped over her and swept his leg out from under him, taking her down to the floor, where she landed flat on her back.

She groaned, letting her arms fall to her sides. She was severely outmatched. Steps approached her, and she looked toward the noise, finding Corym standing over her with an outstretched hand, helping her to her feet.

"That was impressive."

Margot clicked her tongue. "Don't lie. I got demolished."

"You did." She shot Corym a look, and he laughed. "But that man," he pointed to Cillian, "is probably the best combatant on this entire island... perhaps even in all of Faerie, and you landed a hit. You have potential." He turned to Cillian. "Can you help her back to her room? I'm guessing she's about to collapse, and I need to write this report and have it sent to her tomorrow."

Cillian ran his fingers through his hair. "Yeah, I got it."

The heavy door slammed closed, and Margot's knees wobbled, threatening to topple her. Cillian rushed to her side, holding her up.

"Steady there," he murmured, his touch firm yet gentle. Margot could feel the scorching heat from his hand through her training leathers. She glanced up to see his eyes studying her intently; an inscrutable flicker passed through them.

"Thank you."

Cillian merely nodded, his grip on her arm steadying her as they made their way through the corridors back toward her room. The familiar scent of sweat and leather still surrounded them, but it mixed with something distinctly Cillian—pine mixed with a hint of something spicy. She leaned into him, her legs feeling like jelly as they walked in silence through the manor, only the sounds of their footsteps echoing against the floor to keep them company.

As they neared her room, she finally broke the quietude. "It was kind of you to not go all out on me."

He smiled. "I told you I wouldn't hurt you. Besides, you were already struggling enough."

Margot chuckled weakly. "Thanks for the vote of confidence."

"Corym was right. You have potential," he said, his tone swelling with pride. "And I wouldn't have said it if I didn't mean it, so don't even ask." He opened the door for her, helped her to her bed, and cleared his throat. "Do you... need help to get out of these leathers?"

Her cheeks burned, thinking about Vesryn catching them

again. She shook her head. "No... I think I can handle it. Thanks again for helping me to my room."

Cillian's warm smile lingered before he took a step back. "Rest well, Margot. I'll see you for training again soon."

Radiant heat tarried where Cillian stood, making the room seem entirely too small, as if his presence were a permanent fixture. With a sigh, Margot took off her leathers piece by piece and ignored the incessant scraping against her skull.

2 2

A QUEEN INDEED

MARGOT WOKE up the next morning unable to move. Her legs ached and arms were stiff, and she desperately needed water. The fluffy bed was eating her alive, and she didn't know if she could free herself from its tufted confines. After a few minutes of trying, she propped herself up on her elbows and swung her legs over the side, standing on limbs so unsteady her knees knocked together. One step at a time, she made her way over to the desk where the water pitcher sat. She looked at the minuscule water glass with disdain before opting to drink directly from the jug. Water dribbled down her chin as she chugged the precious liquid, feeling it course through her body like a river.

As she set the carafe down, she noticed a parchment scroll with a wax seal that matched the banners lining the training hall. Breaking the seal, she slowly sat, sucking in a sharp breath as her thighs screamed at her and read the document. Corym had written four pages, providing detailed feedback on her training session. He explained where he thought she excelled and where she was weakest, what stretches she should do to help her tired muscles, and what food she should eat to help reinforce her strength. And then, in the postscript, he suggested daily training to hone her skills rather than twice weekly. He said he would mention it to Vesryn, but should she choose daily training, hearing the request directly from her would go further than his words alone.

Setting the letter down, she took another drink and forced herself to go through the stretching motions Corym had detailed. She held each pose for forty-five seconds. Slowly, the tightness gave way and her blood warmed, allowing her to move easily. She was still sore, but nothing a hot shower wouldn't fix.

She towel-dried her hair and put on a thin, white sun dress that hugged her curves nicely. Twirling in the mirror, she tucked a lock of hair behind her ear and gasped when she saw the tip pointing upward. Not fully Elven, but Elven enough. As she inspected her new acquisition, there was a soft knock at the door, and she said, "Come in."

"Corym mentioned you may need some extra attention today, so I figured we could have breakfast to—oh. Oh my. Margot, your ears!" He set the platter on the table and spun her around, his fingers lightly dancing along the newly formed shell. "This happened so fast. Faster than I thought it would, if I am being honest. They look good on you, dear."

"You think?"

"Absolutely." He dragged the tip of his finger down her neck and played with the thin strap of her dress. "And this... is the perfect attire for the queen of a summer isle."

She craned her neck to look at him. "Queen?"

"If the elves had such a thing," Vesryn shrugged, and a devilish smile played along his lips, "you would be perfect for the part." He kissed her exposed shoulder, letting his lips linger. "And I could be your king."

Margot playfully slapped his chest, sidestepping his advances to head straight for the food. "I'm sure there are hundreds of far more suitable elves for that role. I'm barely even an elf!"

"Barely an elf?" he echoed as he sat across from her and scooped eggs onto his plate. "You are so much more than nearly all the elves on the island—you have Ilphas' magic inside of you, and you are *thriving*. At first, I questioned his choice in choosing a human... but it seems he was far wiser than I gave him credit for. May the goddesses watch over him."

Her eyes widened. "Your brothers' magic is inside *me*?"

"That it is." He nodded solemnly. "An unimaginable gift of raw power bestowed to the unlikeliest being."

"I... I don't understand. What does having his power mean? How does it affect me?"

"In due time, all questions shall be answered. Before you learn of elven magic, you must wholly understand the Mana Weave and Faerie's history. Then, and only then, may we dive into the enthralling history of the elves. Fortunately, my recent research endeavors should provide you with more than enough prerequisite knowledge in the coming months. With that being said, you will also be granted additional free time, which you can use to explore Caramis, read, relax... anything your heart desires."

Is this why he's keeping me so close? Because of his brother? That nagging feeling returned, needling the back of her mind. He wasn't telling her the whole truth, that much she knew, but what could she do about it? Questioning his motives seemed like a sure-fire way to bring out the worst in him, and that seemed like a bad idea.

Margot cleared her throat. "With that additional free time, would it be possible to take part in daily training? I know you said two days a week was fine... but Corym thinks I could benefit from daily activity. He said I have potential, and I'd very much like to explore that."

Vesryn's eyebrows shot up. "Corym told you that? Well, far be it from me to keep you from tapping into unexplored potential... yes. I do not see why you could not train daily if that is your desire. In fact, a powerful queen at one's side can only bolster the king. Yes... I like this."

Margot rolled her eyes and took a bite of her eggs. "I'm not a queen, Vesryn."

"No," he chuckled, "of course you are not a queen. But you

have the spirit of one." His eyes were alight with mischief. "Unyielding determination, a heart full of courage, and now," he gestured to her pointed ears, "a touch of elven grace."

She shook her head. "I think you're getting carried away with this queen talk."

"Maybe I am," he admitted, reaching for a piece of fruit from the tray. "But I cannot deny that the elf you are becoming is fit for royalty. How pretty you would look seated upon a golden throne."

"Mm yes," she grinned, ready to play along, "with an irresistible elf at my side. Such a handsome pair we would make."

"Ah, so you find me irresistible?"

"Who said I was talking about you? I meant Corym."

Vesryn's face darkened, shadows deepening around his eyes sent Margot's heart into overdrive. "Is this why you want to take on additional training?" he asked, his tone icy. "To spend time with Corym?"

"What? No. Vesryn, it was just a joke."

His topaz gaze held a stormy intensity that could kill. Clenching his jaw, he twisted his fingers around the cloth napkin. Finally, he exhaled sharply and leaned against his chair, the tension in the room thickening. "A joke," he repeated, his voice tight. "Of course."

A knot formed in the bit of her stomach from the sudden shift in the atmosphere. She scrambled to clarify, her words stumbling over each other in her haste. "I didn't mean anything by it, Vesryn. You know I was teasing." She reached out tentatively for his hand as if to bridge the growing distance between them.

His eyes flickered to her peaceful offering and frowned before meeting her dead on. The storm receded slightly, only to be replaced by something she couldn't pinpoint. "Teasing," he murmured.

Vesryn dropped the napkin and folded his hands neatly in his lap as he stared off into the distance, forcing Margot to withdraw the one she offered him. The shadow of his silence hung in the air, suffocating any attempt at further conversation. She bit her lip, unsure of how to navigate the unforeseen monsoon swelling between them. She toyed with her food, appetite forgotten, as she cast furtive glances in Vesryn's direction, searching for a sign of what he was thinking.

After what felt like an eternity, Vesryn rose abruptly from his seat, the chair scraping against the floor. He towered over her, his chest heaving with suppressed emotion. He looked at her, his lips contorted in disgust, and he paced back and forth before their table. "I need some air," Vesryn said tersely, his voice strained. "Meet me in my study in ten minutes." Without another word, he strode toward the door and disappeared, leaving Margot alone with their unfinished breakfast.

She sat there, stunned by the turn of events, her mind moving a hundred miles a minute, trying to sift through a thousand questions and doubts. It was times like these when she realized she didn't know the elf at all, and it scared her he could alter his personality in an instant. Was it truly a harmless joke that had upset him so deeply? Or was there something more beneath the surface that she had unknowingly stumbled upon?

Pushing her untouched plate away, she rose from her seat to splash some cold water on her face. For long minutes, she stared at herself in the mirror. Within a matter of days she had gone from someone she sort of thought she knew to someone she didn't recognize at all. A quiet ache stirred in her chest as she took in her fading freckles. She loved them. Why did becoming an elf mean she had to lose the qualities that were unique to her? It didn't matter that she didn't remember what kind of person she used to be, she liked the way she looked, and if she were being honest, the elves looked slightly unnerving, unreal. She didn't want to change so drastically. She sighed and left the bathroom to put on her soft-soled shoes before making her way to Vesryn's study.

She hesitated for a moment before knocking softly on the door, the sound seeming unnaturally loud in the quiet hallway.

"Come in," Vesryn's voice called out, sounding strained.

When Margot entered, she found Vesryn standing by the window with the curtains drawn, looking out at the beauty beyond the glass pane. Morning light filtered through thick palms, casting mottled light throughout the room. His silhouette was tense, rigid as a corpse. His breath of fresh air did little to quell the anger that radiated off him. That much was obvious, but she didn't know what to do or how to handle the elf when he was like this.

"I'm sorry if I upset you. I didn't mean to... to insinuate anything about Corym."

Vesryn cracked his neck and pointed to a pile of books in the corner without turning around. "Put those away in the appropriate spots. Once you are done with that, I have countless notes that need to be organized by topic."

Not ready to address the problem between them, Vesryn glided to the other side of the room and cracked open a tome. With clenched teeth, Margot made her way to the corner where the books lay in disarray.

The elf's filing system was as convoluted as the way he researched, and it took her hours to find a home for the books. And during the time it took for her to put everything away, Vesryn hadn't said one word to her. Instead, he created another pile, cleared his throat and pointed at it for her to sort once she was done going through the notes. It was driving her insane. He was penalizing her for a joke that he misconstrued all on his own.

Margot pressed her lips together firmly as she organized the sheaves of parchment, trying to ignore Vesryn's silent treatment. The pressure in the room was growing thicker, each passing moment feeling heavier than the last.

She exhaled sharply as two knocks sounded, and Tahlsia stepped into the room, setting their food and drink on the table. The placid elf's gaze lingered on Margot before she took her leave with a bow.

"Sit," Vesryn said as he took his own seat and piled food onto his plate.

Margot stalled, unsure where she stood with him after their earlier exchange. But when he glared at her, she gave up her standoff and walked over to the table, taking the seat opposite him. She couldn't gauge his mood. He seemed lost in thought, his expression inscrutable, and it unnerved her.

A palpable hush filled the space between them as she ate, her food tasteless, and that nagging returned, letting her know that something had shifted in their relationship, and it didn't feel good. In fact, it felt volatile. Dangerous. Like the elf was a geyser, biding his time until the perfect moment arose when he could blow.

"Vesryn, I—" she started, trying to bridge the divide, but he raised a hand to silence her, his eyes finally meeting hers.

"Margot, I must apologize for my reaction earlier. It was uncalled for and unjust." She searched his face for any sign of insincerity but found none. Instead, there was a vulnerability in his eyes that she had never seen before, a crack in his typically composed appearance. "I overreacted." He laughed as he ran his longer fingers through his silky strands. "It seems I have grown attached to you in such a short time. Even the mere thought of you with someone else... my apologies will never be enough."

"This is unfamiliar for me, too," she whispered. "This world, this magic... *you*. You've been helping me navigate this new life. You chose to spend your time teaching me, guiding me, helping me become a proper elf. Without you... I don't know where I'd be." Her cheeks heated and her gaze dropped to the table. "Maybe... maybe I'm a bit attached to you, too."

"Oh, my dear Margot. You have a way of unraveling even the most impenetrable parts of me." Slowly, she raised her head to meet his burning stare. "Pieces I long thought dead. Components of whom I once was revitalized, making me question my own judgment. But... but I cannot deny that it is welcome." He rounded the table, turned her chair, and knelt before her, resting his head on her lap. "I value your presence in my life more than you know," he confessed, his voice low and intimate. "And while I may struggle to express it, please understand the profound significance you have come to hold for me."

Margot slid onto Vesryn's lap, taking his face in her hands. "To rectify the situation from earlier, I just wanted to say I find you irresistible and would be honored to be your queen."

"Margot," he breathed into her neck as he wrapped an arm around her waist, pulling her closer, "I would gladly build you a throne of stars to sit upon if I could stand beside you as your king. Reign over my heart and soul. Reign over Caramis with me by your side—tradition be damned. We can make our own traditions. The two of us."

His eyes bore into hers. Longing swirled in their depths. He traced a finger along her jawline, then got lost in her hair, gripping the back of her head, and drew her in for a searing kiss that stole her breath. Icy hot fingertips pushed the straps of her dress down, freeing her breasts. She gasped against his lips and let her hands roam over his powerful frame, feeling the steeled muscles beneath his robe before ridding him of it. He hiked up her dress until it was around her waist, hissing when he felt wetness on her cotton undergarments as he pressed his hardened length against her.

"I want you," he whispered, his voice husky with need. "Goddesses know I need you, Margot." She whimpered in response.

With a low growl, he tore the thin fabric away, his fingers sweeping across sensitive skin. Margot moaned, her body responding to his touch with fervor. Slipping through her wetness, he groaned as he stood, lifting her with him, and carried her over to the window. Afternoon light bathed them in a warm glow as he pushed her against the pane, his cock teasing her entrance.

The room was silent except for muffled whines and smacking lips, the only reminder of their near-immortal desires wedding them to the earth. He pulled back, his eyes alight with hunger, and his lips met hers once more, their tongues dancing together in a silent plea for release.

"Please," she panted.

Vesryn's throat vibrated with an unholy sound, and he thrust inside her in a single, powerful motion. Margot cried out, pleasure mingling with pain at the unfamiliar sensation, making her feel more alive than ever before. Their mouths devoured one another as their bodies met in a frenzy, her back squeaking against the glass, the tops of his thighs slapping against her.

He ravaged her, taking her hard and fast with pounding hips and a ferocity that kept her moaning. She clawed at his back, urging him on, wanting more of him, needing to be filled completely. Raw. Primitive. Driven by a spiritual desire that transcended time and space.

Ragged breaths and hot pants grew between them as he pushed deeper, causing her to arch her back. Her body tightened, pleasure building inside, and she dragged her nails across the elf's shoulders. Her muscles squeezed around him, her breaths quick and sharp, and she screamed as release seized her.

Vesryn wasn't done. He plowed into her relentlessly, his movements becoming wilder, his gaze glazed with ecstasy. She locked her legs around his waist, rocking in sync with his motions, and with one last thrust, he emptied himself inside.

Their chests rose and fell in time as they desperately sucked in air. She chuckled as he smoothed her damp hair and admired her flushed skin. Softening, he pulled out, leaving her hollow, but stayed holding her in his arms.

"That was—"

"—Incredible," she said, finishing his sentence.

He rested his forehead against hers. "I do not know if I have ever felt like this before, Margot."

"Perhaps," she laughed, "you've never had a *queen* before."

His lips twitched, the corners barely lifting in a smile. "A queen, indeed."

Margot tapped his shoulder, and he placed her gently on the floor. "I'll finish up the stacks," she said as she adjusted her dress, blushing at the thought of what they had done.

"No need." With the wave of his hand, the books zoomed

about the room, taking care of themselves. He smiled sheepishly. "I was... petty."

"Seriously?"

He shrugged and lazily picked up his robe and put it on. "I am not perfect, my dear. We have quite a bit of time before your training. Shall we finish our meal and call it a day? I have a few things I must attend to, and besides," he smirked, "I am sure you want to freshen up."

"Imperfect?" she snorted as she made her way back to their food. "You're an elf—the absolute embodiment of flawlessness in the flesh." She grinned. "But I suppose we all have our moments."

Vesryn chuckled, the earlier tension melting away like morning mist under the sun and gracefully took his seat. The sharp edges of unease between them softened as the meal unfolded. As they ate, their conversation shifted to a peaceful rhythm, the words flowing freely. Laughter replaced guarded tones, and for the first time, they spoke as equals—not as scholar and pupil caught in a web of circumstance, but as two souls sharing a moment of respite.

The afternoon waned, and the sun began its slow descent toward the horizon. Vesryn reluctantly said goodbye and wished her luck with training, his lips meeting hers for a tender kiss before letting her go.

As she walked back to her room, her thoughts drifted to Cillian, the man she would surely be training with once more. Her steps faltered, and she stumbled, quickly catching herself on the wall. A sudden wave of hopelessness crashed over into her like a stormy sea, leaving behind jagged shards of despair that pierced her very being. Through heaving gasps, she inched along the wall, using it to support her weight, until finally making it back to her room. She fumbled with the knob, cursing her hands under her breath before making her way inside. The door closed, and she fell against it with a *thud*.

She slid to the floor and wept.

VELVET, LUSH AND PLUM-COLORED, BLANKETED Caramis. Elves lit candles and sconces in their homes, making the city pulse like a burning sea of stars. Margot breathed deeply, letting the curtain fall, and made for the door. She probably could have gotten out of training, but she made a commitment. Maybe if she had been training every day for weeks or months, she could get away with it without being judged. Corym wasn't likely to care about her being in bad headspace. She snorted, imagining him shooting her a look that said, "Of course a human couldn't handle the pressure it takes to be a warrior."

As Margot entered, the training hall's unique scent enveloped her in a comforting embrace. An odd feeling, considering this was only her second time in the facility, but probably said a lot about her, not that she was ready to dive into why she found comfort in the redolence of battle. She kept her head down and rushed to get changed, hoping no one would stop to talk to her. She needed just a few more minutes to herself before she was ready to make conversation.

She adjusted her vambraces and stepped back into the center. That she remembered the appropriate term for the piece of armor had a genuine grin tugging at her cheeks. Happiness was fleeting as Cillian stalked out from a corner, giving her pause. Sword in hand, he inched closer to her, taking inventory of her person before settling on her lips. His eyes darkened.

Margot looked nervously around the room. "Where's Corym?"

"Had something to do."

"Oh." She stepped back, trying to put some space between them. "When will he be back?"

In a flash, he was on her, gripping her chin with such force her eyes watered. He leaned in, inhaling deeply. "What did he do to you, Margot?" The rough gravel of his voice rocked her chest. "Did he force himself on you?"

"You're hurting me," she whispered.

Cillian released her, moving his hands to her shoulders. The deafening roar of blood in her ears was all she could hear as her heart struggled to regulate. She was conflicted; terrified that he would snap her in half, and thrilled she could feel his searing heat seep into her bones.

"What did he do to you?" he repeated, searching her eyes as if they held the answer.

She looked away. "Vesryn didn't do anything to me."

"Don't lie to me, Margot!" His words were laced with pain, and she knew that if she looked at him, she would break. "I can smell him on you. Please, if he hurt you, you need to tell me." When she didn't respond, he shook her. "Margot!"

"I already told you he didn't do anything! What do you want me to say?"

"I want you to tell me the truth!"

"You want me to tell you I wanted it? That I wanted to feel his fingers in my hair and his cock inside me?"

Cillian pushed her away and stumbled back. "You *wanted* it?"

"Yes! No!" She winced as her chest constricted tightly enough to hinder her ability to breathe. "I don't know"

"You don't *know*?" he asked, his voice cracking. "You don't even know him, Margot!"

"I don't even know *you!*" Clutching her chest, her knee hit the stone floor with an audible *thud*. "Why do you care so much?"

Leather boots stopped in front of Margot and Cillian knelt. They stayed that way for long minutes until she looked at him. His silver eyes glistened with unshed tears. "Why do I care," he breathed and placed a gentle hand on her cheek. "When I touch you, what do you feel?"

Her eyes fluttered closed. "Pain." A rogue tear settled in the corner of her lips. "Worse... agony. When I'm near you, I could die. Just thinking about you... I can barely take handle it."

"You're not the only one hurting, Margot." He wiped the wetness away with his thumb. "The torment I feel now is more than I have ever felt living on the..." He shook his head. "You can't trust Vesryn."

Margot's laughter echoed like a void throughout the hall. "He says the same about you."

Cillian opened his mouth but snapped it shut and fell into a stretching position. Footsteps sounded outside, and he glanced at her. "Your ears look good, Margot," he said as the door opened and the dark-skinned elf stepped in. "Everything alright, Corym?"

The elf's gaze lingered on Cillian, and Margot swore he shook his head ever so slightly before clearing his throat. "Everything's fine. Let's finish stretching."

WHAT HAPPENS IN THE FLAGON

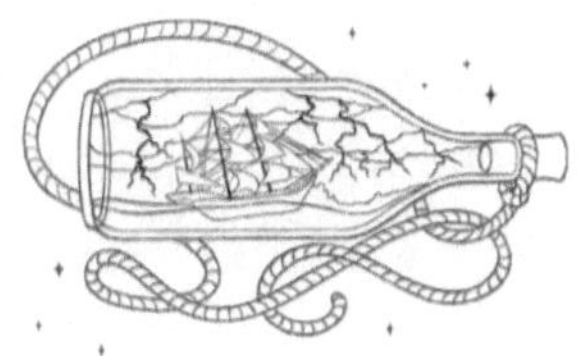

CILLIAN SAT in the corner of a tavern with his back pressed against the wall and elven mead in his hand. The barkeep, a silver-haired elf, kept glancing at him nervously with beady black eyes as he polished glasses and tended to patrons who looked at him with equal suspicion. He didn't blame them for keeping a watchful eye on him—he didn't belong. But after training the other day, Corym, surprisingly, had been the one to tell him to come here, to let off some steam. Apparently, he wasn't confined to the manor. He snorted. *Yeah, because I'd never leave Margot alone on this wretched island.*

He grimaced into his drink. The only promise he had ever made in his life had been to a fragile human girl, and he failed spectacularly. Whatever Vesryn was doing to his bloodsworn was taking her away from him bit by bit and he could do nothing to stop it. He needed to find some way to break Vesryn's hold on her. Killing the elf outright could potentially leave Margot addled forever and that was *not* an option. It was probably the same reason why Cillian was left alive. Vesryn feared the ramifications of a broken blood bond, and the further Cillian was from Margot, the more she would feel it, regardless of the magic he shrouded her under. Bestowing the title of protector upon him was nothing more than a joke—a way to keep him and the bond in check—and Cillian knew it.

"What's with that sour look on ya face?" a short elf with brilliant green eyes and unruly brown curly hair, his skin deep with an olive undertone, said as he slid into the booth next to Cillian.

"No reason."

The elf took a swig of his drink, smacking his lips together, and jabbed Cillian's side with his elbow. "C'mon, don't be like that." Wiping his hand on his shirt, he extended it toward Cillian. "Names Nym. Welcome to the Silver Flagon, a place where all are welcome. Even you, drek."

Cillian scanned the room. Each elf watched their interaction, waiting with bated breath, their eyes wide, tankards and glasses pressed against their lips, but not drinking. He looked back at Nym, then down to his hand.

"Cillian," he said reluctantly as he gripped the elf's sweaty palm. Almost immediately the room seemed to breathe, filling with the sound of libations hitting tables and hushed words floating through the air. "What's a drek?"

"You're a drek, drek. An outsider. Been a long time since I've been able to use that word." Nym grinned over his drink. "Today's a good day. Now c'mon and tell me what's got ya so down." He looked between Cillian and the rest of the patrons, nodding to himself. "Listen, drek, I'm gonna tell you a secret that stays between us, ya hear? The Silver Flagon has sort of a reputation—words spoken here are sacred. What happens in the Flagon stays in the Flagon."

Cillian eyed Nym. The tension in the room had eased, but an undercurrent of wariness lingered. Elves may have returned to their drinks and conversations, but their attention remained divided, sneaking glances at him when they thought he wouldn't notice.

He took a slow sip of his mead, letting the sweet burn settle his nerves. "I'm not exactly in the mood for secrets," he muttered. There was something disarming about Nym's demeanor, a kind of reckless confidence he hadn't found in the elves. He found it strangely comforting.

Nym chuckled, his grin never faltering. "Not a secret meant to cheer ya up, drek. More like... insight into how things work around here. There are places, like this." He waved his tankard around, sloshing mead onto the floor as he gestured to the dimly lit room. "Where the old ways still hold sway. Where Vesryn's shadow doesn't quite reach."

Cillian arched a brow. "And what's that got to do with me?"

Nym shrugged casually, but the look in his eyes was sharp. "Maybe nothin'. Maybe somethin'." He leaned closer, dropping his voice to a conspiratorial whisper. "We know who ya are, drek. And we ain't blind to what Vesryn's doin'. Not all of us are content to just watch."

Cillian's spine stiffened. "I don't know what you're talking about."

"I get it," Nym said, raising his hand in mock surrender. "Trust is hard to come by—especially here. But like I said, words spoken in the Flagon stay in the Flagon. No one's lookin' to rat ya out." His fingers twitched, and suddenly, a miniature forest sprung to life in the center of the tavern. Trees with silvery leaves and twisted trunks shimmered under the lantern light. "I'm just sayin' you're not as alone as you think."

Cillian watched, fascinated, as Nym snapped his fingers, conjuring a stack of slender needles with crisp leaves attached to their ends. He plucked one from the pile and held it out to Cillian. "Fancy a game of leaf darting? Helps clear the mind, almost as well as one of Stog's brews."

"Would ya stop calling me Stog?" The barkeep scowled. "You've known me your whole life, Nym."

"Now why would I go and do somethin' like that, Stog?" Nym waggled his eyebrows. "Just tryin' to make the drek here comfortable since not a one of ya are good at it."

Stog rolled his eyes and went back to wiping down the counter.

"Where was I? Oh yeah!" Nym slapped one of the needles into Cillian's hand. "We're gonna play, drek. I can't, in good conscience, let ya sit here and mope."

Cillian turned the needle over in his hand, the sharp tip pricking his finger. "Alright, I'll bite." He flicked his gaze up to meet Nym's. "How does this game work?"

Nym's grin widened. "Simple. Hit the target, win a round. Hit the mark dead center, and ya get to ask a question that has to be answered truthfully. Miss, and it's my turn. Ya gotta watch out for the forest, though. It'll move and shift as we play." He scratched his head and shrugged. "The trees have a mind of their own."

Much to Cillian's surprise, he found himself smiling. "Sounds fair. And if I win?"

Nym twirled a needle between his fingers before launching it into the moving illusion. It soared straight, piercing the heart of a small glowing orb. "Ya get your answers, drek. And maybe you'll start seein' things differently 'round here." He slipped out of the booth, nicking Cillian's cup and stomped toward the bar, slamming them down. "Two more brews, Stog! Make it snappy!" The bartender grumbled while a few other elves chuckled. Nym looked at Cillian over his shoulder. "You're up, drek. First round was a freebie."

Cillian watched as the trees swayed unpredictably, the little glowing orb flitting between them faster than a glimmerling. He lined up his shot and threw the needle. It whizzed through the air, missing the target by a hair.

Nym handed Cillian a fresh cup and smirked. "Looks like it's my turn." He grabbed another needle. "But don't worry, Cillian. We've got all night." He tossed the needle into the air and grabbed it between his teeth. He narrowed his eyes, then he turned his head so fast Cillian could hardly believe it happened, and the needle whistled through the air, stabbing the orb's center. "Point for me."

"You're cheating," Cillian stared at the orb with his jaw slack. "There's no way."

"Nym doesn't cheat," Stog answered from behind the bar. "But he is damn good at that game."

"Aw, Stog! I knew ya liked me!" Nym turned to Cillian, green eyes glinting mischievously. "My first question is an easy one, drek. Why'd ya come in here?"

"Into the Flagon?" Cillian circled the forest, following the orb, which was far less erratic than the trees. "Corym suggested I come here to relax, relieve some tension."

Nym drank deeply, smacking his lips together once he was done. "Huh, ol' Cory told ya to come here? Interesting. What's going on in the manor that's got your panties in a twist?"

"One question, yeah?" He saw Nym grin sheepishly from the corner of his eye before he threw the needle as hard and fast as he could, piercing the orb. *Speed is the name of the game; the trees are a distraction.* "Oh look, a point for me. Guess I'm up." He smirked at Nym. "What do you gain by telling me not everyone is content watching what Vesryn is doing?"

Nym's grin didn't falter, but there was a sharp glimmer behind his eyes, like he'd been waiting for this question. He casually leaned back against the bar, crossing his arms. "Ah, that's the thing, isn't it? What do I gain..." Nym took a long, deliberate sip of his drink, dragging out the moment. "It's not about what I gain, drek. It's about what we all stand to lose if Vesryn keeps runnin' things the way he is."

"You're skirting around the question," Cillian pressed. "You say you, and others, aren't content with following Vesryn, but you're still here. What's stopping you from doing something about it?"

Nym's smile faded as he tossed another needle, missing the mark this time. "The same thing that's stopped all of us, Cillian. Fear. We're not soldiers—we're bakers, smiths, and tanners. Vesryn has his enforcers, and we're just tryin' to survive. But now things are different." He shot Cillian a meaningful look. "You and your girl? You're the wrench in Vesryn's grand plan, even if he doesn't know it yet."

The elf's words settled like stones in Cillian's chest as he threw another needle into the target, even though they both knew they were no longer playing the game. Nym had expertly weaseled his way into Cillian's space, forcing him to let his guard down. "So, what's the play, then? You're telling me all this, but what do you expect me to do with it?"

Nym titled his head, considering Cillian. "We've been waitin' for someone to light the spark, drek. Someone who's not afraid to take a stand." He jabbed his thumb at his own chest. "I'm not the hero type, but you? You've got that look in your eye. That 'I'll burn the world down if it means protecting what's mine' kind of look. The kind that could get the elves to rally."

Cillian glanced around the tavern, noticing how the other elves subtly leaned closer, listening to every word exchanged between him and Nym. He wasn't just playing a game—he was being tested, measured.

"What do you know of what's going on in the manor?" Cillian asked, eyes narrowing as Nym's needle struck the target with precision.

The elf handed Cillian a needle, his playful demeanor gone, replaced by a seriousness Cillian had yet to see. "Elves are unhappy, drek, and when they're unhappy, they talk. Vesryn's so wrapped up in his own schemes, he doesn't even notice the whispers." Nym's gaze darted to the other elves before landing back on Cillian. "I know he's got a hold on that human girl, and that she's important. She matters to him, sure, but it's clear she means a heck of a lot more to ya."

Cillian's grip tightened on the needle, his voice a low murmur as he stared at the shifting forest. "Not much of a human anymore." He threw the needle, missing the target.

Nym raised an eyebrow, not letting it slide. "What was that?" He asked, his voice edged with curiosity. When Cillian didn't immediately answer, Nym threw his needle, hitting the target dead-on without even looking. "What do ya mean, *not much of a human*? What exactly is the girl now?"

Cillian clenched his jaw, wrestling with how much to reveal. What she was becoming wasn't something he'd fully come to terms with himself. But there was no denying it: the girl he'd risked everything for was no longer the same vulnerable human he'd pulled from the Dreadwood.

He met Nym's gaze. "She's an elf."

Nym let out a low whistle, barely audibly over the murmurs. The room seemed to hold its collective breath. "An elf, huh? Gosh, that's somethin' ya don't see every day. Makes ya wonder…" His voice trailed off, and he looked at Stog, who was gripping the edge of the counter so hard his hands were shaking, "…how that sort of thing comes about."

Cillian grabbed a handful of needles, hurling them into the illusionary forest. Three needles struck the glowing orb in rapid succession, dead center. "Then why don't you tell me, Nym? How does that happen?"

"A powerful elf needs to die." He took a long sip of his drink. "Thought everyone knew that."

Cillian's grip tightened on his remaining needles, his teeth grinding together. "And how often does this happen?"

"Not very often, drek." Nym scratched at his stubbled jaw, glancing thoughtfully at the ceiling as if recalling a distant memory. "The last time a powerful elf died…" He paused, his tone suddenly somber.

"Ilphas," Cillian whispered, the name hanging heavy in the air. "It was Ilphas."

Nym nodded. "And when Ilphas died, he left a legacy. And it's walking around in the form of that girl." He dragged a hand down his face, his body slumping as he sat on one of the stools at the bar. "No wonder Vesryn wants her so bad."

"Who is Ilphas, Nym?"

The elf waved his hand, and the illusionary forest and needles vanished. "Games over, drek. That's a story for another time."

Nym's unexpected strength caught Cillian off guard as the elf shoved him toward the tavern door, his grin unfaltering despite the tension that hung between them. Cillian stumbled, but quickly regained his balance, glaring down at the much smaller elf.

"What in the hells, Nym?" Cillian growled, his voice low and dangerous. He wasn't used to being manhandled, especially by someone half his size.

"As fun as this has been, drek," Nym said in a hushed voice. "I need to have a conversation without ya present. We'll talk another time. I swear."

Without another word, the elf shut the tavern door behind him, the sound of it closing echoing through the quiet streets of Caramis. Cillian stood alone, his mind whirling with doubts and rising dread. He had walked into the Silver Flagon seeking solace, but now he found himself burdened with more questions that were impossible to find the answers to.

FLIMSY DEFENSES

Vesryn tapped rhythmically on the desk. "You are training tonight, yes?"

"Mhm. Every night."

"I shall stop by, then."

Margot slowly set the notes she was reading down and looked at Vesryn. It had been four weeks and three days since she started training, and not once had he asked to watch. She suspected it was because Corym recommended cutting the time she spent researching by an hour and a half so she could train longer a few days ago. Vesryn hadn't taken it well. The elf had grown increasingly clingy and even asked her to share his quarters—she refused. Not that she didn't enjoy being with Vesryn; she just needed time to herself to recover after training, and time spent with him made that *very* difficult.

She cleared her throat. "Why the sudden interest in my training?"

"I have always been curious." He flipped a page in his tome rather than look at her. "According to Corym, you are progressing at an accelerated rate and are even giving the de—*Cillian*," He sneered before he continued, "a run for his money."

"The *de*...?"

"Slip of the tongue, dear."

"Right," she mumbled, moving the heavy burgundy curtain to the side. The sun had set, meaning it was time to go. "It's late... I guess I'll see you there?"

"I shall be right behind you as soon as I finish reading this section." His response was flat. Distant.

Guilt gnawed at Margot's insides, even though she knew his mood wasn't entirely her fault. Vesryn's attachment to her was extreme. Unhealthy. Occasionally he made comments that proved how put off he was that she spent time away from him honing her craft. She enjoyed training, was good at it. And even if she didn't enjoy her time in the hall, she still deserved solitary moments to reflect without worrying about whether the elf had been appropriately appeased that day.

Margot came up behind him, slipping her fingers between his and rested her head against the middle of his back. "I know this has been hard on you, but I appreciate the blessing you've given me to continue practicing. It... means a lot, Vesryn. More than you know."

Vesryn tensed, twisting around almost mechanically, holding Margot's gaze with an ire that threatened to consume everything in his path, but as soon as she released his hand, he schooled his features. Though the room whispered a chill five degrees cooler, tranquility etched itself upon his visage, a serene defiance against the cold he had brought upon himself.

"Should you sit beside me, interfering would be unwise."

"Vesryn, you must stop this," Margot demanded, unable to stop herself. "There is no place for either of us to sit besides this study. Why isn't that good enough for you?"

Speaking so freely would normally be foolish. If it had been weeks ago, she would have expected Vesryn to punish her, but they had grown close, for better or worse, and though his fists were balled at his sides now, she thought she knew him well enough to know he wouldn't physically hurt her.

"Because I deserve more," he whispered, much to Margot's

shock, as she hadn't expected an answer at all. "*We* deserve more. Do you not understand? Power begets power, and together, we can usher the elves into a new era. An era where we are no longer confined to this blasted island, where we do not have to *fear* being overrun by the fae when we can simply take them."

"I cannot, Vesryn, in good conscience, follow your plan to bring *war* to *our* people!"

"Is it suddenly *our* people? Though your evolution is complete, for nearly a month now you have refused to accept that you are, in fact, an elf." He dragged his nail along her jawline and circled her. "Cannot say I dislike this admission."

Margot huffed, jerking away from his touch. "If you can't take this conversation seriously, then I should just go."

As she made her way toward the door, he grabbed her arm, yanking her back. His fingernails dug into her wrist, feeling more like talons. "I am not above taking you over my knee and teaching you respect. You are a *child*," he spat. "Our *people* would welcome war if it meant reclaiming our rightful place on the mainland. Do you know how many years we have spent displaced? No, of course not. Because you have been gobbling up instructional time to train, which I, as you said, have blessed you to continue. So, before you try to admonish *me*, as if I do not understand my kind after *hundreds* of years guiding them, I suggest you rein it in. Or pray to the goddesses for safety, because you will not be able to handle my wrath. Now get out of my sight."

An invisible vice tightened around her chest, squeezing the air out of her lungs as her numb fingers scrambled to open the door. She needed to get out of this cage, needed to get away from Vesryn before the darkness edging her vision pulled her under.

THE TREK TO THE TRAINING HALL DID LITTLE TO improve Margot's mood. After her blowout with Vesryn, she figured he would skip her session, granting her a reprieve.

However, she was sorely mistaken when she saw the elf sitting in a large leather chair with deep button tufting and rolled arms at the edge of the center ring. She had to stop herself from rolling her eyes at how anomalous the piece looked against the backdrop of weapons and equipment.

As she strode past him to change, a sinister curve tugged at the corner of his mouth, his eyes glinting with hidden threats. It made her guts churn and her mind race. She knew he had a temper, but it had been ages since the beast surfaced. *Would he actually hurt me?* She didn't want to think about it.

"You alright?" Cillian asked as Margot entered the changing room. He secured a pauldron to his shoulder. They had fallen into a comfortable rhythm. So comfortable she would even consider them friends. Maybe he was even her best friend.

She undressed and started getting ready as a sigh puffed past her lips. "Vesryn's out there."

"So I saw." His voice was gruff, thick with emotion she couldn't place. It was no secret that he didn't like the elf. Nearly every day he told her to watch her back around him, that he couldn't be trusted. And at some point, if she was honest with herself, she started to believe that Cillian was right. "Why is he here?" he asked quietly.

Margot wrapped her breasts tightly with binding tape before sitting close to Cillian. She looked at him, noting the weariness in his silver eyes, and tentatively placed a gentle hand atop his. "He said he was curious, particularly because I've been doing well against you," she said, keeping her voice low enough so Vesryn couldn't hear her. She frowned. "I suspect it has less to do with my sudden proficiency in combat and more to do with the time I've spent with you. We... fought."

"You *fought*?" He grabbed the sides of her face, and she couldn't stop her eyes from watering. "Did he hurt you?"

"That was a poor word choice... we had a disagreement."

"Did he hurt you, Margot?"

Her gaze shifted to the floor. "He threatened."

"We need to get off this island," he implored. "My ship should still be down at the docks, unless the bastard had it burned." He placed his hand on her chest. Her heart thrummed incessantly, almost as if it were purring like a cat being pet. "Do you feel that? Like an anvil striking your soul with an eternal hammer." He pushed harder against her chest. "You are the blood of my blood, Margot, bone of my bone. Our hearts beat as one, our souls tied like the fiery vines of the sturdy Phoenixwood." He looked toward the door before he returned his focus to her. "We need to leave before Vesryn gets any worse. It's only a matter of time."

Heat bled through her bindings. Its soothing caress calmed her mind but left the rest of her buzzing. For the first time in weeks, she felt like she could breathe despite her needling nerves. Cillian was intense, yet certain in his proclamation. And with that nagging voice quiet, she believed him.

"It's only a matter of time before—"

"—Margot are you—" Vesryn started before cutting himself off. Fury spilled from his pores like a broken dam, drowning them all. The book he had been holding crumpled under his shaking grip. "*What is going on here?*"

Margot looked to Cillian, then down at his hand on her chest, then back to Vesryn, who was seconds away from losing it. Pearls of sweat dotted her brow. Their position was compromising, and for whatever reason, Cillian was disinclined to keep his appendage to himself.

As if Cillian could sense her internal panic, he said, "I was helping Margot with her bindings. If you're not careful, they can get tangled, which is uncomfortable."

"Ah, and the great Cillian knows much about bindings. Of course," Vesryn deadpanned.

"You're right, I do. Having twisted wrapping isn't something you want to think about constantly when in the middle of battle. Losing focus is how you wind up dead. Better she learns that now."

The elf grabbed Margot's arm and dragged her across the

room. "Time to go, Cillian. I can help our dear girl should she struggle getting kitted."

"You're hurting her," Cillian growled as he stepped toward Vesryn. "Let her go."

"It's fine," Margot said, trying to ignore the lack of feeling in her arm. "I'll see you in the ring."

"I suggest you listen to her."

"If you do anything to her, I swear I'll—"

"—You will do what?" Vesryn asked, cutting Cillian off. "That is right." He laughed, the sound sending a chill down Margot's spine. "Not a damn thing unless you are rethinking our agreement. Because to be candid, I am."

Cillian's throat bobbed, and the veins in his neck pulsed. Afraid to speak up or nod, Margot blinked slowly to try to get him to leave before Vesryn did something stupid. A feral snarl rumbled from Cillian's chest as he drove his fist into the stone wall. The impact echoed throughout the room, and he stormed off. Margot held her breath as she settled on the deep, jagged dent his unbridled strength left behind.

"Stupid girl," Vesryn hissed as he pushed her, sending her careening over the bench and onto the floor. "Making friends with the enemy, are we? Or are you just drawn to his looks? Is my elven beauty not enough for you? You yourself mentioned how perfect I am."

The impact with the ground left Margot gasping for air as sharp pain shot through her side. She gritted her teeth as she pushed herself up onto her hands and knees. "The *enemy*?" she questioned incredulously. "He was to protect me, and instead, he is teaching me to protect myself *with* Corym's guidance, I might add."

Vesryn's eyes darkened as he advanced toward her. His movements were deliberate, like a predator closing in on its prey. He loomed over her, his shadow casting an ominous silhouette across the cold stone floor. Her breaths came in short gasps, and she scrambled to her feet, desperate to get away from him. His hand shot out, gripping her throat tightly as he forced her back against the wall, his face mere inches from hers.

"You think you can defy me and seek solace in the arms of another?" Spittle landed on her cheek. "I have told you repeatedly how dangerous he is. Yet here I find you, cozying up with that treacherous swine."

Margot clawed at his grip. She tried to kick him away, but he shoved them apart with his knee, pinning her. "I wasn't—" Before she could finish her sentence, Vesryn tightened his hold. Stars danced along the edge of her vision, inky blackness encroaching and threatening to swallow her whole. Tears streamed down her face. Each breath was a struggle, the air barely squeezing through her constricted airway.

And then he released her.

She took ragged gasps, the sudden influx of air tearing through her throat as she slid down the wall, unable to keep herself upright.

Vesryn crouched and tipped her chin up. "I am your mentor, your master, the only thing you think about. You train because I allow it. You live because I command it."

"I am my own person, Vesryn." She struggled to get the words out. "You can't control me."

"You forget your place, girl," he hissed, his breath hot against her skin. "You belong to me, mind, body, and soul. No one else will care for you like I do."

She lightly touched her throbbing throat. "You think this is care?" she rasped. "This is manipulation. You would have me be a puppet so you can pull the strings."

Vesryn shrugged. "If you have figured it out, why do you continually fight me every step of the way? I know what is best for you and the elves of Caramis. They understand. Why is it so difficult for you to?"

"Because you're suffocating me," she whispered. "You treat me as if I'm a pawn in some game only you're playing. I—I no longer wish to be a prisoner."

Vesryn hummed. "That is a shame." Once he was at the door, he looked over his shoulder. "Best get dressed. I should like to see you in action."

With trembling hands, Margot hurriedly gathered her belongings and changed into her training gear. She laced up her boots and stood in front of the mirror, inspecting Vesryn's handiwork. Though she chose the high leather gorget, she could still see traces of the bruise that had started to bloom. Cillian would know the elf hurt her and feared he would retaliate against Vesryn. *At least he will know to be gentle.*

Steeling her spine, she stepped into the training hall, taking a deep breath of the scent she had grown to love. She scanned the area for Cillian, but he was nowhere to be seen. Vesryn stood at the center of the sparring ring. His fingers drummed against his thighs. Beyond him, Corym stood on the edge, watching with curious eyes.

"Where's Cillian?" she asked as she stepped into the ring. "We were to practice grappling."

Without warning, Vesryn lunged forward, driving his elbow into her ribs. Margot staggered back, pain radiating from her side. Gritting her teeth against the sharp ache, she raised her fists, ready to defend herself from the elf that circled her with lethal grace.

Vesryn sneered. "Cillian will not be joining us, unfortunately. It seems he had other matters to attend to and because I am so concerned that your training should continue, I told Corym I would step in tonight." Margot shot a look at Corym, who kept his face impassive but his form was rigid and tense. Vesryn locked her arms together from behind and leaned in, letting his lips graze her ear. "Do not look at him, dear. He will not save you."

The position he had her in allowed her to grip his fingers. She contorted her body, twisting his hand as hard as she could as she twirled out of his grasp, stepping away from him three paces. The elf hissed, curling his lips in a cruel smile. He advanced with snake-like movements, and with a sudden burst of speed, he flipped around her, touching his index finger to her temple.

Energy washed over her, keeping her in place. "I think it is time you truly learn, Margot. For strength is not just physical; it is mental as well. You must be prepared for any situation, any adversary. Now burn."

Margot's mind screamed as Vesryn's magic engulfed her, searing through thoughts and jumbled memories. He delved into the deepest recesses of her mind, searching for vulnerabilities to exploit regarding Cillian. Every heartbeat felt like a drum pounding against her skull, the heat intensifying with each passing moment. She looked at Corym, who seemed to be yelling something, but the only sound she could hear was the roaring inferno.

Confusion turned to clarity as she focused on Corym's shouts. His words cut through the chaos in her mind, a lifeline in the storm. "You're going to kill her!"

Yes, he is.

She fell to her knees under Vesryn's psychological assault. Desperately, she tried to lay brick after brick, constructing barriers to shield Cillian—the only man she believed could truly protect her. No matter how hard she worked, Vesryn broke through, shattering her flimsy defenses to smithereens. Images and scenarios she didn't recognize whizzed by, melting together to form new memories while others were snuffed out like candles in the wind.

Margot fought against the onslaught, grappling for the splintered pieces of herself and trying to fit them back together. Her vision blurred, and she could feel Corym's panic swirling around her like a cyclone. But he didn't intervene. It wasn't until the tearful anguish of Vesryn's disapproval firmly rooted itself in her mind that the flames ebbed.

Gasping for breath, Margot collapsed on the ground, her mind reeling from whatever happened. Vesryn stood over her, furrowing his brow slightly as a concerned look spread across his face. "Dear, are you quite alright?" he asked, offering her a hand. "Can you stand?"

She hesitated for a moment, unable to remember what

happened, and didn't know if she could trust him. But seeing the genuine concern in his eyes, she let him pull her up.

As she rose unsteadily to her feet, her mind felt like a battlefield strewn with the wreckage of ravaged memories. She tried to piece together the fragments that remained, but it was like trying to assemble a shattered mirror—each shard reflected a distorted image of herself.

"What happened to me?" she whispered. "I don't... I can't..."

"Shh," Vesryn soothed as he smoothed her hair. "I do not know what happened. You collapsed during our practice bout. Corym and I were so concerned! You scared us."

Margot blinked, trying to push through the fog in her mind. She vaguely remembered the intense heat and overwhelming pressure, but other than that, everything was blank, save for the memories of her and Vesryn happily together, in love. She looked at Vesryn, his face etched with worry, and then at Corym, whose eyes avoided hers.

She swallowed. "I think I need to rest."

Vesryn placed a cold hand on her cheek. "I think that would be for the best." He turned to Corym. "Would you mind helping her to her room? It seems there is work to do."

Corym nodded, keeping his gaze lowered as he approached Margot. He offered her a supportive arm, and together, they made their way out of the training hall.

2 5

IMPAIRED

CORYM CLEARED HIS THROAT, shifting his weight from one foot to the other as Margot entered her room. She looked over her shoulder at the elf she had started to consider a friend, a comrade. He glanced at her before picking at a sliver of wood from the door jamb. "Vesryn wants to stop your training."

"What?" She couldn't believe what she was hearing and turned around fully, giving him her full attention. "Is this a joke? Because I collapsed? Look, I may not remember what happened," she began again, talking animatedly with her hands, "but I've been fine every single night we've been training, great even. What happened was a one-time thing, a fluke. Honestly? I've never felt better. I'm stronger. Faster. My memory—"

"—is impaired," he interrupted, letting his gaze fall to the floor.

Those two little words made her stomach plummet like a stone into the depths of the sea. She had finally made peace with the idea that her past might remain a mystery, but now, even her present was slipping through her fingers. *Is my mind unraveling beyond repair?*

"What's wrong with me?" She sniffled.

"Nothing's wrong with you."

"Then... then you can't let him do this, Corym!" Tears rolled down her cheeks. She didn't bother swatting them away. After all those nights spent with him, the elf had seen her cry on more than one occasion. "Training... I-I love it. I'm good at it!"

"I know." He exhaled a rough breath and scrubbed his face before placing a hesitant hand on her arm. "Vesryn isn't only worried about your well-being. He... doesn't want you to be *that* close to Cillian."

"*Him?*" Margot laughed, but it was a sound hollowed out by sorrow, more a lament than a jest. "Why is Cillian even here? Wasn't his duty to protect me? To shield me from... from what, exactly?" Her voice faltered. The elf tightened his grip, steadying her as she swayed. "Instead of simply guarding a vulnerable elf, he chose to forge me into someone powerful. Someone who could care for themself without needing to rely on others. You did, too. Maybe... maybe it's Vesryn who is broken. Not me."

Corym's gaze lingered on her, stretching the silence between them. When it was clear to Margot the elf wasn't going to respond to her, she scoffed and pulled her arm from his hold.

"Feel free to leave."

Halfway through Margot shutting the door in his face, he said, "Wait." The door creaked as she opened it just enough for her head to peek through. "I'll see what I can do about training, alright? Pretty sure I'm in a world of shit with Vesryn, so I can't make any promises. Get some rest, yeah?"

She gave him a lopsided smile. "Thank you, Corym."

"Don't mention it."

Once the elf had disappeared down the hall, she shut the door, grabbed a change of clothes, and tossed them on the bed. Her trembling fingers struggled to peel off her leather armor; she grunted in frustration. Her body was sorer than it had ever been after a night of training. It was a wonder she even made it to her room.

Gingerly, she arose and worked her way toward the bathroom.

As much as she didn't want to, if she didn't at least take a shower, her poor muscles would suffer even more come morning.

"What in the hells happened to you?" Cillian snapped, his voice sharp with a mix of exasperation and concern, the words cutting through the air like a blade.

Margot quickly crossed her legs and used an arm to cover her breasts while using the other one to support her weight against the counter.

"*You can't be here,*" she seethed. "I don't know why you weren't at training tonight, but Vesryn doesn't want me near you."

"*Fuck* Vesryn." Cillian removed her arm from her chest. His fingers skated lightly along her neck; she winced, and he pulled back. "Do you know what you look like? Do you know what that bastard did to you?"

"What are you talking about? I passed out. That's all."

Cillian positioned her in front of the mirror. Margot's eyes widened, her breath quickening as she took in the reflection of someone she barely recognized. Dark bruises marred her once-familiar skin, stark against her pallid complexion. Angry red marks etched themselves into the contours of her body, like the strokes of a mad artist on a violent canvas. She traced the welts, fingerprints snaking across the flesh of her throat, each touch dragging her deeper into a state of abject horror.

"What happened to me, Cillian?"

His jaw clenched, his expression a mask of tightly controlled rage. "What do you think happened?" His fingers hovered over the bruises, ghosting over tender skin without touching her. "Vesryn happened."

"No. He would never do that. Sure, he has a temper, but he would never raise a hand to me."

"You have no idea what happened... you told me in the changing room that you and Vesryn had an argument. Do you remember that?" She shook her head, trying to keep tears at bay. He pressed his palm to her bare chest. "Do you feel my soul?"

Her blood raced as his warmth spread through her like balm. She closed her eyes, focusing on the sensation that was both comforting and unnerving. A steady thrum of energy passed between them, causing her nipples to pucker and her core to go slick. The air crackled with energy, every nerve alive and tingling on the precipice of a plunge she wasn't sure she dared take.

"What is this?" she whispered.

Cillian outlined the curve of her hip, bringing her closer to him. "This," he rasped, his voice heavy, "is how it's supposed to be. You and me, my blood. My heart." His thick fingers slid down the center of her belly, inching closer and closer to the warmth nestled between her folds. "I need you to remember."

"Remember what?" she breathed, forgetting all about the pain Cillian had implied Vesryn inflicted.

His lips brushed against her ear, and she bit down on her bottom lip, stifling a shiver. "Remember who you are," he growled. "You are my flesh, my bone, my blood, my heart... and I need you to remember that."

Margot drew in an uneven breath as he finally brushed against her center. She wanted to resist, to push him away, but instead, her back arched, chasing his touch as that nagging voice urged her on: *Yes, yes, yes.* He cupped her and stroked her sex. Blood rushed between her legs.

"What... what are you doing," she mewled.

"I'm giving you a choice, Margot. You can choose to remember, or you can continue living in darkness, foolishly convinced that your life is yours alone." His fingers delved deeper, rubbing at the dampness between her legs, coaxing it further. She moaned. "What do you say?"

"I-I don't understand," she panted.

"You will," he replied, his voice low and seductive. "Do you want me to make you remember, Margot? Do you want the truth, or do you want to remain ignorant?"

He withdrew his hand, and the warmth was instantly replaced by a cold, hollow void that left her panting and breathless with a sense of emptiness seeping into her bones. Even the relentless chirping in the back of her mind seemed to fade into silence. She turned to the mirror, her reflection a portrait of bruises and exhaustion, then glanced at Cillian. Hunger, raw and aching, swirled in his eyes, a silent plea, as he waited—patient, yet desperate—for her decision. His gaze never wavered, locked onto hers as if he could see her very soul. And deep down, Margot believed he could.

Swallowing hard, she made her choice.

"Make me remember, Cillian."

With a slow, satisfied smile, Cillian stepped closer, wrapping a gentle arm around her and pulling her against him. He pressed languid kisses along the column of her throat, his lips brushing over every bruise, every welt, as if healing each wound with his touch.

"When I found you in the Dreadwood, I think I already knew what you would come to mean to me. You, a human girl from Earth," he murmured as he tended to her injuries. "So fragile. So fair. Not at all built to withstand Faerie. Yet there you were. Withstanding."

"A human?"

He rested his index finger against her lips. "Don't interrupt. It's rude."

She inhaled sharply as if to respond, but a rough hand caressed her breast, teasing her nipple until it formed a peak.

"You were just a visitor here; I was sure you wouldn't become a permanent fixture in my life. Regardless, I knew I couldn't let Ravara or his guards have you. So, I took you." He dragged his finger down her chest and over her belly, the tip just grazing her mound. Her eyes fluttered to the back of her head. "I threw you over my shoulder, gave you shelter on my ship, fed you, clothed you, taught you how to shoot with bow and arrow. My heart, we even fought off a leviathan and lived to tell the tale." He sunk deep into her wetness, curling his digit *just* right. "I made a decision to tell you about the elves. Told you that I would take you to them should you want to learn how and why you came to Faerie." He pushed another finger in, and Margot gasped. "Now, you're not only bound to me, but you're bound to Faerie."

Cillian's voice was like a soothing lullaby, and Margot felt her resolve waver. Her heart pounded in her chest. "I don't," he stilled his movements so she could speak, "I don't remember any of that... I know I'm in Faerie, but I don't remember how I got here or any of the things you're talking about."

He started back up, thrusting deeper, stretching her open and plunging inside her. She cried out, her hips bucking against his hand as a fire ignited between her legs.

"Oh. *Ohhh*," she moaned.

"That's because the elf that fucks you at night wanted you to forget." In one swift motion he had her sitting on the bathroom counter, still thoroughly working her. "Vesryn, the one who keeps me from you, the one who bruises you and makes you feel small. He made you forget." Cillian cupped her face; she could feel her own wetness on her cheek. "I want you to remember, Margot. Not just that you are part of me, but that you're something so much more than what he made you."

Tears limned her lash line. "But why would he do that?"

"Vesryn wants to control you. He wants you—*all of you*— including your power." His gaze bore into hers. "I'm going to make you remember, Margot. I'm going to make you remember everything, even if it kills me."

His lips crashed onto hers with an urgency she hadn't expected, his tongue delving deep, exploring her mouth with a ravenous intensity that left no corner untouched. She gasped for breath, the air searing her lungs as she fought to keep up with his relentless pace, only to have him dive back in, consuming her completely, leaving her reeling in the wake of his passion. A groan slipped past her lips as he licked between her breasts, using his hands to spread her legs further apart so she could feel his hard length against her center. He bit and licked and sucked both breasts until they were raw and sore and aching. She cried out as he engulfed her swollen clit, flattening his tongue and licking in broad strokes.

"Cillian! I'm..." she panted, jerking her hips wildly into his face, her need for release increasing with every passing moment.

"Let go, my heart," he growled, lips still pressed against her core as he pumped his thick cock, chasing his own liberation.

With his free hand, he slid three fingers inside her, pumping in a steady rhythm as his teeth grazed her most sensitive spots. It was too much; her body was on fire, her mind a blur of sensation. She screamed, her body arching off the counter, holding herself upright and digging her nails into Cillian's back as the most intense orgasm of her life washed over her. She rode the wave of her climax, holding him tightly until finally, he let go, too, with a guttural roar that vibrated her ribcage.

He kept his fingers inside her as she came down, her body quivering as she fought to catch her breath. He held her close, his heart thudded against his chest. She closed her eyes, grateful for the quiet in her mind. But in there, in the deepest recesses, was a faint pulse of light. A thread, beating in time with her pulse. With Cillian's.

He wiped away damp hair and pressed a kiss on her forehead. "Do you remember?"

Margot shook her head, a lone tear tracing a path down her cheek. "No." Her voice trembled as she searched his face, desperate for confirmation. "But I remember you."

"That's good enough for today. Let's get cleaned up."

Cillian shed his clothes before he helped her off the counter and guided her into the vast, stone-tiled shower stall. He adjusted the temperature until it was soothing and warm. They stepped under the spray and let the steam envelope them. She reached for the soap, but he got it first and started to wash her, beginning with her face and working his way down. His touch was gentle, as if he were handling something precious and fragile.

Margot closed her eyes, letting the sensation of his hands wash over her. The warmth from the water and the softness of his caresses slowly eased away the remnants of Vesryn. "Thank you," she whispered.

"You're welcome, my heart."

Once they were dressed, Cillian carefully lifted Margot into his arms and carried her over to the bed. With a tender touch, he traced the delicate curve of her cheekbones before skimming along the soft contours of her ear. "Rest now," he said, tucking a lock of hair behind her ear as she nestled into the pillows. The room was warm and cozy despite being so sterile.

As he rose to leave, she gripped his arm. "Stay." She pulled him close, her eyelids heavy with sleep. "Stay with me, please."

Cillian hesitated for a moment, his features softening. "Of course," he murmured, settling into the bed next to her. "Of course I'll stay with you."

Margot closed her eyes, letting a tranquil tide of peace sweep over her as Cillian curled around her, his embrace was a sanctuary. His breath brushed against her ear, gentle whispers muttering sweet nothings that danced like a breeze, while his fingers traced delicate patterns on her arm, leaving trails of goosebumps in their wake. In that sacred moment, cradled in his warmth, she was wrapped in a cocoon of safety, untouchable by the world beyond.

ONE EITHER ADAPTS OR
THEY DIE

THE DIFFUSE LIGHT of the early morning soaked into the stark white walls of Margot's bedroom, bathing the space in a rich, wine-colored glow. She rubbed sleep from her eyes and glanced at Cillian, still beside her. His arms were stretched above his head, lips slightly parted as soft snores wove a gentle melody with a steady rhythm.

From the wardrobe, she selected a pale-yellow chiffon sundress that crisscrossed all the way down to the small of her back, tying into an elegant bow. The gauzy fabric trailed behind her as she stepped into the bathroom to prepare for the day. The scent of their passion still lingered in the air, clinging to her skin like a whisper of the night before. Each breath she took was a reminder, Cillian's essence woven into her very being. A smile touched her lips, but it faltered as she faced the mirror. The bruises looked worse, making her look like the pages of an old book left out in the rain, stained and mildewed.

Margot splashed water on her face, her breath catching as the door creaked open. She whispered urgently, "You shouldn't still be here. Vesryn will surely come check on me."

"I know." She glanced at him, catching the hint of a smirk

playing on his lips. "But I wasn't ready to let you go." The low rumble of his voice sent a thrill through her, making her pulse quicken. He leaned in, his thumb following the hollow of her damp cheek before he kissed her softly.

When he finally pulled away, she murmured, "He's going to know."

Cillian shrugged, a quiet confidence in his gaze as he placed his palm on her chest. "Do you still feel this?"

"Yes," she whispered, fear threading her voice. "How do I know you aren't messing with me like you say Vesryn is?"

Cillian sighed, his eyes pleading as he shook his head. "Margot, I won't hurt you. I would *never* hurt you. This thing between us? It's as real as it gets. Do I look like an elf to you? I have no magic coursing through my veins."

She wanted to believe him, but doubt chewed at her. Yet, that nagging feeling inside told her he was telling the truth. To believe him. Unsure of what to say, she lowered herself on the tufted bench against the wall. All this time spent training together, and she hardly knew anything about him. *Who is this man?*

He was right; he wasn't an elf. All the elves she'd seen were lithe and regal, their skin unmarred, their features delicate and nearly indistinct. Cillian was all hard lines and corded muscle, his body covered in scars, his nose crooked as if it had been broken more than once. If Vesryn didn't want him near her and he wasn't an elf, why would he keep Cillian around? *Maybe he knows more than he's letting on.* Dangerous thoughts. Questions she wasn't ready to ask, no matter how much she wanted to know the answers.

Countless silent minutes ticked by before Margot cleared her throat, unable to bear the quiet any longer. That, and she realized she had been staring at him a little too intently.

"Why are you really here?" she asked.

"I already told you. I wasn't ready to leave."

"No... why are you *here*, in Caramis."

"To protect you."

Margot shook her head, her voice edged with disbelief. "You're lying." Cillian flinched, but she pressed on. "Vesryn doesn't want you anywhere near me. So I'll ask you again—why are you here?"

"I'm here to protect you... from Vesryn."

"Do you honestly think he would kill me?" It was true something was off about Vesryn, and after everything that had happened, she was sure he manipulated her mind somehow, but the elf needed her. *He wouldn't damage something he needed, right?* "Try again."

"I think Vesryn would do a lot of things." Cillian exhaled sharply and sat next to her, resting his forearms on his thighs with his hands clasped together in the center. He kept his head down. "The bond between us... if I were to leave, or if something were to happen to me, you would be fucked. Emotionally. Physically. You could very well tear yourself apart with grief. You would live, but the consequences of either of those things happening aren't worth the effort of getting rid of me."

"I see," Margot said, watching as Cillian's hands tightened into fists. "If this bond between us is so powerful, how did Vesryn... taint it?"

"He had Corym torture me in front of you." A tear slipped down his chin, making her heart clench. "You gave up the bond to save me from more suffering."

"And-and you're sure he tampered with my mind?"

"I'm *positive.*"

Margot's stomach churned with nausea. The thought that all of this had happened without her remembering it gnawed at her sanity. She swiped away a rogue tear that slipped down her cheek and bit down on her bottom lip, trying to stop its trembling. "Why didn't we just leave?"

"Because we needed him to teach you how to control your magic." Cillian's gaze snapped to Margot's. "He *is* still teaching you, right?"

"He... he said I'm not ready." She hiccupped. "He hasn't

taught me anything beyond the magic elflings perform during playtime."

"That bastard," he growled. "And when will you be ready?"

"Once I thoroughly learn the history of the elves. Vesryn said I'm close."

He thumbed her cheek, wiping away her despair. Jolts of electricity coursed through her body. They weren't painful; in fact, the feeling was almost comforting.

"For a little while longer, you'll need to put up with the elf. Can you do that?"

"I can try." Margot inhaled deeply. "Why can't we just... leave this place?"

"In a perfect world, we could. But there was one thing Vesryn was right about: your magic needs to be controlled. Without learning to wield your power, you're a danger to everyone, including yourself."

"I barely even feel my magic. What if it's not there?"

Cillian deadpanned. "Margot, you've literally turned into an elf. Obviously, you have magic. That shouldn't even be a question."

She rolled her eyes, and he chuckled. The sound brought a smile to her face. His fingers drifted to her lips, where they lingered for just a moment before falling away.

"Magic is a fickle thing," he said. "It can be elusive, but it's always there. I've lived a long time, so trust me when I say I've seen it before. So, don't worry so much about where your magic is."

"Why are you helping me?" she whispered.

"Oh, Margot," he murmured, his expression fell as he searched every inch of her face. He brushed a strand of ashen hair from her eyes, glancing at the floor. "I thought that would be obvious. You're my *everything*. I *must* protect you."

Danger surrounded her, and being with Cillian only increased it. Yet here she was, sitting with him in a bathroom, ready to spill her guts. That incessant feeling told her this was the right path, that turning to him was important. She looked at him—truly looked at him—etching the lines and angles of his face and the hard contours of his body into memory, and the world around her faded away. All that was left was the two of them.

"What if Vesryn kills me before ever teaching me?" Her voice nearly broke on the words.

Cillian tipped his chin down, eyes darkening. "That will not happen."

Trusting Cillian with her life was risky, but what else could she do with the hand she was dealt? After piecing together the fragments, she knew Vesryn wasn't the pleasant elf he pretended to be when they first met. He was cold, cunning, and undoubtedly had malicious, self-serving intentions. The fact that he could switch his malevolence off in an instant, assuming a more docile personality, was alarming. Now, she was sure she'd been manipulated into their initial deal because she believed she had no other options.

"I don't know who I am or who I can trust. There... there's a part of me that says I can trust you. Not actually says, but you know, it's more of a feeling."

"That's the bond." Cillian smiled. "I know you've changed, but you're still you, even if it doesn't feel that way now."

"What do I do? Everything's a mess. Memories are missing. Experiences I'm sure I've had are just gone, slipping through my fingers like grains of sand any time I think I finally remembered. Whatever life I lived before coming to Caramis... erased." Her chest heaved with the weight of her sobs.

"This isn't forever. You will get them back." He laced their fingers together and squeezed. "What you've been going through with Vesryn isn't something you can handle alone. Trust me. Lean on me. Use me, Margot, and I promise you I'll stay by your side no matter what happens."

She tried to make sense of what he said through the blaring

sirens going off in her head. They grew louder, pushing her to agree, not even giving her time to think.

"Margot, are you here?" Vesryn asked from the other room. "I intended to be here sooner, but of course there was another mess for me to clean up... Margot?"

She stumbled back from Cillian and wiped away the wetness from her cheek before taking a deep breath. Vesryn's sudden appearance ripped her from her bubble, reminding her of the dire situation at hand. Cillian tucked himself in a corner. He was stiff; she could tell he was struggling to contain his anger.

"O-one mo-moment," Margot said. She tried to compose herself the best she could as she shuffled across the room and opened the door just wide enough so she could slip out without Cillian being seen. "Sorry. I had to use the restroom."

Vesryn narrowed his eyes and assessed her appearance. "Have you been crying?"

Margot turned from him. This conversation wasn't one she wanted to have, but it was obvious she looked disheveled, which was fair, considering what had transpired in the bathroom.

The elf glided across the floor, standing mere inches from her. He tilted her chin and positioned her face in a way that made her look at him. Desire filled his amber eyes as he focused on her mouth. She tried to pull away, but his grip was solid.

"You should not be crying." He dragged his tongue along his bottom lip. "This is your home. Let me care for you."

He placed his hand on the back of her head and pushed her lips to meet his. Margot's insides twisted, squirming against the assault as he forced his tongue inside, tasting every inch of her mouth.

The kisses grew more insistent, violent. She pushed and pushed, but he held her tight as one hand fisted her dress and the other roamed down her backside. Powerless. That's what she was. How could she change her situation if she couldn't change this? He could take anything from her, do anything to her, regardless of what she wanted, and that's exactly what was happening.

A wave of energy rippled through her, working its way through her system. Fear and confusion clouded her mind as she tried to keep her thoughts clear, but it was too late. Overwhelming power claimed her. Whenever there was a moment of clarity, she fought back with what little strength she had, only to fail over and over and over again.

Then, her body betrayed her as nimble fingers traced the curves of her body and cupped the swells of her breasts. Unfamiliar sensations addled her brain further, making her dizzy with lust.

Lips trailed along her neck as his hand slid beneath her dress and rubbed between her thighs. A swell of heat spread from the point of contact, and a moan made its way past her lips unwittingly. Two icy fingers spread her apart and dipped inside. He fucked her slowly, curling his appendages just right. Slickness drenched her, running down her legs. Her apex pulsed, rapidly increasing with each thrust, and she rocked her hips in unison, chasing the pleasure building within her.

Vesryn, Vesryn, Vesryn. His name was a mantra—she couldn't get enough.

She gasped, pushing herself against him impossibly close, wanting to feel more—*needing* to feel more. She lifted her leg, rested it on his hip, and bounced up and down. More. She needed more.

Vesryn bit her lip. "I knew you would be excited. Come all over my hand, Margot."

The sound of his voice brought an image of Cillian to the forefront of her mind, pushing the elf's magic to the side. In that instant, she pushed him away, but his grip tightened like a vice, and he continued working her with an unrelenting force. Her core clenched. She didn't know how much more she could take when a growl commanded her focus.

"Get off her," Cillian spat.

Vesryn pulled his fingers from her, slowly sucking them clean, and turned toward Cillian. "How embarrassing. But you understand, right? She tastes absolutely divine."

Cillian stalked toward the elf with fists clenched at his sides. "Step away from her."

Margot stumbled as Vesryn shoved her aside, her hip slamming into the vanity with a sharp *thud*. She whimpered, clutching the edge for support as Vesryn advanced on Cillian, his eyes blazing with fury. "Did you really think I would not taste you on her lips?" Vesryn snarled, his voice a dangerous whisper. His fingers wrapped around Cillian's throat, squeezing ruthlessly. "Did you think I would not sense the bond you dared return under my nose?"

Cillian clawed at the elf's arm, his face draining of color as Vesryn's grip tightened. "Do you even understand your place here?" Vesryn continued, his tone dripping with venom. "Clearly not, if you have been meeting with my dear Margot at every opportunity. Now, I am left to clean up the mess you have made —and believe me, it will not be pleasant for her. You will regret your choices, Cillian. I shall see to it personally. Now, get out of my sight."

Vesryn released his grip, and Cillian gasped for air, greedily drawing it into his starved lungs. He steadied himself, a flicker of defiance in his eyes as if on the verge of retorting—or worse—but he snapped his mouth shut, biting back whatever words had risen to his tongue. With a look that could have sliced through steel, he glared at the elf before turning on his heel and storming out, the door slamming behind him with resounding finality.

Vesryn's mouth formed a thin line as he turned to Margot.

"It is clear you have learned nothing." He grabbed her shoulder and shoved her into the hallway. "Discipline is not innate. One either adapts or they die. So, now, I must teach you, because dying is not an option."

Margot lurched forward as Vesryn's nails bit into her shoulder, sending a sharp jolt through her body. She jerked involuntarily, and the elf shoved her onto the cold limestone floor. She gazed up at him, tears brimming in her eyes, silently pleading for him to reconsider. The thought of enduring his version of discipline sent a shiver of dread down her spine. She may not remember what happened to her, but she knew what she looked like after he got hold of her and knew she didn't want to face it again.

"You disobeyed me on more than one occasion. You *will* learn to obey."

Air whistled sharply in and out of Margot's nostrils as she struggled to catch her breath, each inhale a battle against the tightness in her chest. Her lungs burned with the effort, her vision blurring at the edges as she fought through the fear to stay conscious. Vesryn, lording over her, merely stared with a detached boredom that sent a chill down her spine. His eyes, cold and unfeeling, betrayed no hint of the cruelty lurking beneath the surface.

Margot's heart pounded erratically, her pulse a frantic rhythm echoing in her ears. She knew that the longer she defied him, the graver the consequences would be. Her body trembled, but she forced herself to meet his gaze, desperate to find some flicker of mercy. There was none. Vesryn's expression remained impassive, almost as if he were growing weary of the entire ordeal.

A faint whimper escaped her lips as she realized the futility of resistance. Vesryn's patience was a fragile thing, and it had worn thinner and thinner with each passing moment. His presence loomed like a dark cloud, suffocating and inescapable. Her mind raced, searching for a way out, but there was none—only the cold, hard truth that she was at his mercy.

Every instinct screamed at her to submit, to do whatever it took to end this torment, but that stubborn part of her that never kept quiet refused to surrender entirely. But even that part had simmered. What had once felt like a roaring flame was now nothing more than a flickering ember.

He tilted his head slightly, the gesture almost lazy, as if deciding whether she was worth any more of his precious time. The silence between them stretched thin, a taut string ready to snap at the slightest provocation. Her breath hitched, the air catching in her throat as she braced herself for whatever cruel punishment he had in store. She knew one thing for certain: nothing good would come if she continued to defy him, and yet the thought of submitting entirely filled her with despair.

Vesryn finally sighed, a long, drawn-out exhalation that seemed to echo in the oppressive stillness. He stepped closer, his shadow falling over her like a shroud, and sheer panic kept her rooted in place. "Follow me," he commanded. "Stay on your knees."

She felt his voice, smooth and cold as iron, whispering against her mind. She didn't dare look up at him. Instead, she stifled a sob, got on all fours, and crawled after him.

Vesryn held the door to his office open. "Get in. Now."

Margot had to force her shaking limbs to move. Once inside, her eyes darted around the dimly lit room, the only source of light coming from a single flickering candle on his desk. Shadows danced along the walls, muttering to one another, as if they knew what was about to happen.

The door creaked closed. The lock clicked. Blood rushed to her ears at the sound of Vesryn's slow and measured steps. He rounded his desk, rummaged through the drawer, and pulled out a long piece of jute rope.

"Stand up."

Margot wobbled to her feet. Her knees and shins were raw from crawling across the floor. The pain almost diverted her attention from how awful and humiliated she felt. Even worse, she wanted to beg Vesryn, to tell him he could do whatever he wanted to her so long as he let her go. But that wasn't an option. She wouldn't give him an ounce of satisfaction.

The elf circled her, studying her with calculated discernment. She could feel him on her skin, mapping out the sinuous curves of her body. A shiver ran down her spine as memories of what happened in her bedroom flashed through her mind. He wanted her. That much was clear. It was also probably the reason he wanted her to distance herself from Cillian. But what if she didn't want him? Did that really matter when he could make her want him?

"Strip," he said. His command was cold and detached.

Margot hesitated. Her hands instinctively moved to cover her body. Fortunately, she had full control of her faculties at the moment. Vesryn wrapped the rope tightly around his hand. She knew it was only a matter of time before he simply took what he wanted. So what good was it to defy him?

She untied the dress and shimmied out of it, wishing she couldn't feel his eyes on her. Her throat tightened as a sob worked its way up. Why didn't she make Cillian leave? She should have pushed harder. Now, she was standing in the middle of Vesryn's study, vulnerable and exposed.

The elf closed in, rope in hand. "Turn around."

Margot obeyed. Goosebumps dotted her skin as his breath spread across the expanse of her back. With a jerk, he moved her shoulders back, aligned her arms with her spine, and tightly bound her wrists together.

"On your knees and spread your thighs."

She couldn't stop tears from falling as she struggled to lower herself to the ground. Once there, she shifted one leg at a time, giving the elf a solid view of her sex. She couldn't decide what was worse, being humiliated like this or being powerless.

"Spread them farther apart," he said.

The strain of her groin made her whimper. Vesryn hummed, clearly pleased with this position, and tied her ankles and thighs in such a way that prevented her from closing them before connecting the end of the rope with her wrists.

"As I told you before, Cillian is not to be trusted." Vesryn admired his handiwork. "Why have you been consorting with him?"

"I d-don't k-know," she stammered through sniffles.

Vesryn gripped her cheeks, squeezing them together so hard

her lips looked like a fish. "Why do you continue to defy my orders?"

"I-it's just a fa-fa-feeling I g-get."

The elf pushed her away, muttering something under his breath. She flinched as he lifted his hand. A stream of magic emanated from his fingertips, and he placed them against her chest. Waves of warmth radiated through her sternum, and she sank into a deep stillness, her breathing shallow and eyes unblinking.

He put two slender fingers in her mouth. "Suck."

Unthinking, Margot hollowed her cheeks and swirled her tongue around the tips. Vesryn smirked, pulling them out with a pop. Her eyelids drooped as he tilted her head back and opened her mouth. A long string of saliva dripped down her throat. Her tongue darted along her bottom lip, licking up every drop.

The elf knelt and petted her head. "Good girl."

Margot's head lolled, and her muscles relaxed further as Vesryn continued smoothing her hair.

"Your love for me is strong, Margot," he said, his tone a melodic lilt. "No one can interfere with how fiercely you love me. You will stay by my side, no matter what."

"Yes Vesryn," Margot said.

"I am always right."

"Yes Vesryn."

"I know best."

"Yes Vesryn."

"You will never go against me."

"Yes Vesryn."

The elf pressed his hand to her chest once more. Lust, desire, need, love—these feelings flooded her. It was like she had forgotten about life's deepest pleasures, and trivial pursuits could distract her no longer because the only thing that mattered was Vesryn. Finally, finally! She knew what she had to do.

"Do you want to show me how much you love me?" he asked.

She panted. Her clit hardened and a gush of liquid pooled beneath her, leaving her impossibly damp. "More than anything."

Vesryn snapped his fingers, and her bindings disappeared. She scrambled to her feet and unhooked the clasps of his robe before sliding the garment down his shoulders, displaying his powerful yet slim body.

Her fingers trailed his tight muscle, tracing the swell before she dropped back to her knees, taking his length in her mouth. She moaned as her head bobbed and her tongue explored every inch of his silky shaft. Her fingers closed around him, pumping the flesh in time with the movements of her head.

His intoxicating scent of juniper berries and mint consumed her, making her wetter. She desperately wanted him to touch her, but this was about him. She needed to show him how much she loved him.

Tangling his fingers in her hair, he fucked her hot, wet mouth with unabated vigor. She gripped his inner thigh. He groaned and his cock twitched. He was close, and she wanted nothing more than to taste him. She slid her hand up his smooth skin to feel his balls tightening. Vesryn grunted, slamming her head to the base of his shaft until, finally, he spilled his salty seed. Greedily, she gulped it down and grinned, letting him ease out of her.

Margot panted softly as she watched Vesryn clothe himself. He ran his finger up her chest and neck before resting the tip gently on her chin.

He cocked his head, giving her a placid smile. "You really are a good girl."

She preened. Being good to him was essential, an intrinsic desire which drove her. She sat nude on the floor, waiting patiently for the elf to guide her. He chuckled and floated across the room, taking a seat behind his desk.

He pointed to the chair across from him. "Take a seat, Margot. We have much to discuss."

Margot reached for her dress, but Vesryn shook his head,

looking pleased. Though she was chilled, if he wanted her to remain nude, she would. Delighting him was a priority.

He set an ancient-looking tome in front of her. "I have not forgotten about your lessons. Before you learn to control your magic, you must first learn where it comes from." He tapped the book. "This text discusses the history of Elandra's Veil, more commonly known as the Mana Weave, in depth. Primordial forces of Faerie gifted this to our kind during the dawn of elven civilization. To understand this would mean to understand our deep connection to natural elements."

Margot hesitated, hovering a hand over the book before carefully opening the cover. Her finger trailed an elegant script, frowning when she found it to be written in a language she couldn't read. Vesryn placed his hand on top of hers and guided her finger along a sprawling sentence.

"Calenon," he said. "The first language."

Though nervous about her magic, her longing to learn from Vesryn overpowered any fear or trepidation she felt. He was a veritable well of knowledge, and if she behaved, he would bestow all he knew. Her lips tugged at the corners.

"The more you learn about Elandra's Veil, the more control you will have over your magic." He dragged his nail up and down her arm. "You can shape magic to your will, drawing it from the world around you."

Her eyes widened, and she looked up at Vesryn. "Teach me to read this so I can learn."

The elf chuckled, eyes glinting. "Learning to read Calenon would take a century. For now, I shall read it to you. Come. Sit on my lap."

"B-but can't you just do what you did before?"

"I could," Vesryn smirked, "but this is more fun, no?"

Margot bit her lip, feeling heat creeping up her neck, and nodded. She straddled his legs, pressing her back against his chest. He reached around her and turned the book toward him as he rested his chin on her shoulder.

"There are four primary elements. Earth, air, water, and fire," he said as he lazily stroked her inner thigh with his free hand, going higher and higher until he made it to her warm center. "Elemental affinity is a fundamental aspect of our magical identity. Without understanding this, we could not master our magic. Are you following along, Margot?"

He gathered wetness and pushed two fingers inside. She gasped, only managing a moan of agreement as he worked her.

"Good," he said, licking her earlobe. "Few elves master two or more elements. Then there is you, the chosen recipient of Ilphas' magic. You, my dear, have an affinity with all four primary elements. This makes you special. As you learn to perfect your craft, you will commune with deities, or so one hopes."

Margot struggled to follow along as he added a third finger, causing her to arch against him.

"Elves are directly connected to the world, Margot." He thrust his fingers deeper, pumping faster. "Nature itself is an extension of the elven race—creation *and* destruction. That power you have... is why you will be my queen, and together, we will take back Faerie."

His voice had dipped to a low rumble, and he massaged a spot inside her that made her toes curl. Every word he spoke dripped with power and authority, captivating her further, making her wetter, hotter.

"Vesryn," she said with a whimper.

"Yes?"

"Please, I..."

"Tell me you will be my queen, Margot. Queen of Elven Kind." His fingers moved even more frantically. "Say I am your king."

She moaned. "Please."

"Say it!"

He rubbed her clit furiously with the thumb of his other hand. Her body shook, and she gasped for air. She couldn't even hold her head up any longer as she luxuriated in each wave that crashed into her.

"You're my king! You're mmf kinf."

Vesryn's hand clamped over her mouth, muffling her orgasmic cries as she convulsed on his lap. Somehow, he pulled his cock free without her noticing and pushed into her with one hard stroke. She whimpered and lifted her arms behind her to wrap them around his neck, letting him pump into her from a better angle. To feel him inside her, to feel his heat, it made her mind feel like jelly. She closed her eyes, feeling complete.

"You are mine, Margot." He grunted and slammed into her. "*My* queen. No one else shall have you."

Vesryn groaned as he came, filling her to the brim. His magic enveloped her like a cocoon. She shuddered. He gripped her chin, turning her head to capture her lips in a heated kiss. She drank in his passionate moans as his cock softened.

"I will take you further than you have ever been," he said. His breath puffed against her ear. "You will be the most powerful elf, and all we need is time. Tomorrow, you will learn about Ancestral Memory. Rest now. Clean yourself up, my queen."

Margot nodded, sliding off his lap, and grabbed her dress from the floor. Dizzy and disoriented, she walked back to her chamber. Her thighs were sticky, and she could still feel his seed, the sensation stirred by the gentle sway of her hips.

"Margot?"

Her brow furrowed, and she turned around, finding herself staring at Cillian. The painful expression smeared across his face scratched at her heart, but she didn't understand why.

"Are you okay?" he asked and reached out for her.

"Why wouldn't I be?" She sidestepped his hand. "I'm to be a queen."

Silver eyes blinked back tears. "You... you agreed to this?" His throat bobbed. "You agreed to this of your own free will?"

"Of course I did! Vesryn is a kind and benevolent king. It is an honor and a privilege to be his queen."

"Please come back to me." His voice was hoarse, and his chest heaved.

Margot pinched her brows together. "Why would you say such things? I don't even know you."

"Don't do this, Margot."

"I really need to be on my way. Busy busy. You know how it is. Also... please don't say these things anymore. It... it messes with my head."

She gave him one last look before turning on her heels. A lonely ache coiled around her heart, and she walked back to her room with her shoulders hunched.

FAINT PULSE

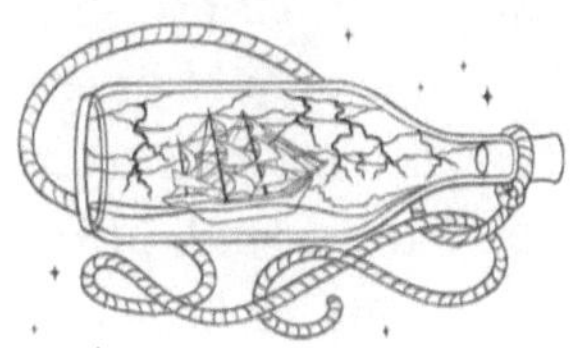

I'm going to fucking kill that elf.

Cillian leaned against the wall, trying to calm himself down. He could fucking smell the bastard on her. Vesryn knew exactly what he was doing, too. Knew that this was a surefire way to get rid of the wicked demon once and for all. Unlike Margot, he wasn't numb to the bond, which was very much still there. And slowly but surely, the bond would kill him. Every time he had to see Margot with Vesryn or smell him on her, another piece of his soul would fade.

He should have left.

Why didn't he leave?

He was grasping at straws, tormenting himself with these redundant questions. Dying didn't scare him—he had started wars and led armies into the heart of battle. He had laughed in Death's face and emerged victorious, living to tell the tale each time. But the thought of leaving Margot? That was a terror that shook him to his core. It was a fate far worse than death, a torment that would sear his soul and char his bones with the unbearable heat of a thousand suns, burning him for all eternity.

Leaving Margot wasn't an option.

"Vesryn is a kind and benevolent king." He rolled his eyes. "Don't make me laugh."

Cillian crossed his arms and looked at the ceiling. Something was wrong with her. Something worse than what Vesryn had already done to her. That woman he saw wasn't *his* Margot; that woman was a specter living in his bloodsworn's body. He couldn't even feel her. Within hours, the elf had shattered her completely, and it was Cillian's fault. He should have endured this burden, laid low, and listened for the shadows to talk. Now it would be that much harder to leave this island. Now he had to figure out what exactly the elf had done to her and if it was possible to unravel that magic.

Unraveling magic wasn't something Cillian had a proclivity for, but his time in Faerie had given him a basic understanding of how this land's powers had worked. Hardly enough information to pick apart what was sure to be some kind of ancient ritual, though, which meant he had work to do.

"Loitering in the hallway, are we?"

Cillian gritted his teeth and glanced at Corym, who had presumably just emerged from his quarters. Inconvenient, but not the worst interruption he could imagine. He made a mental note to avoid this area in the future.

"Looking for another reason to torture me? Is standing here off limits, too?"

The elf's expression soured. "I thought we were past this... look, I'm very good at my job, but I don't enjoy it. By our very nature, elves seek peace, me included."

"Peace? Is that what you call it when Vesryn orders you to flay me alive?" Cillian snorted. "That sure looked like peace to me."

"Watch your tongue," Corym warned, his hand drifting to the pommel of his sword.

"Why?" Cillian shrugged nonchalantly. "I've seen the beginnings of madness before. Was there an actual reason I was sent from the training hall last night? Or was it just so Vesryn could show Margot who's really in charge?"

The elf flinched at the accusation, quickly masking his reaction. *Interesting. So, he's aware that Vesryn is slipping.*

"You know nothing of our struggles," Corym shot back, but his voice lacked its usual conviction. "And as for why you were cut from training... that had nothing to do with me. You know very well I acknowledge your skill in battle."

"Ah, cut from training? Thought it was just for the night. What a shame." Cillian didn't need to know the intricate details of the elves' situation to extract the information he needed. He had a strong hunch that Corym wasn't exactly pleased with the path Vesryn was steering the elves down. If Vesryn's right-hand man was having second thoughts, Cillian wagered that unrest was likely brewing among the other elves as well. "Everyone knows the elves live in an acephalous society—you've never had a leader. Yet I see servants scuttling throughout this house, and it appears Vesryn has taken to calling himself king. I think I know enough."

"Vesryn has never called himself king. He knows the importance of maintaining our society, which allows all elves to thrive. Those that serve this manor chose to be here; they weren't forced." Corym gestured with his hand as if this were obvious. "As I said, we are peaceful."

"Then why resort to torture? Surely a group of elves as peaceful as yourselves could have found some other way to deal with the issue."

"You know why!" Corym snapped. "Even if Margot was less important, bonding with a human... what were you thinking? If her magic had manifested with the bond intact..." He shook his head. "The circumstances were dire and required drastic measures to be taken."

Cillian ignored the slight and pushed off the wall, taking a step toward the elf. "Why is Margot so important?"

Corym paled and averted his gaze. "I'm done with this conversation. There are fresh sweet rolls in the kitchen. I suggest you get some before Vesryn catches wind that you've been sniffing around." The elf was about halfway down the hall when he looked over his shoulder. "I doubt you'll receive punishment for what has happened but do yourself a favor and keep your distance from her for now."

Cillian gave the elf a curt nod and watched him disappear upstairs. *For now, huh?* He didn't know what game Corym was playing, but he tucked that bit of information away for later and headed toward the kitchen. Sweet rolls sounded pretty good right about now.

An elf gripped the basket of baked goods tightly as Cillian entered the kitchen. Flour dusted her cinnamon skin in uneven patches, and her light pink eyes narrowed with a mix of caution and surprise. He could smell the anxiety wafting off her, a subtle scent that kept his awareness keen. Taking slow, deliberate steps toward her, he noticed her knuckles whiten as she tightened her grip on the wicker basket. Their past interactions had been brief and cordial, but he knew his sudden intrusion into her domain was unnerving. His presence was often unsettling to the inhabitants of this world, but years of being shunned or feared had taught him to cultivate a careful charm—no easy feat for a demon from Olvath.

He splayed his palms in front of him and smiled, flashing pearly white teeth. "Just here for the sweet rolls," he cajoled. "Would you mind if I had a few? I'm feeling rather peckish."

Setting the basket down on the counter, she wiped her hands on her olive apron and nodded as she placed two large, sweet rolls on a plate and set the dish on the table in the corner.

"Thank you," Cillian said and took a seat.

As he ate, the elf moved about the kitchen with ease, letting go of—or ignoring—the fear that gripped her moments ago. She removed a few canisters from a shelf and measured dried herbs and leaves before placing them inside an infuser, which she latched closed, and put inside a teapot full of hot water.

"Tea?" she asked. "Goes well with the rolls."

Cillian grinned. "That would be great, thanks."

After a few minutes, she placed a steaming cup of murky

brown liquid in front of him. He raised the cup to his nose, sniffed, and took a sip. A sigh slipped past his lips, and a grimace stretched across his face.

"Something wrong with the tea?" she asked.

"Yes."

The elf placed her hands on her hips and cocked an eyebrow. "And what, exactly, is wrong with it?"

"You burned it, but that's not even the worst part. The ratios of your blend are all off. I don't even need to drink this to know that it's bitter, and the taste of ash probably lingers on the back of the tongue long after the brew has left your mouth. Just look at this color. It's all wrong."

Cillian was being unnecessarily rude, but if there was one thing he couldn't stand, it was poorly made tea. Though he would be lying if he said he wasn't worried about the elf taking back the rolls. Unlike the tea, those were good.

"And you can do better?"

He looked at her and shrugged. "Not sure what ingredients you have to work with, but yeah. Probably."

"Then, by all means," she said as she gestured to the kitchen.

Cillian's eyes widened. He wasn't expecting the elf to give him access to her space but was grateful. Brewing tea was one of life's simple pleasures and his favorite hobby. The repetitive nature of the task was soothing and helped rid his mind of negative thoughts. If he could get this one little thing back, maybe it would help him survive, giving him more time to figure out how to help Margot.

He inspected the containers she had pulled out and pinched the bridge of his nose. The plants here would work to make a decent cup, but it wouldn't be great.

"Do you have any edible flowers? Dried, preferably. Fresh will work, too, in a pinch."

"Flowers in tea?" She placed another container on the counter next to the others. "All I have are fresh flowers. I typically use them to garnish dishes... but never use them in tea."

"If what you served me today is how you usually make tea, it wouldn't matter if you had flowers at all." The elf glared at Cillian, but he ignored her and pressed on. "Dried flowers concentrate the delicate floral flavor and can handle being steeped at higher temperatures than fresh ones. However, if you steep any of these ingredients for too long, they'll burn because they're so fragile, creating a deep and bitter flavor profile."

Cillian portioned everything out, including the flowers. His index finger tapped the counter absently. After a few moments, he turned to the elf.

"Do you have sunmint?"

She placed another container on the counter. "I can't possibly see how this is going to be good."

Sunmint on its own could be overwhelming. The plant was typically used medicinally, but if used sparingly when brewing, the bright taste complimented the botanical flavor nicely.

Cillian packed the infuser and let it rest on the counter as he heated clean water in the teapot. When he heard the water roiling, he immediately took the pot off the heat.

"Why don't you place the infuser inside while heating?"

"I already told you; the plants will burn."

Cillian waited about two and a half minutes and removed the infuser. Then he poured two cups of tea. The resulting brew was far different from what the elf had made. Pale beige, completely transparent, and lightly scented; the tea was perfect. He sat back down and pointed to the seat across from him, and the elf followed.

"Taste it," he said.

She took a sip and grinned. "We haven't been formally introduced. I'm Tahlsia."

"Pleasure to meet you. I'm Cillian."

"Oh, I know who you are. We all do." She took another sip. "I wanted to apologize for my reaction earlier. I wasn't expecting anyone to come to the kitchen."

"No offense taken. I'm sure being a demon didn't help much, either."

"I can't say it helped much, no. Though I would like to know how one from Olvath acts so... well, for lack of a better term, refined. For all the tales we've heard about demons, I expected you to behave like a wild animal."

"Fifty years ago, I probably *would* have acted like a wild animal."

Tahlsia's eyes widened. "You've been in Faerie for fifty years?"

"Closer to fifty-seven, but who's counting?" he said with a waggle of his eyebrows.

"Then... how?"

"I believe many of my instincts have a connection to Olvath. Being in Faerie this long has dulled them. At least that's what I think happened."

Another servant entered the kitchen but immediately left upon spotting Cillian. Tahlsia offered a sympathetic smile.

"They'll come around in time," she said.

"Can't say I want to be here to find out. My time here hasn't exactly been enjoyable."

The elf winced. She must have known what had happened to him. All the elves probably knew. The ones serving this house definitely did. It was difficult to hide wrongdoing when confined to such a space. A fact that made him slightly more uncomfortable.

"It wasn't always like this, you know. When Ilphas died... Vesryn took it the hardest and took it upon himself to try taking his place."

Cillian leaned forward. "And what place was that?"

Tahlsia cleared her throat and stood. "I've said too much. Would you like some rolls and tea to go?"

Damnit. So close.

"That would be great."

She packed a burlap sack and thermos and handed them to

him. "As long as you clean up your mess, I don't mind if you use the kitchen to prepare tea. It was nice speaking with you, Cillian."

"You too, Tahlsia."

He took the goods and headed back to his quarters.

Tahlsia seemed like she knew more than she was letting on. Befriending her could only benefit Cillian. He bet most of the servants here knew what was really going on, and he needed to figure out how to use that to his advantage, and quickly. There really was no telling how long Vesryn had until he completely unraveled.

As Cillian reached the top of the landing, he glanced at the spot where he last spoke to Margot. The hallway felt like it was closing in on him. Claustrophobia gnawed at his chest. He stumbled, using the wall for support as he inched down the hall.

Going to need something a little stronger than tea to get through this nightmare.

Making it to his door, he rested his hand on the knob when muffled voices drew his attention. Curiosity got the better of him, and he sneaked as quietly as a man his size could and flattened himself outside the room where he heard Corym speaking.

"This is a horrible idea, Vesryn."

"Horrible?" Vesryn laughed. "This is our best shot."

"Best shot at what, exactly? The other elves won't go for this, and you know it."

"Who cares what the others think? A human cannot be trusted with that kind of power. This plan ensures we gain control of what is rightfully ours."

"How?"

"Simple. I impregnate her and ensure she transfers her magic to the babe."

Cillian's heart sank as he listened to the callous elf. Margot, the heart of his heart, reduced to nothing more than a means to an end. He clenched his fists. Anger and pain swirled inside him like a tempest. This was not a fate she deserved, but there was no way for him to stop this now. He was just one against many. While he had fought worse odds, never against elves.

"And what do you plan on doing with her after she gives birth?" Corym asked. "Send her back to Earth?"

"Why go through all that trouble when we can just kill her?"

Cillian tried to steady his breathing. Taking the elves on alone was out of the question. He needed to bide his time and endure. Hopefully, he could get through to Margot. The bond was still there; he felt it. He just needed to wait.

"As I've said, this is a horrible plan."

"Do you not trust me?"

Corym said nothing.

"No matter," Vesryn said. "It appears I must deal with a nuisance."

Footsteps shuffled, and Cillian's eyes widened. He backed away and hurried toward his room. The door flew open. Vesryn stood there. Fury flared within his wild eyes.

"What are you doing, demon?"

Cillian shrugged and raised the sack of sweet rolls. "Was hungry. Is the kitchen off limits?"

Vesryn's nostrils flared as he invaded Cillian's personal space. "I should kill you where you stand for taking that tone with me, not to mention all that you have done to Margot."

What *he* had done to Margot? This elf was delusional.

"I didn't know," he said as he held Vesryn's gaze, unflinching. "Won't happen again. Sorry."

The elf stepped closer until the tip of his nose nearly touched Cillian's chin and grabbed Cillian by the collar.

"Do you smell her on me? Is it not sweet?" Vesryn bared his teeth. "She loved every second. Never once did she call your name or think of you. I would know." A sinister curl twisted his lips. "I am in her head."

Cillian's muscles tensed, hands fisting at his sides. Vesryn pushed him back—though he didn't budge—and jerked his head down the hall. "Get out of my sight."

Corym avoided eye contact as Cillian glared at him before he left for his room.

He sat on the corner of the bed, taking deep breaths, trying to quell the anger. Vesryn couldn't be allowed to get the best of him. He needed to remain calm so he could focus on Margot. She needed him now more than ever and she didn't even know.

He sighed and took a sip of tea. Though his assigned room was rather bare, the few pieces of furniture that decorated it were garish. They were made of white stone, intricately carved with elves clad in tawdry-looking garb, sitting on thrones with subjects worshipping their feet. Motifs of a time long ago when only elves ruled the lands.

Cillian missed his ship and the cozy cabin with furniture he crafted himself. He poured his heart and soul into making those pieces. Then, when Margot showed up, it had finally felt like home. Gods, he missed her. He missed the way she smelled and the sound of her voice. He missed her velvet skin and lust-filled looks. She made him feel alive again, and it had been so long since he felt that way.

Deciding there was nothing left for him to do now, he opened the burlap sack. Inside were not only sweet rolls, but a folded piece of parchment. He popped one into his mouth as he unfurled the note and read.

When the moons are at their zenith and the birds have ceased their chirping, meet me two floors down, last door on the right.
-Tahlsia

Perhaps he wouldn't have to handle this alone after all. Admittedly, he was surprised to receive something like this so soon. Maybe Vesryn's spiral had been a long time coming and the elves were tired of it. Even Corym seemed tired of it.

Cillian held the note in his hand, committing the request to memory before holding it over a candle, turning it to ash. *Leave no evidence.* Vesryn was smart, and he wouldn't put it past the elf to ransack his room whenever an opportunity struck.

He stretched out, relaxing in his bed. It was barely midday—

he had hours to kill before he met with Tahlsia. When there was nothing to do, time crawled. Patience wasn't a skill he thought he needed to hone. He was a man of action. Not a man who sat around, twiddling his thumbs.

Margot, can you hear me?

Nothing but silence.

Heart of my heart, I need you to come back to me.

If he kept trying, maybe he could get through to her. All she needed was to remember. Elf magic was powerful, but not stronger than a blood bond. Vesryn could lock away her memories and make her bend to his every whim, but eventually, the bond would win. *Probably why he's so desperate to get rid of me.* Having the bond slowly kill Cillian was the best way to ensure Margot remained ensnared. If Vesryn were to kill him, there was always a risk she would remember who she was, and the elf couldn't have that.

He brushed the thoughts away and closed his eyes. In the back of mind, his end of the bond pulsed crimson, beating with life as if it had a heartbeat of its own. Further down the line was Margot's, dusty, grey. Nearly dead. Hers remained still even as he tried to revive it. The bond was hanging by a thread and was the most painful thing he had ever experienced. He would spend an eternity being tortured if he knew she was alive and well. He *needed* to bring her back.

Eyes still closed, he raised his arm and rested his palm against the wall behind the bed. Beyond the wall, Margot was right there. He knew she was. His imagination ran rampant, conjuring hundreds of ghosts in Margot's image. Each showed a different emotion. A smile tugged at the corners of his lips as he watched them all. He doubted she knew how expressive she was. One showed her straining as she hoisted a sail all on her own, her small frame trembling against its weight. Another, her pale blue eyes wide, biting her bottom lip as he admired the curves of her bare body. She was beautiful. He wanted to show her how beautiful she was every day for as long as they were given.

With one hand on the wall, he let the other wander. Palming his cock through his leathers, he thought of Margot in his shirt, the swell of her breasts showing with berry pink nipples peeking out. He pushed her against the wall, locking her in. She wasn't scared this time, and she wrapped her thighs around his waist, letting him hoist her up. Desire burned within her gaze. Settling into the bed, he groaned as he unlaced his leathers and stroked himself.

Nimble fingers tangled in his hair, tugging, pulling him into a desperate kiss. Their tongues moved together flawlessly, as if they'd had lifetimes to practice. He savored her taste. She slid her hand between their bodies and freed his cock. She opened her thighs wider, granting him access to what he needed, and he thrust himself inside.

Margot.

Repeatedly, he slammed into her, rocking his hips to a rhythm of his own design. The way she clenched around him was exquisite, far too good for him to control his form. He didn't want to scare her, but this was out of his hands. A mighty roar tore from his throat as his limbs elongated and his body bulked up. Horns sprouted from his head just as his cock doubled in size. Her scream turned into garbled moans as he fucked her.

She threw her head back, arching her spine as he roughly massaged her breasts and nipped at her neck. His name slipped past her lips, a blessing and a plea, as she rode out waves of pleasure. He leaned forward, pressing his mouth to hers, and bucked his hips. She gripped his horns like the reins of a horse and rode him faster.

That's it, he said with a growl. *Come for me, beautiful.*

He fisted his cock, pumping furiously, but all he felt was her. Her smell, her taste, her scent—it consumed him. Whatever this was, it was real, vivid, unlike anything he ever experienced. It made him feel less alone.

She was close, but he wanted more time. Slowing his pace, he pulled out and kissed her softly. He stroked her tenderly as his pelvis rolled in circles, the head of his cock brushing against her clit. He filled his hands with her breasts, pinching and pulling her nipples, drawing out whimpers he only dreamed of hearing.

Her thighs clenched around him, holding on as she arched her back again to coax him into her. He licked up the column of her neck before thrusting deep, rasping his teeth against her shoulder.

Come for me. Let me give you what you need.

He slammed into her, feeling himself swell. Her thighs strummed against him, her muscles contracted, and she let out a strangled cry as he filled her.

Feeling his balls tighten, he gripped his cock tighter and groaned before coming all over his hand.

Beads of sweat dotted her forehead as she rested against his chest. He wanted to stay like this for eternity, with her by his side. She panted, hanging limp against him, and his demon form disappeared in a puff of smoke. She slid down his body, and he stood in front of her. Just a man. She flashed him a dazzling smile. He couldn't stop himself from returning one of his own.

Margot, he said, reaching out.

Margot's smile faltered, and she stepped out of the way of his hand, choking with a sob. Her eyes darted around the cabin he had recreated in his mind, lines of confusion etched on her face. She stumbled, trying to get away from him, and then she vanished.

Emptiness flooded Cillian as the vivid dream faded around him, dissipating like a morning mist. All that was left was their broken bond. He ran a finger along it, wishing it were whole. And out of the corner of his eye, he saw the end of Margot's bond pulse faintly, but that was more than enough.

His eyes flew open, and he grinned.

2 8

THREE SISTERS

MARGOT GASPED AWAKE, her body trembling and slick with sweat. The sheets clung to her skin as she tried to calm her racing heart. *That dream...* She pressed her palm to her chest, willing away the sharp ache that had taken root.

She shouldn't have dozed off, not after being with Vesryn, but exhaustion had claimed her the moment her head hit the pillow. Now she lay there, core still throbbing from a dream that felt more real than fantasy. Those silver eyes haunted her, filled with such profound sadness as she'd slipped from his grasp. It was the same look he'd given her in the hallway—like watching her physically pained him.

"Why would he look at me that way?" she whispered into the dim room. That wasn't the gaze of a mere guard toward his charge. It was the look of a lover watching his heart break.

Horror crawled up her throat. What had she done? Here she was, destined to be queen, yet dreaming of another man. The very thought was treasonous. If Vesryn discovered her unconscious desires... She shuddered. Even a king's favor could turn to ice when faced with such betrayal.

With trembling fingers, she reached for the hand mirror on her nightstand. The face that greeted her was both familiar and

329

foreign—delicately pointed ears, luminescent skin that seemed to glow from within, eyes an impossible shade of blue like captured lightning.

"Am I truly fit to become queen?" she asked aloud. She tried to remember what she'd looked like before, but those memories slipped through her grasp like smoke, leaving only certainty that she was an elf now. Perhaps even an elf worthy of holding such a title.

The mirror clattered back onto the nightstand as another bolt of pain lanced through her chest. She stumbled to the bathroom, desperate to wash away the lingering sensations of her dream. The cool marble of the counter steadied her as wave after wave of dull throbs pulsed beneath her breastbone, like a second heartbeat fighting to be heard.

A glint of parchment caught her eye as she passed her writing desk. There, atop an ancient tome, lay a folded note. But first—she grimaced at the state of her skin—she needed to feel clean again.

The hot water did little to ease the ache in her chest, but at least she felt more herself when she finally approached the desk. Her hands shook slightly as she unfolded Vesryn's letter. Heat bloomed across her cheeks as she read his words. The first part was innocuous enough—instructions about studying the companion text for tomorrow's lesson. But the postscript... Her breath caught as she read his explicit desires, the filthy promises of what he planned to do to her. Despite herself, warmth pooled low in her belly. Whatever else Vesryn might be, he knew exactly how to make her want him.

The book itself gave her pause. Its ancient pages were covered in Calenon script, completely unintelligible. But as her finger traced the first line, magic sparked to life. Golden light suffused the pages, and before her eyes, the foreign text transformed into something she could understand. Her heart quickened. She knew elves could harness the elements, but this was something else entirely—something wondrous.

Settling into her chair, Margot opened the cover and the book's pages glowed softly as she began to read, the ancient tale unfolding before her:

In the beginning, three sisters walked the empty expanse of Faerie, their footsteps leaving trails of stardust in their wake. Nidra, the youngest, burned bright with determination and an untamed spirit that set the very air ablaze. Liriel, whose beauty was said to shame the rising sun, moved with ethereal grace between her sisters. And Elandra, eldest and wisest, carried the weight of knowledge in her eyes, deep as the endless void.

Together they stood upon the barren soil of their realm and dreamed of creating something new. Something magnificent. The sisters joined hands, their powers merging as one, and from the heart of Faerie itself, they brought forth a new race.

Nidra breathed into them her fire, gifting them the will to overcome any obstacle. Liriel touched each one with gentle fingers, blessing them with grace and beauty that would rival her own. But it was Elandra who gave them their greatest gift—knowledge itself, the power to understand the very fabric of their world.

Thus the elves were born, children not of flesh but of Faerie's own essence.

The sisters spent countless years teaching their creations. Under their guidance, the elves learned to harness magic, to bend the elements to their will. Elandra showed them the paths to Ancestral Memory, ensuring their knowledge would never be lost. But as the elves grew stronger, the sisters began to withdraw. First Elandra departed, satisfied that her children had learned enough. Nidra followed soon after, called to tend other realms of Faerie.

Only Liriel remained, watching over the elves with a mother's devotion. Yet even her presence could not prevent the schism that was to come.

Discord spread through the elven people like a slow-burning flame. While some wished to remain united, others yearned to forge their own path. Liriel watched as debates turned to arguments, then to bitter feuds. She cautioned those who wished to leave, warning that separation from their kin would weaken their connection to Faerie's magic. But the call of freedom proved stronger than her words.

Those who left took on a new name—the fae. They scattered across the mainland, building gleaming cities and expanding their territories with unprecedented speed. Their numbers grew rapidly, while those who remained true to their origins struggled to bear children. The elves watched in growing despair as their own magic, the very power that made them unique, seemed to turn against them. It wreaked havoc on their bodies, making conception nearly impossible.

Liriel reached out to her sisters for answers, but even their combined wisdom could not undo what had been done. The price of such power, it seemed, was written in their very essence.

As the fae's influence grew, so too did their greed. They claimed more and more of the mainland, pushing the elves into smaller territories, treating them as lesser beings despite their shared origins. The elves endured until they could endure no more. In a single night of fury, they unleashed their power on three fae cities, reducing them to ash.

War erupted across Faerie. Fields burned, mountains crumbled, and the dead piled high on both sides. Only when Liriel could bear the bloodshed no longer did she intervene. With power that shook the very foundations of their world, she spirited the remaining elves away to a hidden isle—Caramis.

There, sheltered from the fae's expanding empire, the elves found peace at last. They built a society without rulers, where each contributed equally to their shared prosperity. And Liriel, though her heart ached for her distant sisters, remained to watch over her children, knowing that her presence was the greatest gift she could offer them.

The soft scratch of Margot's finger trailing down the final page echoed in the quiet room. She closed the book with reverent care, her mind still lost in the ancient tale. Outside her window, the sun had long since set, painting her chambers in a deep magenta glow. How long had she been reading? Hours must have passed without her notice.

A knock at her door startled her from her reverie.

"May I come in, miss?" The voice was familiar—Vesryn's maid.

"Yes, of course."

A slender elf entered carrying a covered tray, her light pink eyes bright against her delicate features. She dipped into a curtsy, somehow managing to keep the tray perfectly balanced.

"Thank you. I don't believe we were ever properly introduced. I'm Margot."

"My name is Tahlsia, miss." The elf set the tray on the small table in the sitting area, the aroma of dinner making Margot's stomach growl. She hadn't realized how hungry she'd become.

Tahlsia's lips curved into a warm smile. "Vesryn mentioned you might forget to eat. Something about a book?" She laughed softly. "In the future, feel free to visit me in the kitchen. I'd be happy to prepare something for you."

"I'd like that," Margot replied, finding herself returning the elf's infectious smile.

"Until then, Margot. Enjoy your evening."

As quickly and quietly as she'd arrived, Tahlsia slipped away, leaving Margot alone with her thoughts and the cooling dinner. She savored each bite, watching through her window as orange lights began dotting the darkening city below. The sight of Caramis at night was beautiful, but something about it left her feeling strangely hollow.

With dinner finished, Margot crossed to the window. The moonlight caught the limestone columns of the manor, casting long shadows across the grounds. She wondered what the other elves were doing now. Did they gather together in the evenings? Share meals and stories? Or were they all as solitary as she felt at that moment?

Exhaustion washed over her, and she made her way to bed. The down blanket enveloped her as she slipped beneath it, but sleep proved elusive. Every time she closed her eyes, she saw Cillian's face. The memory of his touch lingered on her skin, the way he'd filled her so perfectly...

She rolled onto her side with a frustrated sigh. This was wrong. Vesryn had shown her nothing but kindness, offered her a future beyond imagining. She had no business dwelling on thoughts of another man, especially not one meant only to guard her. Yet something about Cillian called to her, stirred something deep within that she couldn't explain.

The sheets rustled as she shifted again, trying to find comfort. Eventually, fatigue won over her troubled thoughts, pulling her into an uneasy sleep. But even in her dreams, she couldn't escape the feeling that something vital was slipping through her fingers— if only she could remember what it was.

A PROPOSITION

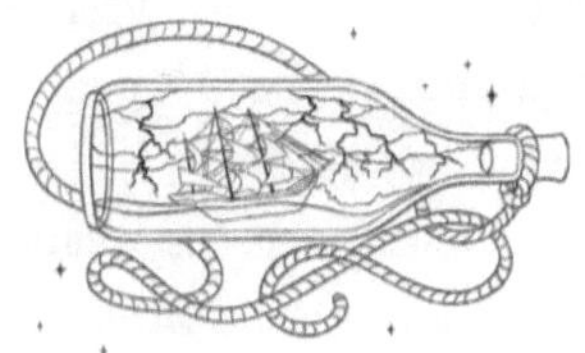

CILLIAN WRUNG excess water from his hair and shook his head like an animal before putting on fresh clothes for his meeting with Tahlsia. He ran a scarred hand down his face and looked at himself in the mirror. Dark circles hung beneath his eyes. The past few days felt like Rahiri fell from the star-studded sky, crushing him beneath its massive celestial weight. Only now could he breathe. There was a light at the end of the tunnel. Barely a pinprick, but it was there, pulsing slowly with life, humming with energy.

With a gentle tug, he pulled back the heavy velvet curtains and took in the deep, luscious hue of the night sky. Stars twinkled like jewels against the rich backdrop, illuminating Caramis below. *Not yet.*

He released the curtains and settled into a chair, drumming his fingers against the desk. One nagging question consumed his mind: why would Vesryn allow him to remain so close to Margot? Keeping him alive was one thing but granting him access to his bloodsworn made little sense. Did Vesryn want him to witness firsthand the torment he inflicted upon her? Was it some twisted form of pleasure for the power-hungry elf? The more he thought about it, the more it made sense—knowing Vesryn's insatiable desire for control, dominance, and power.

Cillian shook his head, dismissing the thought. Dwelling on Vesryn's machinations or the darkness that enveloped everything around him wouldn't do any good. Meeting with Tahlsia, however, could prove worthwhile. He wouldn't put it past her to know exactly what was going on with Vesryn. Typically, servants kept their mouths shut and their ears open, so being kind would lead him to learning what he wanted.

After a while, Cillian strapped his weapons to his body and checked the sky—two moons shone brightly above Caramis. *It's now or never.* He listened outside his door, making sure the coast was clear, then slipped into the hallway.

Cillian stuck to the shadows, letting them coat his skin like a protective veil. With light steps, he descended the first flight of stairs and entered the foyer. Before searching for the next staircase, he stilled, listening for movement. Only the sound of the crystal chandelier tinkling bounced off his eardrums. Someone had spelled the light fixture to sparkle and sway, even though there was no airflow. Living a solitary life here in Caramis hadn't stopped them from displaying their arrogance. Unlike the fae, the elves weren't particularly ostentatious, but they did like their trinkets— they liked them even more when they could show off their power in subtle ways, he had learned.

Silent minutes passed as he searched, finding what he was looking for next to the kitchen. He eased the door open and headed down into the unknown.

The hallway was cramped and dimly lit, with dust motes swirling in the stale air, dancing between the flickering sconces like they were playing a secret game. The stone floor was cracked and crumbling, each step crunching underfoot, a testament to the neglect that Vesryn had shown for his servants' quarters. Clearly, he didn't hold them in high regard if this dark, dungeon-like corridor was where they were housed despite how expansive the rest of the manor was.

Cillian stopped in front of the last door on the right and reached for the knob, but before his fingers could touch the brass, it creaked open. Two sharp, orange eyes peered through the narrow gap, staring him down with an unsettling intensity. Cillian stood there, beads of sweat forming on his brow as he met the stranger's gaze.

The eyes shifted away, and after a tense moment, Tahlsia opened the door wide, letting Cillian inside. The room was packed with elves, each one seated in tense silence and armed to the teeth with rusted blades. Cillian's instincts flared. Without hesitation, he drew his sword and dropped into a fighting stance, canines bared in a snarl. His gaze darted from elf to elf, assessing each potential threat, searching for the weakest link to strike first. Then he spotted Nym among them.

With a burst of movement, Cillian lunged at the green-eyed elf, hoisting him up by the collar with one arm, his sword pressing dangerously close to Nym's throat.

"Fancy seein' you here, drek." Nym grinned, completely unfazed.

"You spout those big, inspiring words, alluding to rebellion," Cillian hissed, his voice low and venomous. "But the moment things get messy, you shove me out and leave me in the dark. When exactly were you planning to fill me in, Nym?"

"Uhh, now?" Nym's grin didn't falter as he scratched his nose, his legs kicking lazily as he dangled in Cillian's grip. "Things got a bit tangled, ya know? Had places to be, elves to chat with."

Cillian's grip tightened, pressing the blade against Nym's throat until a thin line of blood trickled down, staining his shirt.

"No!" Tahlsia rushed between them, holding her hands open, trying to placate Cillian. "Please, we mean no harm."

"I agreed to meet *you*," Cillian snapped, his eyes never leaving Nym's. "Not them. And certainly not Nym."

"And I am here, am I not?" She hesitated for a second before placing her hand on Cillian's and guiding him to lower his weapon. "We have a proposition for you—*all* of us. Please hear us out."

After a moment of deliberation, Cillian sheathed his sword but kept one hand on the dagger at his side as he lowered Nym. He couldn't deny that he was curious about what she had to say. Judging by the size of the group, this wasn't some coalition they threw together. He even recognized some of the other elves, seeing them only in passing around the manor. They had thought about this. He nodded to Tahlsia and took the seat she offered.

She released a long, shaky breath and glanced around the room at the other elves. Many gave nods of approval while Nym tore into a roll.

"I'm just going to come out and say it: Vesryn is bringing our race to extinction, and we would like your help. Reproduction is difficult for our kind, but even more so when we are under duress. The stress on our bodies... the reproductive systems can't handle it and shut down completely."

Cillian leaned forward, resting his elbows on his knees. "You're all under duress? Corym said you were all here voluntarily."

Nym snorted, bits of chewed bread falling into his lap. "Corym's in the same boat as the rest of us. Of course he'd say that. Ya saw how he keeps his staff... just look at this room." He jabbed the half-eaten roll into the air. "He hoards resources, uses his immense power to keep us in check. He tries, and succeeds, to control us. What did ya see when you walked through Caramis, drek?"

"A few elves, some shop stalls, a few stores, a market." Cillian furrowed his brow, thinking back to his walk through the city. "Now that you mention it, there wasn't much. Especially not compared to the size of the city."

"Wasn't always like that," Nym said, brushing crumbs to the floor. "Once, Caramis thrived. There was an economy. Discreetly, we imported goods from the mainland and exported what we could. Elves were happy, thriving. More elflings were being born every year." He shrugged, tossing a hand in the air. "Then Vesryn happened, drek. Put a stop to all of it. Did ya pay for your drinks at the Flagon? 'Course not. No money. All we have is what Vesryn gives us."

"We're not free here!" the orange-eyed elf yelled.

Tahlsia shot him a look, and the elf clamped his mouth shut. She turned her focus back to Cillian. "Nym is right about all of it. And like us, Corym is trying to survive."

Cillian shook his head, swishing his hand around. "Wait, wait, wait. Let's back up so I can get a few things straight. This all started when Ilphas died? You mentioned earlier that Vesryn took his death harder than most and tried to fill his shoes."

"Curse my mouth," she muttered under her breath. "Not all elves can be trusted. One slip-up, and I would have found myself dead. Much like Ilphas did."

Cillian cocked a brow. "So, Vesryn killed Ilphas?"

She nodded. "He killed his own brother in cold blood. They were the oldest, most powerful elves amongst us, always competing with one another to see who was stronger. Ilphas thought it was all good fun, but we all saw the way Vesryn took each loss, the way it grated on him. Eventually, he had enough and killed Ilphas in his sleep. He thought he could take Ilphas' power, but Liriel stopped him, and now she's missing. If she were here... we could have done something about Vesryn a long time ago."

"Well, that explains why he is unraveling so fast... but you're saying this Liriel could stop him? Who is she?" Cillian asked even though he was more concerned with what Margot having Ilphas' magic meant. But now wasn't the time to bring that up.

"One of the three goddesses," Tahlsia explained. "She spent many lifetimes watching over us. Never once did she leave us."

"Not until Vesryn got his hands on her, too," a pale elf chirped from behind a wooden beam.

"We don't accept assumptions as fact, Edea." Tahlsia chided her. "We *assume* Vesryn has done something with the goddess."

"Surely he isn't more powerful than a deity," Cillian said.

"No, he's not. It's possible he gained one of her spell books, though. They were rumored to contain detailed information regarding divine rituals."

Cillian ran his fingers through his hair. "Do you even know if the books exist?"

"They do," Edea whispered. "Liriel documented *everything*."

"Then where are they?" Cillian scanned the faces in the room. "Have any of you looked?"

Tahlsia paced. "We have. Many times, actually, and they would be in this manor. So far, we haven't been able to locate them. But there is one room where only Vesryn can enter."

"And what room is that?" Cillian asked.

"The Grand Archive," Nym said with a grin. "But even I can't get in there. Good luck, drek."

Cillian crossed his arms and looked at the water-stained ceiling. "So, let me get this straight, Vesryn is insane, and you've all known for however long that this was the case. Then he kills his brother, and then the only one who has any hope of stopping him goes missing. Do I have this correct?"

"That's about the gist of it," Tahlsia said, picking at the skin on her bottom lip.

Cillian looked at Tahlsia, then at the rest of the elves. Desperation was in their eyes, save for Nym, who was cleaning his nails. Vesryn enslaved his own kind and forced them to live in squalor and fear. One of the few fates worse than death.

"How do I fit into this?" he asked.

"We want you to kill Vesryn," Tahlsia said, her voice barely above a whisper. "Only then can we be free."

Cillian tilted his head, eyebrows raised. The thought of ripping Vesryn to shreds was something that crossed his mind more than once but killing him would be no small feat. Especially not if he has divine power at his disposal.

"What makes you think I can kill him? You said so yourself... he still has elves on his side. I may be a demon, but I'm not unkillable."

"We know of demons and their strength," Tahlsia started. "However, we don't expect you to do this alone. Everyone in this room will fight with you, and many more of us in town will help, too. Should you agree, we will make haste in our preparations."

Cillian had never been one to shy away from a challenge, but this was different. This task would require precision. Any mistake could mean his or Margot's death.

"I won't risk Margot for a fight that isn't mine."

"As Margot's bloodsworn this *is* your fight. Vesryn's control over her is strong," Tahlsia said. "Without him dead, there is no hope of ever getting her back."

"That's not true. I can bring her back to me, but that isn't her biggest problem. Margot needs time to learn how to control her magic. Vesryn is teaching her."

Tahlsia and Nym cackled, and Cillian shot them both looks. She wiped a tear from the corner of her eye and smiled at Cillian. The rest of the elves smirked.

"Is this really the time to be laughing?"

"Sorry, but whatever Vesryn is teaching her will not help her control her magic." Tahlsia barely stifled her laugh. "Elven magic is innate. Once her magic manifests, she will know what to do. At first, she may struggle, but eventually, she will wield it flawlessly." She moved in front of Cillian. "Look, we need help. You need help. We can create diversions to give you time alone with Margot to break the hold faster, but only if you agree to help us when we call upon you. If he remains in control of her once Ilphas' powers manifest—*her* powers manifest—we'll all be dead."

Cillian stared at Tahlsia, weighing his options. If what she said was true, he could have Margot back sooner than he thought possible. But Margot was barely more than a human, and she would be smack dab in the middle of an elven civil war, possibly with powers she couldn't control very well if they manifested. If he could kill Vesryn quickly, he could leave this place with her and never look back.

Cillian steepled his fingers as he rested his arms on his thighs. "You must guarantee Margot's safety."

"That isn't something we can guarantee, you know that." Tahlsia gave him a sympathetic look. "But we will do everything within our power to ensure she is safe."

Cillian took a deep breath and let it out slowly. He couldn't believe he was doing this. For someone he'd known for such a short time, Margot had completely ensnared him. He would do *anything* to get her back. Even this.

"I'll help you, but as soon as Vesryn's dead, Margot and I get to leave. Understood?"

Tahlsia beamed with delight. "Crystal clear. We'll prepare things on our end. In the meantime, I will be in touch regarding when you can meet with Margot." She grabbed his hand and squeezed. "Thank you for this. You have no idea what this means to us. We've spent years under Vesryn's thumb. To think it will all be over soon... it's almost unimaginable."

Cillian nodded and headed towards the door. He looked over his shoulder. "Don't go making any plans yet. We still have to win."

YOU MUST BE MAD, LOVE

THE NEXT MORNING, Margot paced the room, her thoughts a chaotic whirl she couldn't escape. The dream from the night before clung to her consciousness, so vivid that she could almost believe it had truly happened. The fact that it featured Cillian instead of Vesryn gnawed at her, a troubling secret that threatened to unravel everything. If the elf ever discovered it, disaster would surely follow. There were times when it felt as though Vesryn knew everything about her—his unsettling omniscience both mesmerized and terrified her. *What if he can read my thoughts?* She shook her head, trying to banish the irrational fear, but a persistent voice in the back of her mind kept whispering that he was dangerous. Yet despite that warning, the power he wielded over her was undeniable, pulling her in like a moth to a flame.

Her body and mind belonged to Vesryn—he was her king. And soon, she would be his queen. Yesterday, he had made her feel every bit the queen she was destined to become—the way he looked at her in his study, the way his touch ignited her senses. But as much as Vesryn's presence consumed her, she couldn't shake the memory of Cillian. His gaze had burned into her, searing her soul. Where Vesryn's touch singed her skin, Cillian's had utterly incinerated her, awakening something within that had long been dormant.

Two sure knocks sounded at her door, and she gripped the edge of her vanity, fighting back the bile that curdled in her throat. Vesryn was the only one who knocked that way. *Of course he had to come now.* Quietly, she picked up a cloth square and used it to blot the sweat on her brow before willing her legs to move so she could open the door.

"May I enter?" he asked in front of the threshold with a sly smirk plastered across his face as he lifted a platter full of cream pastries, sparkling indigo juice, and vibrant fruits. "I figured we could have breakfast together, my dear."

Even the thought of eating made her stomach quiver, but she didn't want to disappoint him. She cleared her throat and swept her arm in front of her, gesturing to the table. "I'd love nothing more than to dine with you."

Vesryn sauntered past Margot, his robe brushing against her legs as he moved by, sending an involuntary shiver through her. He set the platter down with deliberate care and began to plate their food. As he reached across the table, Margot couldn't help but notice how the fabric of his robe stretched taut over his muscles, emphasizing every movement. Her cheeks warmed with realization, and she quickly averted her gaze and took her seat.

Vesryn placed the dish in front of her, his hand lingering on her shoulder as he leaned in, his breath warm against her ear. "Is everything to your liking?" he murmured, his voice a soft caress that made a flutter of nerves sweep through her.

She tilted her chin up to meet his gaze, her heart skipping a beat as their eyes locked. His amber pools simmered with an intensity that seemed to burn through her, the morning light filtering through the window behind him, casting a golden halo around his figure. In that moment, he looked otherworldly, like a god descended from the faraway planes, his presence both commanding and mesmerizing. The way the light framed him, highlighting every angle of his face, made her pulse skip.

"Yes," she replied. "Everything looks delicious."

Vesryn threaded his fingers through her cornsilk locks, letting the strands slip away before taking his seat. They ate in silence, the only sounds coming from clicking silverware and the occasional sigh that she accidentally loosed. The elf watched her intently, a faint smile playing on his lips.

"You have been quiet this morning," he said, finally breaking their solitude. "Is there something on your mind?"

His loaded question made her pause mid-bite. She set her fork down, swallowed hard, then took a sip of the bubbly juice, hoping it would calm her nerves.

"Just thinking," she said, keeping her head down. "Yesterday... yesterday was intense."

Vesryn chuckled. "Intense indeed." He walked his fingers across the table and playfully traced circles on the back of her hand. "Did you dream of me last night? Is that why you have been blushing all morning?"

Margot's face flushed, her stomach flipping as she tried to steady herself. Admitting that her dream had been of Cillian would be disastrous. The thought sent a wave of anxiety through her, afraid he might already suspect the truth. *Would he know if I lied?* His penetrating stare seemed to see straight through her, and she feared what might happen if she didn't choose her words carefully. "Yes," she whispered, glancing up at him through her lashes. "I couldn't stop thinking about our study session and... I guess I wanted more." She closed her eyes, not wanting to look at him. The rush of embarrassment that surged through her was all too real.

Vesryn curled his slender fingers around hers and squeezed. "Good. I want you to think of me always, *my queen.*"

Guilt the size of a boulder threatened to crush her. She shouldn't have lied to him. But what other choice did she have? Surely, if she told him the truth, Vesryn would punish Cillian. She didn't want the poor man to suffer any more than he had.

Forcing a smile, she pushed her regret down and cast Cillian from her mind. "I will, Vesryn. Always."

His grip on her hand tightened, making her grimace as pain shot through her fingers. He stood abruptly, the chair scraping noisily across the stone floor, the harsh sound grating against her ears. Without releasing her, he yanked her arm forward, and with his free hand, he lifted her effortlessly, pulling her onto his lap. Goosebumps dotted her flesh as he blew her hair from her collarbone so he could nuzzle the sensitive part of her neck.

"That is my elf," he said as he nipped her earlobe. "I have a surprise for you today, my queen. Follow me to my study."

Vesryn set her down and strode purposefully out of her room, never giving her a chance to decline. Left with no other options, she trailed after him on wobbly legs.

As they walked, Margot struggled to steady her breath, trying to keep her thoughts from spiraling out of control. What could he possibly have planned for her? The blend of fear and excitement rolled uncomfortably inside her, the sensation nearly overwhelming. The way he spoke to her, the way he treated her, made her feel like the most important person in the world. Yet, beneath the surface, she couldn't shake the nagging suspicion that there was something else at play—something she couldn't quite grasp but could feel lurking just out of sight.

Vesryn pushed open the door, rounded his desk, and sat. Folding his hands on top of the dark wood, he nudged his chin toward the chair across from him. "Sit."

The hairs on the back of her neck stood on ends as if someone —or something—other than Vesryn was watching her. Her eyes darted around the room, looking for the source.

"Now, dear. We do not have all day."

Margot wrung her hands together to stop them from shaking and took her seat.

"I had so much fun yesterday," he said with a Cheshire grin. "I thought we could experience it again during today's lesson."

He untangled her hands, taking one to thumb the back of her palm. "Close your eyes."

She did as her king commanded and snapped her eyes shut. Through parted lips, she could hear the quickening of her breath as yesterday's memories played in her mind. The comforting designs he painted on her skin now felt like zaps of lightning, making her part her legs involuntarily as the wetness between them grew—her body was ready before her mind had even caught up.

The door opened behind her, and the sounds of boot-clad feed shuffling around the room filled her ears. *Two people*. After a few minutes, the door opened again, but only one set of feet left the room.

"Take a look," Vesryn said as he turned her chair around and rounded his desk to stand next to her.

The blood drained from her face and limbs, leaving a lingering chill when she saw Cillian standing before her, his body bloody and bruised. Somehow, Vesryn knew what had transpired—or he assumed. She instinctively tried to jump out of her chair, but the elf crushed her fingers in a devastating grip, causing her to whimper.

"Do not move, my queen," he hissed at her, though his eyes never left Cillian. "This is what happens when someone disobeys me. Transgressions cannot go unpunished."

Her surroundings blurred as unshed tears pooled in her eyes. It made her sick to her stomach to look at Cillian like this and she jerked her head away. But Vesryn painfully grabbed her chin with his free hand, forcing her to look.

"P-please, Vesryn," she whispered, her voice cracking. Could her experience last night have been more than just a dream, or was Vesryn grasping at straws? "He didn't do anything wr-wrong."

A pained yelp slipped past her lips as Vesryn slammed her hand against the table with a sickening *thud*. "Keep your mouth shut, demon," the elf spat in response to Cillian's snarls before shifting focus to Margot. His lips brushed against her ear as he spoke. "Do you believe his thoughts pure, dear? Would you truly believe him innocent? As luck would have it, I found him prowling outside your door before we broke fast. His unsavory intentions were obvious."

The menacing tone of his voice sent icy fingers crawling up her spine. It scared her, but she was grateful Vesryn seemed unaware of what transpired in the deep recesses of her mind.

She pulled her hand twice from Vesryn's grip before he let her go, letting her stand in front of Cillian, who, despite his injuries, stood stoically with his hands clasped behind his back. As she inspected him, he didn't spare her a single glance, keeping his eyes forward like a soldier.

Margot ran her fingers through her hair and sighed. "You claim this man is to watch over me, to protect me with his life, yet this is how you treat him for *maybe* having impure thoughts?" She swallowed thickly and chose her next words carefully. "I worry, darling. If you continue to treat him poorly, what is to stop him from taking my life? Is my king a tyrant? I would like to believe you are better than that. Perhaps your feelings for me are clouding your judgment."

The muscles in Vesryn's jaw twitched as he clenched his teeth. Questioning him was out of line. While she wanted to appease the elf, some distant part of her desperately wanted to keep Cillian safe from his wrath. If she continued to sit idly by as Vesryn continued to penalize Cillian for even presumed slights, he would surely die. Standing up to Vesryn now was the least she could do to save him from unnecessary hardships.

The elf's lips twisted into a bitter smile. "You make a fair point. But I fear letting him do as he pleases will be detrimental to our kind. Punishment is required to keep the likes of *him* in line." His amber eyes narrowed. "Do not underestimate the power of demonic desire, Margot. It skews a demon's perception, rendering them unable to discern right from wrong. Thus, assumed transgressions, even ones that lack concrete evidence, must be swiftly dealt with."

Margot glanced at Cillian, who still didn't look at her. Then, it clicked, causing her breath to catch in her throat. He was an *actual* demon. Memories of his massive body, horns and all, making her feel things she couldn't have even imagined if they never happened to her, flashed through her mind. All this time, she thought Vesryn had been insulting him. But no, he *was* a demon, and perhaps her dream had been more than her imagination running rampant.

She gently took Vesryn's hands in hers and smiled. "Would it hurt to cut back on the violence, my king?" She batted her eyelashes. "I very much enjoy living and would rather not jeopardize it. What can I do to prove my loyalty so you can stop this nonsense?"

"Kiss me," he replied. "Touch me tenderly. *Show* me your love and devotion."

Blood rushed to her cheeks, and she whispered in Vesryn's ear, "In front of him, my king?"

The elf chuckled; his hot breath rolled across her skin. "Yes, my love. Show him how committed you are to me."

Margot inhaled deeply, her eyes flickering to Cillian, whose mouth was set in a tight line. She snaked her arms around Vesryn's neck, parting his lips with her tongue as her fingers tangled in his long, silky hair. Kissing the elf was like coming up for air. She needed it—she needed *him* even though she knew what he was. Malicious. Jealous. Hungry for power. None of that mattered, though. He had absolute claim of her body, but her soul... her soul belonged to another.

Passion swelled between them as Vesryn's hands roamed, leaving a scorching trail of embers wherever his fingertips touched. He gripped her bottom and pulled her closer to him, rubbing his erection against her, causing her to hiss as heat pooled between her thighs.

"Did you read the material I gave you?" he breathed, then flattened his tongue and licked up the column of her neck while he lightly circled her clit through her dress.

Afraid she couldn't speak without crying out, she nodded.

"What did you learn?" Vesryn hiked up her dress and slipped a finger between her folds, adjusting her position so Cillian could see her fully. "Something good, I hope."

She gasped as he probed her most delicate spots. "I learned we are a glorious, knowledgeable race created by the three goddesses of the before time. Th-the elves' struggles, triumphs, and their eventual seclusion from Faerie were all de-detailed in the book."

"My, my. You most certainly are the most studious queen." He nipped her earlobe. "And Ancestral Memory? Surely that was written about."

The only memory that came to her mind was the one of Cillian pressing her against a wall, taking her like a wanton woman. But she couldn't say that. Couldn't even think of it. "I-it is the way for an elf to k-keep memories of the Elven race alive even after they p-pass. Each elf holds a palace—a grandiose place filled with a memoir of the ancestor that passed their magic onto them."

Vesryn's fingers sunk further into her, his thumb circling her clit, periodically applying pressure to the bundle. "And who can access Ancestral Memory?"

She moaned, her legs quaking so much she could barely hold herself upright. "O-only the most skilled elves c-can call upon their ancient master for guidance."

"Precisely." He bit her bottom lip and worked her with fervor. Her back arched, and her head lolled. She felt him smirk against her flesh. "Has anyone ever made you feel this way before?"

His words caught her off guard, and she thought of Cillian. The way his rough hands handled her breasts, their intricate dance of teeth and tongue, the way he filled her so completely as if he had been molded just for her. Unable to hold back, an orgasm crashed into her as she writhed on top of Vesryn's hand, letting him bring her to completion as she thought of another.

He licked her clean from his fingers, making her blush as she adjusted her dress. "No, my king. No one has ever made me feel this way before." The lie made her feel hollow, and a sharp pang pierced the center of her chest. It had come from somewhere deep, but she was unable to find the source.

Cillian sniffed, drawing Margot's attention. His silver eyes glistened in the muted candlelight, like tears poised on the edge of falling. The unspoken sorrow in his gaze rippled through her, tugging at the strings of her heart, leaving her adrift in a sea of sadness and confusion.

"As my queen proved her loyalty, I expect you to protect her should she wish it to be so." A grin spread across Vesryn's face as he looked at Cillian. "Now leave. Margot and I must proceed with today's lesson."

Cillian's gaze locked with Margot's as he rested his hand on the doorknob, the intensity in his eyes igniting a deep ache within her—a longing for his touch that left her breathless. He lingered for a heartbeat longer, his presence filling the room with an unspoken promise, and then, in an instant, he was gone. The door clicked shut behind him, and with it, the fleeting warmth she had felt with him just being near had faded.

Margot stared at the spot where Cillian had stood, unable to look away. A hollowness settled in the pit of her stomach. She was broken, empty—another piece of the puzzle gone, the ending of a novel missing. Her heart was screaming, pounding against her chest, telling her this was wrong. Wrong. Wrong. So very wrong. But her mind was a blank slate. Cillian was nothing to her. He *should* be nothing to her. Yet, he meant *something*. And she couldn't quite figure out why he was so important to her.

"Where is that head at?" Vesryn's voice cut through the fog. Margot twisted around to see the elf's widening smile, a dark glint illuminating his topaz eyes. Dread consumed her. "No need to be distant when your king is right here."

Goosebumps prickled her arms. The tone of his voice was sinister, *knowing*. Her stomach lurched, but she willed herself not to quake. "I'm sorry, my king. You're right. I was just shaken up. I promise it won't happen again."

Vesryn hummed as he stepped into her space. He cocked his head to the side and dragged his fingernail up her arm, running it across her jaw until he stopped at the center of her chin. Her throat constricted as anxiety took hold. "See that it does not. Your focus should be on me and me alone." He jabbed his finger into her temple, making her eyes water. "When you are with the demon, you are to think of me. When you are alone, you are to think of me. The moment those pretty little fingers sink into your wet heat, I am the only one on your mind. Do you understand?"

He knows. He knows, and he is going to kill me.

Margot whimpered. Vesryn's touch became a scorching brand, each syllable he spoke hammering into her skull. Tears streamed down her face and her throat was raw as he seemed to cleave her mind in two. Flames had ignited within her brain, searing a merciless path through her central lobe. She collapsed to her knees, drool spilling from her mouth and pooling on the floor. The only sound she heard was the deafening roar of blood pounding in her ears, but she knew she was screaming—and she knew she couldn't stop.

Vesryn knelt beside her, letting his frigid lips brush against her earlobe, his claws wrapped around her neck. "Do. You. Understand?" The words were slow, deliberate, each one a dagger to her soul. When she didn't respond, he slammed her head into the floor with brutal force, holding her down as he withdrew the searing inferno, only to replace it with the sensation of razor-sharp needles stabbing into her psyche. They burrowed deeper and deeper, relentlessly picking apart her brain piece by piece until all that remained was a numbness so profound it swallowed her thoughts, leaving her lost in a void of incoherent nothingness.

The elf sighed. "I grow tired of this game, my dear. Are you truly going to make me ask you thrice?"

Tears and saliva mingled as they dripped from her quivering lips, pooling beneath her hand she couldn't keep from twitching. She couldn't speak—she couldn't even move. The agony was beyond anything she'd ever known, torment that never ceased, torture that paralyzed her. But she knew if she didn't do something, Vesryn would only make this worse. She tried to inch away from him, but before she could, he slammed her head down again, causing her teeth to clamp down on her tongue. The sharp taste of iron filled her mouth, her breath hitching between ragged sobs as she writhed uncontrollably, caught in the vice of excruciating pain.

"Margot, I am so proud of all you have accomplished in such a short time," Vesryn purred, his voice dripping with condescension. "But it seems you still have a soft spot for the demon." With a cruel smile, he grabbed a fistful of her hair, yanking her face up to meet his. "To question my rules, my decisions. To accuse me of being a tyrant." He clicked his tongue. "You must be mad, love." He released her, letting her fall back onto the cold stone with a *thud*. "How do you feel about Cillian now? Go ahead and take a moment to search your mind. I will wait."

Margot squeezed her eyes shut, desperately searching the shattered remnants of her mind for the man who had filled the room —and her soul—just moments ago. But there was nothing. His face was a blur, his voice a distant echo she could no longer grasp. Cillian was nothing more than a fading memory, a man who meant nothing to her.

Nothing.

She groaned as she rolled onto her back and her eyes fluttered open to see Vesryn's twisted expression. A thin sheen of sweat clung to her skin like a veil. Her body trembled, her lips dry and cracked. Exhaustion weighed heavily on her—she needed rest.

"Do you have something to tell me, my queen?"

"I-I don't care about Cillian," she said, her voice hoarse. "I'm loyal to you and only you, my king."

Vesryn held her chin tightly and leaned closer, his breath cold against her cheeks. "Are you sure about that? Because if there is any doubt in your mind, any at all, it would be in your best interest to tell me now."

Margot tried to swallow past the pain in her throat, but it was like trying to choke down sand. She scanned the elf's eyes, searching for any sign of kindness, of mercy. But all she saw was a cold, calculating killer. A monster. There wasn't anything remaining of the elf she thought she knew, and if she didn't play his game, she would wind up dead.

She nodded her head frantically. "I'm sure. There is no doubt in my mind." She stifled a sob. "You are the only one who consumes my thoughts. My heart. My life. I am yours."

He let her go and stood, smoothing the front of his robe. "Good," he said, his tone dismissive. "For your sake, I hope you are telling the truth. Now, rest up. Since you have ruined today's lesson, we will expand upon Ancestral Memory tomorrow."

With a snap of his fingers, the elf magicked her to her bed. Every inch of her body throbbed as if she had climbed a mountain, only instead of making it to the top, she had plummeted right off the side. Her mind was in shambles, the few memories she had of Cillian now reduced to nothing more than a hazy blur. Though she couldn't clearly remember him, the emptiness left in his absence told her all she needed to know—he had been important, crucial even. Vesryn's need for control only confirmed it. If she was to ever break free, she had to be careful, cunning. She needed to outplay the elf at his own game.

She needed to play to win.

31

ALLIES

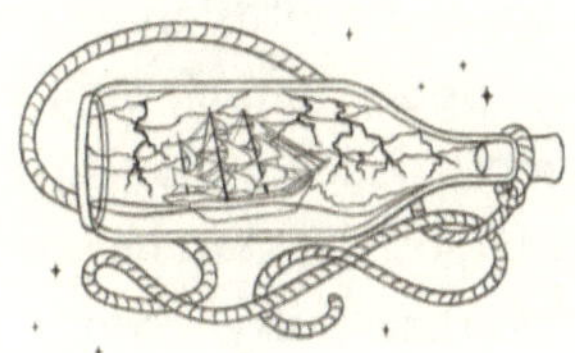

"THAT SON OF A BITCH!" Cillian fumed, stomping around the dingy basement room, kicking chairs and breaking broomstick handles. "I'm going to rip him to pieces. Pull his arms from their sockets, tear his balls off and shove them down his throat. I will bathe in his blood and bask in the glory of that bastard's death. He will regret every damn thing he has done to my bloodsworn."

"You need to be quiet," Tahlsia hissed, her eyes darting around the room. "There are ears everywhere."

"Fuck the ears," Cillian puffed as he threw himself into an unstable wooden chair that groaned in protest under his weight. "Vesryn needs to die. I can just go in there and wrench his heart from his chest. Then we can be done with this, and Margot and I can get the fuck off this gods forsaken island."

The lithe elf placed a hand on her hip and gave him an incredulous look. "That will *never* work. He will kill you on sight."

Cillian snorted. "Vesryn can't take me out. Magic is useless against my kind."

"*Fae* magic doesn't work on your kind." She nibbled on her bottom lip.

"What do you mean?" Cillian leaned in. "It's common knowledge that demons are immune to magic."

355

"Cillian... we've all heard whispers of what happened to you. How do you think you were bound when you arrived on the island?"

That gave him pause, catching him off guard. He had been so worried about Margot that he hadn't even thought about how it happened, and thinking back now, the entire event was a blur—a chaotic rush of violence and confusion. It had happened so fast, too fast. He had always prided himself on his strength and ability to fight off even the most skilled opponents. But one second, he was standing next to Margot, the next, he was shackled by Corym. He was subdued in less than thirty seconds, and he hadn't even realized what was happening until it was too late. Now, as he sat there, the gravity of her words sank in.

What force could have restrained him so completely, so quickly? His mind raced, trying to piece the event together— flashes of light, the grip of cold steel, the sudden, overwhelming pressure that had pinned him to the ground. What had they used against him? And, more importantly, why?

It wasn't just his body they had captured; it was his very essence, his will. When he was strung up in the center of that room, he couldn't even fight back. When he was a fledgling, Hell-wardens would tell tales of ancient magics, of powers that could tame even demons, but he had always dismissed them as myths, stories to frighten the younglings to help hone their survival instincts. How stupid could he have been? Even the most absurd myths held truth at their core.

"Why is elven magic different?" he asked quietly.

"It... is difficult to explain, but I'll do my best." She sighed and took a seat next to him. "Faerie is unique, in that it pulls from two magic systems: the Arcane Weave and the Mana Weave. This is important," she added, when Cillian rolled his eyes. "The Arcane Weave was granted by the deities, but Faerie took what was given and created an even more complex web of magic."

"The Mana Weave?" Cillian asked.

She nodded. "When the three sisters created the elves, they

tied our magic to the Mana Weave, giving us unmatched power, but at a cost." Her throat bobbed. "Too much magic negatively affects the womb, making conception... difficult. The elves were torn, living a near-immortal life without experiencing the miracles of birth wasn't worth having the might strong enough to devastate lands. Half of the elves left. They cast aside the Mana Weave and accepted the Arcane Weave, thus the fae were born, adopting their moniker, calling themselves Children of Faerie. To explain it simply, the Arcane Weave is universal magic, while the Mana Weave is specific to the elves. So, no. You can't just run in there and kill him—or any of us. Not without being severely harmed, or worse, mortally wounded. Faerie herself still bolsters our magic."

Cillian ran his fingers through his hair. Trying to wrap his head around all this made his skull throb, a dull ache spreading from his temples. Tahlsia was right—he couldn't take on the elves alone. He might be as strong as they come, his physical prowess unmatched, but against a barrage of magic coming at him from every direction, magic that could hurt him, he would be at a severe disadvantage. Magic had a way of bending the rules of combat; he had seen it before. It could turn strength into weakness, and agility into futility. It wasn't just about brute force; it was about outmaneuvering opponents who could warm reality with a flick of their wrist. Cillian was good, but even he knew his limitations.

The idea of facing Vesryn and his loyalists without proper support made his stomach churn. Relying solely on Margot and a handful of elves to take down Vesryn was a gamble at best, a suicide mission at worst. Margot was powerful—no doubt the reason Vesryn wanted her so badly—but she hadn't been whole for some time. And the elves who opposed Vesryn, though brave, were few and likely divided. Could he really count on them when the time for battle arose? When the stakes were highest, would they stand beside them or allow fear and self-preservation to drive them to retreat?

The odds were stacked against them, and the more he thought about it, the more apparent it became that they needed a new strategy—something beyond strength and determination. They needed allies, resources, and, more importantly, a plan—a good one. Vesryn was cunning, ruthless, and steeped in ancient magic that, unfortunately, Cillian didn't understand. Underestimating him would be their death.

He exhaled slowly, forcing himself to think clearly. He couldn't afford to be reckless. Not with Margot's life on the line. He didn't know how to protect her— protect them all—when every move he made seemed to be wrong. He needed to be smarter, more strategic. Plotting against Vesryn was nothing like waging war against his own kind—he needed to think outside the box.

"I'm sorry. I know you want to save her, and you will." Tahlsia placed a gentle hand on his shoulder. "But she needs to hone her magic, and you need to work on getting through to her, or else she won't be of any use to us, and we desperately need her."

He stared at the floor with his hands clasped between his knees. "Every time I feel like I get close, Vesryn is always two steps ahead. I keep wracking my brain for the answers, trying to figure out how to get to her, but I... I don't know what to do."

A quiet throat-clearing came from the far corner of the room. Instantly alert, Cillian sprang to his feet, his hands instinctively gripping the hilts of his daggers. His eyes narrowed as he scanned the shadows, searching for the source of the sound. Tahlsia, equally startled, took a few cautious steps back.

"Who's there?" Cillian removed his daggers from their sheaths. "Show yourself."

From the shadows, Corym stepped into the center of the room with Nym trailing behind him. Cillian's stance faltered. *How did he get in without anyone noticing?*

Tahlsia dropped to her knees, crawling across the floor, shaking her clasped hands at him. "This... this isn't what it looks like. Please, you must believe me."

"Stand, Tahlsia. I'm not here to stop this," Corym said to her, though his eyes were locked on Cillian. "I'm here to help you."

Cillian cocked an eyebrow. "Why would you help?"

"Why do ya think, drek?" Nym sat on the floor, throwing small pebbles across the room.

"Vesryn isn't well." Corym dragged a chair next to Cillian's and sat. A pensive look drawn on his face. "I want our species to thrive as much as any of us, but this isn't the way. Ilphas was kind and fair. Vesryn... Vesryn is a savage. I must believe there was a reason Ilphas sought a child of Earth to possess his magic."

"I heard the two of you talking." Cillian frowned as he recalled the memory. "You were all for Vesryn killing Margot after she birthed a child."

"You're right. I agreed the plan could work. Though it's only a theory, he thinks that because she was once human, she will be more likely to conceive. But I know Vesryn. His gears are turning, pushing him over an edge there will be no coming back from."

Cillian sheathed his daggers and sat back down. "What aren't you telling us, Corym?"

"He wants to create an army of children." The elf dropped his face onto the palms of his hands. "He wants to take Ravara's place and reign over Faerie. His new plan is to breed with her for as long as they live."

Vesryn's thirst for power had taken a sickening turn in the blink of an eye, morphing into something far more twisted and dangerous. This wasn't just a play for power—it was a calculated move to reshape Faerie in his image, with Margot as the key to his delusional ambitions. The thought of her being used as a vessel, her life reduced to nothing more than a means to an end, sent anger roiling through him.

"The girl can't handle that," Tahlsia whispered, her voice trembling. "No elf could."

"I know that. That's why I'm here." Corym turned to Cillian. "We work together to take down Vesryn and his followers, and then you and Margot are free to go."

Cillian leaned forward; his eyes narrowed. "Why should I trust you?"

"Because I'm risking everything by coming to you," Corym replied evenly. "If Vesryn even suspects I'm helping you, he'll kill me without a second thought."

"And what do you propose we do?"

"You need to act compliant until Margot has some control over her power. At the moment, Vesryn believes she is wholly under his influence, but I disagree. No amount of magic can eliminate a blood bond—not even ours. I think it's just buried."

Cillian crossed his arms, leaning back in his chair. "I figured that much out already."

"Right. But Vesryn needs to *believe* you've given up." Corym offered Cillian a weak smile. "You'll need to endure Vesryn's need to show dominance. I... I'm sorry."

Cillian's jaw clenched and a bitter taste flooded his mouth. He knew exactly what Corym meant: he would be forced to watch Vesryn fuck his bloodsworn, asserting his control in the most degrading way possible.

"It won't be easy, but after all these years I've spent in Faerie suppressing my instincts, I'll see it done. But I need something from you. Do you have a blacksmith you trust?"

"I do," Corym said, his tone skeptical. "Why?"

"If I draw up plans for a weapon, do you think they could make it for me?" Cillian gave Corym a pointed look. "Discretion is necessary here."

"I don't see why not."

"Excellent. And the rest of the plan?"

Corym leaned back in his chair and looked at Tahlsia. "I assume you're already gathering allies?"

"We are. There are even some fae who are still loyal to the old ways." Her eyes darted nervously around the room. "We've... we've been in communication with the mainland."

Corym's eyes widened. "Is that a good idea?"

She shrugged. "I don't know. But if we invite willing fae to

Caramis, perhaps..." Her voice trailed off as her hand cradled her lower stomach.

Cillian's gaze flickered between the two elves. He could tell that this conversation was veering dangerously close to a topic not yet ready to be broached. He cleared his throat. "I don't care who you choose to ally with as long as they're going to help save Margot."

"So long as ya play your role well," Nym quipped.

"They will help, yes," Corym said, nodding. "We move strategically and carefully. Tahlsia and I will find allies. *Trustworthy* allies. And Cillian?"

"Hm?"

"Don't push Margot too hard. Vesryn will know. You need to be subtle. Can you do that?"

"I'll do whatever it takes."

IT'LL BE A SECRET

"You did well today, dear," Vesryn said, barely looking up as he shuffled through the documents scattered across his desk. His tone was polite, but distracted, his focus clearly elsewhere. "While I would love to spend the day with you, I must get some work done. Will you study in your room?"

Margot fidgeted with the fabric of her dress, her fingers twisting the hem nervously. She glanced between Vesryn and the floor, biting her lip. "Well, I was hoping to get a bit of fresh air. It's been so long since I've been out... and I'd love to see more of Caramis, too. Perhaps you could take a break?" She tried to hide her uncertainty, but there was a slight tremor in her otherwise hopeful voice.

Vesryn sighed, pressing a slender finger to his temple. "I cannot escort you." His eyes finally flicked up to meet hers, cold and unyielding. "Was that not easily inferred?"

Margot's heart sank, the hope she had clung to quickly fading. She forced a smile, though it didn't reach her eyes. "Of course," she murmured, bowing her head slightly. "I didn't mean to trouble you."

She stood silently in front of his desk, her hands clasped tightly in front of her. The soft rustle of papers was the only sound in the room, but it did little to break the uncomfortable stillness. Vesryn flipped a sheet of parchment over, his quill scratching across it for a few minutes more before he finally looked up, his jaw clenched.

"Was there something else you needed from me?" he gritted out roughly, as though her mere presence was a burden he could hardly tolerate.

Margot swallowed, her throat tightening. "I-I hope this doesn't offend you, but... what of my protector? He could escort me, as is his duty."

It felt as though the temperature in the room plummeted. Vesryn's stare sharpened like a blade, his features hardening into an icy mask. His muscles twitched, and the papers in his hands crumpled beneath his grip. With the flick of his wrist, he cast the documents to the floor as if they were nothing more than discarded scraps.

"Do you think Caramis is the type of place where one should wander aimlessly?" His voice was low, dangerously controlled, but the anger simmering beneath the surface was palpable.

The air thickened between them, oppressive and suffocating, as his gaze bore into hers. Margot's pulse quickened, and she instinctively lowered her head, her eyes fixed on the floor.

"Forgive me," she whispered. "It has been days... no, weeks since I've felt the sun, since I've smelled the sweet blooms. I only wished for a walk, even if it's just around the manor... to decompress."

His chair scraped against the floor, the sound grating against the silence. She could hear his footsteps draw closer until the tips of his grey slippers touched her shoes. Her breath hitched as Vesryn tilted her chin up with a single, cold finger. The disparity between his gentleness now and the controlled anger in his voice moments earlier, left her feeling both confused and vulnerable.

He brushed a stray strand of hair from her face, his thumb lingering longer than necessary before he leaned in and placed a soft kiss on her cheek. "I will allow this," he murmured, his voice dangerously smooth, "but only if you stay close to the manor. You will do nothing to break my trust. Is that understood?"

Margot nodded quickly, her heart fluttering as her face warmed under his fingers. She had grown so accustomed to his strict demeanor that moments like this—when he showed glimpses of caring and concern—left her disoriented. "Yes, my king."

His grip on her chin tightened, and he leaned closer. She could feel his breath on her skin. "Remember, Margot," he whispered, "do not break my trust."

She swallowed hard as he released her, watching him glide back to his chair with a fluid elegance. "Now go," he commanded, dismissing her. "I shall send Cillian to your room to escort you."

Relief coursed through her as she hurried back to her chambers, her footsteps echoing in the vast, empty corridors of the manor. The grand halls and meticulously manicured gardens had long since become her gilded cage. Each step reminded her of the invisible chains that bound her here, but soon—soon—she would taste freedom again, even if only for a fleeting moment.

As she entered her room, her breath caught. Cillian was already there, standing with his back to the window, his tall, muscular frame casting a long shadow across the floor. His piercing silver eyes locked onto hers the moment she stepped inside, a familiar shiver running down her spine. There was something about him, something raw and untamed, that set her blood alight, though she couldn't quite put her finger on why. *How had he gotten here so quickly?*

Her protector offered her a grin and his arm, jerking his head toward the door. "Shall we?"

Margot hesitated, her hand hovering just above his arms, nerves buzzing beneath her skin. If she touched him, she feared she might combust, the tension between them crackling like a live wire. But the pull of freedom was stronger. She took a deep breath, placing a delicate hand on his arm. "Yes, let us be off."

Cillian grabbed a basket as they passed through the grand

halls of the manor, his solid presence grounding her in a way she couldn't ever remember feeling. When they finally stepped outside, the warmth of the sun washed over her like a balm, instantly soothing her nerves and lifting the weight from her chest. Her spirit surged, rejuvenated by the simple act of being outdoors.

The gardens stretched endlessly before them, a breathtaking labyrinth of blooms and winding paths that seemed to beckon her further. Bright flowers blossomed in every shade imaginable, their colors vivid against the lush aubergine backdrop. As they strolled along the cobblestone path, Margot caught glimpses of delicate petals swaying in the breeze, the air thick with their sweet, intoxicating perfume. Birds sang from treetops, their melodic tunes weaving through the soft rustling of leaves.

Margot inhaled deeply, her senses awakening to the vibrant life around her. For the first time in what felt like forever, she felt alive again.

She glanced over her shoulder at Cillian, curiosity tugging at her. "What's in the basket?"

He gave her a playful smile. "I thought a picnic might be nice, so I asked Tahlsia to make us lunch. Are you hungry?"

Tahlsia. A knot of jealousy twisted in Margot's stomach before she could stop it, irrational and sharp. She wasn't sure why it bothered her so much, but the thought of that beautiful elf being in Cillian's life sent her mind spinning. *Who is she to him? The question gnawed at her. A friend? A lover?*

"Margot?" Cillian's voice broke through her spiraling thoughts.

She cleared her throat, forcing a smile and pushing the unease aside. "Yes, lunch would be lovely."

A toothy grin spread across his face, sending a warm flutter through Margot's belly. "Perfect. I know just the place. Come on."

He laced his fingers through hers, his grip firm yet gentle as he guided her down a winding path. The soft crunch of gravel beneath their feet created a soothing rhythm, and with every step, the tension that had weighed so heavily on Margot's shoulders began to ease.

Margot gasped as they entered a secluded grove. Dappled sunlight filtered through the trees, casting soft patches of light on the grassy clearing ahead. In the center, a blanket was spread across the ground, and on it, a tantalizing feast awaited—fresh, vibrant fruits, golden pastries, and delicate sandwiches, all meticulously arranged on porcelain plates. It looked like something out of a dream.

Her breath hitched as she took in the scene. "Cillian... did you do all this?"

Cillian shrugged. "I had a little help."

"Tahlsia?"

He nodded. "She helped me prepare this for you."

"Are you two..." Margot put the tips of her fingers together, and Cillian laughed.

"Together? No. She's just a friend. Maybe my only friend here, if I'm being honest."

So, not a lover.

Margot furrowed her brow, meeting his gaze. "Why would you do this for me?"

Cillian's silver eyes held a mischievous glimmer as he slid his hand along the curve of her waist before pulling her down onto the blanket. "Because I think you needed this."

She blinked, taken aback. No one had ever gone to such lengths for her, at least not that she could remember. Vesryn's rare moments of kindness were always tainted by his coldness and cruelty, but Cillian... he was different. He seemed determined to show her a side of life she had long thought unattainable—one filled with care, warmth, and something dangerously close to affection.

"Thank you," she whispered, her voice barely audible over the gentle breeze. "This is more than I could have imagined."

His lips curled into a breathtaking smile; it sent her heart stumbling in her chest. "You deserve more than imagination, Margot. You deserve a lifetime of moments like this."

Her thoughts tangled; knots she couldn't untie. *Why would someone who barely knows me want to do these things for me?* The more she tried to think it through, the hazier her mind became. Perhaps it was the intoxicating scent of flowers surrounding them, making everything feel dreamlike, almost surreal.

Margot exhaled, deciding to let her thoughts drift away with the breeze and just enjoy the moment. She settled onto the blanket, Cillian's presence beside her both comforting and electrifying. His fingers brushed her skin, sending ripples cascading through her body. It stirred something deep within her—an unfamiliar hunger, not just for the delicious food spread before them, but for a connection she had never experienced before. Something real, something profound.

As they ate, Margot found herself stealing glances at Cillian, her gaze lingering longer than she intended. His strong jawline and broad shoulders stood in stark contrast to the delicate features of the elves she had grown used to on the island. Everything about him was raw, powerful, and unrefined in a way that intrigued her. Her eyes traced the movements of his thick, calloused hands as he poured a glass of sweet wine, each gesture deliberate and effortless. The sun's rays reflected off his tousled black hair, casting a dark, almost ethereal glow around him as he tipped his head back to take a sip.

A lump formed in her throat, and she couldn't hold back the question that had been burning in the back of her mind any longer. "What are you?" she blurted out.

He smirked at her. *Smirked!* "I'm Cillian, your guardian."

She swallowed, her eyes narrowing slightly. "But what *are* you?" Her fingers, almost of their own accord, brushed the shell of his ear. Not quite rounded, but not nearly as pointed as the elves. The contact sent a sudden jolt through her body, a strange current that made her wince. He wasn't like the others—wasn't like anyone she had ever known. "You're not an elf."

He leaned in, his face mere inches from hers. "Can I trust you?"

Margot's heart pounded as his silver eyes seemed to burn straight into her, igniting something deep within her soul. The air between them crackled with a strange energy, almost tangible, as though the very atmosphere was alive with the magnetic pull that drew her closer to him. She nodded slowly, curiosity swirling through her veins, piqued by his cryptic question.

"You can't tell anyone," he whispered. His lips curved into a teasing half-smile that caused her skin to pimple. "It'll be a secret just between you and me."

Shadows danced across the sharp planes of his face, the interplay of light and darkness adding to the air of mystery that seemed to surround him. It pressed in on her, making her want to unravel every layer of this man sitting beside her. She craved to know more —who he really was, what he was hiding—but she couldn't ignore the danger that dwelled behind every whispered word. Vesryn's rule had been clear, and breaking them would mean more than just punishment. The smallest misstep could set him off. She'd seen his wrath before, and it wasn't something she ever wanted to experience again.

Still, the risk made her blood sing, and she scooted closer, whispering, "I promise, Cillian. Your secret's safe with me."

"I come from Olvath," he said, his voice dropping to a low, dangerous whisper. His once-smoldering silver eyes darkened, as though the mere mention of that place cast gloom over him. "Do you know what that means?"

She dared to move closer, inching forward until their knees brushed. Her skin prickled at the sudden contact. Shaking her head slowly, she held his gaze.

"It means," he murmured, a low rumble that came up from his chest, sending a shiver down her spine, "I'm a demon—a powerful one. Which is why I'm perfect to protect someone as precious as you."

Her eyes widened as the truth hit her. When Vesryn had called

Cillian a demon, he hadn't meant it as an insult—he meant it literally. Fear and fascination swirled within her, twisting in her gut like a storm. Demons were creatures of malevolence and destruction. No one ever spoke of them openly, only in whispers, and the few things she had read painted them as harbingers of chaos. Why would Vesryn, her king, entrust someone like that to watch over her?

But as she looked deeper into Cillian's eyes, she didn't see the darkness she had read about. Instead, she found something startlingly different—kindness, compassion, and a vulnerability that seemed at odds with everything she believed about his kind. There was a flicker of something more in those mercurial pools, a hint of longing that tugged at her heartstrings, unraveling the fear that gripped her moments before.

It made her question everything she thought she knew about demons—about him—which, admittedly, wasn't much. Could he really be the guardian she needed, or was she being pulled into something far more dangerous?

Margot hesitated, then reached out tentatively, her fingertips grazing the back of Cillian's hand. She needed to understand him, to see beyond the mask he wore. "Why would Vesryn entrust a demon to protect me?"

The warmth in his eyes dimmed instantly, his pleasant demeanor hardening as if a mask of anger had slid into place. His stare became cold, making Margot's pulse quicken. Her breath caught in her throat, her mind racing with sudden fear. *What did I say? Did I push him too far? Should I run? What if he attacks me?* The thoughts hammered at her as his presence seemed to loom larger, suffocating, dangerous, capable of striking her down in an instant.

Before she could fully process the shift in his demeanor, a brilliant burst of light ignited between them. It crackled like lightning, blinding and beautiful, then vanished just as quickly as it arrived.

Margot blinked and searched Cillian's face for any sign that he had seen what she had. But his expression remained impassive, unreadable. Had she imagined it? A soft gasp escaped her as her gaze drifted to the faint, translucent line that now connected them—a delicate thread of spectral energy. It shimmered faintly, like a fragile bridge linking their bodies. She reached out instinctively, her fingers brushing through the gossamer strand, only for it to dissipate into nothingness, leaving her with more questions than answers.

For the briefest of moments, Cillian's mouth twitched, as though a smile had almost broken through the façade. But when she blinked, his face was blank again, the warmth gone.

"What was that? she whispered, her voice shaky.

He shrugged nonchalantly, popping a berry into his mouth as if nothing had happened. "A story for another time, I suppose."

Margot gaped at him. *Is he serious?* An inexplicable phenomenon had just unfolded between them, and he was brushing it off like it was nothing? *I cannot believe the audacity of this man.*

Cillian cleared his throat, cutting through her stunned silence. "To answer your question, I've learned not to question Vesryn's decisions. I was told to protect you, so here I am." He leaned in slightly, his fingers gently tucking a loose strand of hair behind her ear. The gesture, though tender, felt strangely calculated. "Tell me about yourself, Margot. What do you do here? Any plans for the future?"

His words, so mundane and simple, caught her off guard. *Plans for the future?* It was the kind of question normal elves asked each other, but there was nothing normal about this place or her life in it. The buzzing remnants of the strange connection they had just experienced still lingered in her mind, and she struggled to focus.

She held her breath as she searched for answers within herself, but there was nothing. Just an empty void. Distorted images flashed briefly, like fragments of someone else's life, garbled voices echoing faintly in her ears. She furrowed her brow and tried harder. *Who am I? What do I want?* But the harder she tried, the more elusive the answers became.

Nothing. She had no memories of her life as an elfling, no recollection of her favorite activities, or even her favorite foods. Her entire existence seemed to revolve around Vesryn and the manor. *Is that all I am?*

Blinking back tears, she met Cillian's gaze, her voice barely above a whisper. "I don't know."

"Hey, hey, no need for waterworks," he said softly. "It's okay not to have all the answers. We'll figure it out together." His gaze briefly shifted toward the manor. "But I'd keep this from Vesryn if I were you. That elf has a temper."

Temper was putting it lightly, and the thought of what Vesryn might do if he found out she was... broken... made her stomach knot.

"But you work for him. How do I know you won't tell?"

Cillian's grin returned, disarming and sincere, his eyes twinkling mischievously. "I trusted you with my secret. Won't you trust me with yours?"

Trust. The world felt foreign on her tongue, especially when it came to Cillian. But something about him, his presence, the way he looked at her—it made her want to take a leap of faith, no matter how dangerous it seemed.

With a deep sigh, she nodded slowly. "We'll be one another's confidantes."

His smile widened as he stood, taking her hand in his. "I like the sound of that, Margot. But we should get you back to the manor before Vesryn comes looking."

Her fingers slipped between his as she rose to her feet. "Can we do this again?"

"Any time you'd like," he promised. "Just call for me, and I'll come running."

As they walked back to the manor, Margot felt a nagging sensation tugging at the edges of her mind, a feeling she couldn't shake. It was as though something was stirring deep within her—

warped memories pushing against the surface, trying to break free. And then, for a brief moment, clarity washed over her like a fleeting dream. She saw herself standing beside Cillian on the bow of a ship, the two of them gazing out at a vast, endless sea.

It was gone as quickly as it had come, leaving her breathless. She glanced at Cillian, wondering if he had sensed it too, but his expression remained unchanged. Still, the vision lingered, a tantalizing glimpse of something... more. Something important.

MERRY BAND OF DRUNKARDS

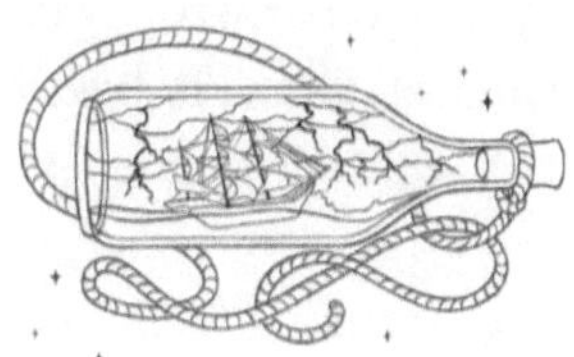

"THIS WILL WORK," Cillian muttered, peeling back the thick rind of a citralon to get to the succulent flesh beneath. His hands trembled slightly as he worked. "I know it will. But it's like Margot isn't even there anymore. She's a totally different person. She speaks differently, acts differently. What in the hells did Vesryn do to her?"

"Nothing good." Corym grimaced. "He used forbidden magic. A ritual that allows the ritualist to control the subject wholly, including obscuring memories or fabricating new ones." He crossed his arms, looking down at the ground. "Why the deities thought it was a good idea to include that in our creation, I'll never know."

Nym scooted his chair along, scraping it against the floor to better join the group. "Vesryn is damn nuts." The green-eyed elf looked between the other three. "Edea heard him talkin' to himself about how it's only a matter of time before the seed takes root. Gross." He kicked up his feet, grinning. "Absolutely bonkers, that one."

"So, the bastard is really going to try," Cillian said, more to himself than the others. He was hoping it had all been conjecture, but it seemed Corym had been telling the truth.

"Try what?" Edea squeaked, peeking around a wooden support beam with wide blue eyes, not unlike Margot's, which made his chest hurt. "Wh-what's he going to do now?"

Cillian looked to Corym to see if the elf was going to enlighten her, but he remained staring at the floor, his gaze far off. *No use keeping the information confidential.* He turned to look at Edea. "Vesryn plans to perpetually keep Margot pregnant to increase the Elven population. He believes that, because she was once human, she will have greater success in bearing young."

The little elf gasped, shrinking back in the shadows, holding herself as if to stop her body from shivering. "Th-that's awful. She'll die."

"That's why we need to keep Vesryn from killing her," Cillian said.

Corym grunted, casually kicking his feet up onto an old crate, his eyes scanning the room before falling on Cillian, cocking his head to the side. "Whether the girl lives or dies depends on you. Not us."

Tahlsia rolled her eyes, her tone cutting through the tension. "You know that's not true. Vesryn could decide to kill her just for looking at him the wrong way."

Nym snorted as he scratched his stomach. "Vesryn could kill *any of us* for lookin' at him the wrong way."

Cillian's hands stilled as he carefully dissected the fruit as the elves murmured their agreement, his mind spinning with thoughts of impending danger. Vesryn's unpredictability looked over everything like a storm cloud, waiting to strike Margot down with the flick of a wrist. Corym was right. Her fate depended solely on him and his actions. The thought twisted something deep in his chest. To protect her would require him to play the role he despised most—subservience. And like a good dog, he would go against every primal instinct to obey his new master. Margot's survival was worth it. He couldn't, *wouldn't*, fail her. So, he would bite back his pride and submit to Vesryn's authority regardless of how much it hurt to watch her slip through his fingers.

"Has anyone secured allies?" Cillian tossed the citralon peel onto the table, popping the last piece into his mouth. "We won't be doing a damn thing with just the four of us."

"Thalindra and Vaeloria are with us," Edea said quietly, now sitting on the floor away from everyone. "Paxim, also."

Nym took a glug of mead from the tankard he brought with him, wiping his mouth on the back of his arm. Cillian's lip curled as he watched the elf, who just grinned. "Everyone down at the Silver Flagon is with us. Rhiannon and her mate—gods, she's a beaut—Zevrik, Tanir, Kaldris, Caelith, uhh, and Ced. Oh, oh! And Stog. I think that's the last of 'em. They're in!"

"Wonderful," Cillian grumbled. "We're just a merry band of drunkards."

"Hey now!" Nym slapped his thigh, his drink sloshing over the rim. "Don't be like that, drek."

"Breton and his mate Shay," Corym interrupted before the conversation could get out of hand. "Timi and Grish," he crossed his arms, leaning back with a lazy shrug, the old chair groaning beneath his weight, "and the ninety-seven elves in the Veilguard— they'll all stand with us when the time comes."

Cillian sat up at that. "How can you be so sure? What's stopping the Veilguard from turning and fighting for Vesryn?"

Corym shot Cillian a sideways glance. "Because I'm the one who's been there for them. I'm the one who picks them up after Vesryn tears them down, after he forces them to fight each other nearly to death just to test their 'strength.' I've been training them, listening to them, and giving them the support they desperately need. I've *earned* their loyalty over centuries, Cillian, by being the friend they don't find in Vesryn's cruelty."

Having trained troops of his own, Cillian knew the depths of loyalty running through a well-led unit. While demons could be tempted by simple comforts, like a home-cooked meal, elves were not so easily swayed. Their loyalty was not unbreakable, but it was steadfast. He wagered they might lose a few warriors when the time came, but the gains would be invaluable. Corym's unwavering commitment to his elves earned Cillian's respect—fostering such cohesion and dedication in a unit required more than just skill; it demanded a full ass and relentless perseverance.

"That's good to hear. We'll need every ally we can get. Tahlsia?" Cillian watched as Tahlsia swept the same spot she had been working on for the past fifteen minutes, her grip tight on the broom handle. "Tahl?"

"I—" She looked up from her broom, eyes filled to the brim with tears. "—I have about forty fae ready to fight on our side."

Cillian walked around the table, placing both hands on her upper arms, squeezing gently so she would look at him. "Tell me what's wrong."

"Oh, good goddesses," She crumpled to the floor, still holding the broom, and she quietly sobbed. "It's so bad. What do we do?"

"Aw c'mon. Nothing's that bad, Tahlsia," Nym said with a grin.

"Shut *up*, Nym," Cillian hissed over his shoulder. He looked at Corym, who was now seated with his forearms resting on his knees, hands clasped together, watching Tahlsia. Edea had gotten on all fours to crawl closer. Cillian knelt and gently tipped up Tahlsia's chin. "I need you to talk to us. What's going on?"

The maid's bottom lip quivered, and she slowly placed the broom on the ground. With one hand on her chest, she took a deep breath, wiping her tears away in one swift motion. "It's Ravara." She met Cillian's gaze, her voice barely a whisper. "Ravara... he—he wants Margot."

"Damn it all," Corym seethed. "How badly does the *glorious* king want her?"

"Ravara? There's another loon for ya," Nym chimed in.

Cillian's fingers curled into fists, nails digging into his palms hard enough to leave crescent-shaped imprints. He had been so preoccupied with the growing tensions among the elves that he had forgotten the looming threat of Ravara—the degenerate, self-proclaimed Fae King who had so ruthlessly hunted Margot. Being exiled to Faerie had made him reckless, and he cursed himself for it now. His existence had once revolved around a singular goal: to conquer anyone who dared oppose the Dread Lord. That singular focus had defined him—until Margot.

She had changed everything. She *was* everything.

Not only did Vesryn have unspeakable plans for Margot, but Ravara wanted her, too. And Cillian had forgotten.

The memory of Margot lying helpless in the dirt haunted Cillian. If he had left her there, vulnerable and alone, Ravara's men would have captured her, exposing her to the twisted dangers of the fae world. And Cillian? He would have continued his hollow, solitary existence, forever tormented by the image of her fragile form amidst the cruel, beautiful landscape. Alone. Always alone. It wasn't a life he could bear to return to.

A humorless laugh slipped past Tahlsia's lips. "Bad enough to have the entire northeastern seaboard lined with troops."

Cillian helped Tahlsia to her feet and looked at Corym. "Do they know where Caramis is?" Corym shifted in his seat, knuckles white as he gripped his knees, but said nothing. "*Corym!*" Cillian growled. Edea whimpered and retreated further back, pressing herself against the wall. "Do. They. Know?"

Nym took another drink, exhaling a contented sigh as he slammed the tankard down. "Course they know. Everyone does. You knew, drek."

Cillian slid a hand down his face, not quite believing their resistance consisted of a maid, an elf who couldn't even stand next to him, a military officer, and Nym, an elf who clearly didn't take a single thing seriously. "Right. Let me rephrase. Do they know how to enter?"

"They know where we are, but all they have to do is wait. Watch." Edea's voice was so quiet Cillian had to strain his ears to hear her over the constant dripping from the leaky ceiling.

"Watch what?"

"The deepweave," Corym said, his voice rumbling like

crushed rock. "All they have to do is watch, and they'll see a ripple in the spell, showing them all of Caramis. It's only open briefly, maybe three minutes, but it's more than enough time for the fae to get through."

Cillian's heart sank as he slumped back in his seat. "How often does this happen?"

"Once every thirteen hours," Tahlsia whispered.

A loud *crack* filled the room as Nym bit into a stoneseed, spitting the shell on the floor before tossing the kernel into his mouth. "They already know, drek."

"We're running out of time!" Edea screeched, causing everyone to flinch.

Silence hung heavy in the room, broken only by the rhythmic plinking of water dripping into a metal bucket. How much time did they really have to prepare? Days? Weeks? For all Cillian knew, Ravara's forces could already be landing on shore, arming his loyal fae to the teeth and readying themselves to storm the city.

"Did you know, Cillian?" Corym asked, expressionless. "Did you know Ravara wanted Margot?"

"I was in Silverbrook, drinking in a tavern, when I heard them talking about her, saying Ravara was looking to 'acquire' a new pet in the Dreadwood." Cillian sighed, letting his head hang. "I got in my ship, sailed up Nyxtrae's coast, and waited. Every night for weeks they'd come out, hunting for Ravara's elusive pet. And then I found her, running aimlessly through the Dreadwood as if there weren't hundreds of creatures lurking in the thicket that could tear her apart. Her body was barely there, translucent like a spirit... until it wasn't. There wasn't much time, so I did the only thing I could think of doing to keep her from Ravara... I—I took her. We ran, hiding against the high cliffs when they tracked her there using some kind of device. Fortunately for us, the incompetent fools didn't look very hard, but the second we got to Elowen, they knew I had her, and Ravara's men were there in droves."

Corym swore under his breath. "This is bigger than you realize, right? He's going to breach our defenses and steal her."

"That prick won't touch a single hair on her head," Cillian growled. "He won't even get close."

Corym shot Cillian an incredulous look. "Even you couldn't take on the entire fae army alone. Ravara's not a threat you can just charge head-on."

"How many does Ravara have?"

"At least fifteen thousand," Tahlsia replied, her tone grim. "At least that's what the whispers say. He called in troops from all over Faerie."

"And the western seaboard..." Cillian's voice trailed off, not wanting to confirm his suspicions.

"Doesn't take a genius to figure out we're surrounded, drek."

"Fuck," Cillian groaned.

"Why didn't you tell us?" Corym stood abruptly, frustration evident as he glared at Cillian. "We could have better prepared! You realize we can't fight on two fronts, right? Caramis will burn to the ground if we do. I understand the bond you have with Margot; trust me, I do. But it's clouding your judgment."

Cillian's eyes flashed with barely restrained fury. "And when exactly should I have told you?" he snarled. "Was it when you were *flaying* me alive, or perhaps when Vesryn was forcing me to watch him..." His voice broke, every syllable pained. "...when he *violated* her? My heartwoven. My lifemate. My *bloodsworn*." Cillian's chest heaved, his deep breaths flaring his nostrils. "And you have the nerve to expect me to tell you *anything*? Sorry, Corym, but I had other things on my fucking mind. Things like keeping her alive."

"These are *my* kin, Cillian. My kin!" Corym puffed up, beating his chest with his fist, his voice strained. "Margot's just one person!"

Edea slipped out from the shadows quiet as a mouse, tangling her fingers together as she looked at the floor, not realizing she had effectively stilted the conversation by her sudden appearance. "Margot's one of us, too." Her fingers curled tightly into the fabric of her dress, and for the first time, she looked at the group.

"Maybe more so than any of us. Ilphas *chose* her! He chose her for a reason."

Everyone, including Nym, had fallen silent. Margot wasn't just a burden, wasn't just a lost soul—deep down, they all knew she was someone with *far* more significance than they initially thought.

"What do we do?" Tahlsia asked tentatively. "Edea is right. She needs to be protected at all costs."

Cillian glanced around at the elves, reading the resolve and fear etched on their faces. There was no more room for doubt. They all knew what had to be done.

"We tear Vesryn limb from limb," Cillian said, his rumbled, simmering with fury that threatened to spill over, "and get Margot the fuck out of here."

3
DOWNFALL

34

PROPERLY MAD

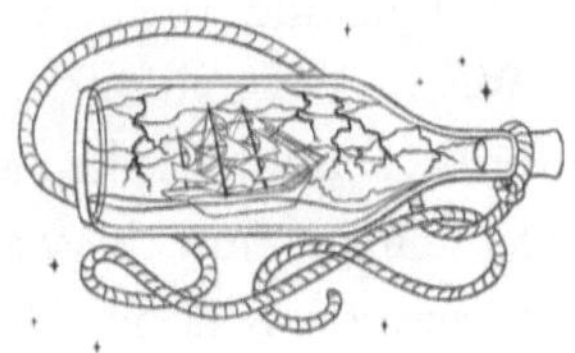

THE MANOR WAS alive with restless energy that pulsed through its walls like a heartbeat. Vesryn's presence was everywhere, an oppressive force that bore down on everyone and everything within his domain. Cillian could feel it creeping into every corner, twisting the air into something thick and suffocating. Servants moved like shadows, silent and swift, avoiding eye contact—and him—as they hurried through the dimly lit corridors. Cillian's own nerves were frayed, stretched thin from days of watching Margot slip further under Vesryn's control, his frustration bubbling, threatening to boil over. Every passing moment drew them nearer to an inevitable confrontation that he wasn't sure they could win. Their plan was fragmented at best, and they needed something concrete to tip the scales in their favor, but with every step he took deeper into Vesryn's twisted domain, the path forward felt more perilous. He knew time was running out.

The hairs on the back of Cillian's neck stood on ends as he felt someone approach from behind. "Come with me," Corym whispered, grabbing his arm. "*Quietly.*"

Corym led them down the dim hallway, guiding Cillian into a shadowed alcove. He nudged Cillian aside, kicked the base of the wall three times and then, with a half-kick, and the wall shud-

385

dered open, revealing a small set of stairs that led to a damp, dusty corridor.

"In you go," Corym said, shoving Cillian through the entrance. Cillian scowled, but Corym shot him a look. "Save the attitude. I need to seal this, and we'll switch spots after if you're that nervous. Now move."

Once the wall closed behind them, Cillian shifted to let Corym take the lead. "Where are we going?"

Corym glanced over his shoulder as he navigated the twisting path with an ease that let Cillian know this wasn't the first time he had traversed it. "Your weapon is done. Meant to tell you the other day, but Vesryn's nonsense kept getting in the way. I'm taking you to where it's stored. It'll stay there until you need it." He smirked. "I still don't get why you need something like this. You're lucky Nym has his... connections. That material wasn't easy to come by."

Cillian's nostrils flared as the scent of saltwater grew stronger. "I need it to fight, obviously. Is this place somewhere I can train privately? I've got a theory, but I'll need you to launch your magic at me."

"You can train there, but Vesryn's got everyone busy today. He's decided to 'inspect' the troops, which means a long day of making sure no one dies and an even longer night of... making sure no one dies. You'll need to find someone else." Corym shot Cillian a sideways glance. "Anyone in mind?"

Cillian's jaw clenched. "Who in the hells is going to help me? Tahlsia's tied up with Vesryn's demands, Edea's terrified of me... I need this, Corym. I have to test this theory."

The passage opened up to a large grotto, its waters shimmering under shafts of light filtering through the ceiling. Vines draped along the jagged stone walls, swaying gently like silent sentinels. Towering sea stacks stood stalwart past the entrance, leaving just enough room for a ship to maneuver out into the Tempest's open waters.

Corym gestured the wide ledge in front of them, where Nym

suddenly dropped from above, landing gracefully on his feet. "Might I suggest Nym?"

"You've got to be kidding," Cillian groaned as he eyed the elf before cocking a brow as he took in his appearance. "What in the hells are you wearing?"

"What do you mean, drek?" He lifted the frayed edges of his tattered brown cloak. Pulling off his cowl, he revealed his usual unruly curls now slicked against his scalp, either from sweat or seawater—it was hard to tell. "How else am I s'posed to sneak around without being recognized?"

"Before this conversation completely devolves, I'm going to take my leave. Nym, show Cillian the goods and help him with whatever he needs." Corym slapped Cillian on the back. "Good luck."

With that, Corym disappeared back into the passage, leaving Cillian and Nym standing at the edge of the hidden grotto.

Cillian crossed his arms as he scuffed the bottom of his boot against the stone, still miffed over what transpired at the Flagon. The carefree elf didn't seem to notice as he started along the shelf further into the grotto.

He looked over his shoulder with a grin, "You comin'?"

Cillian resigned himself with a sigh and followed.

Despite the sweltering heat that perpetually graced the island, the further they moved through the stony corridor, the chillier it became. Cillian's eyes scanned the small cave, the walls much higher than a typical grotto, and the sea level far below the ledge they walked along.

"How often does this place flood?" Cillian asked. Death by drowning wasn't something he wanted to experience.

"Doesn't anymore. Not sure why, but it's become a useful tool." Nym skipped ahead, waving his hand behind him. "C'mon, drek. Just up ahead."

Cillian followed the curving incline, freezing in place as they rounded the corner. Not really quite believing what he was seeing. "Is... is that my ship?" He started walking toward the vessel.

Quicker this time. "Nym, is that my ship?" Not waiting for him to respond, Cillian sprinted toward it, slapping the hull, laughing lightly. "It's my fucking ship! Ah girl, I've missed you."

"Never would've let Vesryn get his grubby hands on somethin' like that," Nym said as he walked up to Cillian. "Ordered it to be burned two nights ago. Old Cory was beside himself, but I came up with a brilliant plan, drek. Not many elves know about this place, not even Vesryn. Too busy lordin' over us."

Cillian turned around, gripping the small elf by his shoulders, an unrestrained smile on his face. "By the gods, Nym. You saved my ship!" Cillian pulled him into a hug, lifting him off the ground as he squeezed. He spun them both around, nearly bouncing on his heels. "You saved her!"

Cillian set him down, and Nym grinned up at him, scratching his cheek and feigning embarrassment. "Yeah, yeah. Ya might want to cool it, else ya girl gets jealous of your newfound love for me."

"I think she'd understand." Cillian patted Nym's cheek twice and laughed once more. Unbridled joy caused his smile to widen so much his cheeks hurt. He didn't think he could feel this much happiness considering the situation they'd found themselves in, but here he was, relishing it. "What a good fucking day."

"Well, it's about to get better." Nym jerked his head toward the deck. "What ya want is in your cabin."

A swift pang of sorrow coursed through Cillian as he sat in his seat, glancing at the empty one beside him. Margot should have been there, celebrating the return of his—*their*—ship. The vessel had become as much hers as it was his. If it were his to give, he'd give her the world. He glanced at Nym, who, for once, looked as if he understood.

The elf placed a hand on his shoulder, giving Cillian a squeeze. "She'll come out of this, ya know."

"How can you be sure?" The words tasted like ash on his tongue. "Even if we do somehow manage to deal with Vesryn, Ravara's going to come—and soon. The elves on this island aren't warriors."

"No, they aren't," Nym agreed as he rummaged through Cillian's chest, pulling out a package wrapped in thick parchment. He placed it in Cillian's hands. "But you are." He rounded Cillian's chair and leaned against the wall in front of him, gesturing to the package. "Open it."

Cillian pulled the twine that flimsily held the parchment closed, and he carefully pulled it away, revealing a stunning demonic fist. He lifted it delicately, turning it in his hands, marveling at the outstanding craftsmanship. Jagged plates of Hellstone composed the outer shell, blending into razor-sharp spiked studs of Infernal Iron that capped the knuckles. Everything about the piece was perfect, right down to the Shadow Leather that would extend up his forearm, keeping the weapon secure as he tore and rendered flesh with every strike.

Unable to wait, he slipped it on, sighing as the metal fused with his skin and the plates started to glow red from the minuscule molten cores within. He unfurled his fingers, wiggling the claw-like extensions, pleased to find that whoever had crafted this piece understood that malleability was necessary.

Cillian threw out a quick jab, and a faint, fiery trail graced the air, the mark of a weapon forged in hellfire and steeped in blood. "Who crafted this? How?"

"Corym came to me after he went to his smith, said his guy couldn't make somethin' like this. You're not the only demon to come to Faerie, drek," Nym muttered, his eyes wide as he took in the sheer lethality of the weapon, as if unaware of what he had helped forge. "The ruins down by Siren's Bay... there's an old Olvathian hellforger holin' up there."

Cillian stared at Nym, taking a moment to appreciate the elf to whom he hadn't given nearly enough credit. "Just who are you?"

A wide grin spread across Nym's face as his eyes flicked up from the weapon. "Someone who gets things done, drek." He pulled his arms across his chest, stretching out his shoulders.

"Corym said you might need help with somethin' else? I'm guessin' it has somethin' to do with that thing."

Cillian ran a finger along the runes etched into the metal of his fist. "Yeah... but we're not gonna do that on this ship. Is there a large, open area near here?"

"How large we talkin'? This big, that big?" Nym measured different sizes with his hands. "There's an open space in this cave to the left of where we come from, but it's not huge."

"Well, that depends on if you're as accurate with your magic as you are with needles."

"Hah! I knew ya liked me, drek." Nym chuckled as he opened the door. "C'mon. Let's get this over with."

Nym cocked his head to the side as they entered the cavern. "Gonna' need ya to say that again. A bit slower this time. What do ya want me to do?"

Cillian was on the ground doing one-armed pushups, getting ready for what could only be described as suicide. "Need you... to try and kill me... but you know, use something... that won't actually..." He grunted as he switched positions to stretch his legs, "take my head off in case this doesn't work."

"When I gave Silas the plans ya drew up, he mentioned that the weapon was extremely dangerous—that there were few demons who could wield such a thing." Nym looked around the cavern, his eyes quickly inspecting the stalactites and stalagmites. "What happens if this doesn't work, drek? I'm not in the business of bein' buried alive."

Cillian pushed himself up from the ground, rolling his shoulders to ease the tension. "It's not going to bring the place down. At least, that's not the goal." He flexed his hands, feeling the burn in his muscles. "If this works, it'll give us an edge against anything Vesryn or Ravara throws at us. But yeah, if it doesn't... let's just say, we'll both have a very bad day."

Nym raised an eyebrow, crossing his arm as he leaned against the jagged wall of the grotto. "You're mad, drek. Properly mad. But... I can respect that." He ran his fingers over his dagger, the blade catching the light that filtered in from the cracks above. "I'll use some basic magic—enough to test whatever the hells you're plannin' without turnin' this place into a graveyard."

Cillian nodded, adjusting the straps of his fist. "Good. That's all I need." He took a deep breath, centering himself, feeling the familiar rush of adrenaline pumping through his veins. "Just keep the pressure on me. I need to see if the runes hold under a real attack."

Nym stepped forward, his stance shifting as he readied himself. A faint glow surrounded his hands, flickering with the emerald hue of his magic. "I'll try not to kill ya, but no promises." His eyes sparkled with mischief, but there was a seriousness there, too—a mutual understanding that this was more than just a test.

Cillian squared his shoulders, extending the claws of the weapon he'd carefully designed, the one forged in secrecy with materials straight from the hells themselves. He could feel the power thrumming within it, mingling with his demonic blood, a volatile force waiting to be unleashed. "Let's do this."

Without warning, Nym lunged, magic rippling from his fingertips in a controlled burst aimed straight at Cillian's chest. Cillian's eyes went wide, and he dodged at the last second. The cavern shook as the blast hit the wall behind him, sending a million pieces of stone flying. Blood dribbled from thin slices where his bare arms were nicked. Cillian paid them no mind.

Nym flipped in the air, lips curling into a wicked grin as he threw two bright green arcs as sharp as razors straight at Cillian. They whizzed through the air, following one another like a boomerang. Quickly, Cillian calculated their trajectory, anticipating where they would hit him. He jumped back to give himself enough room and threw out a mean right hook, slamming into each crescent moon.

The magic stilled as Nym's power twisted, breaking down to their baser elements until they were nothing more than glowing particles. The remnants of energy remained still, but only for less than a second before they twisted into a vortex and were sucked into the runes like a black hole.

Cillian's arm shook so badly that he needed to stabilize it with his free hand. Foreign power seeped into his veins like a parasite, waging a battle between elves and demons below the surface of his skin. His demonic essence had the upper hand, and he was quickly able to sift through the deconstructed magic and put it back together in such a way that made Cillian *thrive*. But it was too much too fast, and Cillian faltered against the sheer force of Nym's attack. His vision blurred, the edges of the grotto spinning as he struggled to keep his footing. If he lost control now, it would all be over.

"You're losin' it, drek!" Nym yelled. Cillian didn't need to see the elf to hear the panic in his voice. "Control it!"

Cillian growled, summoning every ounce of his willpower to stabilize the magic. The weapon thrummed violently in his grasp, teetering on the edge of chaos. With a final, desperate push, he forced the energy back, equally dispersed within his body like a protective barrier.

Taking a moment to catch his breath, Cillian looked at Nym and nodded. "We go again."

"Ya sure that's a good idea?"

"We go again!" Cillian barked. "We go until my body gets used to the influx. *Go!*"

Nym hesitated for a heartbeat before shrugging. "Alright, drek. Your funeral," Nym muttered, steeling himself as the glow of his magic intensified, swirling around him like a living, breathing entity. He raised his hand, and this time, the energy coalesced into jagged spears of light, crackling dangerously.

Cillian braced himself. The runes on his weapon pulsed, ready to absorb and repurpose whatever was thrown at him. Nym thrust his arm forward, sending the spears hurtling toward Cillian at blinding speed. The air hummed with raw power as the spears neared, each one aimed to hit a vital spot.

Cillian swung his weapon, catching the first spear on the flat of the blade. The impact reverberated up his arm, and the spear shattered into pure energy, sucked into the runes like water down a drain. The second spear followed, and Cillian contorted his body, letting the energy flow into him, every nerve alight with the jarring sensation of magic colliding with his demonic core. He could feel the strain, the burn of the invading power seeping into his muscles, but he forced himself to stay upright, to hold steady.

But Nym didn't relent. He pulled a third spear from the ether, this one larger, crackling with unstable magic that hissed and spat. It was a chaotic, volatile mix that could tear through flesh and bone without a second thought. Cillian's eyes widened —this wasn't the kind of magic you tested with; it was the kind you unleashed on an enemy you wanted dead.

"Hold tight, drek!" Nym warned, the playful edge gone from his voice. "This one's got a bite!" He threw the spear, and Cillian barely had time to react as it hurtled toward him, slicing through the air like a lightning bolt.

Cillian raised the weapon, the runes blazing to life in a desperate attempt to absorb the projectile. The impact was immediate and brutal, knocking the wind from his lungs as its energy ricocheted through him, searching for a way out. The demonic etchings flickered, struggling to contain the wild magic as it lashed out, searing through Cillian's nerves. He bit down hard, jaw clenched against the pain, forcing the monstrous energy to bend to his will.

Nym's magic coiled inside him like a viper, and for a terrifying moment, Cillian thought he'd lost the battle. His vision darkened, black spots dancing before his eyes as it threatened to overwhelm him. But he dug deeper, reaching for that uniquely Olvathian part of him that lay at his core, the part of him that was ruthless, unyielding, and had been lost to his time in Faerie. He anchored himself in that darkness, drawing the magic inward until it settled, simmering beneath his skin like a controlled storm.

Cillian stumbled back, panting, his body on fire with residual energy. He met Nym's gaze, the elf's expression a mix of awe and disbelief. "Again," Cillian demanded, his voice hoarse but unwavering.

Nym shook his head, wiping sweat from his brow. "You're gonna kill yourself at this rate, drek."

Cillian grinned, blood trickling from the corner of his mouth. "Better me than Margot. We go again."

Nym nodded, the respect clear in his eyes as he readied another spell. "Fine. But don't say I didn't warn ya."

As Nym prepared the next wave of attacks, Cillian planted his feet, steadying himself. Each round would push him closer to the brink, but he knew he had to master the elven magic, had to make it his own.

For Margot.

For himself.

For the battles ahead of them.

There was no room for failure.

THE VEILGUARD

Corym longed to carve Vesryn open, peel back his skin, and slowly pull out his intestines, foot by foot, just so he could strangle the bastard with his own guts. It wouldn't kill him—no, that would be too merciful—but it would be agony, a slow, traumatizing descent into pain as his skin fused back together around his insides, letting Corym tear him apart all over again. He wanted Vesryn to suffer as he had, as his soldiers had, as those living in Caramis had. No one was safe from his wrath. Not even those elves simply trying to peddle their wares to survive, which had become more and more taxing. Just days ago, Corym had watched Vesryn open the earth, swallowing Almira and her stall, simply because he remembered the look she gave Margot.

If Corym hadn't been watching as Vesryn backhanded Grizsa, sending him flying across the field, he would have thought it impossible for the elf to sink any lower. That was how the past four hours had been spent, with Vesryn barking orders and beating *his* troops, chipping away at the last remnants of their resolve.

"You five," Vesryn singsonged as he pointed to one group. "And you three." He pointed to another cluster of elves. "It is expected that the Veilguard fair well training against one another, but how about fighting someone well and truly strong?"

With a flourish, Vesryn tore off his robe, vanishing it to the ether, revealing his fighting leathers beneath. He knotted his hair on top of his head and brandished his sword, holding it in his left hand while a swirl of magic appeared in his right. "Eight on one." Vesryn chuckled, his lips curling into a vicious smile. "Should be easy for members of the Veilguard, yes?"

The group Vesryn selected murmured amongst themselves, unsure of what to do. Corym remained at Vesryn's side with his teeth clenched. If Vesryn's unfortunate chosen caused him harm, they'd be dead. However, openly defying a direct order would also result in ramifications. This was a lose-lose situation.

Thyna looked at Corym, weary. He dipped his chin in a solitary nod. As bad as this situation was, it would be worse if they didn't follow a direct command given to them by their 'king.'

She gave the group a look that said, *I know this is a horrible idea, but just do what you're told,* as she dropped to a fighting stance. The others followed suit, their eyes bouncing between their comrades and Vesryn as if trying to decide how best to approach what could very well be their death.

Corym pressed his lips together to stop himself from scoffing. *King.* When Vesryn demanded they all refer to him as such, the word just became another reminder of how far the elf he had once called a friend had fallen. The Vesryn of a hundred years ago would have laughed at the notion. Then, he would have performed a tirade that Ilphas and Corym had heard a thousand times about how daft Ravara truly was. How the self-appointed 'Fae King' was all that was wrong with fae society, and if they had any sense, they would stand against him because their kind could never thrive under such a regime.

But that Vesryn was long gone. He had died when he bound Ilphas to his bed and crushed his throat with his bare hands because he thought he would acquire his brother's power that rivaled even his own. Vesryn should have known better, should have known that Ilphas would have never willingly handed over the key to the kingdom to someone likely to break. He should have realized the second he decided to take his own brother's life that Ilphas would *know* who killed him.

Ilphas had.

And just to spite his twisted kin, he chose a recipient so far outside the realm of Faerie that something inside Vesryn snapped when he learned the truth. He fumed for weeks because killing the girl would have been so simple, but Vesryn couldn't take the risk because from beyond the grave, Ilphas had still been in control of the magic he left with a human woman—Ilphas was *still* in control, judging by how little power Margot had mastered.

So, Vesryn took her from the demon. He curated lessons that would never truly teach her how to harness the unbridled magic she harbored deep within and addled her mind. He wanted control so he could lay claim to his empire and expand beyond the borders of Caramis, and unless he was stopped, he would succeed.

Breken walked across the field and stood next to Corym, clasping his hands behind his back as he looked at the skirmish that had unfolded. Vesryn froze six elves with the wave of his hand, laughing maniacally as he beckoned another eight to join the fray. He summoned jagged pillars of earth, launching them in every direction as the Veilguard's paltry attacks bounced off him like light rain.

Soon, two more groups joined. Thirty-two elves against one. Nearly a third of the Veilguard was fighting with all their might, and they were struggling. Vesryn called in two more groups as he summoned a tempest strong enough to send the combatants flying across the field, smashing into the swaying palms that graced much of the island, which shuddered under the impact.

"This exercise is nothing more than a display of power," Corym muttered as an ungodly snap echoed across the field. Jerrod's femur had been broken in two, and he lay in a heap, threatening to be crushed by the chaotic fighting surrounding him.

"Good elves will die today, Corym." Breken grimaced, patiently waiting his turn to be included in the slaughter.

"I can't stop this—none of us can." Corym glanced at Breken before returning to the fight, not wanting to draw unnecessary attention to his best soldier. "Vesryn is no longer listening to reason."

The two stood silently as Vesryn pirouetted across the field, fracturing arms and dislocating jaws like it was a game for elflings. Reluctantly, two more groups joined, throwing spears of ice and waterspouts filled with razor-sharp sea glass across the field, attempting to stop Vesryn as their ire grew. Not that it mattered—Vesryn hadn't been touched. Not a hair on his head was out of place, there wasn't a single bead of sweat dotting his forehead, and he had the energy to keep going until the entire Veilguard had been crushed into oblivion. If every single fae within Faerie piled onto Caramis' shores and attempted to kill Vesryn, Corym wasn't sure they would succeed. Some would consider Vesryn a god, and his power nearly rivaled the goddesses who had all but abandoned them. If they were to have any chance of stopping him, they needed Margot to be in control of her mind as well as her magic. Time was running out.

"Masha... she's carrying," Breken whispered, breaking through Corym's thoughts. "Found out last night." He turned to Corym, the muscles in his jaw ticking as his eyes glistened with unshed tears. "I will not die today. You *must* stop this. That elfling needs me. Masha needs me."

"Breken..." Corym sucked in a breath, wanting desperately to slap his soldier on the back and bring him into a tight embrace to congratulate him, but he remained facing forward out of fear. "Are you—are you sure? How?"

Breken nodded. "I'm sure. It's been weeks since she has bled. As for how, well, we can thank Nym for that." From the corner of

Corym's eye, he saw a smile tugging at the corners of his right hand's lips. "More than once, he brought us to the mainland."

"He didn't... you didn't!"

"Oh, don't give me that, Corym," Breken hissed, though it lacked a venomous bite. "You know as well as I do there's no future here for us—Masha conceiving recently after our trip back confirms what we feared."

"It's too dangerous! The fae will kill us on sight!"

"You see, that's where you're wrong. The fae in those villages? They don't care about us, nor do they treat us any differently. The elves are the only ones who care, hiding on this island, living in fear, defending bigotry." Vesryn called in another group, and Breken balled his fists as he watched his brothers and sisters drop one after the other. "Stop this, Corym. I don't care what you do, I don't care how you do it, but you need to stop this."

Ysolde, Wren, and Finley were the last three standing, barely. The elves were caked in blood, their skin mottled with bruises. They looked at one another, their chests heaving as they drew ragged breaths, and they nodded. Back to back to back, they covered all sides and shifted positions into the Veilguard's Kiss, a fighting stance that would allow them to combine their magic, allowing for quick, lethal strikes focused on disabling their opponent. This was their last-ditch effort, a dangerous attempt to end the senseless battle, and before Corym could stop them, they flickered for a moment, then teleported behind Vesryn, hurling streaks of light no thicker than a parchment cut. It took less than a second for the attack to speed through the air, whistling through the currents, and nicking Vesryn's cheek.

Vesryn gently wiped the wound on his skin and slowly brought his finger eye level to look at the blood dripping to the ground from the tip. His eyes darkened as he lowered his chin, snapping his fingers to send the downed members of the Veilguard to the edges of the field before enclosing Ysolde, Wren, and Finley in a fiery cell. From the outside, blue flames licked up an imaginary wall nearly fifteen feet high, trapping those who dared injure the great king. Their cage was crystalline, allowing onlookers to see what their transgression had earned them.

"Bravo," Vesryn mocked as he circled them. "You managed to hit me. *Once.*" His lips curled into a vicious grin as he stopped, pressing his hand against the flame. "Let us see what you can do should the fae breach our defenses."

The command hung in the air like a death sentence. The three remaining elves looked at the inferno surrounding them, fear flashing in their eyes. There was no escape, no reprieve—only the impossible task of proving themselves in the face of agony.

Corym's heart pounded in his chest, his fury mounting as he watched the revolting spectacle unfold. Vesryn wasn't testing their mettle; it was a calculated torment designed to shatter their spirits, to grind down whatever remained of their courage to make them compliant. Vesryn was solidifying his reign of terror, crushing the last vestiges of hope beneath his heel. And Corym knew, with sickening certainty, they would not make it out alive.

Breken shot Corym a look before stepping away as Vesryn made his way over to Corym.

"What fun this is." Vesryn chuckled as he glanced at Corym. "Do you think they shall prevail? I wonder."

The flames crept closer, inch by agonizing inch, devouring the ground beneath them and shrinking the safe space of their enclosure. Even from twenty feet away, the heat was unbearable, the air thick with the acrid scent of burning earth and sweat.

"You must end this now, Vesryn," Corym pleaded. "There is nothing left to prove!"

The smile in Vesryn's eyes faded. "Tread carefully, Corym. Your insolence grows tiresome." He looked over to the struggling elves, his amusement dimmed but not entirely gone. "In time, you will see this is necessary. Survival is not for the weak, and I will not allow the Veilguard to be anything less than formidable. Should they fall here, well, it will prove you must rethink your training regimen."

Corym clenched his teeth, every muscle in his body tense as

he watched the three elves give their last, desperate effort against a futile battle. Unless he wanted to severely cripple the resistance's efforts, he could only watch in helpless rage.

"What are we supposed to do?" Wren asked, his voice strained as he wiped sweat from his brow. "Run through the fire to the other side?"

Ysolde glanced nervously at the encroaching flames, her face pale. "Somehow, I doubt it's that easy."

Finley dropped his head back, looking to the sky as if he could taste the freedom he hadn't experienced in years, and likely never would again. He looked at the wall of fire that kept shrinking, then to his brother and sister, then to his comrades beyond his crypt. He scanned the field, his eyes falling on Corym. His throat bobbed as it turned back to the other two who were trapped.

"I guess we better test it," Finley said as he stepped closer to the flame.

He held his trembling hand out, close enough that his flesh began to smoke, and with a guttural cry, he pressed his fingertips to the firestorm. The second Finley made contact with the wall, it gobbled his entire arm before swallowing him whole. He screamed and screamed and screamed, his skin turning from pale yellow to pink to a revolting black as he turned to charcoal.

Corym had never felt sicker.

Ysolde fell to her knees, sobbing, repeatedly asking the goddesses why they had let something so horrible happen. Wren rushed around the perimeter, eyes wild, nostrils flaring from how hard he was breathing. And Vesryn just laughed.

"Please stop this," Corym whispered. "No one else needs to die."

Vesryn cocked his head to the side, giving Corym a sidelong glance. "No. I think they do." He clapped his hands once, and the barrier transformed into an obelisk of death, burning Ysolde and Wren simply for doing what was asked.

The flames dwindled to nothing more than a smolder. Those of the Veilguard that remained standing lowered their heads, paying respect to their fallen comrades. Breken looked at Corym, face shining in the sunlight as tears rolled down his cheeks. He shook his head before lowering it.

Vesryn cackled as he donned his robe and headed toward the manor. He looked over his shoulder at Corym. "Clean up this mess."

SAVE MY SOUL

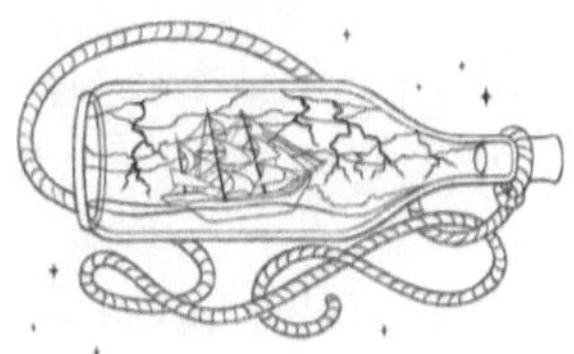

Cillian stretched his aching muscles, now brimming with power. He was no stranger to the demonic fist absorbing demonic blood, but consuming raw elven magic was something else entirely—it left him buzzing, feeling stronger than ever. The sensation was intoxicating, almost *too* good, and he had no desire to sour his mood by returning to the manor, where Vesryn's shadow loomed.

"There a way out of here that'll keep me far from the manor?"

"Not ready to go back? Can't say I blame ya." Nym motioned for Cillian to follow him, leading him to a narrow tunnel that barely looked passable. "This'll do the trick." A wicked grin spread across Nym's face as he gestured for Cillian to crawl through. "Go on, then."

"You first."

"Suit yourself."

Nym dropped to his hands and knees and clambered into the passage. Cillian eyed the small opening. After a few moments, he shrugged and followed anyway. *Nym wouldn't put himself at risk. That damn elf's sense of self-preservation is better than mine.* Halfway through, he realized just how tight the space was, and by the time he reached the end, he was well and truly stuck. With a laugh, Nym grabbed his arms and yanked him out, depositing Cillian in the fresh air just past the city gardens.

Cillian wiped the dirt from his clothes, glancing back at the tunnel. "You enjoyed that, didn't you?"

"Watchin' you squirm in that tiny hole?" Nym's grin widened. "Absolutely. Worth every second, drek."

Cillian shook his head, suppressing a smile. There was probably an easier way out of the grotto, but Nym had clearly enjoyed seeing him wedged in the tunnel. And with how good Cillian felt, he couldn't even be mad.

"Where are you off to?" Cillian asked as Nym started to walk away.

"The flagon, of course," Nym said over his shoulder. "What better way to pass the time than with some sweet, sweet mead? Besides, got a meetin' with ol' Cory later. A nice buzz would help anyone get through that." He turned around and waved three fingers in the air. "See ya' later, drek."

Cillian watched Nym disappear into the distance before he started meandering down the winding path. Even from the outskirts, Caramis was an impressive sight. The lush foliage framed glimpses of vibrant buildings in the distance, their roofs dotting the lavender sky. If Cillian didn't know better, if he hadn't seen the horrors that lurked behind closed doors, he might've been tempted to let Caramis' beauty deceive him, lulling him into a false sense of security.

As he followed the path around the manicured gardens, the stones beneath his boots smooth and well-worn, he noticed how empty it was. No signs of life, no distant chatter, just the soft rustle of leaves in the breeze. Everyone had sequestered themselves indoors, where it was safer from the Vesryn's baleful eye. Though, there was little to stop the elf from tearing through homes just to show that he could. Cillian didn't know how Caramis had been before he arrived, but he doubted the elves could continue to overlook the horrors being committed atop the hill inside the manor where their mad overseer lived.

Cillian reached for his dagger as the wall to his right shuddered. He crouched low, creeping closer when it flickered twice more before winking out of existence, leaving fractured stonework, its jagged edges giving way to an overgrown path beyond. He was certain that Vesryn was the only elf paranoid enough to hide something as innocuous as a cracked wall. And why go through all that trouble of keeping magic in place to dissuade passersby not to inspect the damn thing? Why not fix it? *Unless he has something to keep secret—something he needs to return to.*

Cillian moved a few vines so he could get a better look. The sheer amount of growth led him to believe that this path had been hidden for years. He sniffed. There wasn't a scent he could track. The grass and dirt hadn't been disturbed either. No one had been there in a long, long time, and he was going to find out why.

He unsheathed his blade and hacked through the thick tangle of vines and aerial roots that had twisted together, sending jungle detritus flying. He could only take a few steps at a time before needing to swing again to clear more of the path. The process was arduous and made more unpleasant by the suffocating heat, which became worse as he stepped deeper into the jungle. Thick underbrush and a dense canopy overhead meant there wasn't even a breeze to provide a scrap of relief.

Cillian wiped his brow as he leaned against a tree, taking a moment to catch his breath. He had been cutting away for hours and wasn't sure how much further he had to go to get to the heart of whatever Vesryn was hiding. Would the elf be curious to know where Cillian had gone? If Nym kept his meeting with Corym, maybe Nym would have the foresight to tell Corym that Cillian needed a break from the manor. Though aloof, Nym was full of all sorts of surprises.

He uncorked his waterskin with his teeth, chugging half of the container before dumping the rest on his head, and pushed off the trunk with a grunt, chopping the nearest limb with one quick swipe.

The further away from Caramis he got, the more uneasy he felt. Pain needled his chest, letting him know just how far from Margot he was, while whispers danced on the edge of his hearing, a light, tinkling voice coaxing him forward. He weaved through gnarled tree roots and dodged low-hanging branches, swinging wildly as he carved his way toward Vesryn's dirty secret.

Eventually, the trees thinned, and the uneven ground gave way to a bed of soft moss that cushioned his feet. He breathed deeply, the air crisper, fresh, less dense. A cool breeze ruffled his hair, blowing away the perspiration coating his skin like a veil. The sound of rushing water soothed his weary soul, as if whatever this place was held the power to heal even the most private wounds. Mist kissed his face—a welcomed respite—as he followed the stream around a bend. He stopped in front of a plunge pool, transfixed by the shimmering cascade of waters. Dappled light reflected off the spray, setting it aglow with every imaginable color, making it sparkle like liquid gems.

A subtle shift in the air caught his eye. And there, through the haze and sunlight, stood a figure—a woman with flowing thistle-colored hair that blended seamlessly into the surroundings. She wore a gown of delicate petals, each one shifting like an ever-changing rainbow. The woman glanced in Cillian's direction, green eyes narrowed before widening, suspicion replaced with wonder. Without a word, she extended a hand toward him—an invitation to join her in this sanctuary.

Cillian hesitated before wading through the water toward her. He placed his hand in hers, only to find it wasn't whole. What he felt was magic, not skin, as he let the mist envelop him.

"Who are you?" he asked.

She tilted her head and furrowed her brow as if contemplating. "My name is Liriel. And you, Cillian, are going to help save my soul."

Cillian stiffened. "You knew... you knew what Vesryn was, and you let him live. *You're* the reason Margot is suffering." He knew he should be begging the goddess to help take Vesryn down, but his rage was nearly bursting at the seams. "Why would I help you do a damn thing?"

"You're not wrong. I thought I could guide him, convince him that his path would lead to ruination. My ego was my downfall." Her lips seemed to stretch, leaving an echo of a sad smile. "When Ilphas was killed, it wasn't long after that Vesryn came for me." She scoffed. "The fool used my own magic against me—another mistake on my part for documenting the rituals... but what's done is done. There's no going back. Mother Time is cruel, and even the higher powers cannot alter the past."

"So, you're..."

"...Dead. Quite."

Cillian squeezed his eyes shut, tipping his head back as he slowly exhaled. "Fuck." He scrubbed his face before locking eyes with Liriel. "I'm guessing that means you can't help with Vesryn."

"Not directly, no."

"And indirectly?"

Liriel's viridian eyes sparkled. "As I said, you will help save my soul. I've lingered here for far too long, and it's time for me to return to Arcadia."

Cillian ran his fingers through his hair. *So, she wants to go to the final resting place, huh?* "And how does someone save the soul of a goddess?"

"Simple," Liriel said as she floated higher, just enough to be a head taller than Cillian. "One from another world who can harness the power of both darkness and light breaks the chains."

"I'm sorry." He gave her a half smile and shook his head. "That someone isn't me. Darkness is the only thing coursing through these veins."

Liriel's lips curled into a knowing smile. "Ah, but you've inferred incorrectly. I never said *you* would break the chains." She dipped her chin, lowering her voice. "I said you would *help*. The girl—you will bring her here. She can free me."

"Margot?" Cillian ignored the pain constricting his heart.

"Even if she wasn't under Vesryn's thumb, she's nothing but good. There isn't a shred of darkness in her soul."

"Isn't there?" Cillian cocked an eyebrow, waiting for Liriel to continue. She chuckled and brushed a watery plait over her shoulder. "Perhaps that was true before she became your blood sworn. But now? Your life flows through her veins, tainting her soul. You may have changed *who* you are, but you cannot change *what* you are, Cillian."

"And what of me?" he asked, swallowing the lump in his throat. "Does her life not flow through my veins, purifying my soul?"

"Ah... while elven blood is powerful, it does not breed corruption as a demon's blood does. Her lifeforce isn't trying to humanize you or transform you into an elf, rather it strengthens a bond that never should have existed." She rested her hand against her breast. "A bond that cannot be broken by even a deities' power. It may create beautiful swirls, but it can never change the ocean's essential nature."

The ache in his chest flared, spreading through his body like poison. If Margot wasn't addled, who would she be? Would the blood bond slowly consume her, chipping away at what little of her humanity remained? It was no secret that she was different now. Not the same woman he had found trembling in the Dreadwood. But was that difference caused by the magic she now harbored, Vesryn, or the demon she had grown to care for?

"So, you're saying this is my fault... that I helped create some sort of... amalgamation."

Liriel's gaze softened. "I'm saying it's a consequence. You gave her a part of yourself, and in doing so, you changed her—just as she's changed you, even if only slightly."

Cillian shook his head, stepping back from the pool where Liriel's spectral form shimmered like a mirage. "I never meant to harm her. I was trying to save her."

"Who's to say you didn't?" She floated closer to him, the petals of her dress drifting behind her. "Darkness is not something that can be erased so easily. It lingers, Cillian, as you know. It finds a way to seep into the cracks." She sighed. "Look, I'm not saying Margot is destined to become a harbinger of doom, but once this business with Vesryn is concluded, your work will be far from over."

He stared into the glistening water, his reflection rippling and distorted. For the first time in a long while, doubt crept into his mind—doubt about what he had done. He had thought that binding himself to Margot was the only way to save her. But had he only damned her in the process?

"Your thoughts are so loud I can almost hear them, Cillian. There is no use fretting over what has already been done. Bring her here and free me. Let us be done with this chapter; that way we can all move on to the next."

"Even if I brought her here, Vesryn has her mind locked up so tight even the blood bond has trouble getting through. There's no way she could do what you're asking."

Liriel waved him off. "Nonsense. I may be dead, but I'm not incapable of performing magic." With a slow, deliberate movement, she raised her arms, and the cascade of water behind her froze, halting mid-flow, turning it into an immobile, crystalline structure that shimmered in the light. "Bring her here, and I assure you I can unknot my own magic."

"Your magic? Of course." Cillian scoffed. "And you think you can fix her?" He snapped his fingers in front of Liriel's face. "Just like that?"

"Yes, my magic," Liriel mocked, sneering at him like a petulant child. "Unfortunately, when Vesryn bound me here, he gained access to a veritable trove of knowledge—and not all the knowledge is... agreeable." Her smile faltered; sadness glazed her eyes. "Vesryn is a horrid creature, stubborn, too smart for his own good. I... I can only imagine what he has done to that poor girl. And while I can help her remember who she is... I cannot fix what is broken." Her ghostly magic pressed into Cillian's chest as she poked him. "That is for you to mend."

"You want to use her," he whispered. "Use her for the darkness that is slowly consuming her to break your chains. You're talking about her like she's some kind of tool. Margot's not a weapon to be wielded. She's a person."

"You think I don't know that? Do you think I don't feel the fragility of her spirit?" She jabbed his chest again. "You've set her on this path, Cillian. And there's no turning back now. By breaking my chains, she will find the key to breaking her own. That girl has strength you have yet to fully comprehend—all of you. She most certainly is a weapon, but not for one to wield, no. She must claim that power for herself."

"If I bring her here, what happens next, Liriel? How do I know you won't just use her and cast her aside?"

"I'm not Vesryn, Cillian. I don't seek control or enslave. I want freedom—for both of us. Margot's role in this is not one of subjugation but of choice. She will choose to free me, and in doing so, she will find her own path to freedom."

"And if she refuses?"

Liriel's lips curved into a sad smile. "Then I remain her, bound to this place for eternity, and she continues to fight Vesryn on her own. But I suspect Margot will understand the gravity of the situation better than you think. Besides..." She leaned forward. "There's someone who *desperately* wishes to speak with her. And without that meeting? You have no hope of stopping Vesryn."

Cillian clenched his fists at his side as he painfully remembered Margot discussing what Ancestral Memory was while Vesryn violated her, forcing Cillian to watch. "It's Ilphas, isn't it?"

"That, I cannot say. It's not my place to reveal their identity. But I can tell you this: their connection to her is deeper than you realize. You must trust me."

Cillian's jaw worked, grinding his teeth together as he considered his options. *Trust* wasn't something he handed out easily, especially not to a mysterious being who withheld crucial information. But with the fae threat breathing down their necks and Vesryn ready to explode, time was running out.

"And you'll help Margot?" He eyed her. "How do I know I can trust you?"

"You can't," she said plainly. "But I'm asking you to try."

He hated this—being forced to rely on someone who offered nothing but riddles and half-answers. He swallowed hard, his throat tight. "No promises," he muttered, forcing the words out. "But I'll try to bring Margot to you. She deserves to be free."

"And so do I, Cillian Blackwood, General of the Dread Lord and keeper of Olvath's demonic forces. So do I."

Cillian turned away from the plunge pool, not at all surprised that the goddess knew exactly who he was, despite having abandoned his family name and title long ago. As he began the long, winding journey back to Margot, the cool mist clinging to his skin.

Just before he stepped into the dense underbrush, he glanced over his shoulder. "How close are the fae to breaching Caramis?"

Liriel's eyes gleamed, her form flickering like the water caught in the sun. "You better hurry. Time is not on your side."

ONE HELLS OF A STORY

"Do you think we can really trust the demon?" Stog asked as he placed a tankard of mead in front of Nym. "I mean... he's a *demon*."

"Yeah." Nym gulped the brew and smacked his lips together, sloshing his drink toward Stog, who grimaced as he wiped his face. "And you're a shiesty barkeep who liquors up their patrons to swindle them for all they're worth."

Stog snorted. "Because we're all worth so much nowadays." He pushed a bowl of pitted stoneseeds toward Nym. "Well, can we?"

"'Course we can." Nym popped a few kernels into his mouth, crunching loudly. "When have I ever steered ya wrong?"

"I can think of more than a few..." Stog's voice trailed off as the Flagon's door opened, his face paling. He jerked his chin behind Nym before leaning in close. "Good luck," he whispered.

Nym drained the last of his mead and slid the tankard down the bar for a refill. That Corym deigned to find Nym here spoke volumes of how his day with Vesryn must have gone and he wasn't looking forward to their meeting. He swiveled around on his stool, nearly falling off it when he saw Corym covered in dried blood, soot, and ash. The stench wafting off him permeated throughout the tavern, nearly enough to knock an elf uncon-scious. Nym glanced between Tanir and Ced, raising an eyebrow as if to say, *Well? Are you gonna say something?* Both elves avoided his gaze, staring intently into their cups as if the answers to all life's problems were swirling at the bottom. Nym rolled his eyes. *Buncha skive's.*

Corym trudged up to the bar, chugged a pint that Stog had slid his way, and immediately pushed it forward for another. It was rare for him to drown his sorrows at the Flagon, and Nym knew better than to pry when Corym was in one of his dark moods. The elf had a mean right hook, and after the effort Nym had put into helping Cillian, he wasn't eager to have his face smashed in on top of it.

They sat in heavy silence, the tension thick enough to choke on. Corym didn't utter a word until he downed three more cups, his voice finally piercing through the quiet like a blade. "Ysolde, Wren, and Finley are dead."

The entire tavern froze. Conversations died mid-sentence. Chairs scraped to a halt. Drinks were set down, untouched. Even Stog, who was always cleaning something, stopped wiping down the bar and rested his hands on the counter, his head bowed.

Nym swallowed hard before asking the obvious question since no one else had the guts to do it. "Vesryn?"

"Who else?" Corym muttered as he sighed into his tankard. "And it's worse than that. Half the Veilguard's out of commission. Which brings me to why we're meeting." He shot Nym a sidelong glance. "Back room."

Nym didn't hesitate, hopping off his stool. "Fill me up." He leaned close to Stog, jabbing him in the shoulder with two fingers. "And gimme the good stuff. I know you've been hiding it behind the counter."

Stog grumbled but obliged, and by the time Nym received his drink, Corym had already disappeared, leaving Nym to trail after him.

The door creaked as he entered the back room, taking a

moment to inspect Stog's supplies, slapping a barrel. A hollow sound reverberated inside the cask. *Empty.* There had been hardly anything left. A few sacks of stoneseeds, a couple baskets of dried haloran plums, but not nearly enough mead to get them through what was coming. He moved to the closest shelf, gently opening the only bag that was not empty. Yeast. One sack of yeast. He tipped his head back and exhaled slowly when Corym shifted, drawing Nym's attention to the elf leaning against a barrel.

"Vesryn killed them," Corym whispered. "He killed them because my soldiers did what was asked of them. He killed them because he could." His eyes were distant, haunted, as he scuffed his boot against the floor. "Did you know Masha is carrying?"

Nym paused mid-drink, eyebrow raising. "Masha? Didn't have a clue she was carryin'. That's somethin', for sure. We should celebrate."

"Oh, come off it, Nym!" Corym's voice cracked. He kicked off from the barrel, sending it tumbling and spilling mead across the floor. His boots sloshed through the mess as he marched toward Nym, fists clenched. "I know you've taken them to the mainland. You've been ferrying my soldiers out!"

Nym looked at the mead pooling around his feet, then back at Corym, his eyebrows knit together. "Now, why'd ya have to go and do that?" He gestured to the ruined barrel with an exaggerated sigh. "That was perfectly good booze!"

Corym's face twisted in anger. "This isn't about the damn booze, Nym!"

Nym's usual grin faltered for a moment, his green eyes hardening. "Yeah, well maybe you ought to think about why I'm ferryin' anyone in the first place. Maybe 'cause someone's gotta give those elves a chance. Give them somethin' to fight for." He held Corym's gaze, no longer the flippant elf who let insults slide off him like oil. "And don't pretend *you* didn't know what Vesryn would do. Don't tell me there was nothin' you could do. You know damn well that you're livin' in fear just like the rest of us. Scared that your life will be the next one taken."

"Fuck!" Corym bellowed, his fist slamming into the nearest support beam with a bone-rattling crack. The wood splintered under the force, but he paid it no mind. His chest heaved with ragged breaths as he turned to Nym, hands gripping his dark braids, tugging at the roots. "You're right! I'm fucking terrified!"

He sank to the floor, crouching low, his forearms resting heavily on his knees as his head dropped between his legs. "They're dead because of me."

What followed was a thick, oppressive silence, broken only by the sound of Corym's ragged, uneven breaths. His admission hung in the air like a death sentence, each word a confession of his deepest fears, his failures—and he'd shared them with *Nym*, of all elves. He was left vulnerable and raw; the armor he wore so proudly had finally cracked.

Nym stood awkwardly nearby, picking at his cuticles, sneaking glances at the broken elf before him. Corym's shoulders shook, silent sobs wracked his body, though not a sound slipped past his lips. What Nym wouldn't give to tell a light joke or share a stiff drink with him. But there was no banter sharp enough, no liquor strong enough to piece together something so fragile, something that had permanently ripped away pieces of Corym's soul.

Corym—the ever-stoic, unwavering right-hand elf—had been crushed like a bug under Vesryn's heel. And Nym knew all too well that Vesryn hadn't done it purely for amusement. No, this was deliberate. A calculated, brutal reminder of who held the reins. Vesryn, no matter how mad he became, was still precise in his cruelty. This was his message to Corym: never forget who is king.

"They died," Corym choked out. "Because I couldn't stop him."

Nym yanked Corym up by the collar, hoisting him to his feet. "Cut that out," he growled, locking eyes with him. "You, of all elves, know it's too late to stop Vesryn now. That time passed long ago." He shook his head. "You think throwin' yourself away will fix this? What happens to the Veilguard if you're not here?"

Corym's gaze dropped, avoiding the question.

Nym wasn't having it. Grabbing Corym by the chin, he forced his eyes on Nym. "Look at me. If you fall, they'll all follow. Vesryn will tighten his grip, and those elves who fought and died today? They'll have died for nothin'. But they didn't, Cor. They died for the cause. They're legends now. And you?" His voice dropped low. "You're the one who has to make sure we don't forget that."

Releasing him, Nym reached for his tankard, taking a long drink to settle his nerves. He hated this—being the serious one, the voice of reason. But Corym needed it. He needed to hear it, and Nym knew they couldn't afford to lose him, not now. The fight wasn't over, and Corym had to be strong, no matter how broken he felt.

Nym set his cup on a nearby shelf before wrapping his arms around Corym's stiff shoulders. At first, the elf tensed, resisting the unexpected comfort, but slowly, he eased, and Corym sank into Nym's hold, his body shaking as years of unspoken grief and guilt finally surfaced.

"Let it out," Nym murmured, patting his back in slow, rhythmic strokes as a century's worth of tears spilled onto his shoulder. And for a while, they stood there, the world outside forgotten as Corym, Vesryn's ever-loyal soldier, allowed himself to crumble—if only for a moment.

Corym wiped the tears from his face, his expression hardening as he shot Nym a pointed look. "If you tell anyone about this, I'll string you up by your cock and leave you hanging until it falls off."

Nym gasped dramatically, placing a hand protectively over his groin. "Tell them what?" He mimed locking his lips with a key before grinning wide. With a casual hop, he perched himself atop an empty barrel. "Now, I know ya didn't call me back here just to have a breakdown, so why don't ya go ahead and spit it out?"

Corym straightened, clasping his hands behind his back like the good soldier he was. "In light of recent... developments, I've got a new task for you."

Nym raised an eyebrow, his grin never faltering. "Which is?"

Corym cleared his throat, his gaze darting around the dim room as if he were searching for the right words, or maybe a way out of what he was about to say. "How close are the fae?"

Nym shrugged, grabbing his mug of mead. "Dunno. Close enough."

"Nym."

"Fine, fine," Nym sighed, rolling his eyes. "They're real close, Cor. We've got days, maybe less. If that."

Corym grimaced. "That's what I was afraid of." He took a deep breath. "What I'm about to ask... it's not easy, but it has to be done."

Nym took a long swig of mead, watching him closely. "Out with it already. This suspense is downright painful."

"I need you to broker peace with Ravara."

Nym choked mid-sip, mead shooting out of his nose, spraying all over Corym's chest. He wheezed, half coughing, half laughing. "Peace with Ravara? You're joking, right?" He wiped his face, still struggling to catch his breath. "You've gotta be kiddin' me."

Corym looked down at his chest in disgust, slowly wiping away Nym's spittle and flicking it off to the side. "No jokes. You're the only one who knows the outside world. And with half the Veilguard down... we need this. We can't fight Ravara and Vesryn."

"Uh, ya know who I am, right?" Nym raised his hands in question. "*Anyone* would be better than me, Cor."

"Yes, Nym." Corym sighed, pinching the bridge of his nose as if trying to rein in the mounting frustration. "I know exactly who you are, which is why I'm asking you."

Nym snorted, leaning back against the wall with a dismissive wave. "Oh, sure. I'm just *perfect* for dealin' with Ravara and his royal fae army. Ravara's soldiers practically *love* me. I mean, the last I crossed one of 'em, he tried to skewer me with a glaive." He rubbed his side for emphasis. "Still got the scar to prove it."

"I'm serious," Corym said, his voice strained. "You've got connections in places the rest of us can't reach. You've survived things most elves wouldn't last a day in. And… let's be honest, no one else has your—" he paused, searching for the right word, "—your *charm*."

Nym barked out a laugh. "Charm, huh? Is that what we're callin' it these days?"

Corym leveled him with a hard stare. "I know what I'm asking, Nym. But… just get a meeting with him. I know you can do that. If we can't find a way to stop Ravara, Caramis is finished. You, me, everyone—we're all dead."

Nym's playful expression faltered. "That bad, eh?"

"It couldn't be worse," Corym replied grimly. "And Ravara's no fool. He'll sense the weakness. If we can't get ahead of this, if we don't try something… I'm not sure what'll be left to save."

Nym stared at the floor, his fingers tapping restlessly on the rim of his tankard. "You're really pullin' out all the stops, aren't ya?" he muttered, half to himself. "Fine. I'll do it. But if he stabs me or turns me into a tree or whatever else the fae do when they're pissed, that's on *you*."

"You won't regret this, Nym," Corym said with a small smile.

"Oh, I absolutely will," Nym grumbled, downing the last of his mead. "But at least it'll make for one hells of a story."

He stood up from the barrel, clapping his hands together. "Right, then. Looks like I'm off to charm the fae. Anything else ya want from me while I'm at it? Maybe juggle a few knives? Dance a jig?"

Corym gave him a wry look. "Just come back alive."

Nym winked. "No promises."

EVEN IN DEATH, THERE WILL BE LIFE

MARGOT CLOSED her eyes as the salt-kissed breeze wound through the open kitchen window, caressing her skin as it passed. She relished the way it danced through her hair and warmed her cheeks.

She nibbled on a piece of cheese, glancing at the pretty elf who was preparing for tonight's dinner. After Cillian had mentioned the elf to her, Margot wanted to get to know her and had been coming down to the kitchens every day since.

"Tahlsiaaaaa," Margot whined. "It's such a beautiful day. I'd love to go outside."

Tahlsia hummed, tipping her head in Margot's direction as she wiped down the counter before placing a few root vegetables down. "Every day is beautiful."

"Yes, but today especially." Margot pointed outside. "Look at how many birds there are! I've never seen so many in Caramis, and never this variety! Do you think Vesryn will let me go out today?"

Margot hoped her king would let her explore. After all, she had done exceptionally well in her lesson today. Meditation had come easily to her, quicker than she anticipated. Vesryn had guided her through it with the soothing sound of singing bowls, their tones vibrating through his study like a rhythmic lullaby that relaxed every muscle in her body. Their soft melodic hum enveloped her as Vesryn gently instructed her on how to control her breathing. She imagined Faeries' creation as he described it—threads of fate weaving together, creating a wondrous tapestry of souls.

Eventually, Vesryn's voice had faded, and her imagination took over. Sentient beings unfurled, their radiant forms possessing an ethereal grace as they swished their arms, coaxing towering trees from the ground and raising grand mountains, which rumbled up from Faerie's crust with lush hills rippling from their base before petering off, revealing flat plains with thick fields of swaying grain.

Thunder boomed, and lightning struck the highest mountain, cleaving it in two. Water rushed from the wound, filling ocean basins, rivers, and streams. It flowed purposefully, carving paths through their world, breathing vitality into the land. The rivers curved like silver ribbons, meandering through forests and vast meadows. They nourished the soil, nurturing the flora and fauna that thrived in its life-giving waters.

Margot had felt a surge of power mingling with dormant magic not yet tapped. She raised her palms facing upward and spoke words that came as naturally to her as the sun. *Even in death, there will be life.*

As she commanded those words, the air stirred, carrying with it the scent of blossoms and intangible whispers. The ground beneath her feet trembled, and her eyes had flung open just in time to see a miniature world hovering before her. The planet shuddered as rivers rushed forth and peaks emerged, following the paths she had envisioned. Her heart swelled with pride as she watched the world take shape, spinning slowly on its axis.

When she looked at Vesryn, his eyes were wide with shock, and she couldn't help but smile to herself. *She* had done that—not Vesryn. With a shake of his head, he came to and told her lessons were over for the day before abruptly leaving her alone in his study.

Tahlsia's gasp pulled Margot from her thoughts, and she found her standing by the window, looking out with a furrowed brow.

"What's wrong?" Margot asked.

Tahlsia's tawny skin turned markedly pale, and her fingers gripped the windowsill so tightly that Margot thought she was going to crack the stone. The elf cleared her throat, shaking her head as she moved back to her prep station. "Those birds are not of Caramis, which can only mean one thing..." Tahlsia mumbled, her voice wavering. She cleared her throat. "Vesryn sent word down earlier that should you want to, you can enjoy the gardens today. He..." She sucked in a sharp breath before continuing. "He said he needed to prepare his chambers for this evening."

Margot froze. Vesryn wanted to share his quarters with her that night. How had she forgotten something so important? He said sharing quarters was a rite of passage, one that would allow magic to strengthen their relationship. When Margot asked what he meant, he waved her off, saying he didn't want to bore her with the details, and moved on with the lesson.

"What... uhm..." Margot glanced down at the table, feeling a blush creep up her neck. "What does the magic in his room do?"

Tahlsia's chopping slowed, and she tipped her head back, squeezing her eyes shut as if Margot's question pained her. The elf looked at Margot, concern etched on her face. "The magic woven in the walls of that room... increases the likelihood of conceiving."

"Conceiving? It's too soon!" Margot fretted. "Shouldn't we wait until I have control of my power? I don't understand. Do all elves use magic to procreate? Why wouldn't he tell me?"

Tahlsia wiped her hands on her apron and sat across from Margot, placing a hand over hers. "I cannot begin to understand the inner workings of Vesryn's mind or why he chose not to tell you. However, Vesryn has been alive for a very long time and is probably quite eager to produce an heir. As for the magic, no. Elves do not typically use magic to aid in conception—not that they wouldn't, mind you. They simply do not have access to the kinds of magic Vesryn has at his disposal."

"What do I do?" Margot's voice trembled. She was terrified to have an elfling. She wasn't ready; she didn't know if she would *ever* be ready. This was a huge step in both of their lives, and he had made the decision for her without even telling her his plan.

Tahlsia gave her hand a gentle squeeze. "You do what is expected. Even with magic, the chance of conceiving is low. Especially for someone of your talents." She leaned in and lowered her voice. "You do not, even for one second, let Vesryn catch you off guard. Never let him know your true feelings, especially not on this matter. Never." She pointed to the basket on the counter. "Take that and go get Cillian to escort you to the gardens. Enjoy your time today, and don't worry about this evening. There is no stopping this."

"I-I understand," Margot said as she grabbed the basket and walked toward the door. "Thank you."

Margot rushed through the foyer, her emerald dress trailing behind her like silk wings as she hurried to escape. Freedom was still new, still precious—each stolen second away from the confines of the manor felt like drawing breath after drowning. Her heart soared with possibility, with hope.

Until she collided with something solid.

Vesryn stood before her, a dark monolith in flowing robes. His amber eyes flashed dangerously as she stumbled back.

"My king!" Relief and gratitude spilled from her lips before she could stop them. "Thank you for allowing me this gift, this chance to—"

The crack of his palm against her cheek echoed through the empty hall. Pain bloomed across her face, shocking and sharp. She reeled back, tears stinging her eyes as her fingers found the burning handprint he'd left behind.

Her world tilted, fractured. The hope that had buoyed her moments ago shattered like glass.

A broken sound escaped her throat as she turned and fled

with the basket in hand, vision blurring. Her feet carried her without conscious thought, and she wasn't surprised when she found herself outside Cillian's door rather than her own. Cillian may not be her king, but she had felt safe with him, and she desperately needed to get out of the manor.

Taking a deep breath, she tried to compose herself, but she knew it would do little to help. She could only imagine what she looked like, disheveled, manic. Once she mustered the courage, she shifted the basket that suddenly felt like it weighed a million pounds to the other arm and knocked. Silence greeted her. She knocked again, the fabric of her dress twisting between her fingers when still, there was no answer. A frown tugged at her lips and tears pricked her eyes again. She hadn't considered Cillian might not be in his room. *What does he do all day, anyway?*

Just as Margot turned to leave, the door swung open, and there he was, standing there, dripping wet with a towel slung low around his waist—too small to conceal much of anything. Her gaze drifted, trailing a bead of water as it slid down his chest, tracing scars and muscles before disappearing into the cotton. Her breath hitched, and her mouth hung open. She snapped it shut almost immediately when she realized he was watching her, a glint of amusement in his eyes that quickly changed to concern.

He took her arm and yanked her into the room, closing the door behind them. "What happened to your face, Margot?"

She couldn't hold back the tears, turning into a blubbering mess. Cillian took the basket from her arm and guided her to the bed where he sat beside her.

"Come now, no tears." He tipped her chin up to make her look at him. "Tell me what happened."

"I..." She sucked in sharply before continuing. "I was given permission to leave the manor, so Tahlsia made me a basket to bring to you, and I was so excited I was running, and I ran into Vesryn and..."

"And?"

"And he slapped me. I didn't know what to do so I ran and

ran... then I ended up here." She gripped the edge of his towel and leaned closer. "Please, I need to get out of here."

"That fucking elf," he growled.

"Shh. Don't say that. If he knew I was here..." She took in his nudeness again and swallowed. "If he knew I was here with you looking like *that*, I think he would kill me. Who answers the door with no clothing, anyway?"

He shrugged. "You were going to leave. I didn't want to miss you."

"But you could have found me after you were dressed..." Before she could finish her thought, Cillian walked to his dresser and started rummaging in a drawer, the towel barely hanging on. Her eyes widened as they roamed over his broad, scarred back, down his perfectly muscled—and very exposed—rear. Her face burned.

"I-I'll just go," she stammered, flustered, trying to make her way toward the door.

Cillian was faster. He grabbed her hand before she could get away, his touch sending a shockwave through her.

"Stay," he murmured, his silver eyes smoldering as they met hers. "Besides," he added with a teasing smile, "it's not as if you haven't seen this before."

"What... what do you mean?" Cold dread settled in her bones.

His expression changed instantly, his grip loosening as if he realized he said too much. He quickly turned away, slipping into his leathers with ease. "Nothing."

Margot's mind raced, trying to make sense of his words, of that haunted look in his eyes. There was something there, something important just out of reach. But every time she tried to grasp it, pain needled her temples, pushing the thoughts away. She pressed her fingers against her forehead, willing the ache to subside.

"Margot?" His voice was gentle now, concerned. "Are you alright?"

She forced a nod despite the pain. "Yes, I... yes. I just really need to get out of here."

Cillian hoisted the basket and extended his hand to her. "If Vesryn's unable to control himself outside of closed doors, then there's something I need to show you. Come on."

As they stepped outside, Cillian became rigid, his entire posture shifting from relaxed to tense in an instant. Margot, noticing the change, followed his line of sight. Dozens—if not hundreds—of birds lined the parapet. Far more than she had ever seen before in Caramis.

"The barrier..." he muttered so quietly under his breath she could barely hear him. "There's been a breach..."

"What are you talking about?" Not giving him time to respond, she smiled and extended her hand toward one of the bright yellow birds. "Aren't they gorgeous?" A tiny bird with red spots on its wings fluttered down, landing gently in her palm. It nuzzled its black beak against her thumb, and Margot giggled. "I've never seen them before."

"Don't move," Cillian whispered from behind her. The warmth of his breath brushed the back of her neck as he moved closer. "Don't even twitch. I'm going to kill that bird."

Margot's pulse quickened. *Kill it?* Why would he want to harm something so delicate?

"You won't scream," he warned, his voice steady but commanding. "Just turn around and walk toward the garden. Now."

As Margot started to turn, Cillian snatched the bird like a viper. She had to clasp both hands over her mouth to keep herself from making any noise as she walked swiftly down the switchbacks. The urge to look back at Cillian was strong, but she didn't dare. Every nerve in her body was alight with fear. *What is happening?*

By the time she made it to the bottom, Cillian was already barreling toward her. Before she could even catch her breath, his strong arm wrapped firmly around her waist, pulling her tightly into his embrace.

Margot gasped, clutching at his leathers instinctively as he hoisted her up effortlessly. Her face pressed against the warmth of his chest; the rapid thrum of his heartbeat mirrored her own. She barely had time to process what was happening before he took off, moving at a speed she didn't think was possible.

The world blurred as he ran, each powerful stride sending them hurtling through the air. The wind whipped past her ears, but she felt safe in his grasp, even as the urgency of his movements sent a healthy dose of fear straight through her veins. Her grip tightened as she buried her face deeper against him; the only sound she could focus on was his steady breathing as he carried her away from whatever danger he sensed that she clearly hadn't.

Cillian set her down just past the gardens, next to the base of the rampart, placing his hands on his thighs as he caught his breath. He uncorked his waterskin and drank from it greedily, wiping his mouth off with the back of his hand.

"That's not a native bird," he said. "It's called a netherspar-row. Wildly dangerous. Behind that cute exterior is a mouth full of razor-sharp teeth. When they bite, they inject a deadly venom that can close the eyes of even the strongest creature." He glanced at Margot. "Sorry about the basket. Had to leave it."

"It's fine." She looked around, taking note of the birds that were still around. Their eyes seemed to follow her every move. She shuddered. "Will we be okay?"

"Yes, just don't try making friends with the damn things." He held out his hand. "Let's go."

"Go where?"

He gave his hand a small shake, urging her to take it. "Trust me."

With a deep breath, she placed her hand in his. The moment their fingers touched he tugged her closer. A strange ripple distorted the air, and suddenly, the solid wall before them shimmered, fading away to reveal crumbling stonework and a hidden path beyond. Margot hesitated, her instincts screaming at her to turn back, but Cillian nudged her forward.

"We shouldn't be here," she whispered, her anxiety growing with each step. "Cillian, please... we need to go back."

She turned, trying to pull him back the way he came, but he spun her around, placing his hands on her shoulders. "Do you trust me?"

Though her instincts screamed at her to flee, a small voice inside told her she could trust him. "I do," she whispered.

"Good." He weaved his fingers with hers and pressed on. "I promise, I won't let anything hurt you."

And Margot believed him.

Leaves rustled softly beneath their feet, breaking the quiet as they ventured deeper into the jungle. Despite the towering vines and twisted branches arching overhead like skeletal hands clasped together, the path was surprisingly pleasant. Cillian moved with purpose, his steps sure and steady, and Margot wouldn't have been surprised to learn that he'd cleared the way himself. It felt too precise, too intentional—like a hidden route only he knew.

"Can I tell you a secret?" Margot asked.

"Anything."

"Vesryn... Vesryn wants to try to conceive this evening."

Cillian gripped her hand a little tighter, but he said nothing.

Ten minutes later, he stopped walking and turned to her. "Can I tell you a secret?"

Margot forced a weak smile. "It's only fair."

"One day," he said, his silver eyes burning into hers, "I will kill Vesryn for all he has done."

Margot gasped, her eyes wide with shock as she frantically glanced around. "You cannot say that!" she whispered harshly. "You cannot do that! He is the king!"

"I don't care." He grabbed her hand, guiding her down the path. "It's not much further."

The sound of rushing water greeted them as they stepped into a sunlit clearing. Before them, a magnificent waterfall tumbled over moss-covered rocks, its cascade transforming into a breath-taking display of shimmering droplets that sparkled in the air like scattered diamonds.

"Wow," Margot muttered, breathless.

"Isn't it beautiful?"

"Very much so."

He tugged her again. "As much as I'd love to relax here with you. This isn't what I wanted to show you. Follow me."

Cillian led Margot closer to the waterfall, where, shrouded in the mist, stood the most beautiful woman Margot had ever seen. Her translucent form bowed graciously to Cillian, her gown appearing as though woven from the mist itself, reflecting the glistening droplets in the air.

"No petals today?" Cillian asked, gesturing to her dress.

The ghostly woman chuckled. "One of the few things I can still change about my situation." She turned her glowing, green eyes to Margot. "I'm so glad you came. My name is Liriel, and I am here to help you."

"Liriel?" Margot instinctively took a step back, her heart pounding in her chest. "The goddess?"

Liriel floated closer, her ethereal face only inches from Margot's. "Has Cillian explained why he brought you here?" she asked, her voice soft yet probing. "Because truly, I wish to help."

"Uhm... no." Margot wiped her sweaty palms on her dress. "I'm sorry... but how can you help me? Do I even need help?"

Cillian stepped forward and knelt in front of her, taking her hands in his. "I'm sorry I didn't tell you the full truth before." Sorrow flashed across his face. "I wasn't sure you'd believe me. Margot, Vesryn controls your mind."

She recoiled, trying to pull her hands from his grasp, but Cillian held firm. "You're lying," she whispered, her voice trembling. "He wouldn't... he couldn't do that."

"Think about it," Cillian urged as he searched her eyes. "Don't you find it strange that you can't remember anything about your life before Caramis? Your family, your friends... lovers? Don't you wonder why?"

A cold shiver ran down her spine. She frantically tried to recall something, anything about her life before Caramis, but her mind was blank. The more she pushed, the sharper the pain in her head grew. How could she not remember?

"I don't believe you," she murmured, though the words felt hollow, lacking conviction. Deep down, she knew Cillian was right.

"Margot," Liriel breathed as she glided to the water's edge, placing a hand on Margot's shoulder that buzzed with magic, "sometimes we don't realize we need help until it finds us."

Tears welled in Margot's eyes, and she jerked away from the goddess.

"Shall I prove it to you?" Liriel asked softly.

Before Margot could respond, the surface of the water rippled, revealing images that rose from the depths. Scenes of a life she didn't know unfolded before her—holding the hand of a loved one through sickness, laughing with friends, celebrating birthdays. Each image flickered in and out, but one lingered: her and Cillian, standing on the bow of a ship, the wind tossing her hair as they sailed toward a horizon painted in vibrant shades of purple and pink. She could almost feel the salty breeze, the gentle rocking of the ship beneath her feet.

Nostalgia swept over her, tugging at her heart. She had once known this life, had shared part of it with Cillian, and somehow Vesryn had torn it from her mind, leaving her adrift in a sea of forgotten memories.

"Do you see it now?" Liriel gestured to the pool. "The life you've unknowingly left behind? The connection you once had with the demon standing beside you?"

Tears rolled down Margot's cheeks as she looked between Cillian and Liriel. "Sometimes... sometimes I see pieces, fragments," she whispered. "It feels like something is there, but every time I reach for it, it slips away."

Liriel's expression softened. "Memories are fragile, easily manipulated. Vesryn is strong, there is no disputing that, but there is a way to reclaim what has been taken from you."

Silver eyes bore into Margot's, silently pleading for her to accept. She hadn't been the only one hurt by Vesryn. While Margot had been blissfully unaware of her past, Cillian had never forgotten. It broke her heart.

Margot looked at Liriel. "Can you really help me?"

"I can, and I will, so long as you help save me from what binds me here."

"I don't know how I could possibly help you," Margot choked back a sob. "I barely have any power."

"Oh child..." Liriel tilted her head, and her brows softly creased. She swiped her thumb across Margot's cheek, turning her tears to glitter that drifted away. "You have more power than you know. Come." The goddess motioned toward the plunge pool and the mossy ground. "Place one hand atop the water and another on the ground, then close your eyes."

Margot's fingers pushed past the dense moss and plunged them into the dirt. Soil embedded itself under her nails as she rested her other hand atop the water as instructed. With a furrowed brow, she tried to draw from Faerie, to use its gift to break the binds. She imagined them, could see them clearly in her mind's eye, but nothing came.

"What now?" Margot whispered. "I don't feel anything. We should wait until I have control of my magic."

"Shush." Liriel's voice floated around her as if the goddess were circling her body. "There's no need to wait when the power is already within you. All you need to do is *accept* who you are and release it."

"Accept who I am..." Margot echoed. How could she accept who she was when everything she thought she knew was built on lies? The shards of who she was were scattered like shattered glass. Nothing more than fleeting shadows she couldn't hold onto.

"*Focus*," Liriel chided. "I can feel you wandering." She paused as if letting the words sink into Margot's psyche. "Picture the cool water resting in your palm, the essence of life itself—purity given form. Feel how it contrasts with the damp earth beneath your hand, grounding you, tethering you to your mortality. Let them coalesce, find balance. Where there is life, there is death. Where there is darkness, there is light. Neither is greater than the other, for too much of either invites chaos and destruction."

"I don't know how. I don't even know who I am."

Warmth enveloped Margot as the goddess' ghostly presence seemed to draw closer. "You are more than the sum of your memories. A clouded past doesn't change who you are, your power. You can feel it, can't you? The pulse of light and dark, flickering within you."

With furrowed brows, Margot sifted through the jumble in her mind, trying to pinpoint the potential Liriel was convinced she had. It seemed impossible. Nothing made sense, and what little she could see appeared out of order. She waded through thick haze and murky images until stumbling upon something that beat with a subtle, steady rhythm. It wasn't bright or blinding like she'd imagined light would be. Nor was it cold and oppressive like the darkness she feared. Calming. That's what it was. The presence of both righteousness and corruption, merged in harmony.

"I feel... something," she admitted. "It's there."

"That's it," Liriel whispered. "Now release it. Let it flow, Margot. Melt these shackles that bind."

Margot's hands tingled, her fingers twitching as if drawn by invisible threads. She looked down, watching in awe as soft tendrils of light and shadow unfurled from her palms, twisting together like roots.

"Now let go," the goddess urged on.

Margot exhaled slowly, releasing the tension in her body. The light and darkness surged from her hands, stretching out toward Liriel. As the energy reached for the goddess, the mist around them shimmered, the water from the falls catching the glow.

For a moment, everything was still.

Then, with a soft hum, the energy wrapped around Liriel. Shafts of crepuscular rays burst through black smoke, hissing as the two shattered the chains binding her spirit before dissolving into nothing.

"Incredible," Cillian breathed.

"You did it!" Liriel's tinkling laugh filled the grove. "Oh, Margot, you did it! I knew you could." She spun around, kicking up water with her bare feet. "For far too long, I've been trapped here. Finally... finally I get to rest." She pressed a kiss to Margot's forehead, placing both hands on her shoulders. "Are you ready?"

Margot wrapped her arms around herself, looking down. "I'm scared."

"The unknown is always frightening, dear one. But the question remains." Liriel tipped Margot's chin up. "Do you want to know who you are?"

A sharp pang of guilt tore through Margot's stomach when her gaze rested on Cillian. Unshed tears limned his waterline. He knelt, staring at Margot like she was everything. She scooted close, knee to knee, and took his calloused hand in hers.

"What do I do?" Margot asked, barely able to keep her voice steady.

A solitary tear broke free, trailing down his cheek, tracing the sharp line of his jaw before slipping from his chin. "I miss you, Margot," he croaked. "I miss *you*. Not... not what Vesryn's turned you into. But I can't make this choice for you."

No. Cillian wouldn't make this choice for her, unlike Vesryn, who decided to use Margot to produce an heir. Forcing her into a future she hadn't asked for. Using her as a means to an end. *His* end. With all she knew now, she understood Vesryn didn't care for her. He would never let her choose. But here, with Cillian, the decision was finally hers.

Exhaling a shaky breath, Margot looked over her shoulder at the goddess. "I think I'm ready."

"Even now, what little power I have left is barely enough to tether me to this world. Once I release Vesryn's hold on you, I'll be gone," Liriel warbled, her voice faint. She gestured toward Cillian. "Stay with Cillian Blackwood. And do not refuse the one who wishes to speak with you. Without being whole, Vesryn will prevail, and nothing—no one—will be able to stop him."

Margot didn't know who would want to talk to her, but judging by Liriel's flickering image, time was running out. She allowed herself one moment of reprieve before she stood before the goddess. Liriel smiled like a doting mother and pressed a finger to Margot's forehead.

Every experience that helped shape Margot slammed against her skull like a battering ram, bringing down the fog. Like the sharp turns of a river, the channels of her life twisted and knotted together. Thousands of images assaulted her, fragments of a shattered mirror, piecing themselves back together.

The veil Vesryn had cast upon her mind slowly unraveled, revealing glimpses of her past self and leading her toward self-discovery. With each passing moment, she was more connected to who she had once been, a puzzle finally coming together after years of being scattered.

There was Janey, the woman who was always there for Margot. They were at a bar on karaoke night, singing some terrible song from the 90s—poorly. Margot's face was flushed from liquor and she and Janey tipped their heads back, hanging on to one another as they nearly peed their pants laughing.

Then, her mother. Iris' frail body resting on her bed as the hospice nurse administered medication to ease the pain. Margot sat on the floor crying while holding her hand that was nothing more than skin and bones. The death rattle had come, and this was her mother's final moment, the last day her soul traversed the mortal plane and would be taken from Margot forever.

The hurt from the barrage of memories she was assaulted with was nothing compared to the hurt from seeing her mother's last breath. Tears rolled down her cheeks as another memory unlocked.

Nineteen-year-old Margot walked into the kitchen in the home where she grew up. Iris was leaning against the farmhouse sink crying. Her mother looked over her shoulder, her bottom lip quivering. Leo Hawthorne had walked away from his family.

Another memory materialized. Six-year-old Margot's nose was pressed against the glass as a shark swam past. Her blue eyes were wide with wonder, taking in the sights the aquarium had to offer. Her father knelt beside her, resting his hand on her shoulder pointing to the fish, explaining what they were while her mother snapped photos with a disposable camera.

With bated breath, Margot watched as the last piece of the puzzle fell into place. A vivid memory, so exquisitely beautiful, yet tinged with a hint of pain, which caused her to fall to her knees. The slice of her flesh, the taste of his blood, the burning desire to consume him in a fiery blaze of passion. She remembered everything. And in that moment, deep within her being, a bond shone brightly, like a beacon in the dark.

39

THE MNEMOSYNE WEAVE

BLACK ICE slowly crept up the bond, turning its warmth to a bitter, frigid ache. Soil and grit dug under Margot's fingernails as she clenched the earth, the cool moss pressing against her palms. The brief relief of seeing the blood bond again was snatched away as reality came crashing down around her. Like everything else Vesryn had touched, the bond was tainted, and the truth clawed at her insides.

"Oh god," she heaved, gagging on bile that worked its way up her throat. "Oh god." Her gaze snapped to Cillian; a sob welled in her chest. "What did I do to you? I—" She jerked her head to the side and retched up a stream of vomit.

Memories she wished could have remained hidden stayed at the forefront of her mind. Cold fingers digging into her thigh, pushing inside her. His lithe body, crushing her against a window as he took her. Thin lips pressed to hers as she mewled for more.

She heaved, vomiting again.

The scenes kept rolling in vivid clarity. Cillian being flayed alive because he chose to bond with her. Vesryn slamming her head into the floor, threatening her life if she didn't forget the demon who saved her on more than one occasion. Cillian being forced to watch as Vesryn *raped* her. Over and over and over again.

And my body wanted *it.*

"Margot," Cillian said, his voice a deep rumble that finally broke the dam holding back her tears. "It's not your fault."

"I'm so sorry, Cillian," she cried, smearing dirt and snot across her face as she tried to wipe away the tears that just kept coming. "I'm so, so sorry."

Cillian moved close and thumbed her cheek. She flinched, scrambling away from the *very* large man in front of her, nearly falling into the plunge pool where no trace of Liriel remained. The pain behind those silver eyes made her heart seize, but the calloused skin against hers had the bile rising all over again.

Heat that had once ignited her blood, made her yearn for passion and love and acceptance, had turned vile, fetid. Like a pool of tar, thick and suffocating, threatening to swallow her whole if she dared let Cillian in.

And that fucking elf was to blame. Vesryn made her betray their bond. And here she was, betraying Cillian again. He just gained the missing half of his heart, and she could barely look at him despite the bond screaming at her, telling her to go to him.

But she couldn't. Vesryn clung to her like a parasite, burrowed under her skin, invading every part of her life, every inch of her body. When she closed her eyes, all she saw were those cold, calculating eyes. She could smell him, taste him; he was everything she didn't want—yet the only thing she could think about.

"You have nothing to be sorry for," Cillian choked out, his voice ragged as if the words were sandpaper. "He would've killed you."

Margot let her arms fall limp at her sides, her face tipping toward the sky as a gut-wrenching wail tore from her throat. She gasped between sobs. "I wish he had," she spluttered. "I wish he killed me the moment I stepped onto this godforsaken island, so you didn't have to live this. More than that, I wish you had left me in that damn forest where you found me, because I've been nothing but a burden."

"Never say that." Cillian edged closer. Margot stiffened and she felt him still. He audibly swallowed. "Bringing you with me that night was the best decision I've ever made. You breathed life into my soul, made me feel again. I would endure Vesryn's wrath one hundred times over if it meant you survived, Margot. If it meant I got this chance to be with you, right here, right now."

"Be with me," she echoed, shifting her watery gaze toward him. "What's there to be with? I'm a broken woman—no, not even that, an *elf* because my humanity was ripped from me, too—who can't stand to be touched." She clutched the fabric of her dress. "Look at me! You don't deserve this, Cillian. You deserve to be with someone whole, someone *good*." She sniffed, swatting away the wetness on her face. "Someone who can love you the way you deserve. Not the measly scraps of affection I don't even know if I'll be able to give."

"You love me?" Cillian's voice was barely a whisper. The muscles in his right arm twitched as if he wanted to reach out to her, but his hands remained firmly planted on his thighs. "Margot, do you love me?"

She opened her mouth to answer, but before the words passed her lips, a sharp pain needled her heart making her whimper.

"Margot?" he croaked. "Blood of my blood, talk to me."

She was voiceless, the pain incessant, her heart constricting faster and faster. It felt like it would explode. Then, without warning, an invisible force wrenched her backward, sending her spiraling through an endless void of colors. Twisted trees, swirling mountains, and crashing waves blurred past in a dizzying rush, until she was violently assaulted by a blinding light so intense she thought it would sear her eyes. Then, suddenly, everything stopped. She stood still, surrounded by an endless expanse of stark, empty white.

Margot's manic laughter rang out, reverberating into forever as she looked at the nothing around her. She had died—trapped in some kind of purgatory—without ever getting the chance to tell Cillian she loved him. Not that she expected a happy ending, but she thought fate might have spared her a small mercy, some fleeting moment of joy. Instead, fate had stolen even that from her grasp, leaving her stranded in a place where nothing existed but her own despair.

She sighed, resigned herself, and picked a direction at random, the sound of her steps and rogue sniffles were the only things keeping her company.

Time slipped away from her—hours, days, months, *years?* There was no way of knowing. She just kept walking. She never grew tired or hungry or thirsty; she never needed anything at all. Nothing more than a wandering soul adrift in an empty eternity. This was how she knew she was dead. If she was alive, she would have kicked the bucket long ago from exertion and lack of nutrition.

Though her body may have been gone, her mind was still very much intact, and she had ample opportunity to sift through the mess Vesryn made. The bastard had spelled her multiple times, and each time, the palls of magic became more complex, stacking on top of one another—but not before mussing up the natural order of events. Layers upon layers of cognitive detritus needed to be cast out, giving her room to rearrange her thoughts in the correct timeline. One by one, she sequenced her memories, sequestered her emotions tied to each experience, and breathed steadily.

For the first time in what could have been a millennium, her steps faltered. A gentle breeze stirred, teasing loose strands of her hair as it brushed past her, caressing her skin and tickling her nose. Her senses flickered to life. The endless white of the world shifted, hues slowly bleeding into existence—pale yellow fading into a soft lilac, like dawn breaking over the horizon of the Tempest Sea. She turned sharply on her heel, her pulse quickening as she spotted it: a solitary hill rising in the distance, crowned by a single, towering white tree with teal leaves standing sentinel at its crest.

Then, the wind gusted, as if urging her toward the peaceful scene. With the shake of her head and a slight tug at the corner of her lips, she followed the element. *Maybe I'll meet God.* She snorted at the thought.

Blossoms the color of dragon fruit flitted about as she climbed the hill, carrying with them the redolent scent of daffodils—a fragrance that reminded her of her mother. Every spring, just before summer's warmth settled in, her mother would take her to the Blue Ridge Mountains. Margot hated it. Iris would laugh, bouncing along as Margot grumbled about bugs and itchy grass.

"If you'd just wear the clothes I got you, you'd be more comfortable," her mother would say. Margot would roll her eyes, insisting the hiking pants were just as itchy as the bushes—and if she had to be uncomfortable, she might as well look cute.

Miles later, they'd reach a small clearing where daffodils bloomed in a bright, unruly patch, stretching like a burst of sunshine in the green shadows. Iris would stop, her eyes lighting up, and drop to her knees, beckoning Margot to join her.

"See? Isn't it beautiful?" her mother would whisper, her voice soft as if not to disturb the flowers. She'd pluck a daffodil and tuck it behind Margot's ear, beaming with the same unfiltered joy she always had for life's smallest beauties.

Margot had been too young to understand then, but something about the gentle crinkle of her mother's smile or the way she traced the edge of a petal with her fingers made her pause, even as she'd roll her eyes and cross her arms in protest. She remembered the itchy feeling and aching limbs, sure, but now—standing alone in the memory—she wished she could feel that itch and burn again, just to be there with her.

The memory faded like morning mist as Margot ascended the hill, her steps slowing as she approached the majestic white tree. Its teal leaves fluttered in the breeze, casting marbled shadows that danced across the grass. As she drew closer, she noticed a figure seated beneath the sweeping branches, their back resting against the pale trunk.

Margot's nerve endings buzzed. After walking for what felt like an eternity through endless white nothingness, finding another soul here seemed impossible. Yet there they sat, as still as the ancient tree itself, waiting. The wind died down to barely a whisper, as if nature itself was holding its breath.

With trembling legs, Margot forced herself to take another step forward. The seated figure lifted its head, and her world tilted on its axis as recognition dawned on her. There was no mistaking the midnight blue hair, amber eyes, and pale complexion—it was Vesryn. Her throat tightened, and panic flooded her senses. She stumbled backward, scrambling to escape, kicking at the ground in a desperate attempt to hurl herself off the hill, but the earth beneath her stretched and shifted, trapping her at its peak.

Through the blur of her tears, she saw the elf frown, lifting his hands to gather his dark hair into a loose knot. He closed the distance between them in a few long, purposeful strides, extending a hand with an unsettlingly gentle smile that carved a dimple in his right cheek.

"At last, we meet face to face, Margot," he murmured, crouching down and offering his hand once more. "My name is Ilphas."

His words reverberated against her ears, distorted and muted, like echoes trapped underwater—sluggish, surreal. She wanted to scream, to crawl away, to do anything but sit there frozen, but her body refused to obey.

He crouched before her, his elbows resting casually on his knees, as though they weren't standing on the edge of a nightmare. She flinched as his gaze roamed over her, assessing.

"My brother sure did a number on you," he said, his tone disturbingly soft. "For that, I'm sorry."

Margot's chest heaved from the effort to break free from the invisible weight pressing down on her. His words pierced through her haze, and her eyes snapped to his face. *Brother?* The word coiled around her, sharp and unwelcome, but her voice remained trapped in her throat, silenced by fear and confusion.

Ilphas tilted his head, his amber eyes narrowing with quiet curiosity. A soft gust of wind stirred the loose strands of midnight hair framing his face, brushing them across his cheek like fleeting shadows. "I know it's difficult, but I need you to think. Remember."

Margot's stomach roiled, a sickening twist that left her breathless. She had worked so hard to bury those terrible memories, locking them away in the darkest corners of her mind where they couldn't hurt her anymore. And now, Ilphas was asking her to unearth them—to sift through the wreckage for some elusive answer to a question he hadn't even bothered to explain, as if she should already know.

"I won't," she whispered, her voice trembling. "I won't go there again."

Ilphas sighed and dropped to the ground in front of her with an air of practiced nonchalance, folding his legs beneath him. From somewhere behind his back, he produced an apple as if by magic, the vibrant red skin catching the light. Without a word, he sank his teeth into it, the crunch sounding sharply in the stillness.

"I won't pretend that I understand how you feel—simply put, I can't." He paused, turning the apple in his hand as though searching for inspiration. "How do I say this without sounding like an absolute tal."

He bounced the apple off his knee, the rhythmic thud filling the silence. "Elves of a certain... caliber... aren't exactly known for their empathy. It's not that we're incapable of it, mind you. But for most, there's little incentive to bother learning." His words were as casual as the toss of the apple, but how his gaze flicked to her sent a chill creeping down her spine.

"That said," he continued. "I like to think I'm an exception." A faint smile curved his lips, disarming and dangerous all at once. "And seeing as we have nothing but time, Margot, you're going to tell me what happened."

Margot blinked absently. Tell him what happened? *No. Not happening.* She shook her head slowly, her body trembling. She didn't owe him anything—least of all the fractured pieces of her soul.

"I don't care what you think you are," she spat, her voice cracking. "I won't do this. I won't relive that nightmare."

Ilphas arched a brow, his expression caught somewhere between amusement and disappointment. He set the apple beside him, brushing a speck of dirt from his hand. "That defiance—admirable, really. But you misunderstand, Margot. This isn't a request."

The cold weight of dread settled over her as she clenched her fists, her nails digging into her palms, grounding herself against the rising tide of panic.

"You don't get to demand anything from me," she said through gritted teeth, the words torn from her throat. "Not after what your brother did. Not after—" She stopped, choking on bile.

"And yet, here we are," he said softly, gesturing to the world of white before them. "You're stronger than you realize, Margot. Strong enough to survive my brother's... ministrations. But that strength won't last if you keep letting him win."

She flinched, her body instinctively curling in on itself as his words hit their mark. Her pulse hammered in her ears, and her vision blurred with unshed tears. "You don't know anything about me."

Ilphas leaned forward. "Don't I?" he murmured maddeningly calm, the words sharp and precise. It was too similar to Vesryn—too measured, too calculated—and the familiarity sent a cold swear prickling down her spine.

"I know what he's capable of." His gaze bore into hers. "I know what he can do. Hells, Margot, the bastard killed me with his own hands." His lips curled into something between a smirk and a grimace. "Trust me when I say, I think I know better than most. And when I look at you..." he paused, his stare piercing through her like a blade. "I see someone worth saving."

"So..." Margot wiped at her face, smearing tears across her cheeks as her earlier assumption was confirmed. "I *am* dead."

Ilphas tipped his head back and laughed—a smooth, deep

sound that sounded strange against the backdrop of nothingness. It was too much laughter, almost manic, and it set her on edge. When he finally looked at her again, his eyes glittered.

"Dead?" he repeated. "No. Of course not."

Her lips parted, the question spilling out before she could stop herself. "Then... then where are we?"

"The Mnemosyne Weave," he said simply, as though the words should mean something. His eyelids grew heavy as he tilted his head, studying her reaction. "Not ringing any bells? How about Ancestral Memory?"

At that, Margot stopped breathing. Her lungs refused to cooperate as the Rolodex in her mind spun frantically, flipping through page after page of painstakingly curated memories. Her grip on them was tenuous at best, but among the fragments she had managed to piece together were Vesryn's lessons on elven magic.

Ancestral memory—every elf carried the ability to pass down their knowledge and a spark of their magic to their descendants, ensuring part of them lived on, regardless of whether their bloodlines met ill fate or lived on for ages. But only the most powerful elves—like Vesryn, like Ilphas—could transfer their entire magical essence to another. And those elves with the ability to exchange such vast amounts of magic could enter a place that acted as a bridge between realms of consciousness, where time unraveled and stood still all at once. It was where the recipient of such power could commune with its giver—a place outside of life and death, of reality itself. Though Vesryn never gave this place a name, Margot assumed the Mnemosyne Weave was that place.

Margot jerked back, meeting his eyes as rage simmered deep in her belly. "You brought me here. *You* are the reason I went through those horrors." She shook her head, exhaling forcefully through her nose. "You chose me. You gave me your magic and pulled me into Faerie. Why?"

"Because I knew what my brother would become. I saw the madness festering inside him long before he wrapped his hands around my throat." He leaned forward, closing the gap between them that Margot had created. "I needed someone who could stand against him. Someone whose soul could handle both light and shadow."

"You mean Cillian's darkness," she said quietly. Her heart ached at the mere mention of his name. "The blood bond."

"Precisely." A knowing smile tugged at his lips. "I didn't just choose you, Margot. I waited. I watched. Until I found someone who could not only wield my magic but merge it with something far more dangerous—demon blood."

Margot scoffed. "How could you have known I would bond with Cillian?"

"I didn't." Ilphas shrugged. "I only knew that you would survive should it ever come to that. Cillian isn't the only demon in Faerie, you know. The chances of you going through with the ritual, however, were slim but never zero."

"You used me," she accused, anger finally breaking through her fear. "You manipulated my entire life, just like your brother."

"No." His voice cut through her rising fury. "I gave you a choice. The magic, the bond—none of it would have taken if you hadn't chosen it yourself. That's the difference between me and Vesryn. He takes. I offer."

"And now?" Margot asked, her hands trembling. "What are you offering now?"

"The truth and guidance," he stated. "But first, you need to face what happened. Every moment, every violation, every scrap of dignity he stole from you. Because until you do, you'll never be strong enough to stop him."

40

I'VE SHOWN YOU THE PATH, BUT YOU MUST WALK IT

TIME TRICKLED like grains of sand through Margot's fingers in the stark expanse of white. Each breath felt suspended between moments, stretched thin across an eternity that had no beginning and no end. Ilphas sat calmly, watching her with those piercing amber eyes—so like his brother's, yet holding none of Vesryn's cruelty—as she wrestled with his demand.

"I won't do it," she whispered. The pristine emptiness around them seemed to swallow her words. "I won't relive what he did."

"You already are," Ilphas said softly. He picked up the apple he had discarded earlier, turning it thoughtfully in his hands. "Every time you flinch from Cillian's touch. Every time you try to bury those memories deeper. Every time you avoid looking too closely at yourself." He met her gaze. "The magic I gave you—it's not just power, Margot. It's consciousness. Memory. And it's trying to show you something important."

A warm breeze stirred the teal leaves overhead, carrying the haunting scent of daffodils. The fragrance wrapped around her like her mother's embrace, and for a moment, she could almost hear Iris' voice telling her to be brave. Her mother had always been brave—right up until the end—and so could she.

"What could possibly be important enough to make me

remember?" Margot twisted her hands in her lap. "He—he violated everything. My mind, my body, our bond..." Her voice cracked on the last word. Cillian's painful expression flashed through her mind, and she pressed her hands to her face and as if the act of covering her eyes could block the memory.

"Exactly that." Ilphas stood, the apple forgotten at his feet. He began pacing in slow, deliberate circles, his voice gaining an urgency that caught her off guard. "The bond. Think, Margot, think. Why would my brother be so desperate to break it? Why would he want you to carry his child?" He paused, letting the questions hang in the air between them. "What happens when elven magic and demon blood coalesce?"

The white expanse around them rippled like disturbed water, and something stirred deep within her—a power that was neither light nor dark but somehow both, waiting to be understood.

The rippling white stilled. Margot pressed her palm to her chest where the blood bond pulsed, damaged but not destroyed. "The magic... it changed when Cillian and I bonded," she muttered, her brow furrowing as fragments of understanding pieced themselves back together. Her breath hitched and eyes widened. "That's why Vesryn was so intent on breeding. He thinks a child born between us would have the power of a god."

"Close." Ilphas said, a faint smile playing on his lips. "But you're missing the crucial detail. Vesryn doesn't just want *any* powerful offspring. He wants one specifically from *you*—the only being in existence who successfully merged elven magic with demon blood." He extended his hand, palm up, an invitation. "Let me show you."

Margot hesitated before taking it. The moment their fingers touched, the Weave around them transformed. The stark white gave way to swirling colors that blended into scenes from her time with Vesryn. She tried to look away, but Ilphas turned her face, forcing her to watch.

"No," Margot breathed, attempting to pull away, but Ilphas' grip was firm yet gentle.

"Watch," he commanded softly. "Not the act itself, but what happened to your magic during those moments. Look past the terror and *see*."

Fighting back bile, Margot forced herself to look. Through the lens of the Weave, she could see threads of power emanating from both her and Vesryn. His magic—brilliant and cold—tried repeatedly to dominate hers. But beneath the surface of her pain and humiliation, something extraordinary was happening. Her magic, infused with Cillian's darkness, didn't just resist Vesryn's assault—it absorbed it, transformed it.

"You see it now?" Ilphas asked, his voice cutting through the suffocating atrocities Vesryn committed. "Every time he tried to break you, your magic grew stronger. The bond with Cillian didn't weaken you—it made you capable of something unprecedented." He released her hand, letting the vision fade. "Vesryn thinks breeding with you will give him access to that power. But he fundamentally misunderstands what makes you unique."

"What do you mean?"

"Your magic can consume both light and shadow because you chose to embrace both. The bond wasn't forced upon you—you and Cillian forged it together, *willingly*." Ilphas' expression hardened. "There are certain inalienable truths to magic. No child conceived through violation could ever achieve what you have. Vesryn's obsession will destroy him, but first, he'll tear apart everything in his path trying to prove me wrong."

The scene morphed again, but this time into a visualization of her merged magic—threads of light and shadow weaving together as if they were one and the same rather than two opposing forces threatening to combust.

"What you can do, the way your magic has evolved—it's incredible," Ilphas said, gesturing to the display. "But understanding it and actually wielding it are two very different things."

"I can barely think straight," Margot whispered, wrapping her arms around herself. "How am I supposed to control this kind of power when I can hardly..." She trailed off, her mind drifting to everything that still lay ahead.

"You don't have to be whole to be powerful," Ilphas said quietly. "The scars my brother left—they won't fade quickly, if ever. But you can learn to channel even that pain into strength."

Margot's throat tightened. "And Cillian? How can I face him when I can barely stand being touched?"

"That's not something I can fix," Ilphas admitted. "Healing will take time—time we don't have. But right now, you don't need to be healed. You need to be ready. Vesryn will not stop until he gets what he wants. And what he wants will destroy you and everyone you care about."

He held out his hand again, his gaze steady. "Are you ready?"

Margot stared at Ilphas' outstretched hand, her heart hammering against her ribs. "I thought you said we had nothing but time."

Her eyes flicked up to Ilphas, catching him smiling as he scratched the side of his nose.

"Ah, well, that would have been true were we just sitting here talking. Alas, magic is a finite resource, and I can only maintain Mnemosyne Weave for so long. It truly is a pain, what with being dead and all. The amount of time it takes for magic to recharge is rid—I digress." He cleared his throat and presented his hand again. "Are you ready, Margot?"

Everything within her screamed to run, to hide, to protect what little remained of herself. But she couldn't. Not with Vesryn's madness threatening to tear apart everything she held dear.

"I'm ready," she whispered, placing her shaking hand in his.

The moment their fingers touched, power surged through her —raw and ancient, neither light nor dark but something more primal. It resonated with the magic already flowing through her veins, amplifying it until she could feel every thread of the Weave around them.

"Good," Ilphas murmured. "Now, close your eyes. Feel how the magic moves through you, how it responds to your will."

Margot did as instructed, letting her consciousness sink into the flow of power. It was different now than before—no longer just a tool to be wielded, but an extension of herself. She could sense how it curled through her body like smoke, filling every hollow space with potential.

"The key," Ilphas continued, his voice seeming to come from everywhere and nowhere at once, "is understanding that your magic isn't solely about your power. It's about balance. Light and shadow, creation and destruction—they're both part of the same whole."

He guided her through the motions, teaching her how to draw from each aspect of her magic simultaneously. How to let them dance together without fighting for dominance. With each passing moment, the power grew more familiar, more natural.

"Remember," he said, "Vesryn's strength comes from control —from forcing his will upon others. Yours comes from harmony. From choice. That's what makes you different. What makes you stronger."

Margot's eyes fluttered open. Tendrils of light and shadow twisted around her arms like living vines. "But will it be enough?"

"That," Ilphas said, releasing her hand, "depends on you. I've shown you the path, but you must walk it. The path will not be easy." He stepped back, his gaze lifting to the white tree overhead. Its branches nearly naked, the few remaining teal leaves trembling. One drifted down, spiraling slowly before gently landing at their feet. "Our time grows short."

"Wait," Margot called, panic rising as the world began to dissolve into shimmering white. "There's still so much I need to know!"

Ilphas smiled sadly. "Trust yourself, Margot. Trust the bond. And remember—" His form started to blur. "You're stronger than you think."

"Ilphas!" Margot yelled. She took a step forward. "Will I see you again?"

He hesitated, tilting his head with a faint, almost teasing arch of his brow. "You will. When the time is right."

Then he was gone.

The void shattered like glass, and reality crashed over her. Margot gasped, her body jolting as she found herself back by the waterfall. Cillian still kneeling before her, exactly as he had when she'd left.

41

THE GREY

"Please." Drawing in ragged breaths, Cillian's chest heaved. His fingers dug into his knee as his eyes bore into hers. "Please say something, Margot."

"I... I'm sorry. Can you repeat what you said?" Guilt needled her gut. She remembered what Cillian asked. How could she forget? But she needed time to think. She was being bombarded with too many emotions, too many external stimuli. She hated that part of her missed the quiet peace the Mnemosyne Weave offered.

"Do you love me?" Cillian asked. He looked as though he aged thirty years from the stress he was wearing on his face.

The word "yes" caught in her throat as she stared at the man in front of her—her bloodsworn, her anchor, her salvation. Cillian remained frozen, silver eyes brimming with unshed tears, waiting for an answer he'd been denied by her sudden departure to the Weave. But she wasn't the same woman who had left mere seconds ago. Understanding coursed through her veins like liquid fire—demon blood and elven magic finally, perfectly aligned.

"I love you," she whispered, her voice stronger than it had been in weeks. "I love you enough to face this." She held up her hand, watching as shadows and light danced between her fingers

—no longer fighting for dominance but working in tandem. "Vesryn thought he could break me by forcing me to forget you. But remembering you..." Her eyes met his, and this time, she didn't flinch away. "Remembering us... that's what makes me strong enough to end this."

"You love me..." Cillian murmured, his voice a whisper of disbelief. Shock and awe and adoration washed over him as his gaze darted between her hand, roiling with magic, and her face. "Really? How could you love me, knowing what I am? Knowing that I brought you here."

Margot blinked back tears, steeling her spine as she drew closer. She sank to her knees before him, their legs brushing. Tentatively, she placed a shaky hand on his thigh, inhaling sharply as his muscles moved against her palm. Slowly, she raised her chin to look at the man she loved, her mate.

Her hand moved upward, trembling as it brushed over his jaw, tracing the lines and scars etched into his face—marks of battles fought, victories won, and losses endured. The imperfections made him devastatingly real, devastatingly him.

She cupped his cheek, her thumb brushing against the rough stubble. "I've loved you long before the bond," she whispered. "Before I was your bloodsworn. Before I even understood what it meant to be your mate. Cillian, you captured my heart in a way I never thought possible."

Cillian's throat bobbed as he swallowed hard, but he stayed still, letting her take the lead. Her voice dropped, intimate, reverent. "I love your scars and your bruises and the way you laugh like you don't believe you deserve it. I love the timbre of your voice—rough, steady, grounding—and the way you always fuss over your tea like it's some sacred ritual."

Margot leaned in, her forehead pressing lightly against his, the warmth of his breath mingling with hers. Her heart thundered in her chest, loud enough to drown out the screaming in the back of her mind. She closed her eyes, letting herself feel the moment, refusing to let Vesryn ruin this one, too. "I love the way you see me. The way you hold me up when I'm breaking, even when you're breaking too. The way you put me first without ever asking for anything in return."

Her nose brushed his, the faintest, most delicate touch, and she felt his breath hitch. "You're everything, Cillian. Everything good in this world and the next and the one after that. Because life isn't just black and white. It's not light versus dark or good versus evil. It's all the messy, complicated shades of grey in between. And you—you are the grey I choose."

Her voice faltered, but she pressed on, her hold tightening. "I love you because you're here. Because even when bad things happen, even when the pieces shatter, you're still here, helping me put it all back together."

Cillian's hand shook as he slowly lifted it to cover hers where it rested on his cheek. The touch sent a jolt through her system— part fear, part longing—but she forced herself to stay present, to focus on the gentle way his calloused fingers curled around hers.

"I will spend every day of my life trying to be worthy of that love," he whispered, his voice thick with emotion. "But Margot, you don't have to push yourself. What Vesryn did—"

"—Is exactly why I need this," she interrupted, her other hand rising to frame his face. Magic stirred beneath her skin, light and shadow moving together in sync. "He tried to take everything from us. Our bond, our memories, our choice." She thumbed his cheekbones. "But he failed. Because this? This is mine to give. My touch, my love, my power."

He pulled back, scanning her face. "Can I kiss you?"

Her heart lurched, anxiety flooding her veins like a tidal wave. She saw it—the quiet desperation he tried so hard to hide. He wasn't asking for much, just this one moment, this one kiss that would be hers to give. Slowly, she nodded, a small, hesitant gesture. Closing her eyes, she braced herself for impact.

When his lips met hers, it wasn't what she expected. There was no crash, no urgency. Instead, his touch was soft, tentative, as though he was testing the waters of something fragile and sacred.

His tongue brushed lightly against her bottom lip—a question, not a demand.

She yielded, just an inch. He took no more than she offered, his movements unhurried, devout, like he was afraid to break the moment. The kiss deepened, not with hunger but with purpose, every touch deliberate, every shift a silent promise: he would never take more than she was willing to give.

Her fingers hesitated before finding their way to his chest, resting lightly against his leathers. Beneath her touch, the steady beat soothed her in a way her own erratic rhythm couldn't.

When he pulled back, just enough to break the kiss, his breath lingered on her lips, warm and ragged. His forehead pressed against hers, and for a moment, neither spoke.

"Margot," he whispered, her name barely audible as though he was afraid it might shatter the tenuous progress they made. "I love you."

As if responding to his words, Margot's magic flared, casting them both in an ethereal glow. Muted purple light danced across Cillian's features, highlighting the wonder in his silver eyes.

"Your power," he breathed. "It's beautiful."

"It's us," she corrected, smiling softly. "Light and dark, demon and elf. Everything Vesryn feared we could become." She leaned back slightly, letting her magic flow freely between them. "Ilphas showed me the truth. Vesryn doesn't just want an heir— he wants to replicate what happened when we bonded. But he can't."

Cillian's brow furrowed. "What do you mean?"

"Our bond changed my magic, made it stronger because we chose each other." She moved her hand down his chest to where their bond bound them for eternity. "But Vesryn's way—taking what isn't freely given—it could never work. He'd destroy himself trying."

"When exactly did you meet with Ilphas?" Cillian asked, his voice low and careful.

"Just before I told you I loved you." She sighed and put some space between her and Cillian. The distance made it a little easier to breathe. "It's complicated, and I was gone for a really long time, but for you, almost no time passed."

Cillian cleared his throat. "What did he show you?"

Margot closed her eyes, remembering the visions in the Weave. "Every time Vesryn... every time he forced himself on me, he was studying my magic. Testing it. He could see how the demon blood in our bond transformed everything it touched." She winced. "But he never understood why. He thought if he could just break me enough, control me enough, he could replicate what we have."

"That's why he was so obsessed with having heirs."

"Not just any heir." She opened her eyes, meeting his. "He wants a child born of elven magic and demon blood—a being powerful enough to rival the goddesses themselves. But Ilphas showed me what Vesryn couldn't see: magic born of violation is corrupt, unstable. The more he tried to force it, the more my power rejected him."

Cillian's jaw clenched. "And the ritual in his chambers tonight?"

"Was meant to be his masterpiece." Bitterness crept into her voice. "He's woven spells into every stone, every beam. Ancient magic he stole from Liriel's texts. He thinks if he can conceive a child there, surrounded by that much power..." She shuddered. "But it would have destroyed us both. The magic would have torn us apart trying to merge what was never meant to be joined."

"Because it wasn't freely given," Cillian murmured his understanding.

Margot nodded. "Our bond works because we chose it. Because there was love, trust—even before we understood what we were to each other." Her magic stirred, casting shadows on the ground. "Ilphas knew this when he gave me his power. He knew someday someone would come along who could show me that true strength isn't about dominance or control. It's about choice."

"That's why he chose you." Cillian took a step forward, reaching out to touch her cheek, but not quite touching. "He knew you would understand."

"He knew Vesryn wouldn't. His own brother..." Margot's voice caught. "Ilphas showed me Vesryn's descent into madness. How the desire for power consumed him until he murdered his own brother in his sleep. How he bound and killed Liriel, using her own magic against her. But even then, Ilphas had the last laugh." A small, sad smile tugged at her lips. "He made sure his magic would find someone who would use it the way it was meant to be used—not to dominate, but to protect. To heal."

"And Ravara?"

"Is the least of our problems right now." She took a deep breath. "We need to get back to Caramis. Vesryn will know something's wrong when I don't return to his chambers tonight, and I need to be ready."

Cillian's expression darkened. "You're not going anywhere near the bastard."

"Yes, I am." Her tone left no room for argument. "Because this time, I'm fighting back. Not just for us, but for every elf he's terrorized. For Ilphas, for Liriel—for everyone who's suffered because Vesryn couldn't understand that true power comes from love, not fear." She lifted her hand, watching as light and shadow twined around her fingers. "He wanted to create something unmatched by forcing light and dark together. But we've already done it, simply by choosing each other."

4 2

LITTLE SPY

THE SILVER FLAGON had gone quiet with Nym's impending absence looming overhead, its usual raucous energy replaced by the anxious pulse of anticipation. He wondered if the place would still be standing when—*if*—he returned. No sense dwelling on it now. He had a job to do, even if that job meant walking straight into the maw of the beast.

"You're going to come back," Stog said, cleaning the same tankard he had in his hand five minutes ago. "This place... this place doesn't work without you."

Nym grinned, jabbing Stog in the gut with an elbow. "See, I knew ya liked me."

Stog gripped Nym's shoulder, shaking him a little. "I'm serious. Don't do anything stupid to get yourself killed."

"I won't." Stog dug his fingers into Nym's shoulder, giving him a pointed look. "I'm serious, alright? I won't do anything stupid." Nym sniffed. "I'm not sure if ya know this, but I'm pretty fond of livin'."

With a final squeeze of his shoulder, Stog stepped back, his gaze steady. He pounded a closed fist against his chest, the sound resonating like a vow.

The scrape of a chair broke the silence. Nym turned to see

461

Ced rising to his feet, his movements deliberate despite the copious amounts of liquor he'd ingested in the short time Nym had been at the Flagon. One arm folded behind his back, the other pressed to his heart in silent salute.

One by one, the others followed—Tanir, Zevrik, Kaldris, and the rest of their battered company. Each stood tall, their fists to their chests, their eyes fixed on him with solemnity.

Their belief in him was heavier than armor yet stronger than steel, and in that moment, Nym had never been prouder to be part of this movement. They offered no grand speeches, only their unwavering resolve, a shared strength he hadn't realized he needed.

He swallowed hard, offering a salute of his own before walking to the door. This mission was his to bear, but he wouldn't carry it alone.

NYM PULLED HIS CLOAK TIGHTER AS HE CREPT through the thick fog rolling off the Tempest Sea. Dawn was still hours away, but he could make out the shapes of Ravara's war galleys dotting the horizon—massive shadows lurking in the predawn gloom. The fae weren't even trying to hide their presence anymore. Why bother when victory seemed assured?

From his vantage point in the craggy hills overlooking the northeastern coast, Nym could see the true scale of what they faced. Hundreds of ships stretched as far as the eye could see, their black sails billowing like storm clouds. The beach below teemed with activity as more fae soldiers made landfall, their armor gleaming dully in the torchlight. He'd known the situation was bad, but this... this was an extinction-level event.

"Quite the view, isn't it?" a lilting voice asked from behind him.

Nym managed not to flinch as he turned to face the speaker. The fae who emerged from the mist was tall and lithe, with silver-white hair that seemed to capture what little light there was. His crystalline blue eyes were sharp, cunning, and cruel.

"Lord Ravara," Nym said, dropping into a bow that was only slightly mocking. "Fancy meeting you here."

The Fae King's lips curved into a smile that didn't reach his eyes. "Come now, little spy. Did you really think I wouldn't know you were coming?" He gestured to the armada spread out below them. "I've been waiting for Corym to send someone. Though I must admit, I didn't expect it to be you."

"What can I say?" Nym shrugged, keeping his tone light even as ice slid down his spine. "I'm full of surprises."

"Indeed." Ravara's gaze sharpened. "Just as I'm sure you have some interesting information to share about a certain girl with rather... unique abilities."

And there it was—the real reason Ravara let this meeting happen. Not that Nym had expected anything else. The Fae King's obsession with Margot was well known to everyone outside of Caramis, even if the reasons behind it remained murky.

"Might have some insights worth discussin'," Nym said carefully. "Though I reckon that kind of information comes at a price."

Ravara laughed, the sound was like breaking glass. "Oh, you precious thing. You think you're here to negotiate?" His smiled turned predatory. "Let me be clear: you're here because I allow it. And you'll tell me everything you know about the girl, or I'll extract it from your corpse."

As if to emphasize his point, shadows began to coalesce around them, taking the shape of armored fae warriors. Nym counted at least twenty before he stopped trying. *Well. This is going about as well as expected.*

"See, that's where you're wrong," Nym said, forcing himself to meet Ravara's gaze. "I'm here because ya need me to be here. Because what I know about Margot? It's not just about her power. It's about why ya want her so badly." He paused, watching

Ravara's expression carefully. "And about who else is coming for her."

The temperature seemed to drop several degrees as Ravara's eyes narrowed. "Explain."

"Might want to send your friends away first," Nym replied, nodding to the shadowy figures surrounding them. "What I'm about to tell ya... well, let's just say some secrets are best kept between *friends*."

For a long moment, Ravara simply stared at him, those eyes seeming to peer straight into his soul. Finally, he waved a hand, and the shadow warriors melted back into the mist.

"Speak quickly," Ravara commanded. "My patience grows thin."

Nym took a deep breath, knowing his next words would either save them all or damn them completely. "Tell me, my lord... what do you know about the Void Lords?"

Ravara's gaze bored into Nym, searching for traces of truth. "The Void Lords? You expect me to believe such fairy tales?"

"Got your attention, though, didn't it?" Nym was playing a dangerous game, but then again, he always did. "Look, the truth is—"

Ravara's hand shot out, fingers wrapping around Nym's throat before he could finish. The Fae King lifted him effortlessly until his feet dangled above the ground. "The truth," Ravara snarled, "is that you're stalling."

Through the spots dancing in his vision, Nym saw more fae warriors materializing from the mist. Their armor clanked as they formed a circle around them.

"Not... stalling," Nym choked out. "Creating... leverage."

"Leverage?" Ravara's laugh was cold as winter frost. "You insignificant little worm. Did you really think you could bargain with me?" His grip tightened. "I have an armada. I have an army. And soon, I'll have the girl. What could you possibly offer me?"

"Time," Nym wheezed.

The horn blast that cut through the morning air was so loud

it shook the ground. Ravara's head snapped toward the sound as more horns joined the first, their urgent calls echoing across the water. On the beach below, the fae army erupted into chaos.

"My lord!" A warrior appeared beside them, dropping to one knee. "The elves—they're gone!"

Ravara's eyes widened. His grip on Nym's throat loosened just enough for him to draw a ragged breath. "What do you mean, gone?"

"The deepweave, my lord. We can't find it. The island... it's vanished."

Nym couldn't help the grin that spread across his face, even as Ravara's fingers dug into his flesh. "Funny thing about Caramis," he rasped. "Sometimes it likes to play hide and seek."

Ravara hurled him to the ground with a roar of fury. "Find them!" he commanded the assembled warriors. "Tear apart every inch of this coastline if you have to, but find that island!"

As the warriors scattered, Ravara grabbed Nym by his hair, yanking him up. "You think this clever deception will save you? Save them?" His voice dropped to a venomous whisper. "You've only delayed the inevitable. And now you'll watch it unfold from my ship's brig."

Through the thinning fog, Nym could see the first rays of dawn painting the horizon in shades of purple and gold. He hoped he'd bought enough time. Hoped Corym had gotten his message. Hoped the resistance was ready.

"Take him," Ravara ordered two of his remaining guards. As they seized Nym's arms, the Fae King leaned close. "When we find the island—and we *will* find it—you'll have a front-row seat to its destruction."

"Seems I hit a nerve," Nym said, unable to resist one last jab. "What's wrong, my lord? Afraid someone else might get to her first?"

The backhand caught him across the face with enough force to split his lip. Blood trickled down his chin as Ravara grabbed his jaw. "I'm going to enjoy breaking you, little spy. But first..." He turned to the assembled army below, raising his voice to carry across the beach. "Find me that island! I want every ship, every soldier searching. The first one to spot it will be rewarded beyond their wildest dreams. The first one to bring me the girl…" His cruel smile widened. "Well, let's just say their name will live in legend."

As the fae warriors dragged him toward the waiting ships, Nym watched hundreds of vessels pull away from the shore, spreading out across the Tempest Sea like a net. He'd known this was coming. Had planned for it, even. But seeing the sheer scale of Ravara's forces—the glint of weapons, the thunder of boots, the overwhelming sense of inevitable doom—he couldn't help but wonder if they'd all badly miscalculated their chance of survival. Nym spat blood onto the deck of Ravara's flagship as they shoved him below.

The brig was cold, the damp air thick with the scent of salt and iron. Chains clanked as Nym was shoved into a corner, his wrists shackled to the wall. The guards left without a word, the heavy wooden door slamming shut behind them. There was silence, broken only by the distant creak of the ship and the muffled roar of Ravara's forces preparing for war.

Nym shifted, testing the restraints. Solid iron, etched with faint runes that glimmered in the low light. No breaking through those—not with brute strength, and not with magic. He leaned back, letting his head rest against the sodden wood of the hull, and let out a slow breath.

The resistance couldn't be more ready. And yet, sitting here now, with Ravara's army closing in on Caramis, doubt crept in. What if they weren't ready? What if the resistance fell before the island could reveal itself again?

No. He couldn't afford to think like that.

Footsteps echoed outside the door, and Nym straightened as the lock turned. A young fae warrior stepped inside, her sharp features illuminated by the glow of a lantern. She looked barely out of training, her eyes hard but not yet hardened.

"You're the one causing all this trouble?" she asked, her voice clipped.

"Trouble's a strong word," Nym replied, his grin lopsided despite the ache in his jaw. "I prefer 'complication.'"

She didn't smile. Instead, she crouched down, placing the lantern between them. "Lord Ravara won't tolerate your games for long. Whatever you think you're stalling for, it won't work."

"Good thing I don't play games." Nym sniffed. "I deal in truths. Sometimes uncomfortable ones."

Her brow furrowed. "Truths? Like what?"

"Like the fact that your king's obsession is blinding him. Margot's not just some weapon to be wielded. She's the key to something bigger—something none of you understand." He leaned forward as far as the chains would allow, his voice dropping. "You think this war ends with Caramis? It doesn't. If Ravara succeeds, he'll unravel something none of us can put back together."

The warrior hesitated, her fingers twitching on the hilt of her sword. "You're lying."

"Am I?" Nym tilted his head. "Tell me, does Ravara ever explain why he wants her? Or does he just demand obedience?"

Her silence was answer enough.

Nym pressed on, his tone softening. "You're on the wrong side of this. You know it, even if you can't admit it yet. You think you're fighting for a better world, but all you're doing is helping him tear it apart."

The door creaked open again, and the warrior jumped to her feet, the spell between them broken. Ravara stepped inside, his presence filling the room like noxious gas. He glanced at the young soldier, dismissing her with a single look. She hurried out, her lantern casting flickering shadows across the walls as she went.

"Making friends already?" Ravara drawled. "That was fast."

"Just sharin' stories," Nym replied easily, though his pulse quickened.

Ravara stepped closer, his boots heavy against the wooden

floor. "You think your little games will buy you time, but you're mistaken. Caramis will fall, the girl will be mine, and you..." He crouched down, his face mere inches from Nym's. "You will be for death before I'm through with you."

Nym held his gaze, refusing to flinch. "Big talk for someone who doesn't have all the pieces yet."

Ravara's eyes narrowed, his patience clearly thinning. "You think you're clever, don't you? But your cleverness won't save you. Or her."

He straightened, turning to leave, but paused at the door. "Enjoy your last hours, little spy. They'll be your most painful. And I assure you, I know exactly how to get you to tell me what I want to know."

The door slammed shut, and Nym exhaled, his bravado cracking for just a moment. He glanced at the faint light filtering through the cracks in the hull, the rays of dawn growing stronger. If the resistance didn't act soon, there wouldn't be a Caramis left to save.

He closed his eyes, forcing himself to focus. This wasn't over. Not yet. He just needed to play his cards right.

And far away on Caramis, Margot would be preparing. He could only hope she was ready for what came next.

Because when the deepweave revealed itself, all hells would break loose.

TIME TO GO

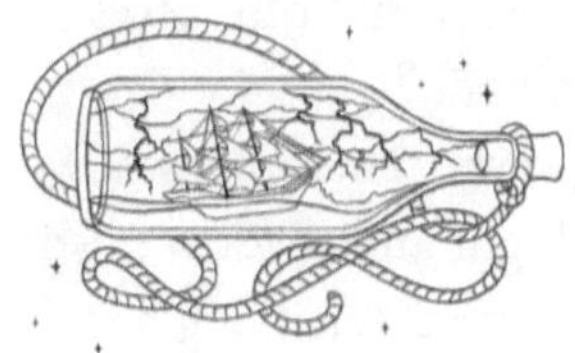

CILLIAN WATCHED from the shadows of the training hall as Margot moved through the space, her steps silent against the stone floor. They'd hidden in the jungle to wait out Vesryn—Margot's idea—and it had thrown the manor into chaos. Periodically, they'd do recon, hoping activity would die down. Eventually, it did. Hours of searching led to sleepy elves—even Vesryn. She'd insisted on coming just before dawn, that the risk of discovery would be at its lowest. Even now, after everything, her pragmatism carved through his chest like a blade.

Morning's first light caught on her new armor—leather and steel mixed with something older, etched with runes Cillian didn't recognize. The hellforger had outdone himself, crafting protection that could withstand both physical and magical attacks. He wasn't sure how Nym had the foresight to have the expert crafter create armor on top of the fist, but that little elf continued to surprise him.

"You're brooding again," Margot said without turning around. She flexed her hands in the reinforced gloves, assessing their stretch. "I can feel it through the bond."

"Can't help it." He pushed off from the wall but maintained his distance. "Walking into his chambers alone is suicide."

"Which is why I won't be alone." Now she did turn, meeting his eyes with that familiar steel in her gaze. "I'll have you."

"Outside the door," he reminded her bitterly. "Unable to reach you if—"

"If I fail." She lifted her palm, calling forth a sphere of pure light that cast harsh shadows across her face. With her other hand, she summoned darkness until both forces swirled around her like twin serpents. "I won't fail."

The display of power sent shivers down his spine. This was what Vesryn feared. Light and shadow existing not in opposition, but in harmony. A perfect, terrifying agreement between deadly elements to work in tandem, to provide balanced destruction for one blessed—or cursed—to wield. And at the center of it all was Margot. A human who somehow was able to harness elven magic as well as demonic blood when both should have torn her apart from the inside out.

"Show me," she said, letting the magic fade. "Show me how to channel demon blood without letting it consume me."

"Demon blood responds to emotion," Cillian said, rolling up his sleeves. "Rage, fear, desire—they all feed it. But the secret isn't controlling those feelings." He called forth his own darkness, tapping into raw emotion that the bond offered and let it coat his skin like oil. "It's accepting them."

Margot's eyes tracked the display, analyzing every detail. She'd been different since returning from wherever Ilphas had taken her consciousness—more focused, almost predatory in her attention. "That's what I've been doing wrong. Trying to master it instead of working with it."

She closed her eyes, and Cillian felt the bond between them pulse. Light bloomed around her once more, but this time, she didn't fight when tendrils of shadows weaved through it. The magics twisted together, neither overtaking the other, until she was wreathed in twilight.

"Good," he breathed, forcing himself to stay rooted in place when every instinct screamed to go to her. His touch wasn't what she needed now. "Now channel it through your core, like we practiced with the bow."

Margot's breath hitched as the combined power surged through her. The runes on her armor flared in response, creating a feedback loop that made the air crackle with energy. A small smile curved her lips.

"It doesn't hurt anymore," she whispered. "Before, it felt like I was dying, but now..." She opened her eyes, and for a moment, they blazed silver like his own. "Now it feels right."

"Try the offensive forms." Cillian adjusted the fist, summoning a shield of pure darkness tinged with his own blood. "Hit me with everything you've got."

"Cillian—"

"I can take it." He met her gaze steadily. "And you need to know you can do this without holding back. Vesryn won't show mercy."

Her jaw tightened at the name, but she nodded. The light and shadow around her condensed, forming jagged spears that hummed with deadly intent. Cillian braced himself, knowing this was going to hurt like hells.

Margot raised her hand, getting ready to assault Cillian, but he dropped his shield and held up his hand. "We can't stay here." The training hall suddenly felt confining, every echo a potential betrayal of their presence. She lowered her magic, letting it dissipate. "I know a place. Follow me."

They moved like ghosts through the manor's winding corridors, Margot's footsteps now as quiet as his own. Dawn had barely broken, casting long shadows that provided additional cover as they made their way outside. The nethersparrows still lined the parapets, their beady eyes tracking their movement, but they kept their distance. Wherever the breach was, it was likely some fae were able to slip through as well. They needed to hurry.

Cillian led her down the worn path to the hidden grotto entrance. He grumbled as he stuffed himself back into the tunnel he barely fit into. Inside, the vast cave opened before them, the sound of gentle waves lapping against the stone providing a soothing backdrop. He followed Margot as she hooked left toward the water, her steps stalling as she spotted the familiar ship bobbing gently in the protected waters.

"How?" she whispered, taking a step toward it.

"Nym." Cillian's lips quirked. "That pain in the ass has become one of my favorites."

Margot reached out, running her fingers along the hull. Through the bond, Cillian felt a surge of emotion—nostalgia, longing, and beneath it all, a deep ache that made his chest tight. But she pulled away before he could say anything, squaring her shoulders as she walked back to the central room.

"This is perfect," she said, gesturing to the open space. "No one will hear us here."

Without waiting for a response, she called forth her magic again. The combined forces of light and shadow danced around her, illuminating the cave in an ethereal glow. This time, she didn't hold back.

Spears of twilight magic crashed against the shield Cillian barely had enough time to raise, the impact sending him sliding backward several feet. He grunted with the effort of maintaining his defense, wincing as he siphoned more blood to reinforce the shield. Her power had grown exponentially in such a short time, but more importantly, she was finally trusting it—trusting herself.

"Again," he called out, holding steady. "But this time, let the demon blood guide your instincts. Don't think—feel."

Margot's next assault came faster, harder. The merged magics responded to her emotions, feeding off both light and shadow until they became something entirely new—something grey. Each strike carried the raw force of demon blood tempered by the precision of elven magic. It was beautiful and terrifying—just like her.

A particularly powerful blast shattered his shield, forcing him to dive and roll. When he came up, she had already closed the distance between them, twilight coalescing into blades around her hands.

Their eyes met, and for a moment, time seemed to stop. They were close enough now that he could see the flecks of silver in her eyes, could feel the heat radiating off her skin. The bond hummed between them, strong and vital despite everything Vesryn had done to break it.

Margot sucked in a sharp breath, and Cillian instantly stepped back, giving her space. But she shook her head, jaw clenched.

"No," she said. "I need to learn to fight in close quarters. I can't..." She swallowed hard. "I can't let this control me. Vesryn will expect me to be broken and take advantage of that."

"You're not broken," Cillian said fiercely. "Changed, yes. But not broken."

She met his gaze again, and this time, there was something else in her eyes—something that made his heart stutter. "Help me prove it."

Cillian nodded slowly, drawing more blood and directing it to the fist. If she was ready to face this, he would be there every step of the way. "Your move."

Their deadly dance continued, each strike and parry bringing them closer to the edge of what they could endure. Sweat ran down Margot's temples as she wielded her merged magic, the twilight energy responding to her will with increasing precision. She was learning to channel both aspects of her power—using the demon blood's raw force while maintaining the calculated control of elven magic.

"Good," Cillian called out as she executed a particularly complex sequence. "Now try—"

The cave shuddered violently, sending loose rocks clattering to the ground. Both froze, eyes meeting in shocked recognition. The vibrations intensified, and the water in the grotto began to churn.

"No," Margot breathed.

Another tremor rocked the cave, stronger this time. The ship's moorings creaked ominously as waves crashed against the hull. Above them, through the cracks in the ceiling, they could hear the screech of hundreds of wings—not nethersparrows, but something larger, more ominous. *They're in. Time to go.*

Cillian grabbed her hand. "We need to move. Now."

They raced through the tunnel system, emerging into mayhem. The purple sky had turned an ugly crimson, thick with the silhouettes of winged fae warriors. Below, the first wave was already breaching Caramis' shores.

"The Flagon," Cillian said, his voice tight. "Nym and the others—"

"I'm right behind you."

They sprinted through the streets, dodging panicked elves as they ran. The tavern came into view, its windows already boarded up. Cillian kicked in the door to find the resistance in disarray.

"They weren't supposed to be here for days!" Tanir shouted over the din, frantically distributing weapons. "The wards should have held!"

"Where's Nym?" Cillian asked, running through the mess. He glanced over his shoulder to make sure Margot was still following.

Stog threw a hefty sack across the room to Caelith. "Went to negotiate with Ravara." He turned to Cillian, a grimace on his face. "Little good that did."

"Corym? Tahlsia?" Cillian asked urgently.

The building shook as something massive impacted nearby. Stog cursed as bottles crashed behind the bar. "Corym has been with the Veilguard, running around looking for her." He pointed at Margot. "Tahlsia never left the manor. Considering what is happening, she and Edea are aiding with evacuations."

"How many made it to the safe points?" Cillian asked.

"Maybe half the city," Zevrik answered as she adjusted her vambraces. "The rest..." She trailed off as another explosion rocked the foundation.

"We need to get to Vesryn," Margot said, her magic coiling around her protectively. "He's only going to make it worse."

Stog snorted. "You'll never make it to the manor. The fae will have it surrounded by now."

"They're not the only ones who can fly." Cillian's eyes gleamed dangerously as he felt his demon form stirring beneath his skin. "But we need a distraction."

Ced cackled as he tightened the straps across his chest. "A distraction we can do." A grin spread across his face, reminiscent of Nym's. "Remember those explosives you helped me get, Kaldris? Time to put them to use." He looked around the room at the gathered resistance. "Who's ready to wreak havoc?"

The answering roar was drowned out by another impact, even closer this time. Dust rained from the ceiling as the fae lay siege. Through the empty door frame, they could see orange flames beginning to paint the horizon.

Caramis was burning. And somewhere in his tower, Vesryn was watching it all unfold.

44

CHANGE OF PLANS

THE BIRDS HAD GONE SILENT.

Corym stood atop the eastern rampart, watching the horizon blur as thousands of fae soldiers emerged from the deepweave like wraiths materializing from smoke. Their numbers seemed endless, their gilded armor catching the light of dawn and setting the coastline ablaze. Behind them, more shadows twisted in the mist —siege engines, war machines—fae technology—instruments of absolute destruction that would soon tear through Caramis' paltry walls as easily as parchment.

How many lives would be lost today because of his silence? How many had already been lost to Vesryn's madness while Corym stood by, telling himself that loyalty meant something? That by staying close to power he could somehow temper it, guide it, keep the worst of it at bay?

Lies. All of it.

He'd been lying to himself for decades, watching as Vesryn descended further into darkness, as the vibrant streets of Caramis withered under his rule. Now, the consequences of his cowardice were marching toward their shores, and the blood of every elf who fell would stain his hands as surely as it would stain Vesryn's.

"Commander!" Breken's voice cut through his thoughts. His

second-in-command sprinted along the wall, face flushed. "They're coming through on the western front as well. We're surrounded."

Of course they were. Ravara wasn't going to leave anything to chance, not with a prize like Margot at stake. The Fae King would crush them between hammer and anvil, grinding Caramis to dust.

"How many?" Corym asked, though he already knew the answer wouldn't matter.

"Too many," Breken replied grimly. "The Veilguard is spread thin as it is, and half our forces are still recovering from..." He trailed off, but Corym could see the accusation in his eyes.

From Vesryn's "training." From the senseless deaths of their brothers and sisters. From Corym's failure to protect them.

"Sound the horns," Corym ordered, his voice steady despite the storm raging in his chest. "Get the civilians to the shelters. Any who can fight or is able to hold a spear should report to the central square for arms and assignment."

"And the others?" Breken asked carefully. "Those who sided with—"

"All of them," Corym cut in. "We don't have the luxury of division anymore. Caramis stands or falls together."

Breken nodded and turned to go, but Corym caught his arm. "How's Masha?"

A flash of fear crossed his second's face before he could mask it. "Safe. For now."

"Good." Corym squeezed his arm. "Keep her that way. No matter what happens today, we need to ensure there's a future for us."

As Breken hurried off, horns began to echo across the city—deep, mournful notes that hadn't been heard in generations. The sound made Corym shudder. How many times had he imagined this moment? How many nights had he lain awake, wondering if his choices would lead them here?

Movement from the manor caught his eye. Vesryn stood on his balcony, his form rigid as he surveyed his domain. Even from this distance, Corym could feel the rage radiating off him in waves. Their eyes met briefly, and in that moment, Corym saw something that chilled him to his core: not madness, but perfect, crystalline clarity. Vesryn knew exactly what he was doing, had always known. And he would watch the world burn before relinquishing his grip on power. Before relinquishing his grip on Margot.

More horns joined the chorus—not the deep resonance of Caramis' warning system, but higher, more martial notes. The fae were signaling their advance. Time had run out.

Corym drew his sword, the steel singing as it left its sheath. Three armies would clash today: Ravara's forces, intent on claiming Margot and crushing any who stood in their way; Vesryn's loyalists, who would defend their mad king to their last breath; and somewhere in between, those who still believed in something more than power and conquest.

The resistance would have to move quickly if they wanted to succeed. The chaos of battle might be their only chance to strike at Vesryn while his attention was divided. But first, they had to survive the initial assault.

Corym sucked in a breath as the sound of flapping wings overtook the sound of horns. He raised his hand, sights set on the horizon as Ravara's Reavers headed straight for Caramis. "Form ranks!" he bellowed, his voice carrying across the ramparts as elves scrambled into position. "Archers to the walls! Shield bearers forward!"

The remaining members of the Veilguard moved with practiced precision, but Corym could see the fear in their eyes. They had trained for this their entire lives, but nothing could truly prepare them for what was coming.

The first volley of fae arrows darkened the sky like a cloud of locusts.

Caramis' last stand had begun.

"Shields!" Corym roared as the arrows descended. Magical barriers flickered to life along the ramparts, most holding against the onslaught. But not all. Screams pierced the air as arrows found their marks, and the acrid scent of blood mingled with sulfur from deflected spells.

He had positioned the strongest among them along the eastern wall, knowing Ravara would lead the main attack there. But even their combined power couldn't hold forever. Already, he could see the strain in their faces as volley after volley tested their defenses. Elves were strong, stronger than the fae, but even the strongest fall.

Movement to the right caught his eye—Zevrik, darting between defenders like a shadow, whispering to select members of the Veil-guard. The ones they could trust. The ones who would act when the moment came. Corym pretended not to notice, just as he pretended not to see the growing number of "injured" soldiers being escorted to the deep chambers where their real forces were gathering.

"Commander!" A young elf—barely more than a boy—sprinted toward him, breathless. "King Vesryn demands your presence in the manor. He says—"

"Tell him I'm needed here," Corym cut in, gesturing to the chaos around them. "The defense of Caramis—"

"He insists," the messenger pressed, trembling slightly. "He says... he says if you don't come now, he'll consider it treason."

Corym struggled not to roll his eyes. Vesryn wasn't a fool. He had to suspect something was coming, even if he didn't know the details. Keeping Corym close was just good strategy. Though Margot not returning to the manor had thrown even Corym for a loop, and even if Vesryn searched his mind, he'd find no information regarding that little detour.

A thunderous crash drew their attention to the western wall. One of the fae siege engines had found its mark, and a section of the ancient stone was crumbling. Defenders scrambled to shore up the breach, but Corym could see it was only the beginning.

"Sir?" The messenger's voice cracked. "What should I tell him?"

Corym's jaw clenched as he watched another volley of arrows darken the sky. The choice he'd been avoiding for decades had finally come due. There would be no more walking the line between loyalty and rebellion. No more pretending he could serve two masters.

"Tell him—"

The rest of his words were drowned out by an explosion that rocked the entire city. Corym spun toward the sound, his heart stopped as he saw flames erupting from the manor's eastern wing. Not fae artillery—the blast had come from inside.

Someone had moved early. Or been discovered. Either way, their carefully laid plans were unraveling.

The messenger was already running toward the manor, but Corym caught the glint of metal just before an arrow took the boy to the back of the head. He fell without a sound, another casualty in a war that had barely begun.

"Breken!" Corym shouted, and his second materialized from the chaos as if summoned. "Take command here. Hold the walls as long as you can, but be ready to fall back to the secondary positions when I give the signal."

"Where are you going?"

Corym's grip tightened on his sword as another explosion rocketed the manor. "To make right what I should have stopped years ago."

He took off at a run, weaving between defenders and debris as more arrows rained down. The fae hadn't breached the walls yet, but it was only a matter of time. They needed to deal with Vesryn quickly if they were going to have any chance of mounting a real defense.

The streets of Caramis were a maze of panic and confusion. Civilians fled toward the shelters while soldiers rushed to their positions, the two streams of bodies colliding in pandemonium. Somewhere in the distance, a child was crying; there were so few children on the island that he could have guessed who it was.

Corym forced himself to keep moving. He couldn't save everyone. Not anymore.

As he neared the manor, a figure emerged from the smoke—one of Vesryn's personal guards, sword drawn.

"Stand aside," Corym ordered, letting centuries of authority ring in his voice.

The guard's stance widened. "King Vesryn's orders. No one enters."

Corym's hand hovered over the hilt of his sword. "I was summoned."

"And then you weren't. Move along."

Corym gripped the handle, not yet drawing his weapon. "Last chance."

The guard's blade came up. "Long live the king."

Corym's sword was moving before the words finished leaving the elf's mouth. The guard was good—all of Vesryn's chosen were—but Corym hadn't survived this long by being predictable. He let the guard parry his first strike, then dropped and swept the elf's legs while simultaneously driving his blade up through the gap in his armor.

Corym's strike was true, and blood spurted with every slowing beat of the guard's heart, coating Corym's face. The guard's eyes widened, and Corym took advantage of his shock by unsheathing his dagger and burying it into the poor soul's skull.

"I'm sorry," he whispered as the light faded from the guard's eyes. Another death he would carry. Another choice he couldn't take back.

He wiped the blood from his blades, securing them both at his side. More explosions sounded from the manor as Corym raced inside. The grand entrance hall was already a battlefield—bodies lay strewn across the marble floor, smoke curling from blast marks on the walls. The resistance had clearly made progress, but at a terrible cost. A familiar voice echoed from above, followed by the distinctive crack of Vesryn's magic. Corym took the stairs two at a time.

Just as he reached the top-level landing, a body barreled into him, sending him stumbling backward into a room as the door swung open in the same instant. He hit the floor hard, his shoulder slamming into the unforgiving stone, drawing a low groan from his lips. The smaller figure that had crashed into him rolled off in a tangle of limbs.

"Edea?" Corym rasped, staring at her in disbelief. How could someone so timid hit with that much force?

"*Shhh*," Tahlsia snapped as she closed the door quietly, stepping into view. She offered him a hand. "Be *quiet*. There's not much time so—"

"I need to get to Vesryn, Tahl!" Corym interrupted.

"Stupid, stupid male," she muttered, shaking her head. "No, you need to intercept Margot and Cillian *now*, before this entire manor and every innocent soul inside it is obliterated. Take it to the square if you must, but you *cannot* let them fight here."

Corym scrubbed his hand down his face, bits of dried blood flaking off. "You're not even supposed to be here." His sharp gaze shifted to Edea, making her shrink back. "Neither of you."

Tahlsia slapped a torn scrap of parchment into his hand. "Plans change. Stog couldn't talk Margot out of this asinine idea." Her voice faltered, her eyes flickering downward. "Cillian couldn't, either."

Corym grimaced as he scanned the hastily scrawled dispatch. The words burned in his mind before he crumpled the paper in his fist. "What makes you think she'll listen to me?"

"She trusts you," Edea said softly, her voice so small it almost didn't reach him. Her wide eyes darted to the blood on his face and chest. "And... you're covered in blood." She winced as if the word physically hurt to speak. "I'm sure you can think of some way to redirect them."

Tahlsia sighed heavily, folding her arms. "And Vesryn? He can't stay here much longer. It's only a matter of time before the fae breach the manor."

Corym's jaw tightened as he looked between Edea's trembling frame and Tahlsia's grim expression.

"Fine." He flexed his blood-covered fingers. "But if this goes sideways…"

Bits of stone fell from the ceiling as another explosion went off. Edea whimpered, hugging her knees to her chest.

Tahlsia threw her hands in the air. "As if it all hasn't gone sideways already!"

Corym shot her an annoyed look but didn't argue. Instead, he made for the door. Edea scrambled to her feet, grabbing his bicep before he could head out into the fray.

"Be careful," Edea breathed. "Please be careful."

He hesitated, just for a moment, before pulling away. "You two, stay out of sight. If—*when*—the fae breach the manor…" His words trailed off, and a puff of air pushed past his lips. "Do whatever it takes to stay alive. Surrender. I don't care. Just don't get yourselves killed."

Without waiting for an answer, Corym stepped into the hallway, the sounds of distant chaos bleeding through the walls. Somewhere, Margot and Cillian were hurtling toward disaster. And he needed to find them. Fast.

45
HOPE

CORYM'S HANDS shook as he read the dispatch for the third time. The parchment, stained with ink and what looked suspiciously like blood, was concise and to the point: Margot was better—rife with magic—and she and Cillian were moving through the city, heading toward the manor.

Something had happened, something big that prevented Margot from returning to Vesryn. Cillian had said it was possible to bring her back. It was unlikely he would succeed so soon, but it wasn't impossible. Considering they were now moving toward the manor with one purpose in mind, it suggested that is exactly what occurred. Margot was going to kill Vesryn.

Black wings beat dangerously close to the western wall—Reavers—or what was left of them. Corym directed bolts to his fingertips, lighting crackling up his forearm, and with a mighty growl, he unleashed a torrent of lightning, taking down the rest. Those soldiers were nothing more than fodder, meant to distract, and it was working.

He scrubbed his face, sighing through his fingers before catching Ravara's men loading up the siege engine with boulders that were dragged from the beach. Soldiers ran past him toward the merlon to prepare their defenses. How could he be searching for Margot when his soldiers needed him here?

Corym ran to the center of the wall walk. "Hold!" he bellowed over the thunderous crash of siege engines. The ancient walls of Caramis shuddered beneath his feet as fae weaponry hammered their defenses. Through gaps in the predawn mist, he could make out the first wave of Ravara's forces—their armor glinting like stars as they advanced across the beach in perfect formation. "Wait for my signal!"

Breken appeared at his side, blood streaking his leathers. "West wall's failing. Vesryn's loyalists pulled half our forces for the manor's defense." His voice cracked, exhaustion seeping through. "What are your orders?"

Before Corym could respond, a horn blast cut through the chaos—three sharp notes that made his stomach turn. "Belay that order!" one of Vesryn's chosen shouted from further down the wall. "All units to the manor! The king commands it!"

Corym's jaw clenched as he watched nearly a third of his remaining forces abandon their posts. The Veilguard was fracturing, torn between their oath to protect Caramis and their loyalty to a deranged king who would sacrifice them all.

"Sir?" Breken's hand tightened on his sword. "What do we do?"

Another impact thundered against the walls. Through the settling dust, Corym could see grappling hooks arcing up from the beach. The fae were done testing their defenses. The real assault was beginning.

"Hold this section," Corym said finally. "Whatever forces you have left, whatever it takes. We can't let them—"

A blast of magic lit up the eastern quarter of the city, so bright it left spots dancing in his vision. Not fae magic—something different. Something that made his teeth ache. When the glare faded, he saw two figures moving through the streets below, heading straight for the manor. Even from this distance, he recognized them. Margot and Cillian.

Unbelievable amounts of power swirled around Margot like a tempest, neither light nor shadow, but something new, something grey. Something that shouldn't be possible. He had just seen her yesterday, still firmly under Vesryn's control. How could she possibly have changed this much? And more importantly, what would she do with that power now?

"Corym!" Breken's shout snapped him back to reality. "We need orders!"

Another explosion rocked the eastern quarter. Through the smoke, he could see members of the Veilguard moving to intercept Margot and Cillian. If they engaged... if whatever it was that she wielded was turned loose in the cramped streets...

"Take command here," he said, already moving toward them. "Hold them as long as you can. I need to—"

"You can't leave us!" Breken grabbed his arm. "The fae are coming! The walls are falling! We need our commander!"

Corym pulled free, hating himself for what he was about to do. "No. You need *a* commander. And right now, that's you." He clasped Breken's shoulder. "Keep our people alive. If a battle can't be won—get out. That's an order."

Before his second could protest, Corym turned and raced down the wall steps. The streets below had descended into chaos as civilians fled the approaching fae army. He pushed through the crowd, trying to plot an interception course. If he cut through the market district...

A horn blast from the western wall made him stumble. That signal could only mean one thing—another breach. They were being surrounded. How many more would die while he chased after Margot? How many more lives would be lost because he wasn't where he was needed most?

But he couldn't ignore what was happening. Whether Margot was still Vesryn's puppet or had broken free, her power made her the most dangerous piece on the board, and both sides wanted her. With everything falling apart at the seams, he needed to control one thing; they needed some advantage—*any* advantage

—and this was the surest way to mitigate even more senseless death.

He rounded the corner onto the high street just as another blast lit up the predawn sky. The sight stopped him cold. Margot stood in the center of the road, power radiating off her in waves. The demon stood at her back, his own darkness rising to meet hers, the hellforged weapon on his arm glowing with barely contained violence.

Six of Vesryn's personal guard lay scattered at their feet among countless winged fae warriors. Not dead—Corym could see their chests rising and falling—but broken in ways that would never fully heal. A seventh guard charged forward, sword raised and crackling with lightning. Margot didn't even look at him. A tendril lashed out, catching the elf mid-stride and hurling him through a shop front in a spray of glass and splintered wood.

"Seven down," Cillian growled, his voice carrying despite the chaos. "How many more want to die for him?"

The remaining loyalists exchanged glances, their weapons wavering. They'd been trained to fight elves, demons, fae—but this? This was something else entirely.

Corym stepped into view, forcing himself to breathe past the suffocating effect Margot's magic had on him. "Stand down," he ordered the guards. "Get to the walls. That's where you're needed."

"But sir," one started to protest. "The king—"

"I said stand down!" The words cracked like a whip. "This isn't your fight anymore."

The guards hesitated for only a moment before breaking ranks, hurrying toward the sounds of battle at the walls. Corym watched them go, knowing he'd just sentenced some of them to death. But better a clean death in battle than whatever was about to unfold here.

Margot took tentative steps toward Corym with Cillian trailing behind, uncertainty painted the demon's face before he carefully schooled his features. Corym's hand hovered over the hilt of his blade, his own magic sparking at the tips of his fingers.

"He needs to die, Corym." Margot stalled no more than two paces from him, her magic whipping up dust and debris. "You can't stop this. I won't let you."

"Corym's on our side." Cillian let his shadows fall, sliding his fingers through hers. He sighed when she tensed but released her all the same. "He knows Vesryn needs to die."

"Does he?" she said, eyes wild as she gestured to Corym's hands. "Does he really?"

Corym snuffed his magic and raised his hands in surrender. "I agree. Vesryn needs to die, but not at the manor. There are too many innocents there. Take it to the square. Give them a chance to run." His voice caught. "Let me save what little I can."

"How is that supposed to work?" Cillian jerked his head toward the manor high up on the hill. "He's fortifying his castle."

"We draw him out," Margot breathed. "He wants me, right?"

"Everyone wants you, Margot." Corym grimaced.

"I've got an idea." She sucked in a sharp breath and turned to Cillian. "But you're not going to like it."

Cillian crossed his arms, his eyes darkening. "What's your idea?"

"You're going to transform—*fully* transform—and fly me around the manor. If he knows where I am, he'll come. I know he will."

"No," Cillian said plainly.

Corym stepped forward, placing a firm hand on Cillian's shoulder. "It's madness," he said quietly, "but it's our best shot—and you know it."

"It *is* madness," Cillian growled. "It's too danger—"

Another explosion shook the city. Through the billowing smoke, Corym could make out the distinctive silhouettes of Ravara's siege engines being wheeled into position. The fae hadn't just breached their outer defenses—they were establishing a foothold.

"We don't have time to argue," Corym urged. "Look around you! The city's falling. If we don't draw Vesryn out *now*, there won't be anything left to save. You will never get your shot at taking him down."

Margot stepped between them, her magic coiling around her like smoke. "I can do this," she said, meeting Cillian's gaze. "I have to do this."

The demon's jaw worked as he looked between her and the chaos engulfing the city. Finally, he gave a curt nod. "Find. But we do this my way." He shed his human form in a burst of darkness, muscles bulking, horns sprouting as he transformed. Black wings burst through his leathers, rising high above his head while the bottoms dragged along the cobblestone. Deep red veins with an iridescent sheen spiderwebbed throughout the patagia. Corym winced as the sound of bones clicked into place. Cillian's voice was deeper, rougher when he spoke again. "Get on my back. If there's even a hint that he's going to—"

"I know," Margot said softly, already moving to climb onto his now-massive frame. "Trust me."

Corym watched the exchange with a mixture of awe and trepidation. The bond between them was palpable, stronger than any magic he'd witnessed in his centuries of life. *And even that may not be enough...*

Corym cleared his throat. "I'll coordinate the ground forces," he said, mapping out positions in his mind. "Draw him toward the central square. It's the only space big enough to—"

The rest of his words were drowned out by another impact against the walls. This one was different—not the thunderous crash of siege engines, but a high, keening sound that had him gritting his teeth. He squinted to see through the smoke, catching glimpses of something massive moving through the breach. Something that shouldn't exist outside of legend.

"Corym!" Breken shouted as he ran toward them. He hunched over with his hands resting on his thighs as he tried to catch his breath. "Gods... took me so long to find you—we need you at the wall! They're bringing in—"

"Go," Margot said, now secured on Cillian's back. She looked over her shoulder at Corym. "We'll handle Vesryn."

"I'll meet you there soon." A grim smirk played on his lips. "Just... try to leave some of the city standing."

As he sprinted back toward his troops, Corym heard the leathery beat of Cillian's wings. He glanced back just in time to see them rise above the rooftops, Margot's magic trailing behind them like a banner of war. A reminder that some fights couldn't be won with traditional warfare.

He just prayed to any deity that would listen that they all survived long enough to see tomorrow.

The stone beneath his feet trembled as another of those piercing sounds split the air. Whatever Ravara had brought to break their walls, it was unlike anything they'd faced before. He rounded the corner to find Breken organizing what remained of their forces, his face streaked with blood and ash.

"Report," Corym barked, falling easily back into command.

"Sir," Breken's voice was strained. "They've brought wyrms."

Corym's blood ran cold. The ancient beasts were supposed to be extinct, hunted to death centuries ago by the giants living on Zarandor. Yet there they were—massive, serpentine forms moving through the breach like living battering rams, their scales gleaming unnaturally.

"How many?"

"Three that we can see. But sir..." Breken swallowed hard. "That's not the worst of it. Vesryn's loyalists—they're opening the deepweave."

"They're what?" Corym grabbed Breken's shoulder, spinning him around. "On whose authority?"

"Vesryn's." Breken's eyes were wide with fear. "He says if Caramis falls, it falls to everyone."

Above them, Cillian banked sharply, making a pass near the manor's highest tower. Margot's magic flared like a beacon, impossible to ignore. A challenge that even Vesryn, in all his madness, couldn't refuse.

The deepweave rippled, reality distorting as the magical barrier protecting their home began to fail. Soon, all of Faerie would know exactly where to find them.

Corym released Breken, his mind racing. "Sound the evacuation. Get everyone who can't fight to the tunnels." He drew his sword, steel singing against the scabbard. "The rest of us... we hold the line. As long as we can."

It wasn't much of a plan. But with wyrms at their gates, the deepweave failing, and their king about to engage in magical combat that could level the city, it was all they had.

He just hoped it would be enough.

I'D SOONER LIGHT MYSELF ON FIRE

WIND TORE through Margot's hair, its icy fingers knotting strands against her neck as Cillian banked sharply to the left. Caramis' air had changed. Weather that had been warm and inviting just hours ago now held a chill like autumn clinging to the doorjamb while winter pulled with all the strength of the Arctic.

A bolt of molten green magic streaked past them, exploding against a crumbling tower in a cascade of rubble and fire. The impact lit up the sky and illuminated the city below in a brief, brutal flash. Margot tightened her grip around Cillian's horns; her knees clamped against his muscled sides as his wings fought the turbulence.

The air was thick with smoke and ash, the pungent scent burning her nose and lungs. Below them, Caramis was a ruin. Fires painted the streets in eerie shades of orange and red, and dark plumes of smoke spiraled into the heavens. She could hear the faint cries of soldiers—elves *and* fae—interspersed with the deep, guttural roars of the massive beasts that had joined the fray.

Margot swallowed hard, forcing herself not to look too long at the destruction. Every moment spent above the city was a gamble.

The longer they lingered, the more likely Vesryn's forces would find a way to clip their wings.

Another blast of magic ripped through the dawn, this one closer. The heat of it prickled her skin, and she ducked instinctively as it passed overhead.

"Hold steady," she called, her voice barely audible over the roaring wind.

Cillian didn't answer, but his muscles shifted beneath her as he angled into an updraft, his wings catching it with honed skill born of centuries of flight. She couldn't understand why he would keep his wings hidden; they were beautiful. What he was capable of amazed her.

The manor loomed ahead; its pristine limestone towers silhouetted against the burning horizon. Margot's heart thudded against her chest as she let her magic seep outward, a deliberate display of power. Her skin tingled with the effort, and the air around her glimmered faintly.

She didn't need to call for Vesryn. She knew he would feel her as she still felt small parts of him attempting to eat away at her.

"There," she shouted, pointing as a shadow moved on the balcony. Her magic surged, a deliberate pulse that screamed, *Here I am.*

Cillian's growl rumbled through her as his chest vibrated with the sound. "Let the bastard come," he snarled.

The balcony was just close enough for her to make out Vesryn's form. His midnight blue hair caught the light of the flames, and even at this distance, the force of his magic pressed against hers. He raised one hand, and the air around him rippled, bending under his command.

"Higher!" she yelled as another bolt streaked toward them, this one winding and twisting through the currents like a living vine.

Cillian obeyed instantly, his wings straining as they climbed. Margot gritted her teeth, but she didn't falter. Her eyes remained locked on Vesryn.

They made another pass. Close enough for Margot to see Vesryn's face twisted with rage as he tracked their movement. His magic raged around him like a bottled monsoon, raw power barely contained.

"A little higher," she said in Cillian's ear as another spell sizzled past them. "We need him to follow."

Cillian's wings beat harder as they climbed. Through their bond, she could feel his concern warring with determination. He didn't like this plan—didn't want her anywhere near Vesryn—but he trusted her implicitly. That trust meant *everything*.

Below, chaos engulfed the city. Fae forces pressed in from three sides while massive creatures battered the remaining walls with their meaty tails. The resistance fought desperately, but they were overwhelmed, outmatched. How many would die while she played this deadly game of cat and mouse?

A burst of magic exploded above them, forcing Cillian into a nosedive. Margot's stomach lurched as they plummeted, the ground rushing up to meet them. At the last second, he pulled up, powerful wings catching them just above the rooftops.

"Careful," she breathed, heart pounding. Through their bond, his silent apology soothed her.

They wheeled around for another pass, and this time, Margot saw exactly what she'd been waiting for. Vesryn had left the balcony. He was moving.

"It's working." She gathered her power, letting it build until the air around them hummed. "Take us to the square."

Cillian banked toward the city center, his massive form casting a shadow on the streets below. The square opened up before them, eerily empty amid the surrounding chaos. The perfect stage for what was to come.

They landed near the center, the cobblestones cracked, forming a crater beneath Cillian's feet. Margot slid from his back but kept one hand pressed against his side, drawing strength. Her magic swirled around them both, covering them like a veil.

"He's coming," Cillian said through gritted teeth.

Margot nodded, feeling Vesryn's approach like a storm gathering on the horizon. All around them, the sounds of battle grew more distant, as if the city itself were holding its breath.

"Stay close," she said, though she knew he would anyway.

Magic erupted at the edge of the square as Vesryn materialized in a flash of gold light. His steps echoed against the cobblestones, slow and deliberate, each one striking like a war drum. The glow of his magic bathed his angular features, highlighting the cruel twist of his mouth and the cold fury burning in his amber eyes.

"My queen," he said, his voice a mockery of reverence. He stopped just short of the swirling barrier Margot's had created. "How fitting of you to bring the fight to me."

Margot didn't flinch. Her power coiled tighter around her, sharper, waiting for her direction. "This isn't your fight, Vesryn. It's *mine*."

He tilted his head, a slow, reptilian movement. "Oh, but it *is* mine. Everything here is mine. The city. Power. *You*." His lips pulled back in a sneer. "Have you come to bow before me, finally? Or are you here to beg for mercy?"

A bitter laugh slipped past her lips, cutting through the tense silence. "Beg? For you? I'd sooner light myself on fire."

Cillian shifted beside her, his wings unfurling slightly, but Margot raised a hand to steady him. Vesryn's eyes flicked to the motion, his sneer deepening.

"Still hiding behind the demon, are you?" Vesryn shot Cillian a dismissive look. "You disappoint me, Margot. I thought you would have learned by now that these... *creatures*... cannot protect you. They only weigh you down."

"You have no idea what he's done for me," Margot said, her voice low but steady. "What he's sacrificed, what he *would* sacrifice. That's something you could never understand."

"Sacrifice?" Vesryn's laugh was sharp as broken glass. "Do you think loyalty matters in the face of power? Of destiny?" He gestured around them. "All of this—everything I have done—has been for you. To show you what we could be together. And yet you continue to defy me, clinging to scraps of mortal ideals."

"For me?" Margot nearly choked on the words. "You let the deepweave fall; you chose not to fight for your people. Don't you dare for one second say you did this for me."

"Oh, but I did!" A manic grin spread across his face. "Would you let all these poor elves die? No... that is not the *queen* I know. The only way to save them is if we do it *together*."

"You did this for control." She stepped forward, her magic blazing brighter. The ground beneath her feet cracked as twilight energy spilled into the stones. "You did this for some twisted fantasy you've built in your head." Her voice hardened. "You don't want a queen. You want compliance."

Vesryn's face darkened, fists shaking at his sides. "You don't know what you're saying," he snarled, taking another step closer. "You don't know what you *are*."

"I know exactly what I am," Margot said, her chin lifting as her power swirled higher. "I am what Ilphas chose. What Cillian bound himself to. And what you will *never* control."

"Ilphas was *weak*." Vesryn's expression twisted, his anger sharp enough to cut. "Ilphas chose you to spite me, nothing more."

"You're wrong." Margot voice's voice didn't waver. "Ilphas chose me because I'm stronger than you'll ever be. You only break things, Vesryn. You destroy. You think that's power?" She shook her head, her tendrils snapping like a whip. "True power is creation. Building something worth fighting for. And I will fight for it. For them. For love. I *will* end this."

"End this?" His chuckle was low and menacing as he moved closer, his nose mere centimeters from her shield. "Oh, my dear. This is only the beginning." He raised his hands, golden light gathering between his palms like the sun's rays. "I offered you everything. Power. A throne. *My love*." His features twisted into something barely recognizable. "And this is how you repay me?"

"Your love?" The words taste like ash in her mouth. "You don't know the meaning of the word."

"I know more than you could possibly imagine," Vesryn snarled. "I know what we could be together."

"I know what we'll *never* be." Margot's magic swelled, responding eagerly to her call. No more hesitation. No more doubt. "And I am done being your puppet."

Light and shadow exploded between them as their magic collided. Vesryn's power was staggering—pure, ancient elven might that made the air tremble. But Margot held firm, the grey meeting his force for force.

"Beautiful," Vesryn marveled, his lips curling into a cold smile. "I knew you would be something magnificent." He slammed his palm to the ground, calling the earth, sending shattered cobblestones at her feet to force her back. "But still so naïve. Did you think I was showing you everything during our lessons? That I would give away my secrets?"

He raised both hands, and the world seemed to bend. Faerie responded to his call—the earth's crust crumbling, air distorting, water vapor crystallizing mid-air, lightning cracking overhead. The elements were at his bidding. Margot's blood ran cold. She had never seen anything like it, and it took everything she had not to let fear overcome her.

Cillian's wings snapped out as he lunged demonic fist forward, but Margot stopped him with a thought. *Not yet*.

"I have lived centuries," Vesryn continued, power building around him like an elemental storm. The ruins of Caramis churned around him, creating deadly projectiles. "Mastered magic you cannot even comprehend. While you studied and relished the idea of being queen, I was preparing." His eyes blazed with madness as the remaining buildings at the edges of the square began to crumble. "It is time for Faerie to have a new king, the *rightful* king!"

The full weight of his magic crashed down like an avalanche. Margot threw up a barrier which Cillian reinforced from his iron palm. She gritted her teeth as the force threatened to overwhelm her. Heavy stone and wood and metal ricocheted off the shield. With each bit of detritus that smashed into her, Margot winced, struggling to keep hold. This was the real Vesryn—not the calculating manipulator, but a being of pure destructive potential.

"You're insane," she gritted out. "You'll destroy everything."

"Does it make a difference?" He flicked his hand, launching a large chunk of the flower shop into the sky behind him. "I will rebuild it!" His laughter echoed as another wave of his power tore through the square, taking a row of homes with it. "A new Faerie. A better one. With you at my side," His eyes darkened as they narrowed in on Margot, "whether you want to be or not."

A guttural boom tore from Cillian's throat. He moved with a flash, impossible to follow, his massive form providing cover as Margot rolled away from a blast that would have ripped her apart. The demonic weapon flared to life as Cillian clenched his fist. Black and red smoke hissed from the hellforged runes. Margot scrabbled to her feet at Cillian's side, where their bond hummed, and they struck and parried in fluid coordination. Cillian weaved through rocky pillars Margot pulled from Faerie's core to provide some level of protection. He siphoned his blood to power up his fist and intercepting the elf's errant shots which he launched back at a terrifying rate.

But Vesryn was relentless. Each spell more devastating than the last. Buildings toppled. The ground buckled. The very air burned from the intensity of his assault, stinging Margot's skin. This wasn't about control anymore. This was about absolute dominion, no matter the cost.

"You can't even feel it, can you?" Margot called out as she deflected another attack with the flick of her wrist. "What you're doing to Faerie?" She pushed back with her own power searching for gaps in his defenses. "You're tearing it apart!"

"I am its master!" His voice echoed across the ruins. "Its power is mine to command!"

But Margot could feel the truth through her connection to

Ilphas' magic. Every spell Vesryn cast was ripping at the fabric of reality itself. The power he wielded wasn't meant to be used this way—wasn't meant to destroy the very world it came from.

She threw everything she had into her next attack, a rush of grey singing through her veins. Cillian's darkness gave it weight, while Ilphas' light gave it purpose. Not to destroy, but to restore balance.

Razor-sharp vines the color of pitch shot from her fingertips, crashing into Vesryn with a force that reverberated through the square. The impact sent them both reeling, her boots skidding against the cracked cobblestones while Vesryn smashed into a wall.

Vesryn recovered first, his shoulders heaving as he straightened. The golden light of his magic flared brighter, spilling out like lava. His face twisted, not with pain, but with unbridled rage —a storm of hatred that roared louder than any spell he could cast.

Margot wiped blood from her lip and froze as the realization hit her like a blade to the chest. It wasn't just his power pressing against her—it was his madness. The deep, spiraling hunger that had devoured everything he once was. Those fleeting moments she spent with him where she thought she saw vulnerability were gone. All that remained was this hollow shell, burning with ambition and wrath.

Her vines receded, curling back toward her like obedient dogs. She steeled her spine, meeting his furious gaze.

"It's over, Vesryn," she said, her voice quiet but edged with razors. "You've already lost."

His unbridled yell tore through the air, more magic than sound, a violent ripple that cracked the sounds of war raging around them. In an instant, he lunged, faster than thought, his form a blur of blazing power.

A spear of golden light erupted in his hand, so bright that Margot had to throw up an arm to shield her eyes. She heard the weapons hum, and before she or Cillian could counter, it collided with the barrier she and Cillian barely had time to throw back up.

Her breath caught as the impact resonated through her chest, the sharp crackle of his power spiderwebbing across the twilight-grey surface. For a heartbeat, the world seemed to slow. Veins of gold etched themselves deeper into the shield, each one a splintering warning.

Fragments peeled away, shimmering like glass as they dissolved into the air. Her pulse thundered in her ears as she watched the barrier unravel, each piece crumbling into nothingness until, with a final, shattering burst, it fractured completely.

The magic dissipated in a puff of iridescent dust, leaving them exposed.

47

DELICATE WEBS

THE CHAINS BIT into Nym's wrists as he dangled from the ceiling of Ravara's war galley. His shoulders burned from supporting his weight, but he kept the easy grin plastered on his face. No sense letting his captors know how much it hurt.

Through the porthole, he could see the lilac glow of dawn tinged with orange painting the horizon—or maybe that was just Caramis burning. The sounds of battle carried across the water, punctuated by the occasional earth-shaking roar of wyrms. Above it all, flashes of strange purple light lit up the sky like silent lightning.

"Quite the show, isn't it?" Ravara hadn't stopped pacing since he'd started his interrogation. The self-proclaimed Fae King's crystalline eyes never left the distant battle. "Your Vesryn proves more resourceful than expected, keeping the girl hidden all this time."

"Girl?" Nym cocked his head to the side. "What girl? Ya know, drinkin' does funny things to the mind sometimes. Makes ya see things that aren't there."

A backhand caught him across the face, snapping his head to the other side. The taste of copper flooded his mouth. Still, he kept grinning.

"Your act grows tiresome." Ravara's voice was soft, dangerous.

"I can feel her power from here. That... unusual magic." A cruel smile played on his lips. "Tell me what you know about her. About Margot."

Nym spat blood onto the pristine deck. "Don't know much 'bout any Margot. Just a drunk who causes trouble, remember?"

"Is that so?" Ravara moved closer, his presence cold as winter frost. "Then perhaps you can explain why a simple drunk was caught trying to send messages to the mainland." He pulled a crumpled piece of parchment from his robes. "Or why you seem so... valuable to, let's say, our mutual friend, Corym."

"You've been quite busy, haven't you?" Ravara flicked the parchment with a long, pale finger. "Ferrying messages, moving goods, helping elves slip away to the mainland. Tell me, how does one so... unremarkable manage such feats right under Vesryn's nose?"

"Just lucky, I s'pose." Nym's shoulders screamed in protest as he shrugged. "Right place, right time, ya know how it goes."

"Luck." Ravara's laugh was like breaking ice. "No. You have something far more valuable than luck, little spy." He began pacing again, his boots clicking against the deck in a measured rhythm. "You have influence. Connections. The ability to move without drawing attention." His eyes gleamed. "Such talents shouldn't be wasted rotting in a cell... or a grave."

"Awful kind of ya to notice." Nym's grin widened despite the pain in his jaw. "But I think I'll pass on whatever you're offerin'."

Ravara stopped in front of a gilded table, running his fingers along its surface. "Tell me, what do you know of the western territories?"

"Heard they're lovely this time of year."

"They're in chaos." Ravara's tone sharpened. "The fae houses squabble amongst themselves like faelings fighting over scraps. They lack... direction." He turned, fixing Nym with that penetrating stare. "Unity."

A particularly violent explosion had the ship swaying. Through the porthole, Nym could see one of the wyrms demolishing what remained of the eastern wall. His heart clenched—he'd grown up near there, spent countless nights stumbling home from the Flagon along those streets. Now it was all being reduced to rubble.

"And ya think you're the one to give it to 'em?" Nym asked, keeping his voice light. "Seems to me they're not too keen on followin' anyone these days."

"They will be, once I have what I need." Ravara moved closer to Nym. "That girl's power is only the beginning. With her capabilities under my control, the other houses will fall in line. But to maintain that control..." he gestured to the parchment again. "I'll need allies who understand how to move in the shadows. Allies with connections. Allies like *you*."

"Sounds fascinatin'. Still passin', though."

The backhand caught him across the other cheek this time. Nym's head snapped to the side, but his grin never faltered. Blood or no blood, he wouldn't give Ravara the satisfaction.

"Your loyalty to Caramis is admirable, if misplaced." Ravara pulled a chair close, sitting with unnatural grace. "But surely you can see the futility of it? Look around you. The city burns. Vesryn's madness has doomed you all. The only question the remains is what rises from the ashes."

"Ya really love the sound of your own voice, don't ya?"

Ravara's eyes narrowed. "Perhaps a demonstration would be more persuasive." He raised a hand, frost crystallizing in his palm. "I understand you're quite fond of that tavern of yours. The Silver Flagon, isn't it? I wonder how many of your friends sought shelter there when the walls fell?"

Hopefully, none, he thought, but it wasn't enough to stop the threat from punching him in the gut. He had to force himself to maintain his careful demeanor. "Threatenin' a male's drink? Now that's just mean."

"Mean?" Ravara stood, looming over him. "You have no concept of mean. Not yet. But you will learn. Everyone learns eventually." He began pacing again, his movements predatory.

"The mainland nobles you've been dealing with—did you think I wouldn't find out about them? The deals you've brokered, the safe passages you've arranged?" His smile was sharp as a blade. "How many lives hang by the threads you've woven, I wonder?"

Nym's stomach dropped. He'd been careful—so careful—with those arrangements. If Ravara knew about them...

"See? Now we're getting somewhere." Ravara's voice dripped with satisfaction. "You're not just some drunk causing trouble. You're a spider at the center of a *very* delicate web. And I..." Frost spread from where his feet touched the deck. "I own that web now."

A distant roar shook the ship, different from the wyrms. This was followed by a flash of purple light so bright it made Nym's eyes water.

The cabin door burst open. A fae soldier stumbled in, his gilded armor scorched and smoking. "My king! We've found them —the girl and the demon. They're in the central square, but—" He doubled over, coughing. "The power... we can't get near them. It's like nothing we've ever seen."

Ravara's head snapped toward the porthole. The purple light had intensified, illuminating the water with an ethereal glow.

"Well, would you look at that," Ravara murmured. "It seems our dear Margot has finally shown her true potential." He turned back to Nym, that cold smile returning. "Think carefully about your position while I'm gone. When I return, you'll either be a valuable ally..." His hand drifted to the sword at his hip. "Or a dead drunk."

"Don't hurry back on my account!" Nym called after Ravara's retreating form. Only when the cabin door slammed shut did he let his grin fade, his eyes fixed on the supernatural display of power lighting up Caramis.

"Give 'em hells, Margot," he whispered. "Give 'em all hells."

Through the porthole, he watched Ravara disappear into the chaos of the burning city. His shoulders were on fire as he tested the chains, but his mind was already racing, plotting. Ravara might own the web, but Nym? Ravara was right: Nym was still a spider. And spiders were patient.

TAHLSIA CLUTCHED HER FROCK AS THE CHANDELIER IN the foyer swayed, the crystals clanking against the metal like funeral bells. The caustic stench of smoke had begun seeping through the manor's walls, and each distant explosion brought it closer. Whatever was happening outside—whatever chaos Ravara had unleashed—was moving toward them fast. She needed to hurry.

With quiet steps, Tahlsia made her way toward the kitchen, trying to ignore how the floor trembled beneath her feet. Edea was handling the upper floors, leaving Tahlsia to guide the servants hiding in their quarters to the tunnels beneath the city. The loyalists had left the manor to drop the deepweave, making it safer for her and Edea to move freely, but without having that ancient protection, nowhere was truly safe anymore.

She wiped sweat from her brow before lifting the oil lantern from the hook beneath the center island. The flame wavered with each impact, casting errant shadows as she descended to the servant's quarters. Another blast shook the foundation, and fine dust rained from the ceiling, coating her shoulders in centuries of grime.

"Sariya?" Tahlsia knocked on the door, keeping her voice steady despite the urgency coursing through her. "Sariya, I need you to open the door." Her forehead hit the wood with a dull *thud* as she pressed her palm against its cool surface. "We need to leave, Sariya. I know this is scary… but we need to go. The tunnels will keep us safe."

After what felt like an eternity, the door creaked open to reveal Sariya, barely more than an elfling. Tears limned her bottom lashes, her dark skin slick with them, her nose swollen and red. Tahlsia's heart ached at the sight.

"Is Ama dead?" Sariya didn't bother wiping the tears now flowing freely. "She-she left so long ago... a-and all the explosions. The whole building keeps shaking."

"Oh, sweet one..." Tahlsia pulled her against her chest, pressing a kiss atop her head even as another tremor sent the lantern light dancing wildly across the walls. She couldn't promise the girl's mother was alive—not with the carnage she'd glimpsed outside—but she could offer hope. "Your ama is strong, and with the Veilguard at her side, she is stronger still."

"Dust was falling from the ceiling." Sariya sniffed before continuing. "Ama told me to stay here. She said that she would c-come back. What i-if she comes home and I-I'm not here?"

A distant roar rattled the manor—not an explosion this time, but something worse. Something alive. Tahlsia's grip on Sariya tightened instinctively. She had seen them from the top-floor window, but was hoping the smoke had been playing tricks on her. Judging from the sound, that hadn't been the case. The wyrms were getting closer.

"Your ama is a smart elf and knows how to find you." Tahlsia smoothed Sariya's hair, forcing down her own fear. "But more importantly, your ama wants you to be safe. And right now, we need to go. The tunnels will protect us until this is over."

"But Ama!"

The manor shuddered violently as another explosion ripped through its walls. The dilapidated ceiling cracked, raining mildewed splinters and chunks of stone. Sariya ducked, covering her head with her arm. The lantern nearly slipped from Tahlsia's grasp as she shielded the girl with her body.

They were running out of time.

"Your ama will understand." Tahlsia steadied herself and tipped Sariya's chin up, meeting those tear-filled brown eyes. "I need your help to gather the others. Can you do that? The sooner we get everyone to the tunnels, the sooner we'll be safe."

"I can help," she whispered, her bottom lip quivering. "Ama would like that."

"Yes, she would." Tahlsia led her into the hallway, where the smell of smoke was stronger. Through the tiny windows near the ceiling, an orange glow painted the pre-dawn sky. *Fire.* "You take the left side. I'll take the right. Quickly now. There isn't much time."

As they separated, Tahlsia sent up a silent prayer to the goddesses. *Let us reach the tunnels. Let us survive this madness. Let there still be a Caramis to return to when this is done.*

"We're here," Sariya wheezed, one hand clutching her side as the other supported her while she caught her breath. "I-I gathered everyone."

Tahlsia scanned the terrified faces of the elves she had worked with for hundreds of years. Worry lines creased their foreheads, their hands clasped together so tightly their knuckles whited. They were all there. Shaken, but there.

"Great job, Sariya." She drew a slow breath to steady herself as the ground rumbled and nodded to herself. "Now, we run before whatever is out there makes it inside. Keep up, everyone!"

Tahlsia took off, running back up the stairs, tearing through the kitchen out into the foyer, up to the second floor with the hurried steps of her friends—her family—behind her. She hooked a right, then a left, and ran straight down the hall toward the alcove, where she quickly opened the false wall, ushering them inside. One by one, the elves carefully descended into the darkness far beneath Caramis, far away from the battle raging on the surface.

As Chariss passed, Tahlsia gripped her arm, pulling her to the side. "Watch over Sariya, please." Her voice wobbled as she continued. "Her ama, I don't..."

The elderly elf patted Tahlsia's hand. "I understand." She stood on her tiptoes, scanning the line of elves, spotting Sariya. "Sariya! Come with me, dear."

"We must go," Chariss said as Sariya made her way over to them.

Tahlsia nodded as the young elf's gaze lingered on her. "You *must* go. Everything will be fine."

Sariya said nothing, and with a few gentle tugs, she finally made it through the passage, heading down to safety.

"Top is clear," a low whisper sounded from Tahlsia's side, causing her to jump.

"Goddesses, you scared me, Edea." Tahlsia placed her hand against her beating heart. "You're sure everyone was accounted for?"

"Yes. They're in line now." Edea tucked herself in the shadows, watching the elves. "They need to move faster."

"They probably can't see very... oh!" Tahlsia placed her hand along the stairwell, sending a faint glow through the cracks in the stone. She stepped back in place, a bead of sweat trickling down the side of her face. "Quickly now! Pick up the pace!"

"You should conserve your energy." Edea gave her a chiding look. "You're going to need it."

"*They* need it more."

Some elves thanked Tahlsia and Edea as they passed, and others mumbled prayers beneath their breath. The only thing left for Tahlsia to do was hope they were heard. Genocide of an entire race... no. She wouldn't let that happen. The resistance wouldn't let that happen.

A thunderous boom reverberated through the walls, followed by a loud crash, which came from inside the manor. Edea's eyes widened, and she rushed to the back of the line, urging the elves forward. Ravara's forces had gotten through. Tahlsia readied herself to close the passage.

Heavy footsteps echoed through the hall from the central stairs. "Close it!" Edea yelled from the back of the line.

"Not until the rest are through!"

Edea looked over her shoulder, said something quickly to the elf in front of her, who relayed the information to the elf in front of him, and then they were running. "Now!" Edea shouted, pushing the last elf into the passage.

Tahlsia inputted the sequence to close the door, and just as the final *click* sounded, Edea was grabbed around the waist by a gilded soldier. Four more soldiers appeared, cornering them.

"Well, well," the soldier said, his armor gleaming in the dim light. "What do we have here? Servants of the manor, perhaps?"

Tahlsia backed against the wall, her heart pounding. Through the window, she could see the sky turning an unnatural shade of purple. Whatever was happening out there, she prayed it would end quickly.

"Take them to the king," another soldier commanded. "He'll want to know how many escaped through these tunnels. Let him get the information out of them."

As they were led away, Tahlsia caught Edea's eye. At least they'd gotten the others to safety. At least they'd done that much.

48

READY

Margot and Cillian staggered back. Her heart hammered against her ribs. The force of Vesryn's attack had torn through their defenses as if they were paper—something she wasn't expecting. Behind her, Cillian snarled, his darkness surging forward to meet her own. Their combined power rippled across the square, causing the cobblestones to shudder beneath their feet.

Through gaps in the vortex surrounding them, she caught glimpses of the larger battle raging through Caramis. Fae warriors clashed with the Veilguard in the streets while fires consumed entire blocks. The sky had turned a sickly shade of purple. Even the air felt wrong—heavy, charged, as if reality was buckling under the strain.

Vesryn shed his robe with a flourish, revealing battle leathers underneath, and tied his hair in a tight bun. Messy strands of midnight framed his face, making him look less like a crazed dictator and more like the warrior he truly was. From the sheath at his side, he drew a thin sword. The hilt burst to life with a flash of gold, snaking up the blade as he readied for the fight of his life. The raw power emanating from him made the grey within Margot surge in response, wanting to find balance.

"You truly are magnificent," he marveled, his eyes following the graceful curves of her shadows. "However, it is not enough."

He blinked forward faster than the eye could see. Margot's breath caught in her throat, certain she was about to die before the fight truly began, but Cillian had already anticipated the attack. Her bloodsworn dashed forward, demonic fist crackling with blood-infused power, and swung. Vesryn was faster still. He twisted his body, avoiding Cillian's blow, and redirected his magic to the hilt. The impact, when it connected with Cillian's spine, sent him flying. Her mate howled as he hit the cobblestones, the road cratering beneath him with a disheartening crack.

Margot lurched forward, a cry catching in her throat, but Vesryn had already recovered. He advanced with measured steps, each one deliberate, predatory. The power surrounding him pulsed in time with his movements. The very elements he had taught Margot to command were bending to his will.

I'm fine, Cillian's voice echoed through their bond. *Stay calm. I've got you.*

His next attack came without warning. A wave of pure energy ripped across the square. Margot didn't think—she reacted, this time pulling lightning from the clouds above. Her twilight magic collided with Vesryn's in a spectacular display that sent tremors through the entire island.

"Oh, my dear queen," Vesryn delighted as glittering magic residue showered them like deadly rain. "All this power... did you think the demon helped you achieve this? No, no... it was my guidance, my teaching, which brought you to this precipice."

"You taught me? Guided me?" Margot's laugh was hollow. "Get over yourself, Vesryn. You broke me down and violated me in ways that are unthinkable, immoral. The only thing you taught me was how to hate. How to hate *you*." Her throat tightened, but she pushed back harder, her magic spreading like ink through water. She would never give Vesryn the satisfaction of seeing just how badly he ruined her, and it took everything she had to keep her voice steady, to mask how he had left her shaken. "Everything else? That was mine to choose."

"*Choose?*" Pure venom dripped from his voice. The air around him began to crystallize, frost spreading across the broken cobblestones. "You still cling to such petty concepts. Choice? Free will? These are luxuries we cannot afford, not when you are so simpleminded." His smile twisted into something cruel, something that made her blood run cold despite the inferno of magic surrounding them. "I had hoped you would understand willingly, but it seems I must teach you one final lesson."

A distant roar shook the city—not from their battle, but from something massive moving about the streets. Through the magical haze, Margot caught glimpses of scaled hide and razor teeth. The wyrms were getting closer.

Cillian shot up from the crater, his wings unfurling as he launched himself toward them, but Vesryn was ready. Three bolts of concentrated magic erupted from his fingers, tracking Cillian like guided missiles. The demon managed to absorb two with his fist, the weapon glowing brilliantly as it struggled to contain the vast amount of power. The third bolt caught him in the stomach, sending him careening into the rubble of a collapsed building.

Before Margot could react, Vesryn appeared behind her. His icy fingers found her throat, and suddenly, every horrible memory, every violation came rushing back. Her body betrayed her, trembling uncontrollably as those memories threatened to drown her. Vesryn leaned in close, his lips brushing against her ear as he whispered, "See? You remember."

The words sparked something in her—not fear this time, but rage. She forced back the bile, focusing instead on her magic. The twilight energy responded eagerly, forming thousands of spectral needles made from ore formed beneath Faerie's crust that she drove into Vesryn's gut. He hissed, releasing her instantly as he flipped away. He landed just inches from her, palm already blazing with power. The blast that followed was tinged with blue fire, and though Margot dove aside, she wasn't quite fast enough.

Pain exploded through her shoulder as the pauldron punctured her skin. The demonic runes etched into her armor flared to life, eager for more power. They greedily devoured Vesryn's magic, channeling it directly into her bloodstream. She hit the ground hard, writhing as the foreign invader threatened to tear her apart from within.

Vesryn was on her in an instant, pinning her legs with his thighs as he forced her down against the broken stones. "Stealing Ilphas' magic was not enough?" he hissed, spittle hit her cheeks. "Must you steal mine, too?"

The noise inside her head was deafening as Vesryn's toxicity fought to find purchase. She squeezed her eyes shut, trying to block it out, but then his cool fingers pressed against her forehead. Those deadly, precise tendrils of his power probed her mind once more, seeking entrance, seeking control. But this time, the twilight magic responded, furious at the attempt. Light and shadow moved as one, forming a barrier that even Vesryn couldn't breach.

She inhaled sharply, choking on his familiar scent. Every instinct screamed at her to flee, to get away from his touch, but she forced herself to focus. She needed to seal away these memories, the trauma, if she had any hope of winning. *Help me*, she called through the bond.

A deep, resonant roar erupted from the rubble. Stones ground against each other with an ear-splitting *crunch* as Cillian burst free. Through barely open eyes, Margot saw him hurl a massive boulder at Vesryn. The elf raised one hand almost lazily, reducing the projectile to dust—but Cillian had anticipated this. He charged through the debris cloud, colliding with Vesryn's lithe form and sending them both rolling into a pile of broken limestone.

The demon's hellforged fist came down again and again, each impact releasing bursts of stored magic and blood. Smoke and red mist rose from the weapon's joints as it made contact with Vesryn's blood, but Cillian didn't relent. The brief reprieve gave

Margot precious seconds to gather herself. *He can't control me anymore, he can't control me anymore.* She repeated the mantra as she methodically locked away every memory of Vesryn's abuse. There would be time to process later—if they survived. For now, she needed clarity.

The ground trembled, and not from their battle. Margot's eyes widened as she saw what was approaching—a wyrm, its serpentine body plowing through the streets as if the buildings were made of sand. The creature moved with impossible speed for its size, and the magic swirling around their battlefield intensified as it drew near. Its scales scraping against rock was like the grinding of tectonic plates—a leviathan, but on land.

The wyrm hit their vortex at full speed, and for a moment, time seemed to slow. Vesryn, still locked in combat with Cillian, raised one hand. Golden ribbons of magic wrapped around the beast, and Margot watched in horror as they began to flay it alive. Each glowing strand cut through scales and muscle with surgical precision, sending arcs of blood raining down across their battlefield. She couldn't look. The wet sound of tissue being rendered made her stomach turn.

The wyrm's arrival had caught Cillian off guard. Vesryn seized the opportunity, hurling him into the creature's remains before turning his attention back to Margot. She was on her feet in an instant, the grey surrounding her like armor. When Vesryn charged, she ducked right, using the momentum to pivot behind him. Her magic coalesced into a blade—a kris forged from light and shadow—and she drove it deep into his arm.

Blood dripped from Vesryn's limb where Margot's twilight blade had struck, but his cruel smile never wavered. If anything, the wound seemed to excite him. His magic surged, golden light consuming the injury, knitting flesh back together before her eyes.

"Did you think it would be that easy?" he taunted, rolling his newly healed shoulder. "That a simple blade could end this?" His power exploded outward in a dome of pure force.

Margot braced herself, channeling her blood and magic into a shield of intertwined light and shadow. The impact when their powers met sent her sliding backward, her boots leaving deep grooves in the cobblestones. Through gritted teeth, she pushed back, refusing to yield.

We need help, Cillian's voice echoed through their bond. *You feel it too, don't you? The way the magic is building.*

She did feel it. The vortex surrounding them had become a maelstrom of competing forces—Vesryn's raw power, her twilight magic, Cillian's darkness, all churning together in ways that defied Faerie's natural laws. The air seemed to crack with the strain of containing it.

Corym, she thought back. *He's out there. I can sense him.*

Create an opening, Cillian commanded. His wings unfurled as he took to the air, drawing Vesryn's attention. *I'll keep him busy.*

Margot watched as Cillian soared above them. Vesryn's attacks followed, golden bolts streaking skyward like angry stars. The demon wove between them with surprising grace, each near miss feeding more power into his hellforged weapon.

She understood the plan without needing to discuss it. While Vesryn was focused upward, she could work on the vortex. But it wouldn't be easy. The competing magics had formed something approaching a wall—a barrier that even she, with her unique abilities, would struggle to breach.

Taking a deep breath, Margot reached out with both hands. Light gathered in her right palm while shadow pooled in her left. Instead of combining them immediately, she let each force build, growing stronger, purer. The pressure inside the vortex increased, making her ears pop.

Above, Cillian dove straight at Vesryn, forcing the elf to create a shield of his own. Margot seized that moment of distraction, bringing her hands together, forming that perfect twilight grey that was only hers.

"What are you doing?" Vesryn snarled, catching glimpses of her work between exchanges with Cillian. "That barrier is the only thing keeping Ravara's forces at bay!"

He wasn't wrong. Beyond their magical arena, she could hear the sounds of battle growing closer. The fae army was advancing, and somewhere out there, wyrms still prowled the burning streets. But they needed Corym. Needed his strength, his knowledge of Vesryn's fighting style. Most importantly, they needed him to witness this—to see firsthand that Vesryn could be defeated.

Margot pulled her hands apart slowly, her twilight magic forming a wedge that she drove into the vortex wall. The barrier resisted, magic crackling and spitting as she forced it wider. Sweat beaded on her forehead from the effort. This close to the vortex's edge, she could feel just how powerful Vesryn was.

"No!" Vesryn's fury manifested as a wave of golden fire that swept across the square. Cillian barrel-rolled to avoid it, but the elf was already moving, racing toward Margot with his sword raised.

She saw him coming but couldn't move—not without losing her grip on the opening she'd created. Through the gap, she caught Corym's face, his violet eyes wide with recognition. *Just a few more seconds...*

The impact never came. Cillian dropped from the sky like a stone, crashing into Vesryn with enough force to carve a gaping wound in the earth. They rolled away in a tangle of wings and magic, buying her the precious moments she needed.

"Corym!" she screamed, forcing the gap wider. "Now!"

The elf didn't hesitate. He dove through the opening just as her strength gave out. The vortex snapped closed behind him with a sound like thunder, briefly drowning out the chaos of the larger battle. He rose smoothly to his feet, drawing his sword in one fluid motion.

"You dare?" Vesryn's voice was barely recognizable as he untangled himself from Cillian. "After everything I have done for you? After all these years?"

"I dare," Corym replied simply, falling into a fighting stance. "For Caramis."

Margot felt the shift in the air as Corym's magic joined the fray—not as powerful as Vesryn's, perhaps, but skilled, controlled. The vortex stabilized, no longer threatening to tear itself apart. Three against one. Now they had a real chance.

Vesryn's laughter echoed across the square, high and wild. "Then you shall die with them." His magic exploded outward once more, but this time, Margot was ready.

This time, they all were.

49

PURE POWER

THE VORTEX of competing magics swirled around them, wild and unrestrained, casting strange shadows across the ruined square. Power thrummed through Margot's veins as she faced Vesryn alongside Cillian and Corym. The elf who had tormented her, controlled her, now stood before them with his golden magic blazing—but he was outnumbered.

Three against one should have given them the advantage, yet Vesryn's energy level was staggering. Each blast that erupted from his hands carried enough force to level buildings. The cobblestones beneath their feet had been reduced to rubble, and still, the elf pressed his attack, his amber eyes wild and crazed with nothing behind them but the drive to win, to conquer.

Beyond their magical arena, Caramis burned. The sounds of battle grew closer—clashing steel, screaming soldiers, and the earth-shaking roars of wyrms. Through the gaps of the vortex, Margot caught glimpses of fae soldiers advancing through the city's broken defenses. Buildings crumbled in their wake, centuries of Elven architecture reduced to ash and limestone. The city she'd come to know, despite everything, was being systematically destroyed.

But Margot couldn't focus on any of that. Her entire world

had narrowed to this moment, this fight. Her magic responded eagerly to her call, light and shadow moving in perfect harmony as she prepared to end this once and for all. The power surged through her blood, her soul, different from anything she'd ever experienced—stronger, disconcerting, more dangerous.

They had to stop him here. Before he destroyed everything.

"Your magic is unstable," Vesryn snarled, his voice carrying over the sounds of war. Sweat dotted his brow; the first sign their combined assault was taking its toll. "You cannot hope to contain what you do not understand. What you were never meant to possess!"

The truth of his words stung, but Margot held her ground. Sparks sputtered and crackled around her as her magic responded to emotions she embraced. With each pulse, she could feel something deeper stirring—something bad. Something beyond her control.

Cillian's concern vibrated through their bond. They both knew this was different. Volatile. But there was no turning back now. It was do or die. And Margot planned to do.

Corym moved first, violet bands streaming from his blade as he engaged Vesryn from the left. His movements were precise, calculated—each strike aimed at weak points in Vesryn's defense, born from lifetimes of learning how the deranged king operated. The elf deflected most, but a few drew blood that sizzled as it hit the ground.

Massive wings darkened their battlefield as Cillian took to the air. The hellforged weapon hummed, ready to unleash devastation. Their coordinated attack forced Vesryn back, but the elf's manic smile never wavered.

"Fools," Vesryn spat, deflecting Corym's strike while simultaneously launching a bolt at Cillian. "Do you really think you can defeat me? I am power incarnate! I am—"

His words cut off as Margot's magic slammed into him. Shimmering black chains materialized, trying to bind his arms and legs. For a moment, it seemed to work. Vesryn's eyes widened in genuine surprise as the grey began to seep into his flesh.

Then everything went wrong.

A torrent of power cascaded outward from Vesryn's body, tearing through the air like a shockwave. Margot's constructs shattered, the chains dissolving into mist. The force of it sent all three of them reeling backward. Corym slammed into a half-collapsed wall while Cillian was thrown into a spiral, barely managing to right himself before hitting the ground.

The backlash hit Margot like a physical blow, driving her to her knees. Her magic tried to absorb the excess energy, just as it had done before, but this was different. This was too much, too fast. The power burned through her veins like liquid fire, and she could feel something tearing inside her—something fundamental.

Margot! Cillian's voice carried through their bond. He was trying to share her burden through their connection, his darkness reaching for her light, but even that wasn't enough. The power was too vast, too unstable.

The vortex surrounding them began to collapse, reality rippling and distorting where competing magics clashed. Strange patches appeared in the air where the unseen ether seemed to fold in impossible ways. Through these rifts, Margot saw... somewhere else. Somewhere familiar.

"You see?" Vesryn's laugh was errant, almost hysterical. "This is what happens when you defy the natural order. When you try to create something that was never meant to be created!" He spread his arms wide, channeling even more power into the maelstrom. "The walls between worlds are thinner than you know, my queen. And now they break!"

The sky above them fractured like tempered glass, revealing an endless void beyond. Magic poured from the cracks—raw, untamed power drawn to their battle like moths to the flame. It swirled around them, seeking a vessel, seeking control.

Margot screamed as her body tried to process the influx. Light and shadow warred within her, threatening to tear her apart. She could feel Cillian's desperation through their bond, feel Corym's mounting horror as reality continued to unravel around them.

They had to end this. Now.

But as the void yawned wider above them, Margot realized that ending Vesryn might not be enough to stop what they had set in motion. The magic was too wild, too hungry. It needed somewhere to go.

Together, Cillian's voice echoed through their bond. *We end this together.*

Cillian's darkness surged forward, with Corym's magic joining theirs as they launched a final, desperate assault. Vesryn tried to dodge, but there was nowhere to go, and the power consumed him. For the first time, real fear flickered across his face.

"No," he growled, trying to maintain control. "I will not let you—"

Corym's shadows skittered across the cobbles, manipulating stone which morphed into chains and wrapped around Vesryn's legs, anchoring him to the broken ground. Before the elf could break free, Cillian's massive form descended from above. The demon grabbed Vesryn's arms, forcing them behind his back as his wings created a cage of darkness.

"How *dare* you." Vesryn thrashed against their hold, and his golden magic flared again. But for once, his raw power couldn't break free. They had him.

Margot approached slowly, drawing Cillian's ceremonial dagger. Her twilight magic coiled around the blade, merging with ancient runes that pulsed with grey light. Each step was heavy, loaded, carrying the weight of what Vesryn had done to her—to all of them.

"No more games," she said, her voice steady. "No more control."

Vesryn thrashed harder, but their grip was iron. "You think killing me will save you?" His laugh was sharp, desperate. "You are nothing but a vessel—a failed experiment! You cannot contain—"

The dagger's edge pressed against his throat, silencing him. Cillian's savage satisfaction washed over her. *Hold him steady.*

The blade bit deep. Vesryn's mad laughter turned to choking as she dragged hellforged metal through flesh and bone. His magic sputtered desperately, trying to heal the wound even as she sawed deeper through his neck. Blood sprayed across her face, hot and sticky, but she didn't stop. Couldn't stop. This had to end.

With a final, terrible wrench, Vesryn's head separated from his shoulders. Corym and Cillian released his body, letting it crumble to the ground like a sack of flour. The head rolled away, those amber eyes still blazing with hatred and madness, even in death.

Everything stopped. The air stilled.

Then, Vesryn's untethered magic burst free.

It rushed toward Margot like a tidal wave. Her twilight energy reached out instinctively, eager to consume this new power.

"No!" she gasped, but it was too late.

The magic plowed into her with the force of an avalanche. Pain exploded through every nerve as Vesryn's power forced itself in, seeking a new vessel. This wasn't like absorbing Ilphas' gift—this was violent, uncontrolled. Pure power with nowhere else to go. One last effort made by Vesryn to manipulate the narrative.

The void above them flashed brilliantly, after images of that familiar world growing stronger. Reality buckled under the strain as Margot's body tried to contain what it was never meant to hold. She was being torn apart, being pulled between worlds as the magic threatened to consume her entirely.

"Hold on!" Cillian shouted, sounding so far away. "Just hold on!"

But she couldn't. It was too much. As consciousness began to fade, Margot caught one final glimpse of that familiar place through the void above.

Then, everything went white.

WHAT HAPPENED TO YOU?

BLINDING white gave way to a fractured reality—shards of two worlds colliding in impossible ways, threatening to tear her apart from within. The void pulled at Margot like a hungry beast, its maw stretching wider with each pulse of unstable magic coursing through her veins. Through rapidly closing gaps in the ethereal fabric, she saw a place she never thought she'd see again. Dingy cream walls, worn hardwood floors, and the soft glow of morning light filtering through gauzy curtains filled her vision.

Home.

"Hold on to me!" Cillian's voice cut through the noise as his massive arms wrapped around her waist. His wings unfurled, trying to stabilize them against the void's relentless pull, but even his demon strength couldn't fight this. Blood and shadows surged from the fist, creating a protective cocoon around them.

"Can you close it?" Corym shouted over the deafening roar of collapsing magic. The elf's violet eyes were wide with a mix of terror and awe as reality continued to splinter.

Margot's body shook within Cillian's hold as tears pricked the corners of her eyes. Pain radiated from deep within her bones as she tried to control the fissure, to seal it with her magic. Any time she thought she came close to knitting the crack in the sky back together, it grew two inches wider.

"I can't!" she cried, trying again and failing. A sob tore from her throat. "I don't know how!"

"I think the only way to close this thing is to go through." Corym inched over to them, his arm raised, shielding him from flying debris. "The power is too much! It needs somewhere to go!"

Margot knew he was right. She could feel Vesryn's magic writhing inside her, mixing with her own in ways that defied the natural order. If they stayed, the mounting pressure would tear not just her, but all of Caramis apart, maybe even all of Faerie. Already, she could feel the fabric of space warping around them, threatening to rip open permanently. The choice was being made for them.

"Together then," she gasped through the pain, gripping Cillian's forearms where they crossed her stomach. Through the bond, he tried to help contain the storm raging within her, but there were far too many emotions running their course.

She took one last look at Caramis' burning skyline, orange flames licking purple clouds as wyrms prowled the ruined streets. Screams and the clash of steel carried across the wind—the death throes of a city that had been her home for so long. And through the smoke, a figure in resplendent armor drew nearer, his crystalline gaze finding hers through the falling ash.

"Ravara," Cillian growled, tightening his hold on Margot.

The self-proclaimed Fae King's power roiled off him as he strode across the ruined square, stepping over Vesryn's headless corpse without so much as a glance. "Did you think I would let you slip away so easily?" He glanced at the void, looking mildly concerned, but he quickly schooled his features. "After everything I've done to find you?"

Ravara rushed forward, but it was too late. The void's pull was too strong, reality already crumbling around them. Margot caught one last glimpse of Ravara's face contorting with fury as he reached for her with frost-covered fingers—then the darkness swallowed them whole.

Falling between worlds was like being unmade. Colors that shouldn't exist painted impossible patterns across the darkness. Time stretched and compressed, meaningless in this space between spaces. Margot screamed, but no sound emerged. The only constant was Cillian's iron grip and the steady thrum of their bond.

Her body felt like it was being pulled apart at the atomic level, every cell fighting to maintain cohesion as they passed through the barrier between realms. Vesryn's stolen magic thrashed inside her, seeking escape, seeking control. The runes etched into her armor blazed with protective light, but even they struggled against the chaotic forces buffeting them from all sides.

Corym's presence flickered nearby—sometimes right beside them, sometimes impossibly far away. The elf's natural magic seemed to resist the journey, creating strange ripples in the void. His form blurred and sharpened, flickering in and out of view as if reality couldn't quite decide how he should be translated.

Memories flashed through Margot's mind: her first steps into Faerie, lost and afraid; meeting Cillian in the Dreadwood; the blood bond that changed everything; Vesryn's cruel manipulation; and finally, their desperate battle in the square. Each image burned like brands against her consciousness before dissolving into the swirling confusion.

Without warning, gravity reasserted itself.

They hit her apartment floor hard enough to crack the wood. Margot's legs gave out instantly, but Cillian caught her before she could collapse completely. His wings had vanished, his demon form receding as they crossed over, but his silver eyes still blazed with otherworldly light. The hellforged weapon on his arm pulsed once before going dark, overloaded from containing so much wild magic.

"He'll find a way," she gasped, still feeling the phantom chill of Ravara's reaching hand. "He won't stop hunting us."

"Let him try," Cillian growled, his arms tightening protectively around her. They both knew Ravara's resources were vast, his influence far-reaching. Even here, they might not be safe.

Corym landed more gracefully beside them, though his usual composure was shaken. "Ravara doesn't know this realm," he said, but his voice lacked conviction. "And the deepweave... without it, finding a stable crossing point would be nearly impossible."

"Nearly," Margot echoed. The power inside her still felt volatile, unpredictable. Sparks of grey magic occasionally leaked from her fingertips, leaving scorch marks on the floor. Would Ravara be able to trace that power? Track them across worlds?

The sudden silence amongst them was deafening.

Margot's magic roiled beneath her skin, struggling to adjust to this new reality. The familiar scents of her old life—coffee, laundry detergent, the lavender candle she always kept burning—felt alien now. Everything was exactly as she'd left it: dishes drying in the rack, the half-finished smutty pirate novel dog-eared on the coffee table, running shoes kicked off by the door. Yet nothing was the same.

She tried to step forward but stumbled, her equilibrium shot from the crossing. Cillian's powerful hands steadied her, his touch grounding dizziness overwhelmed her senses.

"Are you alright?" His voice was rough with concern as he helped her stay upright. His hands lingered on her waist.

"I don't know," she admitted. "Everything's... different. *I'm* different. And the magic here, it's—" She struggled to find the words. "It's like trying to breathe underwater."

"We all are," Corym said quietly, taking in their surroundings with wary fascination. The elf looked absurdly out of place—hell, they all did—in her modest kitchen, his blood-covered battle-worn leathers a stark contrast to the typical human things like modern appliances. "This realm... it dampens everything. Dulls it." His hand went to the sword at his hip, seeking comfort in its familiar weight.

"Can you feel it?" Margot asked Cillian, leaning into him as another wave of dizziness hit. "The difference in the magic?"

He nodded, his jaw tight. "It's heavier here. More resistant." His eyes scanned the apartment, tactical assessment warring with curiosity. "But the bond—it's stronger somehow. Clearer."

She felt it too. Their connection hummed between them, a steady anchor in this strange, familiar place. Perhaps here, where magic was scarcer, their bond stood out more prominently against the background noise of reality.

The sound of keys in a lock made them all freeze.

Corym's hand flew to his sword while Cillian pushed Margot behind him, his body tensing for combat. The hellforged weapon might be temporarily depleted, but his protective instincts were as sharp as ever.

"Margot?" a familiar voice called out. "I heard voices from the hall—are you finally home? Because girl, we need to talk about you ghosting me..."

Margot's heart stopped as Janey Kim rounded the corner into the kitchen, paper coffee cup in hand. Her best friend looked exactly as she remembered: yoga pants, oversized sweater, pin-straight, jet-black bob. A slice of normalcy that felt completely surreal after everything that had happened.

Janey's eyes went wide as she took in the scene before her: Margot in her torn armor, covered in blood and dirt; Cillian's massive form, hovering protectively nearby, his silver eyes gleaming unnaturally in the morning light; and Corym, ears pointed and magic still crackling faintly around his fingers despite the dampening effect of Earth.

The coffee cup hit the floor with a wet splash. Dark liquid spread across the hardwood like spilled blood, steam rising in lazy spirals.

"What the fuck?"

Margot opened her mouth to respond, but what could she

possibly say? How could she explain everything that had happened? The magic inside her stirred restlessly, responding to her emotions, and grey sparks danced between her fingers.

Janey's eyes fixed on the display of power, and her face went impossibly paler.

"Oh my god," she whispered. "What happened to you?"

AFTERWORD

Dear Reader,

Thank you for joining Margot and Cillian on their journey through Faerie. When I first began writing their story, I wanted to explore what happens when someone is thrust into a world of magic and wonder, only to discover that beauty often masks darkness. Through Margot's eyes, we see how power can corrupt, trauma can reshape us, and love can give us the strength to reclaim ourselves.

The blood bond between Margot and Cillian represents more than just a magical connection—it's about choosing to trust someone completely, even when everything else has been taken away. Their relationship reminds us that healing isn't linear, that sometimes we must fight for the people we love, and that real strength often comes from vulnerability.

Vesryn's character explores themes of control and manipulation, showing how abusers can present a benevolent face while systematically breaking down their victims. Through Margot's struggle to break free of his influence, we see the difficult but vital journey of reclaiming one's agency and identity.

The elves of Caramis, too, demonstrate how systemic oppression can make us complicit in our own captivity. Characters like

Corym, Tahlsia, and Nym show different ways of resisting tyranny—some through direct action, others through small acts of defiance and aid.

As Margot and Cillian's story continues, they'll face new challenges on Earth while grappling with the consequences of their actions in Faerie. The power they've claimed comes with a price, and Ravara's hunger for control won't be easily satisfied.

Thank you again for reading my debut novel. I hope their story resonates with you as much as it has with me.

Paige Annabentleah

ACKNOWLEDGMENTS

First and foremost, my husband, Matthew, deserves recognition. None of this would be possible without his constant support and belief in me. He puts up with the crazy, gives me peace when I decide I need to work every hour of the day, and is the most amazing father. I love you.

Samantha, you have been with me every step of the way and have read and reread and reread again. Without you, Margot and Cillian's story may not even exist. You are the best friend, the greatest sounding board, and the biggest cheerleader I could ever ask for.

Magdalena, the amount of beautiful artwork you have created for this installment is one of the most amazing things that has ever happened to me. I am eternally grateful that I took the plunge and reached out because not only do I have an amazing artist in my corner, but I also have an amazing friend.

Kate, you pushed through this monster and guided me toward making Sea of Exiles the best it could be without adding fifteen more chapters. Thank you.

And to you, my readers. If you made it this far, thank you for taking a chance on a new author. Without you all, there would be no story to tell.

ABOUT THE AUTHOR

Paige Annabentleah lives with her husband and two children, surrounded by towering stacks of books and an ever-present cup of coffee. When she's not writing dark fantasy romance or epic fantasy, she can be found immersed in video games or curled up with her latest reading obsession.

With a background in psychology, Paige brings depth and authenticity to her characters, exploring the complexities of trauma, healing, and relationships through the lens of fantasy. Her stories blend the wonder of magic with the raw emotional journey of self-discovery.

Sea of Exiles is her debut novel, combining her love of romance, dark fantasy, and character-driven storytelling. She is currently working on the next installment of Margot and Cillian's story.

Curious about what's in the works for Paige Annabentleah next?
Follow her on social media.

Subscribe to the newsletter for updates!

Join the Discord community!

facebook.com/annabentleahpaige

instagram.com/annabentleah

threads.net/@annabentleah

tiktok.com/@annabentleah